Praise for Cecelia By Moonlight

"Author Ross Alan Bachelder weaves a sprawling, intricate tapestry in *Cecelia by Moonlight*, showing us how a young and brilliant girl's past can influence her in ways both exultant and calamitous. As this romping, picaresque adventure unfolds, he leaves us wondering, moment by harrowing moment, just what the future will finally have in store for someone as gifted as Cecelia Middling so obviously is."
— **Sharon Hilton**, *skilled actress, beloved artistic director, and natural-born dramaturg*

"In *Cecelia by Moonlight*, the young and precocious Cecelia Middling soon realizes she's been born into a family of loud, lewd, barely literate oddballs who have little tolerance for her independent ways. When she openly rebels against her parents' attempt to turn her into a "proper" young lady, all Hell breaks loose. Bachelder's obvious ear for human voices makes this lively tale leap off the page with sparkling energy."
— **Dona Masi Layton**, *passionate wordsmith and author of The Taking*

"As with anything author Ross Alan Bachelder writes, *Cecelia by Moonlight* is a wild literary toboggan ride—a ribald and trenchant tale bursting with richly drawn characters, emotionally charged dialogue, and shrewd reflections on human behaviors both noble and negligent. You'll get your money's worth with this Rabelaisian outburst!"
— **Edouard "Eddie" Langlois**, *actor, director, set designer, costumier, and visual artist without equal*

Cecelia by Moonlight

The Problem with Intelligence

Cecelia by Moonlight

The Problem with Intelligence

Ross Alan Bachelder

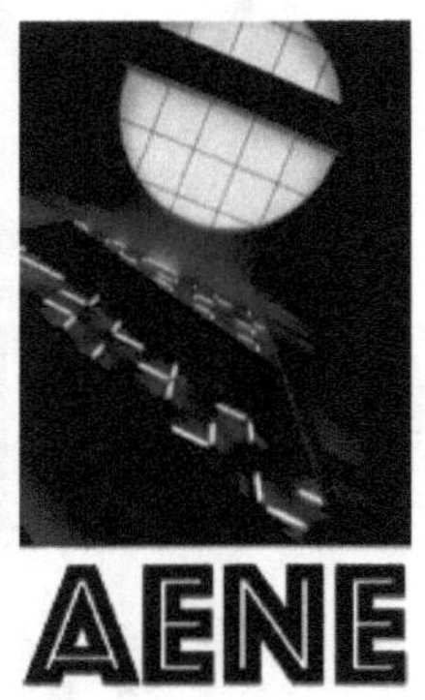

Cecelia by Moonlight: The Problem with Intelligence

Copyright © 2024 by Ross Alan Bachelder

This book is a work of fiction. Names, characters, places and incidents either are the product of the author's imagination or are used fictitiously, and any resemblance to actual persons, living or dead, events, or locales is entirely coincidental.

Printed in the United States of America

Published By
The Publishing Pad
www.thepublishingpad.com

Paperback ISBN: 978-1-963732-02-3
Hardcover ISBN: 978-1-963732-03-0

This book was produced in coordination with Artful Endeavors New England (AENE), Berwick, Maine.

Dedication

In memory of Essex, Massachusetts artist Bonnie Jean Malcolm (1922–2023), who, for ten wonderful years, through her inspiring late-in-life correspondence with me, gave me the unconditional love Cecelia so badly needed.

"It is a sad fact I have noticed with
humans. By the time you share
what a loved one longs to hear,
they often no longer need it."
—Sebastian Krispin, in Mitch Albom's *The Little Liar*

Contents

Chapter One..11
Chapter Two...25
Chapter Three...29
Chapter Four..37
Chapter Five..41
Chapter Six...47
Chapter Seven...51
Chapter Eight...65
Chapter Nine..73
Chapter Ten...79
Chapter Eleven..99
Chapter Twelve.......................................121
Chapter Thirteen.....................................133
Chapter Fourteen.....................................141
Chapter Fifteen......................................145
Chapter Sixteen......................................177
Chapter Seventeen....................................187
Chapter Eighteen.....................................195
Chapter Nineteen.....................................217
Chapter Twenty.......................................251
Chapter Twenty-one...................................281
Chapter Twenty-two...................................295
Chapter Twenty-three.................................305
Chapter Twenty-four..................................319
Chapter Twenty-five..................................343
About the Author.....................................353

Chapter One

As Stanton Middling headed north on the 101, it was nearly 7:00 p.m., long past the usual end of his workday. The cool, off-the-Bay breezes that make March in San Francisco the envy of anyone east of the Mississippi—and, for that matter, south of Nogales—were gone now. In their place was the kind of sticky, moisture-heavy atmosphere that can make nooses out of neckties and turn a well-ironed shirt into a sopping-wet car sponge.

Scheckel & Newbury, a fortress-like building just off Kearny Street, south of Telegraph Hill, was about as lively as a barn dance in a morgue, even on a good day. *Jesus,* Middling thought to himself. *It's bad enough being trapped behind a stinkin' desk on what was supposed to be my day off. But in weather like this? It's Saturday, for Christ's sake! And crunching numbers all day long was even worse. I shoulda been down at Smitty's by now, sippin' margaritas and checkin' out the chicks.*

It wasn't just the long hours and lousy weather that had Middling so worked up. The traffic was horrendous, and after a long week of labor, the hordes of homebound commuters were even more short-tempered than usual. The war in Vietnam was spinning out of control, and thanks to a well-planned protest of unprecedented size and fury, people in London, Paris, Rome, and nearly thirty other cities around the world were having their say and saying it loudly.

All across America—Chicago, Boston, New York, Philadelphia, Washington, and dozens of other cities—people were sick and tired of seeing planeloads of dead soldiers in tin boxes on the Evening News while trying to eat their supper. Cars with bumper stickers saying *War Is Not Healthy for Children and Other Living Things* could be found in more and more cities, small and large, from coast to coast.

In San Francisco alone, thousands of battle-weary peaceniks were pouring out onto the streets, demanding an end to the war and making Middling's mood ten times more wretched than usual. His head was throbbing, his stomach growling. Right now, his idea of heaven was to get his ass home to Sausalito, take a short drive down to Smitty's, and, for a few precious hours, reclaim his little Patch of Paradise. *To hell with war and politics,* he grumbled. *Bring on the drinks! Is that really asking all that much?*

Traffic was nearly at a standstill now, so to kill some time he dialed up Station KMPX. *I could use some soothing, middle-of-the-road stuff right now,* he thought.

But it didn't happen. The very first song that came roaring out of the dashboard was Janis Joplin's "Piece of My Heart." He'd hated that song the moment it hit the charts. *Brooke's nuts about Joplin,* he chuckled. *Surprise, surprise! But me? I'd rather run my nails across a goddam chalkboard than listen to that 'singer' howling like a drugged-up banshee. She's just got to be pourin' whiskey on her Froot Loops in the morning!*

Once he was back in the air-conditioned comfort of his oceanside home in Sausalito—his son, Clay, wasn't home yet, so he knew he'd have some peace of mind for a while—he yanked off his tie, hung his sport jacket in the closet, put his briefcase in the den, then kicked off his Florsheims—*fucking foot killers, they are!*—and padded out to the kitchen to claim the nightly drink his wife always had ready for him when he got home. *What a sweetie she can be,* he grimaced, *when she's not bein' a Grade A bitch!* He'd gladly have said it to her face—she actually liked it when he said things like that—but she was no doubt upstairs as usual, poring over the latest issue of *House Beautiful*.

Typical money-hungry woman, he sneered. *She sucks the life out o' my bank account month after month. I've no doubt she expected a castle on the Rhine once we were engaged. But then she married me—poor thing—and ended up with nothin' but a cheap little shack on the rim of the Pacific. Well, tough luck, honey! We don't always get what we wish for, do we. I know I sure as hell didn't.*

Moments later he was stretched out on the living room couch overlooking Richardson Bay, nursing a Mai Tai and watching Walter Cronkite drone on about the arrival of yet another four hundred coffins full of dead soldiers—young men barely out of high school when they were drafted—all set to be flown home from Vietnam after being slaughtered in a conflict they didn't understand and never really wanted to be a part of in the first place.

Stan wasn't about to see his own son get sent off to Vietnam. After all, he himself had found a way to stay the hell out of Korea. And the way he saw it, a Middling had better things to do than fighting a senseless war in some faraway, good-for-nothing land.

Cronkite! The most trusted man in America? You bet he is, thought Middling. *Every goddam night I can count on that pompous old fart to spoil my supper with that morbid little cadaver fest of his. If he'd wanted to count dead GIs for a living, he should have become an embalmer, not a friggin' news anchor.*

Stan was getting a serious buzz on by now, talking back to the television. "Have any trouble with that, Wally Boy? Well, too damned bad! That's the way it is, at least in *my* house—478 Bridgeway, our very own Citadel by the Sea. And guess who's the Head Honcho!"

Of course, Stan Middling might very well have become a GI, too, had it not been for a well-timed assist from his self-serving Uncle Theodore—at the time a proud member of a Bay Area draft board whose members were in the habit of taking "special care" of their college-bound kids—"true patriots" who found a way to bend the rules just enough to keep their favorite boys out of Korea.

The unpleasant truth was that Stan hadn't really seen a good reason to even care about Korea. After all, without even trying, he and his male friends and neighbors had been the proud beneficiaries of a smug, patently racist society. And because of it, he really couldn't see why Uncle Sam shouldn't send the Blacks and working stiffs of the world to Vietnam in place of his son. Worse, he conveniently ignored what every one of those unfortunate inductees knew all too well: they had a very good chance of coming home in the belly of a transport plane along with dozens of other dead soldiers, laid out in identical, sealed aluminum boxes more like sardine cans than coffins.

It all seemed like such a long time ago. After all, he and his uncle were the only two people in town who knew The Rest of the Story. As for everyone else, he wanted them to think he'd copped a medical discharge because of a screwed-up kidney caused by too many hard drinks. *What harm could there be in that,* he thought to himself. *Let 'em think it!*

He soon fell asleep, and before long he was dreaming— yet again—about the time he'd been down at Smitty's one Christmas Eve, thoroughly trashed and socially undisciplined, nibbling on Trixie Tannenbaum's earlobe as "Oh Come, All Ye Faithful" blared out from the jukebox.

It was the same fantastical narrative every time he dreamt about her. He'd be burrowing his moist, prehensile tongue into her ear while she walked her fingers up the inside of his thigh—destination, womb-broom. The fact that the restaurant was crammed full of half-crocked celebrants didn't really faze him. *Hell,* he figured, *if they don't like it, they can read the menu or pack up and go to HoJo's.*

He'd vowed to himself long ago never to share dreams like that with the Mrs. It made his transgressions all the more delicious. They were at the very heart of his most passionate yearnings, and he could never get enough of them.

He'd just reached the most memorable moment in his dream—the one where he pops open a bra cup while she's stroking his Willy—when the front door swung open, and in came Clay with a six-pack in one hand and the latest issue of *Playboy,* still sealed in cellophane, in the other.

He'd only recently turned nineteen, but at 5 foot 11 and still growing, with broad shoulders, a shock of curly red hair, impressive biceps, and a lantern jaw, he could easily have been mistaken for a twenty-five-year-old. He was also nearly half a foot taller than his father now, and that reality didn't please his Old Man. The truth was that the taller Clay got, the more discontented Stan became, and yet he was too ashamed to admit it to anyone but himself—and only when alone, brooding, in the middle of the night.

"So who's on the cover this time?" said Stan.

"Oh, just another scantily clad sorority babe," said Clay, then held the cover up so his father could see it. "As you can see, she's snuggling up to a six-foot-tall snow bunny. Kind o' dumb, considering it's a friggin' steam bath today in Sausalito. But hey, it's what's inside that counts! Right, Dad?"

"I get your drift," Stan chuckled. "But believe me, I'd do a hell of a lot more than snuggle up to a babe like that." He sighed, closed his eyes, and smiled dreamily up toward the ceiling. "Anything worth reading inside?"

Brooke—who, unknown to them, had been standing at the top of the landing when Clay came home from work—stayed right where she was and listened to every lurid word of their conversation.

"Plenty!" said Clay. "I probably shouldn't tell you this, Pops, but this month they're running Part One of *Octopussy*! You know, that James Bond story that's about to become a book. Can't wait to read it! And by the way, you ain't gettin' your filthy hands on it 'til I'm good 'n' done with it."

Stan clicked off the television, then turned away from his son and buried his face in his Golden State Warriors pillow, hoping to get a little more rest before supper. Clay headed upstairs, and as he was leafing through the magazine he bumped into his mother.

"Oh, shit!" he said, then stepped out of the way, rolled the magazine up, and held it guiltily behind his back.

"Don't you 'oh, shit' me, young man! That's no way to talk to your mother."

"Sorry, Mom," he said. "Didn't see you up there. You weren't listening, were you? I hope not!"

"Heard every damn word," she said. "But no need to worry. It doesn't really faze me. Let's face it, Clay. Now that you're done with puberty, you're a chip off the Old Man's libido. I should have seen it coming. Now, instead of having just one horny degenerate under my roof to contend with, I've got *two*."

"*Playboy*'s not just about girls without their clothes on," said Stan. "There's serious literature in it every month! You know, stuff for the *thinking* man."

"Oh, yeah," she sneered. "You mean like Fellini, or Nabokov? Or better yet, that provocative pictorial on 'The Girls of Rio'? I found the February issue under your side of the bed last week while cleaning your bedroom, Einstein. You're a man of *taste* now, aren't you. A real scholar! Next you're gonna tell me you never really look at the pictures."

"One or two of 'em, maybe," Stan said. "Same with Clay. It's damn harmless if you ask me."

"Jesus, Stan! Do we have to wade through this kind o' brain sewage every goddam night?" She headed down to the living room, with Clay dutifully following behind her as if he were being dragged down to the principal's office. He knew it was Lecture Time again, and he figured he might as well sit himself down, listen patiently to yet another motherly rant, and get the whole ordeal over with.

The three of them now formed themselves into a tight little triangle, with Stan on the couch, Clay near the bottom step of the staircase, and his mother in the overstuffed chair near the coffee table.

"Now look," she began. "You probably won't believe it, but I really don't give a damn what the two of you read to get your rocks off! I'm a lot smarter than you think I am. Besides, I've got more important things on my mind. It's about time we had ourselves a little pow-wow, don't you think?"

"A pow-wow?" said Clay. "I thought we just *had* a pow-wow."

"*Some* of it," she said. "You need to stay put and hear the rest. A pow-wow about work-work! Labor! Employment! Starts with a J and ends with a B. It's called Doin' Your Share!"

At this point, Clay's ears were burning.

"I mean, other than that crummy part-time job of yours at City of Paris—the one you call in sick to every three days—what have you done lately to help carry the load around here? Name one thing! Of course, I doubt you will, because the truth is you've done absolutely *nothing*."

"Not fair!" he shouted. "Just last week I took out the trash three nights in a row."

"He did!" said Stan. "I saw him do it all three times."

"That's not a job," she said, "it's a *chore*. Why don't you get some training and find a *real* job—something creative—something that pays well?"

"Like what?" asked Clay. "Like *what*?"

"Like Village Fair," she snapped. "I mean, where do you think I go every morning—Golden Gate Fields? Sorry, I'm not into racing. The Christian Science Reading Room? I'm a *window dresser*, for Christ's sake. Remember? Certificate and everything. It's great fun! It's creative! It pays well! And, best of all, I get to gawk at all the famous people who go in and out of the stores I service. Thirty-eight of 'em! Artists, poets, philosophers—you name it—come through that place every day. Timothy Leary and his wacko buddies from the Houseboat Summit are regulars at Village Fair. Alan Watts, too! Saw Gary Snyder and Allen Ginsberg chowin' down at a local burger joint one time. We won't even *talk* about what they do in their spare time. I've even seen Janis Joplin! What a cheap tart *she* is. Can't sing worth a shit, does drugs up the yahoo, and sleeps with anyone who happens to have a penis, I've been told. I liked Jerry Garcia a hell of a lot better."

"Honestly," said Clay, "I couldn't care less about all those sleazy misfits you think are so cool. The dregs of society, far as I'm concerned. Listen, I'm glad you like your job, but if I were you, I'd be looking for something more ambitious."

"Don't preach to *me*, junior," shouted Brooke. "You don't know what the word 'ambitious' means!"

"And just in case it slipped past the two of you somehow," said Clay, not really listening to his mother, "I've been working at City of Paris warehouse since last *October*. Got a framed Employee of the Month certificate for filling in on Thanksgiving Day so the boss could have a day off. Forgot to tell you."

"And *that's* the truth, too!" said Stan. "It's still up on his wall. Go look! It's right next to the Patti Reynolds centerfold I gave him for Christmas." He looked over at Clay, tossed him a knowing wink, and whispered to him from the couch. "Jesus—what a smokin' hot princess *she* is!"

As Brooke sat through yet another of her husband's tasteless preadolescent regressions, she couldn't help laughing. "You know what, Stan? You can't whisper worth a damn. Never could! If anyone would know who the Playboy centerfold was—usually some totally forgettable, know-nothing babe with boobs the size of cage balls—it would be you. I'm surprised you don't have one tacked up over the toilet in the upstairs bathroom, where you can get to it while I'm sound asleep. You know, strike while the iron's hot!"

Clay and Stan looked over at each other and shrugged. They could tell she meant business now, so they went silent, donned the most cherubic smiles they could come up with, and waited politely for Reverend Middling to continue her homily.

She pointed toward Clay, then turned to Stan. "In case you've forgotten," she said, "I weaned your son off Momma's Milk nearly two decades ago." Then she walked over to her husband, cupped her hands under her breasts, and bobbed them up and down for emphasis. "But you? You're still breastfeeding your Little Lord Fauntleroy as if he were some sort of undernourished infant Heir to the Throne. Look, I know you care for Clay! But it takes more than sweet talk and lame excuses to make a family. So let's get *serious* for a change. Your son is a young man now. He's reached *voting age,* for heaven's sake! He could even be down in Phú Yên Province right now, pickin' off some gooks like all the other grunts!"

"Ain't no son o' mine gonna be cannon fodder for a bunch o' peewee slants!" said Stan.

Brooke glared contemptuously at her husband, then shut him down with one angry sweep of her arm.

"*Knock it off*, big guy. If Clay's number comes up, he'll go! I know *you* would have, if you hadn't been rejected for medical reasons—or so you claim. What a shame, huh? I'd have been so proud of you!"

"Oh, yeah," sneered Stan. "I'd have been a gung-ho member of the Armed Forces, wouldn't I—a real gun-totin' John Wayne. So of course it jus' broke my heart when I got that rejection notice."

"But it'll be different for your son, won't it. He won't have any choice in the matter!" Then she turned to Clay, beaming in her motherly way. "I mean, would you just *look* at that boy! He's healthy as a Triple Crown winner! But he's here on the home front right now, so, in the words of the Silhouettes, it's time for our little offspring to get off his ass and 'Get a Job' until Uncle Sam needs him."

Clay got up from the staircase and stood defiantly in front of his mother, his hands trembling, his face red with anger.

"OK, OK! So I've no doubt I'll go if I'm called up! Wouldn't wanna bring shame on the Middling family, would I. But in regard to employment, here's the truth you seem to want so badly. Today was my last day at City of Paris. I decided I couldn't take any more of Conklin's abuse, so I flew off the handle and lit into him. Told him I was done kissin' his ass for a lousy buck-forty an hour. Then I flipped him the bird and walked out the door—but not before I swept all the paperwork off his desk, like confetti in a parade. God, was *that* fun! It was one sweet, unforgettable moment. Ain't nobody gonna treat me like dirt and get away with it!"

Brooke grew quiet, then adopted a softer tone.

"But why, Clay? Don't you realize you're shooting yourself in the foot when you do things like this?"

"Things like what?"

"You *know* what," she snapped. "No more 'let's pretend'!" She did her best to stay cool, then turned philosophical. "Everyone has to learn to take a beating in the workplace in the early years. It comes with the territory! So now you've walked away from yet another perfectly good job—a resume-building job, I should add. So what's next, Mr. Know-It-All? Who in his right mind is gonna want to hire you this time around?"

Stan listened to her trim-down with no small amount of envy, and then, feeling guilty for being too soft on his son, he finally chimed in.

"Listen up, ace, and listen carefully," he said. "I'm sick to death of watching you squander your future, and at our expense! If you think you're gonna continue to mooch off my hard-earned salary by lounging around here all day and refusing to help us financially, you've got a lesson or two to learn. Now if you really want that entry-level job I've been promising you, then first things first: get your butt over to that telephone, right now! Call Conklin, apologize for your stupidity, and beg him to rehire you. Then, once you're back on the job—and once you've proven to me that you can keep your mouth shut and perform well for a few months—I'll get you all set up at Scheckel & Newbury. It'll be a job more than worth having—a Golden Opportunity!"

As Clay listened patiently to their counsel, he couldn't help being amused by his father's sudden transformation into a take-charge, pants-o'-the-family guy. Then he turned toward the two of them and quietly issued a rebuttal.

"No need to make that call," he said. "Things are gonna be different from now on."

Brooke and Stan looked up with raised eyebrows, then exchanged polite but skeptical smiles.

"Remember my pal Dori? You know, Dorian Breitmeyer. They used to call him 'Pizza Face' in high school because his forehead was absolutely swarming with zits! Luckily for him, he looks a lot better now. Kind o' grew out of 'em, I guess. Anyway, Dori got me a part-time job at Marin City Flea Market, where he works. Nothing fancy, but it'll pay the bills."

Stan bolted upright and glared at his son. "Oh, my God!" he cried. "Marin City Flea Market?" He buried his face in his hands, then shook his head. "I wouldn't get caught *dead* in that place! And by the way—aren't there a lot o' Coloreds up there?"

"Yes, Dad," he sighed, "there are a lot of 'Coloreds' up there. What century were you born in? Not everyone around here grew up rich 'n' privileged like you did! Not everybody was born with pale pink skin. And have you noticed? The spoons they use at Marin City are *plastic*, not silver." Then, hoping to win his father over, he tried another, gentler approach. "The place is really kind o' cool! I mean, Jack Kerouac used to hang out there in the '50s. They even called Marin City the Golden Ghetto!"

"Oh, that's a swell name," said Brooke. "White picket fences, ornamental gardens, drug dens plentiful as dandelions. The perfect place to raise a family."

"Look," said Clay, "I'll grant you the town has a few warts here and there. Bad press, mostly; they never tell you about the good stuff. But Sausalito ain't exactly Shangri-La, is it. Just the other day, Dori told me they had another big drug bust just down the street from the Yacht Club! Those corporate high rollers aren't the civic-minded choir boys you make 'em out to be."

Then Clay stooped down, tightened a stray shoelace, and headed back toward the staircase. "Better wages, better conditions, better boss. That's what Marin City means to me! I can live with the negatives. And just think: you won't have Clay to kick around any more. Won't *that* be nice! I'm gonna live with Dori and split the rent with him. So, you see, everything's gonna work out just the way you wanted. Hope you're happy now!" Then he grabbed his copy of *Playboy* off the staircase, stuffed it into the back pocket of his Levi's, and bounded upstairs to his bedroom.

With Clay upstairs, the only sound in the Middling household was the steady whoop-whoop-whoop of a ceiling fan in the living room. Then Stan, who was still stretched out on the couch, turned toward Brooke and broke the silence.

"Dinner all set?" he purred. "I'm so starved, I could eat a truckload o' pork roasts!"

"You can forget the pork roasts," she frowned. "Look in the refrigerator. There's lots o' leftovers in there—the *healthy* stuff. The last thing you need is more fat around your middle. Looks like you've got a truck tire under your T-shirt."

She got up and turned off the television—another news bulletin showing swarms of angry protesters marching in downtown San Francisco—and headed down to the family room in search of a little quietude.

Once inside, she turned the lights down low, flopped down on the fainting couch she'd picked up at an antique sale in Tiburon a few years ago, and lit up a Winston Light. When she first set her eyes on the chair and learned that at one time it was thought to have been the property of screenwriter Stirling Silliphant, she was unable to resist it, despite the two-thousand-dollar price tag. *Yeah, Stan was really pissed,* she chuckled. *But tough titty, I told him. We all need indulgences on occasion; you get yours, I get mine.*

But at this particular moment, she had no interest in the historical value of the chair. She simply wanted a room of her own and an hour to herself, and she would have been willing to stretch out on a cold, hard floor to get it.

"Thank you, Mr. Silliphant," she chuckled, then took

a deep, satisfying drag on her cigarette. "It may be hell in Vietnam, but for one brief interlude, it's heaven in Sausalito!"

Chapter Two

Clay, who was now proudly and gainfully employed at Marin City Flea Market, liked Fridays the most. They were the one day of the week when he was paired up with Dori, and that meant the two of them could let down their guard and talk dirty, just like they did in the old days. It was like a savagely executed game of badminton, with insults and obscenities in place of birdies and rackets. Their tasteless end-of-the-week banter never failed to make the workday go by a whole lot faster.

Today it was their turn to clean up the inevitable accumulation of litter that carpeted the vast expanse of Flea Market property after an especially busy day. No fancy equipment, either. Just a pair of crude but functional trash pickers—long, heavy poles with a sharp prong at one end—the better to harvest everything from poop-filled diapers to day-old condoms, all cooked to imperfection by the relentless onslaught of Marin City's legendary sunlight. On days when the air was static, their distinctive odors always managed to come together, creating a perfume that no woman in her right mind would want to wear and no man would ever want to smell.

"So how are things goin' between you and your Old Man?" said Dori. "He must be proud of you for taking this job."

"Are you shittin' me?" said Clay. "He's rippin' mad! Said he's even *ashamed* of me. Nothin' new about that, though; I've just kind o' learned to live with it. But if you want the truth, he and Mom are clearly thrilled to have me out of the house."

"I'd be thrilled, too!" Dori laughed. Then he realized it hadn't struck Clay as all that funny. So he threw down his pole, walked over to him, and slapped him affectionately on the back.

"Come on, pal," he said. "I was just havin' a little fun—jerkin' you around for a sec! But, joking aside, I can't help thinking that all three of you are better off apart than you were when you were living under the same roof. You must o' woke up every morning thinking you were over in 'Nam, bein' carpet-bombed by the gooks."

"You're not all that far off," said Clay. "I thought seriously of wearing a flak jacket whenever they were around." Then he turned to Dori. "Oh—I almost forget to tell you! I turned on the TV while you were in the bathroom this morning and heard they bombed the hell out o' Hanoi yesterday for the first time. Haiphong, too. We're gonna beat the crap out o' those little Kewpies, by God!"

"Cute," said Dori, "but it's starting to look like it ain't all fun and games over there. And right now, here at home, there's a whole lot o' protesting going on. The natives are obviously getting restless. Just the other day, a trio of soldiers down in Texas refused to go to South Vietnam! Said the war's 'immoral'! The word I'm hearing is that if those Three Stooges don't get their act together and do what Uncle Sam says, they may get three years' hard labor."

Dori looked over at Clay, frowning. "Hey!" he said. "Weren't you all set to be drafted a few weeks ago? And yet here you are in Marin City now, fishin' for Pampers and Trojans! I always wondered how the hell you managed to wriggle out o' that little dilemma! As for me, I guess I was just lucky. My number never came up, and then the next thing I knew, I . . ."

"I *told* you why," said Clay. "Medical problems!"

"Oh, yeah—medical problems! I kind o' forgot that.

Anyway, no big deal! We'd better cut the chatter and get back to work. There must be at least another ton or two of rubbish ahead of us, begging to be rescued." Then he suddenly stopped cold and turned toward Clay with a look of blazing eureka written all over his face.

"Whoa, big guy!" he shouted. "Call me Mr. Matchmaker, but for some reason, I just remembered this chick I know who'd fit you like a custom-tailored jockstrap!"

Clay stopped what he was doing and gave Dori his rapt attention. "This better not be another one of your sick-minded teasers," he said. "My social life's been drier than a desert fart lately. I could use some action—not yesterday but right now!"

"Her name's Avis," said Dori. "Avis Guertner. And let me tell ya, brother, she's just got to be the sweetest meat in the deli!"

"And you know this first-hand?" said Clay. "Or tongue or whatever?"

"No, I don't know it 'first-hand or tongue or whatever,'" said Dori. "Don't be a pig! Any guy with two eyes and a pair o' gonads can tell the difference between FDA Approved and a plateful o' roadkill."

"How old is she?" asked Clay.

"A few years older than you," said Dori. "So a few years ahead of us in school. Not sure how many. But don't worry 'bout that. She's in incredibly good shape for a woman her age. And I've no doubt she really knows the ropes, too! When I was in school, she was already a legend. We all got a kick out of telling stories about her exploits, trying to imagine what she'd done and who she'd done it with."

Clay was excited now—so whipped up, he was actually licking his lips. *Jesus,* he thought, *she sounds way too good to be true! Then again, don't they all? But Dori'd never intentionally mess around with me. We've been buddies since third grade. Might's well give it a shot. I hear opportunity knocking; better answer the door!*

Clay knew Dori was a sucker for flattery, so he leaned in on him right away and began laying the groundwork for a meeting. "Nice work, Cupid!" he said, "but now that you've gotten me all titillated, what's my next move? I mean, how should I go about hooking up with this Sweet Little Thing?"

"Not all *that* little," said Dorian. "You'll see. But oh, so sweet! Anyway, my friend Tommy Dolliver is having a keg party on the Fourth. It'll be up in Mill Valley, not all that far from Mount Tamalpais. Perfect timing, too; his parents are down on Half Moon Bay right now, ridin' the waves with the surfers. They won't be back until the 14th. Also, I've been told Mill Valley's absolutely teeming with redwoods—another dividend for a tree hugger like you. And it gets even better! Tommy said we can each bring one good friend, no questions asked. So guess what, pervert? You can go ahead and slap a 'sold' sticker on your pee-wee, 'cause you're coming with me. And if you play your cards right, Romeo, you might just end up on the forest floor with her, long before the booze starts flowin'."

Chapter Three

As Dori and Clay wound their way up the hill to Tommy's place, they needed only their ears to know that the keg party was at full tilt. They could hear Meat Loaf's "Runnin' for the Red Light" screaming out from a pair of tube amps Dolliver had set up on the front lawn, and the beer was flowing like tap water.

"Johnson's really stickin' it to them gooks, ain't 'e!" laughed Clay, making light conversation in hopes that it would calm his nerves.

"Don't know why the hell you're worryin' about 'Nam right now," said Dori. "You've got some quality snatch to take care of! Time to get your priorities in order, sausage."

"You're right," said Clay. "That girl's about to find out just how good a nice big link o' kielbasa can be. Should be a dietary staple for the discriminating woman, huh?"

A powerful thumping sound invaded the Dolliver estate, and Dori was captivated.

"Would y' listen to that!" he said, then rolled his window all the way down to get the full effect. "That's a Univox U-45B. I can tell just by listening to it. Best damn amp on the planet."

"For the price, anyway," said Clay. "Or for people who don't know shit about amplifiers."

"Let's not go down that rabbit hole again," said Dori. "It's party time! First up, we've gotta track down Avis Guertner so's I can introduce you to her."

"Guertner, Squirtner," said Clay, then moved his pelvis licentiously while climbing out of the car. "I'm already in fourth gear!"

The Dolliver residence, more like a Victorian mansion than a normal abode, was artfully positioned on a steep bluff overlooking Mill Valley. The valley itself was dotted with homes not nearly as nice as Tommy's—simple, affordable dwellings for soldiers home from World War II and bent on starting families—but they were far enough away from the Dollivers that Tommy didn't have to worry about the drunken reveling bothering anybody.

Dori wormed his way into the crowd nearest the kegs, dragging Clay behind him. The two of them made no effort to avoid rubbing up against the revelers—especially the women.

"Nothing like pressing the flesh in a crowd of half-naked Decent Ritas," he said. "Did you see the tits on the one with the blue tank top?"

"Missed *both* of 'em," said Clay. "I was too busy wondering what it would be like to bury my face in that fine booty of hers!"

"Better save your pocket change for someone you can actually handle," said Dori. "That girl's one high-classed piece o' jail bait. But let's face it—she's way out o' your league."

Clay, who was only half-listening to Dori's one-liners, caught sight of a long-legged, blonde-haired beauty just ahead of him and couldn't stop gaping at her. She was nearly a head taller than he was—not the size he was usually attracted to. But in this case, her sparkling eyes and statuesque physique only whetted his appetite. "Oh, my God," he said to himself. "What I wouldn't give to park my Bad Boy in *her* garage!"

"If you could *reach* her," laughed Dori. "Anyway, you'd better zip your lips and cool your tool! That's Birdie Guertner—the girl I said would fit you like a custom-tailored jock strap. Her name's really Avis, but they've been calling her Birdie ever since she was a tiny thing."

Clay blushed a deep red, then looked the other way, pretending he hadn't really seen her. "Sorry," he said. "If I'd known it was her, I'd never have said what I said."

"Just let it go, numb-numb," said Dori. "No harm done—not yet, anyway."

Then he yanked Clay off to the side and half-whispered into his ear. "Tell you what, dude. I'm gonna jump ship now so you can sail over to Miss Birdie on your own and show her what a true Christian gentleman you really are—a young man with only the purest of intentions. Now get a move-on, boy. Get over there and show that sweet young thing what a Man on a Mission can do!" Then he shoved him in the direction of Birdie, wished him well, and went off on his own to pour himself a beer.

Clay ran his fingers through his hair, checked his breath to make sure it wasn't disgusting—he could tell right away that it was—then popped a breath mint, found the nearest keg line, and fell in, conveniently, right behind Birdie. Then, just as he was about to tap her on the shoulder and introduce himself, the guy clowning around directly behind him accidentally pushed him, front-first, straight into Birdie's tightly packed pair of short shorts.

"Sorry," yelped Clay, "I didn't mean to do that. Promise!"

"Really!" said Birdie. "Are you sure?"

"Yes, really!"

"Well, intentionally or not, I can't say I really minded it all that much," said Birdie. "I've had worse things happen." Then she abruptly reached down and chucked him under the chin. "Guess you're not the bashful type, either. I mean, you sure don't waste time getting to know people, do you."

The moment she touched his face, Clay could feel an involuntary swelling in his chinos, and he was hooked. *Holy shit,* he thought, *Dorian's a regular fucking Nostradamus! All I can say is, carpe diem, baby!*

When the two of them had gotten their beers, they slipped away from the horde of revelers and found a shady spot beneath a grove of tall, stately maidenhair trees.

"Guess I should introduce myself," said Clay.

"Guess you *should*," said Birdie. "So let's hear it!"

"Clayborne Middling! But they call me Clay now. Born in Sausalito, currently living in Marin City." He didn't want her to know that Dori had told him about her, so he played dumb. "And you?"

"Birdie! Birdie Guertner."

Clay couldn't help laughing at the idea of a girl named Birdie. "Really!" he said. "Birdie! Is that your real name?"

"Authentic! Certified! Government approved!" She'd never really liked the name Avis, so she was more than happy to be known as Birdie.

"Good," he said, "because I really like it."

"Anything *else* you like about me?" she asked, then flashed him a coy 'Come Up and See Me Sometime' wink. "Weekend special! Everything's thirty percent off, now through Sunday." She blew the foam off her beer and took down the remainder in one sloppy, theatrical chug.

"Whoa!" said Clay. "Not sure I can keep up with that kind o' drinking. I'm more the slow, deliberate type."

Birdie handed him her empty glass, then jabbed her thumb back toward the keg line they'd been in only moments ago.

"Deliberate?" she said. "Maybe so, maybe not. So let's find out! Do me a favor, sweetie, and go fetch me another beer. And another one for *you*, Mr. Hot-and-Foxy. The proof's in the pudding, right? We'll get to it one pint at a time."

Clay did as he was told, then came back to Birdie with two filled-to-capacity tumblers and handed one of them to her. Then they held their libations up toward the sun, admiring their rich, amber glow.

"Three . . . two . . . one!" laughed Birdie, and Clay, who by now had pretty much bid adieu to his inhibitions, gladly followed suit. They polished off round two in record time, and three rounds later they were up in Tommy's guest bedroom, urgently yanking their clothes off and feasting on the sight of each other's soon-to-be-buck-naked bodies. Dori, knowing all too well the intensity of Birdie's needs and desires, had given her the house key and directions to the bedroom two days ago.

"Don't be so bashful!" said Birdie, giggling like a schoolgirl as she unhooked her bra and stepped out of her panties. "A slim, tight-assed young stallion like you? You've just *got* to know all the good moves by now!"

She wondered why Clay was taking so long—most men, in their hyper-masculine eagerness, would be sprinting toward the finish line by now—then looked down and saw that he'd gotten his shirttail stuck in his zipper.

"Same old story!" she laughed. "But no need to worry, big guy. Mommy'll fix that for you!" Then she dropped to her knees and unjammed the zipper, and out popped his Johnny—a well-built Jack-in-the-box, all set for playtime.

They were soon locked in fleshly combat, with Birdie—by far the more experienced of the two—in the lead and Clay, still obviously a sexual apprentice, playing catch-up. They assumed the usual positions and tried the usual moves, but what the two of them had fully expected to be a long, joyful Battle of the Hormones never made it beyond a skirmish.

It was over far more quickly than either of them wanted it to be. The sun was setting now, and inside, the bedroom was bathed in half-darkness. Other than the sound of their rhythmic postcoital breathing, the only thing that could be heard was the slow, steady ticking of a mantel clock overlooking the bed. Birdie could tell Clay's ego had been wounded, and he could tell she was obviously less than fulfilled.

Still, in spite of their unspoken disappointment, they lay stretched out on the bed, slick with perspiration, smiling and embracing as seemed only appropriate under the circumstances. They may have been coupling with abandon only moments ago, but because they hardly knew each other, their minds had already gone in very different directions. They were anything but a couple.

Guess I should have gone easier on the booze, thought Birdie while buttoning her blouse. *Am I stupid, or what? I clearly pressed his button way too soon!*

That girl's got one hell of a snatch, Clay thought to himself as he pulled up his slacks and slipped into his shoes. *A guaranteed wet dream!*

But deep down inside, he knew he was ashamed of himself. He'd been reasonably certain it was going to be nothing more than a guilt-free summertime romp in the hay, so he was quietly shocked to discover that, to him, she was much more than a simple conquest. He was attracted to her as a *person*— as a personality. Even worse, he knew he hadn't really been up to the challenge as a lover, and as he stood there in the darkness, watching Birdie move slowly toward the door and out of his life—perhaps forever—his eyes filled with tears.

"Don't worry," she said, then blew him a kiss from across the room. "You were terrific! The way I see it, it's good when it's wild and it's good when it's tame. Good when it's fast and good when it's slow. Yes, you were in a hurry today. Kind o' businesslike, if you ask me. So big deal! Honestly, I thought you were *adorable* as a bedmate. So what's the problem, then, Captain?"

"The problem," said Clay, "is that the moment I saw you today, I was genuinely *attracted* to you. *All* of you! And I wanted to impress you! But as you know all too well, I got smashed instead. And even though I know from experience that I can't handle that much booze and make things happen in bed, I went ahead and tried—and ended up making a complete ass of myself!"

"We'd better leave it at that for now," said Birdie. Then she stepped back across the room and handed him a slip of paper with her phone number on it. "Put this in your wallet," she said. "You'll have it for a rainy day. And don't you *dare* think I'm gonna forget you, because I won't! The fact is I *like* you. Really! And who knows? Someday we might have the good fortune to cross paths again. Wouldn't that be lovely?"

"Maybe so," said Clay. "Maybe so. I'll think about it."

Birdie found her way downstairs, then stepped out onto the lawn and headed for her car. Though it was chilly outside now, she stopped for a moment to watch, shivering, as a spectacular series of blue and yellow chrysanthemums brightened the late-night sky. Only a handful of guests were still on the property, some of them still tanking up, others either passed out in their lawn chairs or groping each other in the lush, clandestine nooks and crannies of the Dolliver estate.

Clay watched Birdie glide across the emerald-green, expertly manicured lawn, her sleek blond hair shimmering in the moonlight, then turned wistfully away and set out to find Dori. He finally tracked him down in the caretaker's utility shed, putting lawn chairs away. He pitched in and helped him finish the chore, and moments later, weak-kneed from boozing and audibly short of breath, they climbed into Dori's car and settled in for the trip back to Marin City.

Exhausted from the long afternoon of partying, they said nothing to each other for nearly all of the five-mile trip home. It wasn't until they could see the Golden Gate looming ahead of them in the fog that Dori broke the silence.

"So how'd it go?" he asked. "Did you seize the moment and shag the Birdie?"

"Cut it out!" said Clay, then turned angrily away from him and stared out the passenger window. "We talked and talked and had a really nice time! That's all that happened—nothing more!"

"Oh, yeah," said Dori. "And have I told you? I've decided to get the hell out of this shithole of a town, find myself a nice, cozy seminary, and study for the priesthood! Sex is for the sinners; friendship's for the saints. The Bible tells me so! Anyway, I've no doubt you and Birdie will make swell passion-free long-distance pen pals. That's because I just happen to know she's heading to New Jersey next month. Has family there and wants to spend some time with them."

The two of them went silent again, and twenty minutes later they were back in Marin City, nursing their headaches, sorting out their emotions, and doing their best to fall asleep. They badly needed the rest, because in less than five hours they'd be back on the grounds of Marin City Flea Market, plucking trash off the lawn.

Until then, Clay knew he was doomed to torment himself with thoughts of Birdie Guertner and how it was that he'd managed to fail so miserably to please either her—a stunningly beautiful girl with a captivating personality—or his own fragile, mortally wounded self.

Chapter Four

Five months had passed since Tommy Dolliver's Fourth of July party, and 1967 was only a few weeks away. He and Clay were still living together and working at the Flea Market, but their patience for the mind-numbing work they were doing was wearing thin. Clay was especially fed up with his circumstances.

Dusk was fast approaching now, and as they continued to pick up trash, they watched with great relief as a long, asymmetrical necklace of cars, buses, and Harleys headed out to 101 South, glowing a rich metallic orange in the sunset. It meant their workday was nearly over.

"This place is an absolute disaster!" said Dori, then speared a half dozen gummed-over cigar butts—two of them stained with lipstick—and tossed them into the nearest trash bucket.

"Holy shit!" said Clay. "What kind o' woman sucks on a stogie?"

"The kind you wish would suck on *your* stogie." said Dori, then made a fist and jabbed Clay on the shoulder. "Listen, Janis Joplin smokes cigars. Bet y' didn't know that."

"Oh, I know it, all right, but it ain't *all* I know. I also know she's smokin' hot in bed. Loves screwing! I read all about it in *Rolling Stone*—first person narrative."

"Shut your fat mouth!" said Dori. "What the fuck do you know about screwing? You didn't even grab the snatch when you had it right there 'neath your wiener on the Fourth!" Then he reached into his pants pocket and pulled out a beat-up leather-bound flask he'd found inside an abandoned Camaro a few days ago.

"Take a swig o' *this*, Romeo," he said. Then he unscrewed the lid and handed him the flask. "Maybe it'll perk up that dysfunctional pecker of yours."

"No thanks," said Clay, one insult away from losing his temper. "You know we're not allowed to drink on the job. Use your noodle, for Christ's sake."

"I use my noodle quite often," he said. "Trust me! But you? You don't use yours 'cause you don't even know what the fuck it's *for*. Now, come on, pussy," he sneered, "*take* some! A *real* man ain't afraid to take a little snort or two on the job."

Clay, tired of fielding insults and innuendos about his sexual prowess, waved Dori's outstretched arm away, then grabbed him roughly by the shoulders and drew him so close their chins were touching.

"One more smart remark about my sex life, Breitmeyer, and I'm gonna turn that ugly face of yours into a plate o' hash browns!" Then he shoved him down, pounced on him, and pinned his arms to the ground.

"*Jesus*, Clay," shouted Dori. "What the hell's come over you? We used to have fun making fun of each other."

"That was then, and this is now," said Clay. "Listen, you don't know shit about my sex life. It's usually people who don't *have* a sex life who get a kick out of tormenting people who *do*." As he struggled to keep Dori pinned down, he saw Simon La Branch, the groundskeeper, leap out of his truck and come running toward them, his face contorted with rage. He was big and beefy, with dark, wiry hair carpeting his chest and an array of colorful tattoos—including a swastika and a blood-dripping knife—on his Popeye-like forearms.

"Let me up," shouted Dori. "The boss is coming, and from the looks of things, it ain't for afternoon tea!"

Clay immediately climbed off Dori and helped him get into a standing position. Then the two of them brushed the dust off their Levi's, raked the grass out of their hair, and stood like a pair of cardboard cutouts, waiting for their Moment of Truth.

"So this is what I've been payin' you little pricks to do while I'm back in the office, fillin' out forms and dealin' with assholes just like you!"

"We were all done for the day," said Dori, shrugging his shoulders.

"It's 5:30 now," said La Branch. "Your workday ends at 6:00."

"We always horse around at the end of our shift," said Dori. "It's just our way of unwinding after a hard day's work."

La Branch shook his head in disgust. "Did you say 'done for the day'?"

"Yes, sir," said Clay, and, like a pair of humiliated bobbleheads, the two of them nodded in unison.

"True enough," said La Branch. "But not just for the day. You're done for good! *Forever!* Now gimme those pickup sticks and get the hell off my property. Time to go home and horse around on your own damn time."

He grabbed the two poles, stormed back to his truck, and climbed in. "I should o' stuck 'em up your asses," he said, "but I've get better things to do. Gotta get on the phone and find me a couple o' guys with *brains*!"

Depressed and angry, Dori and Clay stopped at the Trident on the way home to lick their wounds while polishing off burgers and a round or two of beer. The murals on the restaurant's interior walls, poorly designed and sloppily painted, were a perfect complement to their disillusioned, devil-may-care mood.

"Jesus," said Clay, "I don't know why I ever agreed to take that job. I mean, let's face it. It was pure, slow-dripping torture just to get up and go there every day."

Dori took another swipe at his Lucky Lager, wiped his mouth on his shirtsleeve, then turned away and let loose a belch so loud, so frat-boy theatrical, that it made the prim and proper couple at the next table over stop their eating and glare at him in disgust.

Then he turned back to Clay. "Don't be stupid!" he said. "You know why you took that job. You took it because you needed the friggin' *money* and wanted desperately to get the hell away from your Old Man."

Clay winced, then went silent because he knew that, once again, Dori had gone straight to the heart of an issue uncomfortably close to home.

"I suppose you're right," he said. "But I still hated working at the Flea Market. What a dump. What a dead-end way to make a living! I need to get my shit together right away and find something better to do—something worth my time—something that pays a hell of a lot more per hour than we were ever gonna get from that toad La Branch."

"How about doin' some temp work?" said Dori. "It would keep the dollars rollin' in, and you'd be able to slow down and search for something really lucrative."

"Maybe I will, maybe I won't," said Clay. "I mean, temp work ain't no picnic, either. Now let's pay the fuckin' bill, then get out o' this place before the cops come by and slap a fine on us for talking dirty!" He stood up from the table, fired off his very own belch, even more horrendous than Dori's—this time directed spot-on at the same couple—then sat down and waited quietly as Dori went up front and paid the cashier. Moments later, they were on the road again, driving home to their apartment and into a future so uncertain—so hard to imagine—that Clay couldn't bear to think about it.

Chapter Five

Nearly a month after Clay's and Dori's firing, Clay still hadn't found a job. Without a recommendation from La Branch, his most recent employer, he was forced at every turn to make excuses, shade the truth, and lie outright just to land an interview.

Dorian, true to his word, went out the day after he was sacked and landed a three-month-long temp assignment as the truck driver for a restaurant supply business. If at the end of the three months his boss was happy with his performance, he was told, he'd be offered a permanent position with a decent salary, a two-week paid vacation, and medical insurance.

After three months without a nibble, Clay was falling headlong into depression bordering on despondency. To fill the long, painful hours of waiting for the phone to ring, he began spending his days on the couch, either drooling over the centerfolds from past issues of *Playboy* or watching reruns of *Petticoat Junction* and *My Favorite Martian*.

More and more frequently, Dori would come home from work and find Clay sound asleep on the couch, an empty beer bottle and a half-eaten wedge of pizza beside him on the TV table. By now the scene had become old news for Dori. He missed flopping down on the couch after work and resented seeing Clay monopolize the one piece of furniture that he, not Clay, had bought for the two of them in a rare moment of selflessness. He'd also begun to wonder if his roommate, who was falling behind on his share of the rent, would ever listen to his conscience, get up off that couch, and pound the pavement like everyone else does when they're unemployed.

The following Monday after work, Dori hung his jacket in the foyer, kicked off his work shoes, then stepped up behind the couch and, without warning, shook it violently, jarring Clay from a deep, dream-filled sleep.

"What the fuck!" shouted Clay. "Can't you see I was sleeping?"

"You *bet* I saw you were sleeping," said Dori. "It's all you ever *do* any more. But guess what? Your time has come! Your train has arrived! Enough is enough! Now get your ass off my couch and clean up the mess you've made on the carpet. Are you a human or a pig?" He made a club out of the *Sausalito News* and brought it down, forcefully, on Clay's head.

"Time to get reacquainted with the Hometown Classifieds, Bozo! And it's your last chance, because this is the last issue. They're goin' out o' business—just like you've been doin' for the past three months!"

Still groggy and disoriented from hours of fitful sleeping, Clay dragged himself up off the couch, picked up the beer bottle and pizza from the TV table, and stormed out of the room, leaving a trail of crumbs and chopped onions as he went.

"The last issue? Fine!" he growled. It's nothin' but a rag anyway. Good riddance! And good riddance to *you*, asshole. Tonight will be my last night livin' with a jerk like you. I'm movin' out tomorrow!"

"Gonna run back to Daddy again?" said Dori, shaking his head. But the truth was that he wasn't at all surprised. "Father Knows Best," he chuckled. "Hasn't that always been your plan?"

"None o' your damn business!" said Clay. "I'll do whatever the fuck I feel like. And by the way, you owe me twenty dollars, deadbeat. Remember? I paid for your Jerry Garcia ticket when you forgot your wallet last week. So leave that

Andy on the kitchen table tomorrow before you go to work. And when you get home, that sorry excuse for a couch will be all yours again, and I'll be long gone from this dump!"

Dori went to the kitchen and put a TV dinner in the oven, but Clay, too angry to stick around, caught a taxi to the Guernica, one of his favorite restaurants, and drowned his sorrow in the specialty of the house, bouillabaisse. He topped it off with a double order of garlic bread, and when he'd finally had his fill, he washed it all down with three quick shots of pacharán liqueur. The waiter could see right away that he was overdoing it. He was soon listing like a sailboat in a derecho—so he cut him off, brought him his check, thanked him for his patronage, and sent him on his way.

That boy must be in a heap o' trouble, he thought to himself while clearing the table. *He dined alone, and he never cracked a smile the whole time he was here.* The waiter saw Middling's kind nearly every night of the week, and he knew from experience that only someone in deep emotional trouble would be dumb enough to eat that much food, then guzzle three straight pacharáns in a row. *Christ,* he snorted. *He may as well have chugged a bottle o' Clorox; it's a whole lot cheaper than booze. Mark my words: he's gonna wake up tomorrow with one hell of a hangover, facedown in a pool of vomit.*

The waiter's hunch was right on the money. Clay went to Dori's place to crash—he realized too late that he had no other place to stay that night—then woke up late the next morning with a splitting headache and, on his pillow, a ghastly billabong of recycled halibut, pacharán, and banana cream pie. His bedsheets and pajamas were caked with vomit and smelled to high heaven. *Think I'll let Dori take care o' this mess,* he laughed. *It'll give that asshole something to do when he gets home from work.*

He cracked open a window for relief, then took a shower,

threw on a pair of jeans and a shirt, and poured himself a cup of coffee. He found his twenty dollars on top of the breadbox, and beneath it a small white envelope with his name scrawled on it. *Gotta give Dori some credit,* he mused. *He can actually be true to his word if you put enough heat on him.*

He stuffed the bill into his wallet, then opened the envelope and unfolded the note. It was written on a scrap of oil-stained butcher paper and had the unmistakable odor of fresh fish and seawater. He held the paper up to his nose and sniffed it. *Halibut,* he smiled. *He must have been down to Alioto's again. Christ! Stuff's damned expensive there. The bastard never scrimped on fish, and yet he was too cheap to buy a box o' Cocoa Puffs. Go figure!*

The note didn't mince words. As Clay read it, his ears burned. It was as if he were suddenly back in Our Lady of the Sacraments, being trimmed down by the head nun for some unpardonable sin he'd committed in study hall. However, Dori's choice of words wasn't especially nun-like. He was good at talking truths, but he also had the unfortunate habit of using words a lot more colorful than the average Religious would have chosen, especially while in the service of the Lord.

Listen up, Middling. You've gotta get your shit together! Find yourself a job—any job! Won't really matter what you choose; it'll sure as hell be better than camping out on that couch day and night, watching stupid, warmed-over sitcoms.

And while you're at it, find yourself a woman! Are you still seeing Birdie Guertner? If you aren't, then either get yourself back in the sack with her or find a suitable replacement.

Work and women: they go together like a fucking horse and carriage! Let's face it: It takes a whole lot o' cash for a guy to keep his hottie feeling taken care of. Haven't you heard? No money, no nookie! I mean, how long do you wanna go without some snatch? C'mon, man!

Clay hated being preached at. He'd endured enough tongue-lashings from his parents over the years to last a lifetime, but this time he knew Dori was right. Being penniless was a pain in the pocketbook, and while jerking off might meet an immediate need, it had become more and more a genuine drag for him—a poor substitute for hidin' the salami.

First things first, he mumbled to himself. Then he sat down, suddenly full to overflowing with resolve, and tied his shoelaces. *Time to get the fuck outta here and find myself a steady supply of simoleons!*

Chapter Six

Two weeks after enduring Dori's rant, and badly in need of putting distance between the two of them, Clay still hadn't made a serious effort to find work. To cope with his restlessness, he drove north to El Verano, then headed down to Juanita's for breakfast. Formerly known as Juanita's Galley when it was on Gate 5 Road in Sausalito, the new Juanita's wasn't nearly as colorful now as it was then. But it was still a popular gathering place for the more rough-and-tumble locals. It was forced to move out of Sausalito after a melee involving forty bikers and a handful of Galley regulars shut it down.

While Juanita Musson wasn't exactly Clay's idea of beautiful—she was undeniably overweight and unkempt, even slovenly—it didn't really matter. And though she was notoriously hot-headed when crossed, if you behaved yourself she was nearly always fun to be around and had a way of making you feel good about yourself every time you went there.

Not a harpy in hair curlers like my Old Lady, he thought to himself, wincing as he recalled the more and more bitter exchanges he'd had with his mother over the last few months. *More like your sweet, acid-tongued Aunt Lillian from Tuscaloosa, home for Thanksgiving, on her game, and ill-behaved at the dinner table. And yet empathetic,* he smiled. He could always count on Juanita when a storm was brewing in his head.

He pulled up a chair, settled into Table No. 7, and waited for someone to come and take his order. To his delight, instead of another nameless, dime-a-dozen bimbo, it was

Juanita herself who came to his aid, gliding adeptly over the greasy, uneven floors that had sent so many unwitting Juanita's customers down on their asses—even to the ER—over the years.

"Well, if it ain't the one and only Clayborne Middling!" squealed Juanita. She immediately leaned down and bear-hugged him, smothering the greater portion of his face with one of her huge, pendulous breasts. It was a little like being suddenly embraced by The Blob.

"Juanita!" he shouted, but his voice, usually crisp and staccato, sounded at the moment as if he were speaking through a ball of socks.

"So how's it goin', chum?" she bellowed. She let him loose and backed away, then stood there, hands on hips, and smiled affectionately at him.

"Things could be better," said Clay. "I was having trouble with my parents. They were always bitchin' at me about my need to find steady work. So I finally packed up and moved out. Hooked up with my friend Dorian Breitmeyer, who needed a roommate to keep his expenses down."

"Bet that was a good deal for both of you!" she smiled.

"It *was*," said Clay, "at least in the beginning. He even found me a job at Marin City Flea Market! That's where he'd been working for the last couple of years, so getting me hired was a cinch. Anyway, things were going well until the boss happened by one afternoon, saw us horsing around, and fired us on the spot for failing to work right up until closing time. I tried to tell him we were tired—that we'd done all of the work we were supposed to do that day and just needed to unwind for a minute or two before checking out. But he didn't buy my argument. We didn't think it was such a big deal, but he obviously did!"

"Listen," said Juanita, "I'd have done more than just fire the two of you. I'd have pulled your ears off and dumped you into the nearest waste bin. Bosses don't pay the help to screw around on company time!"

"I haven't even told you the worst of it," said Clay. "Dori found another job right away, but I didn't. And before long he got tired of having me lying around at home while he was at work. So he came home one night, saw me sound asleep on the couch, and started shouting at me. Told me to get the hell out of his apartment and find myself a job, just like *he* did!"

"Well, shit!" said Juanita. "But you know what? Dorian was right! You've got to do something about that right away. And about you and your parents, too. Listen, I was just messin' around with you a minute ago. You know I've always been fond of you and your family. But Mommy and Daddy do have a point, don't they? Their little boy is no longer all that little."

She leaned over him again, then put one beefy, water-burned hand on his shoulder and gave his hair a motherly tousle. "You're at the age, Clay, when you've just *got* to have steady employment. Time to grow up and take charge of yourself. Ain't nobody gonna do it *for* you!" She stepped back from him again and gave him a thorough once-over. "You know what, Clay? You're lookin' kind o' scrawny! What's happened to the Big Guy I remember?"

Clay shrugged.

"Don't know?" she said. "Well, *Juanita* knows. You need to fatten up them ribs o' yours! And because I kind o' like you, it'll be all you can eat. On the house!"

Oh, my God, he wondered. *Have I stooped so low I'm taking handouts now?* He went silent for a moment, then reached up, gave her a grateful smile, and patted her affectionately on an elbow. "I'll *take* it," he said.

Ten minutes later she was back again, this time with a generous plateful of piping hot pancakes, home fries, and sausage.

"Now, I don't wanna see even one little scrap o' food on that plate when I come back!" she laughed. "Understand? And I hope I'll be seein' you again one day soon—but not until you've landed a job. And not just any job, either! This time it's got to be a job worth *keeping*."

He finished his breakfast in record time. Minutes later, when Juanita came back to check on him and clear the table, he stood up and gave her a long, sincere goodbye hug. "That was so sweet of you!" he said. "I had to come here to get what I never got at home—a little *empathy*."

"Come any time, honey," she said. "I've got plenty more lovin' where that came from!"

He blew her a kiss, then headed out to his car and drove straight back to Sausalito. As he drove listlessly through the late-morning traffic, he found himself thinking fondly of his uncle Leandro Constantine—his houseboat in Sausalito, his colorful personality, his all-around decency over the years—then decided to go straight to Galilee Harbor and ask him to put him up for a few nights until he could find a job and another place to live.

Chapter Seven

Clay arrived at Leandro's place with a knapsack slung over his shoulder, and as he inched his way toward the entrance of the houseboat, he could feel the gangplank swaying with the help of a stiff breeze off the harbor. Leandro heard him coming, then jumped up from the couch and peered through the peephole. He swung the door open and, like the bird in a cuckoo clock, stuck his head out.

"Giásou, Clay!" he said. "What brings you to my watery abode? And what's with the knapsack?"

"Nothin' special," said Clay, then removed the knapsack and dropped it by his feet. "I was just walking around the harbor for a bit and thought I might stop by and see what my Uncle Leanie, the Sausalito Greek, is up to these days."

"Just out walking? With a *knapsack*? Don't you go jerkin' me around!" he laughed. Then a warm, welcoming smile quickly spread across his leathery, sunbaked face.

"A Middling never does just 'nothin' special.' He's always got a plan—or more likely a scheme—up his sleeve. And it's nearly always got somethin' to do with money. I mean, *Jesus,* Clay. You're a regular chip off your Old Man's block, aren't you. The spittin' image!"

Clay shot his uncle a dirty look. "Thanks a lot!" he snapped. "The last thing I am is the spittin' image of my father! And I'm not here for money, either—not exactly, anyway." Then he shrugged his shoulders and looked awkwardly down at his feet. "The truth is, I was just hoping you might be willing to help me save some money. I've just lost my job, and I'm in a real pinch right now. I thought you might let me stay here for a few days until I can find another way to make some cabbage—I mean *serious* cabbage, not the chump change I've been making for the past few months. It's about time I moved up a rung or two on the job ladder. I'm tired of living like a freakin' hobo."

"Slow down!" said Leandro. "Take a deep breath!" He moved in close on his nephew and put one gnarled index finger under his chin. "Did I just hear you right? Did you say you've lost another job?"

"Well, yeah," Clay answered. "I 'lost another job,' if you wanna put it that way. Ain't no use pretending! By the way, I'm accustomed to getting smears like that at home, but I didn't expect to hear it from my Uncle Leandro—not today, anyway!"

"You expected me to send you a sympathy card? Listen, son: you're knockin' on the wrong damn door if that's what you want."

"It's not like I just lost some Big Dollar position—a job worth having in the first place! I was a common yard worker—the lowest rung on the ladder—at Marin City Flea Market. And trust me, Leanie, it was mindless, buck-forty-an-hour grunt work—the kind of no-future gig that only dimwits and derelicts ought to be doin'!"

"The way I see it," said Leanie, "it was pretty damn dimwitted of *you* to have taken that job in the *first* place. You need to think better of yourself than that."

"So can you help me or not?" said Clay. "All I'm asking for is a place to sleep and a working toilet—nothing fancy."

"I don't know," said Leandro. "I just don't know. I mean, it's already crowded here with me and Latrice."

"Latrice?" Clay shouted. "You've got a babe named Latrice in the sack with you now?"

"No, stupid! Latrice is not a 'babe'—she's my pet macaw!"

"A *macaw*? Who the hell wants a friggin' macaw in his house?"

"I do," said Leanie. "*I* do! And to be precise, she's a hyacinth macaw. Thirty years old, too! For a bird like Latrice, that's middle age."

"But don't they squawk all the time?"

"Well, she does get noisy on occasion; I'll grant you that. But most of the time, she's sweet as sugar."

"Well," said Clay, "I suppose I could learn to live with a macaw for a few days."

"All right," said Leanie. "If that's how you feel, then you're on! I must be losin' my mind, but let's give it a shot. And as for Latrice, we'll have to wait a few days to see if *she* can put up with *you*."

"Oh, yeah!" said Clay, beaming. "I just knew I could count on my Uncle Leanie in a crunch!"

"We'll see about that," said Leandro. "Now grab your knapsack, matie, and come with me. For the next few days, this boat's gonna be your home. But before I get you settled in, you need to get something straight. This place ain't gonna be no Nirvana by the Sea! No keg parties! No chug-a-thons! No late-night pussy on the poop deck!"

"I *get* it," he said. "I really do! The chicks can wait. Besides, there'll be plenty of time for messin' around once I've landed a job. Plenty of money, too! Right now, though, I'm all business!" Clay looked around, then remembered Dori's couch and screwed up his face. "But where will I be sleeping? There's so much crap around this place."

"Might be crap to you, my boy, but it's essential equipment to Cap'n Ahab. You'll find out! Anyway, see that series of coat hooks? The ones high up on that bright orange panel between the bookshelves and cupboards?"

"Yeah, I see 'em," said Clay. "What about 'em?"

"Grab that leather loop near the top of the panel, then yank down hard on it—not *too* hard, but hard."

He did as he was told, and seconds later a wall-mounted

bed, fully made and all set to sleep in, came creaking down like a drawbridge and settled into position on the floor of the houseboat. It nearly touched the wall opposite the panel, but there was just enough room between the two to allow someone to get wherever he needed to go without disturbing the sleeper.

"Sweet!" said Clay. "A hell of a lot better than that shitty little matchbox I slept in at home!"

"You won't wanna get too comfortable in that bed," said Leanie. "You aren't gonna *live* here, you're gonna *stay* here. And whenever you're not working for me, you'll need to get out and pound the pavement!"

"Pound the pavement?" said Clay. "What's that mean?"

"Pretty simple," said Leandro. "It means get a job! But one thing at a time, young fella. I'll see you bright 'n' early tomorrow."

The message came through loud and clear. Clay realized his uncle meant business, so he drove into downtown Sausalito right away and picked up the latest edition of the *Chronicle*. Then he went to Fred's Place on Bridgeway, and over a bowl of chili and a slab of cornbread—to his surprise, he was still hungry in spite of the mountainous breakfast he'd devoured at Juanita's—he scanned the Help Wanted section. He knew he had to move fast, so he couldn't afford to be picky.

The first opening that caught his attention was for a part-time delivery and maintenance person at the legendary Tides Bookstore, also on Bridgeway.

Can you read? Doesn't matter. We need your brawn, not your brains. Must start immediately and be able to lift 50 lbs. Tides Bookstore, 501-4229.

Clay hardly ever read books. *What's the point?* he asked himself. *I can get whatever I need to know right off the Boob Tube.* So this job looked perfect. *They aren't looking for an Einstein; they're looking for a muscly, meat-and-potatoes kind o' guy—like me! And I wouldn't have to read the books, anyway, only lift 'em. Yahoo!* He found a phone booth, fed some coins into the coin slot, and dialed up the number in the ad. A half dozen rings later, a gruff male voice barked into the receiver.

"Receiving!" it said. "Ernie!"

Clay suddenly realized he hadn't planned what to say.

A man sighed exasperatedly into the receiver. "So who is it this time?" he snarled. "I mean, my fuckin' phone's been ringing every three seconds. How's a fella supposed to get any *work* done?"

While truly appalled by the man's rudeness, Clay was determined to keep his cool. *Maybe he's just being playful,* he thought, *having a little fun with me, keeping things light.*

"Good morning, sir!" said Clay. "I'm calling about that job opening in today's *Chronicle.* Sounds like a good fit for me."

"Well, that's just dandy," said Ernie. "A good fit, huh? I should think I'd be the judge of that, not you! Anyway, what took you so long, smart guy? I mean, how bad do you actually need a job? Not very, I'd say."

"Badly!" said Clay, swallowing his pride and preparing for battle. "I'm genuinely interested. Really! There just has to be something I can do to help you. And besides, I've always loved books. I'd read every damn book in the library if I only had the time. Honest! I got an A in American Lit in high school!"

"To tell you the truth," said Ernie, "I really don't give a shit about your A in American Lit. I mean, did you really read the ad? Look: I have to listen to phonies like you every day at work. I'm not dumb enough to hire one."

Fed up, Clay slammed the receiver back into its cradle—loud enough, he hoped, to give Mr. Grouchy a serious ear-ache. *I wouldn't work for an asshole like that anyway,* he laughed. *Guess I'm gonna have to be more discriminating.*

Determined to land a position, he dove back into the Help Wanted section, and two long, arduous pages later, he'd finally found another nibble under the heading Hospital Support Staff.

Wanted: Food service trainee, Ross General Hospital. Steady part-time work with multiple responsibilities including food prep, dishwashing, cashiering, kitchen maintenance, and delivery. Previous experience not necessary. Must provide at least three letters of rec-ommendation for reliability, character, good health, and ability to work in a friendly, fast-moving team-work setting. Must be available for training beginning Monday, July 17.

"Jesus!" shouted Clay to the display of XXX-rated call girl flyers wallpapering the phone booth. "Are they hirin' a dishwasher or the Surgeon General?" He knew it wasn't exactly his cup of tea, but he decided to give it a try any-way. He had just enough change left in his pants pocket to cover a second call, so he laid the coins out on the platform, put in the amount needed, then dialed 1-800-774-ROSS.

"Hello," said a jittery, high-pitched voice. "Who am I speaking to?"

"Clayborne Middling," he said. "I hear you're looking for a food service trainee, and I'm interested. Is it you I should speak with about it?"

"Food service trainee? I'm not looking for a food service trainee. I've been doin' my own dishes for nearly forty years. My husband, God bless him, doesn't think he should have to! So why would I need a food service trainee? You must have a wrong number."

"No, I do *not* have a wrong number," said Clay, growing impatient. "I have the *right* number. I know it's the right number because I checked it three times before I dialed. By the way, I'm also good at math! I never make mistakes with numbers."

There was a long, uncomfortable silence, followed by an obvious sigh of exasperation—all too familiar to Clay by now—and then a loud, indignant slam-down at the other end of the line.

Touché, he muttered. *The bitch hung up on me! Another hot prospect down the drain. Hot as a friggin' ice cube.*

He jerked open the accordion door, then stepped out and slumped down on a nearby park bench, discouraged, desperate, and disillusioned.

My God, he lamented, *there's got to be a better way out o' this mess than job hunting the old-fashioned way. Besides, why should a guy with my talents settle for some mindless, dead-end position that pays less than shit? These corporate guys are all alike—a bunch o' goddam cheapskates. They reduce their overhead by working their employees to death, then squander the excess on yachts and junkets and one-night stands. That's corporate greed for you. I can do better!*

He sat there, nodding and reflecting, for nearly an hour, trying his best to come up with an idea while watching car after car of gainfully employed working stiffs roll through the intersection, smiling cheerfully on their way to and from steady, rewarding, well-paid positions. He knew it wasn't right, but he hated them, if only for their good fortune. And at this particular moment, he hated their *guts*.

Badly in need of sleep yet too ashamed to go back to his uncle's place empty-handed, Clay made a pillow out of his jacket and stretched out on the bench. He watched as a flock of sparrows swept down onto a nearby rooftop, lined themselves up like soldiers on roll call, and stared inquisitively down at him.

He remembered from his World History class that Buckminster Fuller was famous for a great many reasons, one of which was his passion for napping. Whenever Fuller had a problem that needed solving, Mr. Jennison said, he'd just lie down and fall asleep, and when he woke up the solution would come to him like a flash of lightning.

If it worked for Bucky, maybe it'll work for me, Clay thought to himself. *I'll give it a try!*

Before long he managed to fall into a deep, rejuvenating slumber, and when he woke up an hour later, the sun blazing down on him, he was shocked to realize that the answer to his problems had indeed been delivered to him like a Gift from the Gods—or maybe from Bucky—while he was sound asleep on a park bench. He saw the same flock of sparrows still staring down at him, chattering amongst themselves, and wondered if they were able to tell how happy he was to have found a solution while sound asleep.

He sat up, yawned and stretched, then dialed the just-in-case number he'd stored in his wallet long ago. A dozen ear-shredding rings later, he finally made the contact he needed.

"Who's this?" said a sharp, contentious voice, obviously a male—and, even more obviously, his father.

"It's Clay!" he said. "Remember? Your son, Clay!"

"Oh, my God!" said Stan, genuinely surprised and then more than happy to have heard from his son again so soon after their quarrel. "Do me a favor," he said, "and tell me you've finally landed a job!"

For a moment, he'd sounded to Clay like the father he remembered from his childhood—jolly, upbeat, almost musical. But he knew the music was about to die, because he was about to disappoint his father yet again, Big Time.

"Not yet," he said. "Almost, but not yet. The truth is, I was having trouble trying to live with Dori. He was getting on my nerves, and I was clearly getting on his, too. He found a job right away, but I didn't—and that only made things worse."

"Well, that's no surprise," said Stan, who quickly realized that nothing had really changed. "So *now* what are you gonna do? What's next? Have you patched things up with Dori?"

"Not really," said Clay. "He got so fed up with me moping around the apartment, he kicked me out! I tried other job leads but got nowhere, so I went down to Galilee Harbor and asked Uncle Leandro if he'd be willing to put me up on his houseboat until I land a position. He finally said yes, so I'm supposed to come back tomorrow and start doin' odd jobs for him to earn my keep. I'm thankful, and yet I can't quite see how it's gonna . . ."

"How it's gonna *work*? Listen, I can finish the fucking sentence *for* you! You can't quite see how it's gonna work because it *isn't* gonna work! You know that and I know that."

Shaken and humiliated, Clay prepared himself emotionally to ask the impossible, knowing full well that it would be like tossing a lit match into a tankful of gasoline.

"Anyway, I was wondering if you and Mom might . . ."

"I know, I know," said Stan. "If your mother and I might be willing to bail you out for the umpteenth time. Let me guess: you want to come home right away—tonight—and sponge off the Old Man again. Right?"

Clay bit his tongue, then waited to see what further abuse he was about to be subjected to. But, to his surprise, instead of showering him with another round of insults his father offered him a rare moment of tenderness.

"Listen, Clay," he said. "I do still love you. But I'm only human! And to tell you the truth, I've been more and more sick and tired of your floundering around in the work world—of taking shitty, no-future assignments that always seem to end in failure. So this is what we need to do: I want you to call your Uncle Leandro—*tonight*—and tell him, No way, José!"

"But Uncle Leandro's *Greek*," Clay said.

"I *know* he's Greek," said Stan. "Don't jerk me around! But seriously: can't you see? You'd be wasting your time on that silly houseboat, and so would he! So be a *man* for a change! Put your foot down and tell him you're not coming. Tell him you'll find your own way out o' the mess you've created for yourself."

"Jesus, Dad!" said Clay. "My own way? I mean, what the fuck would I do after that? Set up shop on a park bench? Report to the nearest homeless shelter? Those don't sound like workable solutions to me."

"Just shut up and listen to Papa," said Stan. "How 'bout doing me a favor and *trusting* me for a change!"

Clay went silent.

"I was hesitant to call you about it—didn't know where the hell you were and what you've been up to—but we have another opening for a manager trainee down at S&N headquarters, and we'd like to offer it to you."

"Me? Why me?" said Clay. After all the abuse he'd just endured, it was the last thing he expected to hear from his father.

"Don't be stupid. You *know* why! You need a steady job—a good one, not a lousy one. And, by God, you're gonna take it whether you want to or not. Understand?"

"I think I get it," he shrugged, feeling deflated. "I mean, I'm finally getting the picture."

"'Bout *time* you did! So consider it done, my boy. You're

gonna come home, and you're gonna live with us until you're financially solvent enough to be out on your own again. But I'm tellin' you here and now, this will be your last chance to listen to Daddy—to take his advice and run with it. Got it?"

Clay realized that this time he was trapped. He had no choice but to either suck it up and be an ass-kissing S&N trainee working under the same roof as his father, or go back out on the road and continue to grovel for yet another low-paying, dead-end position.

"All right!" said Clay, resigned to his fate. "I'll call Leanie right away and tell him the deal is off. And I'll get to your place later tonight, soon as I can."

"Good! We'll leave the light on for you. But I'd better tell you in advance: until you prove you can actually succeed in the job we're training you for, I'll be keeping twenty percent of your take-home for household expenses. We're not running a homeless shelter at the Middling residence. Until you prove to us that you can find your wings and fly off on your own, you'll be our *tenant,* not our son. Now go make that call, then get your ass home before sundown or damn close to it!"

"Will do," said Clay. "Will do." Then he hung up on his father, called Leanie, and told him he'd changed his mind and wouldn't be staying with him after all.

"Well, I'll be damned," said Leandro with more than a hint of sarcasm. "So me and Latrice won't be having the pleasure of your company after all, huh?" He could feel the nasty side of himself welling up deep inside him, so he tamped it down, took the high road, wished his nephew well, and signed off as gracefully as he could under the circumstances.

Back home again late that night, tucked into his childhood bedroom, Clay wanted desperately to believe that the entire familial nightmare he'd been living through for the last few years—a weaponless army of ghosts from his troubled past—had finally faded out of existence. But the ghosts came back with a vengeance, hell-bent on tormenting him with memories of a severely mishandled, profoundly dysfunctional childhood. As he drifted off to sleep, he found himself praying that his life would soon take an upward turn and bring him close to something like a normal, crisis-free existence.

He woke up late the next morning to an ear-shattering ring from the Mickey Mouse telephone next to his bed. He loved nearly everything about that phone, a long ago gift from his grandmother Mavis, who knew, at the time, that he was a proud, enthusiastic member of the Mickey Mouse Club. But the phone's shrill, relentless ring—a sound so obnoxious it could wake a stone fence—made owning it a mixed blessing.

He tried to ignore the sound and fall back asleep, but Mickey clearly had other plans for him. He gave up and picked up the receiver, imagining for a split second that it might be his mother, calling him down for a delicious, lovingly prepared Welcome Home breakfast.

But it wasn't. It was Stan, who'd left earlier than usual for work and was calling him from his office. He sounded unusually surly and ill-tempered—which was saying a lot about a man who surely had been born surly and ill-tempered—so Clay braced himself and prepared for a lashing.

"Where the fuck *are* you, Clay?" he shouted. "I told you to show up promptly at 9:00 a.m.!"

"Show up?" said Clay. "Show up *when*? You never told me precisely when to 'show up,' so I figured I'd get a good night's sleep, then pull myself together and get down to S&N around midmorning."

"Midmorning, my ass!" he ranted. "Just get your sweet tushy down here as fast as possible. Can't you understand?

This is the very first day of your brand new life! You're now the newest recruit at Scheckel & Newbury, and your time with Henley Tuckerman, our training coordinator, will be unlike anything you've ever experienced—especially compared to those crummy jobs you've had in the last few months. By the way, Tuckerman is both my immediate supervisor and a longtime friend. He's also highly intelligent—an amazingly knowledgeable fellow—so he doesn't take any shit. Be prepared to do as he says or suffer the consequences, not just from him but from *me*. Understand?"

"Understand! I'll get down there ASAP. But I need an hour or so to whip myself into shape. I know you don't think so, but I can be a fast worker when I have to be."

He hung up, then grumbled to himself as he scrambled to prepare himself for Day One at Scheckel & Newbury. *But twenty percent of my take-home? Even Uncle Sam isn't as greedy as that!*

Chapter Eight

Clay managed to show up, properly attired and emotionally prepared, a little before noon, just in time to see a portly, smartly dressed man, probably in his late fifties, standing next to his father just inside the main entrance to the guest lounge. There could be no doubt it was Tuckerman, and Clay could see right away that his new boss was pointing down at his wristwatch, a look of hard-boiled disapproval etched across his brow. *Uh-oh,* thought Clay, *looks like this guy's gonna be a heavy hitter!*

He could also see that Scheckel & Newbury, which must have considered itself to be at or near the top of the list of nationally known real estate enterprises, didn't mess around with decor, either. The lounge was impeccably swank and luxurious—the sort of corporate touch that could easily have been in a scene from *Goldfinger.*

It was Stan, by far the most gregarious man on the S&N roster, who got the ball rolling.

"Meet your new underling!" he chirped to Henley. "I know he's a little late, but there was a bit of a mix-up. First-day jitters, I guess—as much my fault as his!" Stan turned to Clay and gave him a stern, disapproving look. "It won't happen again, will it, my boy?" Then he turned back to Tuckerman. "This boy of mine is a real go-getter, Henley—a hard worker and a quick learner. He'll absorb your words of wisdom like a sponge!"

"My pleasure," said Tuckerman, nodding warmly but patronizingly at Clay. "And by the way, Stan was right: you *do* look a lot like your father—though you're obviously a whole lot taller than him. Guess I'll know in a day or two whether you're a whole lot *smarter*, too!" He winked playfully at Clay, then smiled mischievously at Stan.

Clay—who, like most teenagers, had a high opinion of himself in spite of his insecurities—was instantly flattered. But his father, who'd been enduring comparisons like this more and more frequently whenever his son was around, was stung.

"Height alone can't make a man out of a boy," he sputtered, then glanced over at his son with an unmistakable aura of contempt. "Clay is still very much a work in progress! And yet maybe—just maybe, with a little help from the two of us—we'll manage to get him to the finish line in one piece."

"Thanks for the 'encouragement,' Pops," said Clay, who was equally stung but for very different reasons. Then he turned to Henley and, without looking back at his father, delivered an equally painful touché. "And who knows," he snickered, "you just may turn out to be even better at mentoring than my Old Man!"

Stan turned green as a chameleon and started for his office, then turned back toward the two of them.

"And may the best man win!" he said. "My guess, Henley, is that you're going to need more than a day or two to see what, if anything, this boy has between those two finely sculpted ears of his. As for me, I must confess that after years of uncertainty, I'm still looking for something—*anything*—in there."

Henley reached into his briefcase, pulled out a two-inch-thick stack of official-looking documents, then handed it to Clay. "I've no doubt I'll get an early and definitive measure of your gray matter just by seeing how you handle these documents," he said. "You need to go to your new office right now—second door down, on the right—then study the charts and record your observations. There's also a Q&A section on pages 17 through 26. It's just as important as everything else in the stack, so don't give it short shrift!"

"Promise!" said Clay, perhaps a little too unctuously. "It would be neither wise nor professional of me to do so, now, would it."

"And once you're finished, young man, you can bring the documents back to me. But no later than 3:00 p.m.! Your father said you're a fast worker and a stickler for details. So now, my boy, here's your one big chance to prove it. By the way, around here we call my approach to hiring the Sudden Death Analysis. An S&N candidate either swims like an Olympic gold medalist or sinks to the bottom on the very first lap, dead in the water."

Clay, by now thoroughly pissed at his father for playing Wise Old Owl in front of Henley, went into his office, closed the door with the words Clayborne Middling artfully displayed on it, then laid the stack of papers down on his desk and began sifting through them.

Wowzer, he thought, *they've put me only two doors down from the Grand Poobah himself! I've been here less than an hour, and I'm already three rungs up the ladder. That crap about 'Sudden Death Analysis' is just a playtime gimmick—another silly corporate shenanigan. I'll be at the top rung before Thanksgiving!*

But when he went back through the papers and had a closer look, what he saw did not please him. *Building a Productive Database: Strategies for Assembling and Keeping Track of Your Company's Inventory—How the Masters Do It,* read the document.

This sounds like nothin' but a trainload o' bureaucratic bullshit, he whined. It all sounded intolerably dull to him, and he could see right away that his brain would be fried after only one hellish week—or even one hellish hour—of immersion in this kind of rubbish. *By the time I get done with this stuff,* he grumbled, *I'll be more than eager to go back to Marin City Flea Market and pick up trash for a living. If, of course, La Branch would be dumb enough to hire me again.*

But Clay really didn't want to suffer another failure so close on the heels of his most recent one. So he bucked up, bore down on the documents, answered the questions in considerable detail, and had the stack of papers fully and meticulously executed nearly an hour ahead of time.

He stepped into Henley's office, handed him the completed documents, then went back to his desk and waited nervously for his response. Half an hour later, Tuckerman stepped out with a broad smile on his rosy-cheeked, Pillsbury Dough Boy face and motioned to Clay to come back into his office. Then he closed the door behind them, turned to him, and spoke to him in hushed tones.

"You mustn't tell your father I said this," he whispered, "but you're not only a head taller than your father, you're a hell of a lot more *intelligent* than he is!"

Clay, caught completely off guard, simultaneously blushed and beamed at Henley's assessment. He'd have loved for his father to be in the room just then to hear the words of praise, but he knew from years of experience that it would have spelled a very bad ending to what little remained of their father-and-son relationship.

"The masterful way you interpreted the data in those charts," said Tuckerman, "and the clever way you answered my questions make it clear to me that you're smart as a whip." He drew Clay close to him, then continued. "I hate to say it, Mr. Middling—may I call you Clay?—but compared to you, your Old Man is dumb as a fence post—a kind of hapless Dagwood figure around here. To be honest, I'm more than a little shocked that Stanton Middleton is actually your father!"

He continued: "Of course, I kind of knew that already. Your father and I were in the same chemistry class in high school, and honestly, he didn't seem to know a proton from a pig's foot! Everyone knew he'd never be a scholar. Fact is, he was nothin' but a friggin' *goof-off*—the class clown of Tamalpais High."

"Really!" said Clay, doing his best to conceal the fact that he was truly shocked at what Henley had just told him about his father. Then he quickly tried to change the subject.

"I never expected you to actually *like* what I did with those documents," he said. "But if you're serious—if you really do want me to come on board—I'd be more than happy to do so. Matter of fact, I think being a part of this place would be really cool! I mean, oh, my God! Wait 'til *Dori* hears about this!"

"Dori?" said Tuckerman. "Who's Dori?"

"Sorry," said Clay. "Dorian Breitmeyer! But we've always called him Dori. Anyway, we were good friends in high school—same one you and Dad went to—but he's had a few more breaks than I've had since then. Thinks he's some kind o' Big Shot now. And every time I see him these days, he finds a way to tell me that compared to him, I'm a loser."

"Don't be silly!" said Tuckerman. "There's no need for you to beat yourself up like that. And you can forget about your friend Dori. Sounds to me like *he's* the one who's the loser, not you. Anyway, you've just assured yourself a bright and lucrative future with Scheckel & Newbury. Come back tomorrow at 9:00 sharp, and I'll plug you into some of our most challenging, vexing projects. Are you ready to rock 'n' roll?"

"Wow!" said Clay. "So you really are serious. And you *bet* I'm ready!"

"Of *course* I'm serious!" Didn't I just say so?" Then Tuckerman reached across the desk and tapped a knuckle on Clay's forehead. "That stuff between your ears? We *need* some o' that stuff—a hell of a lot more of it, in fact—around here."

"I'll do my damnedest to please you," said Clay. "I'm gonna make you proud!"

"I'll be right up front, Clay," said Henley. "The projects I'm giving you have been damn tough nuts to crack. Everyone agrees they've got great potential, but no one around here has been able to come up with plausible ways to turn a profit on 'em. And yet, from what I've seen on these documents"—he smiled, then whacked the stack of papers on the top of Clay's head—"I've no doubt you've got what it'll take to make 'em work."

Then Tuckerman suddenly appeared to be unsure of himself, more than a little worried about the impression he'd just made on the son of one of his most loyal employees.

"Listen," he said, "I really shouldn't have said what I did about Stan, you know. Guess I owe you an apology! But your father really does fumble around at work. He can never quite find a shoe that fits when we're strategizing. Oh, he *means* well! Everyone knows that about your father. And every once in a while, he even comes up with an idea worth kicking around. Anyway, it won't happen again. Promise! And please remember: mum's the word. What your father doesn't know can't hurt him."

Clay sipped the last of his coffee and got up from the table, then looked out into the hallway and saw his father heading toward the elevator to his office on the third floor. Given what Henley Tuckerman had just said about him, Clay couldn't help wondering if S&N thought of that floor as more burial ground than workplace—an out-of-the-way area where only employees with no real future were left to doze through hour upon hour of quasi-clerical grunt work. At any rate, he knew it wasn't a good idea for anyone to be chummy with a family member while at work, especially on day one of a brand new job. So he waved briefly and kept on moving.

As he watched the elevator door close, he felt ashamed that he'd been given a plum location at Scheckel & Newbury while his father was still languishing away upstairs, six feet under, where he'd been for nearly two decades.

He spent the entire next day in Henley's office going over the projects he'd be working on. Meanwhile, he vowed to himself not to say one word, either to his father or anyone else, about the conversation he'd had with Henley Tuckerman.

Chapter Nine

It was now February, 1968, nearly two years since Clay joined Scheckel & Newbury. Henley Tuckerman was immensely pleased with his new hire. The projects he'd put Clay in charge of had dramatically improved the S&N profit margin—so much so that the Board of Directors was seriously considering reinstituting the annual Christmas/Hanukkah bonus.

Moreover, Clay had discovered, to his great surprise, that he enjoyed—*really* enjoyed—his new job. In the weekly strategy sessions, the younger Middling—still in his early twenties and fresh out of the starting gate—impressed everyone around him with his high-voltage enthusiasm and his extraordinary attention to detail. And after work each night when Clay came bounding into the living room, Stan and Brooke could see right away that he was genuinely happy to be a part of Scheckel & Newbury. "Our son," they told anyone who would listen, "is finally growing up!"

Then, one afternoon, Henley stopped by Stan's office near closing time and invited him to join him later that night for a meal at Sam Wo's, a favorite Chinatown lunch-and-dinner spot for the Higher-Ups at S&N. Sam Wo's was just as popular for the outrageous conduct of Edsel Ford Fung—known as "The World's Rudest, Most Insulting Waiter"—as it was for its top-rated cuisine. And because of both, Sam Wo's was nearly always filled to capacity.

The locals took Fung's insults in stride. For them it was just another ho-hum dining experience, San Francisco style. But for first-timers, and for the hordes of tourists passing through Chinatown, to go home well-fed and tell their friends they'd been abused, ridiculed, and entertained by Fung was a badge of honor and a source of pride.

Stan had never dined at Sam Wo's, so he was more than happy to let Henley do the ordering. "The barbecue fried rice is a real knockout here," he said. "You wouldn't want to miss it, so I'm gonna make sure you don't!" He placed the order, and then, in a gesture of workplace solidarity, he raised his cup of tea to Stan.

Food seldom came fast at Sam Wo's, so the two of them had more than enough time to settle in and strike up a conversation. "Don't worry about the cost," said Henley. "Tonight is on me! It's the least I can do to thank you for bringing that wunderkind son of yours into the fold. He's helped turn S&N into a financial juggernaut in just ten short months."

Stan half-heartedly nodded his approval, but he was tired of hearing Henley and his colleagues heap praise on Clay, so he did his best to change the subject.

"So how's the little woman? Good as ever?"

"So-so, as usual," said Henley. "But I gotta tell you, she can be a real nag in the morning! The other day she went after me like a buzzard on a skunk. Said I shouldn't leave my wet towels on the floor when I'm done showering. Said I shouldn't hang my dirty underwear on the vanity, where she keeps her toothbrush. 'I'm not your personal attendant,' she says. 'Pick up your *own* friggin' skivvies—and leave my damn toothbrush alone!'"

"Been there, done that," said Stan. "But why the big fuss? She could o' just picked up that pecker pouch of yours and put it in the hamper like a good wife should." He shook his head in disgust, then took another sip of tea. "Women: they're worse than a bunch o' Wagnerian Valkyries when they get their backs up, aren't they! Anyway, how's things at home otherwise?"

"A pain in the ass!" said Henley. "That's what they are! I go to work every day, bust my hump for a few measly greenbacks, then come home and get fed into the meat grinder with tales of my son's dastardly misdeeds!"

"Wait a minute," said Stan. "You have a *son*? I had no idea!" He arched an eyebrow, then winked slyly at him. "What'd you do—have a little late-in-life mishap?"

"Not a mishap, my boy, just a situation. But the truth is I don't usually talk about things like this away from home. Y' know, to me it's just a family matter, and it should *stay* that way."

"Whatever you say, boss," said Stan. "Anyway, what kind of misdeeds?"

"Little ones and big ones," said Henley. "First, the little one: Before I left for work yesterday, I gave Ephram— that's my son—a firm order to pick up all of the crap he'd left on the living room carpet—comic books, a bag of chips, a gummed-over banana—*that* kind o' crap. So I got home around 7:30 that night and walked in the door, then stepped on what was left of the latest fallen banana and fell flat on my ass. Thought sure I'd landed on a pile o' fresh dog poop! I'm tellin' you, that boy's a born slob!"

"OK," said Stan. "Not good! And the *big* one?"

"All right, you asked for it," said Henley. "I headed out to the kitchen to get a paper towel and clean off my shoe, and my wife, who'd just come in through the back door after her doctor's appointment, was slumped down in the breakfast nook, looking as if she'd just been told she has stage IV cancer of the liver! So, dutifully, I said, 'What's happened, honey? Why the long face? You get some bad news?'

"'You wanna know why I have a long face?' she snarled. 'In a moment, it's *you* who's gonna have the long face.' So here's what happened: I ran into our daughter at a convenience store up in Mill Valley the other day, and . . . oh, my

God! There she was—standing there like the Hindenburg in a hatching jacket. Had a belly like a goddam Halloween pumpkin!"

"Holy Christ!" said Stan. "You have a *daughter*, too? You have a son *and* a daughter?"

"Oh, yeah," said Henley. "Older than her brother, but yes, we do indeed have a daughter. Ain't no doubt about *that* now, is there!" he chuckled.

"The eyes tell all, I guess," said Stan. "Anyway, I'm so sorry. What a shocker! No *wonder* your wife was so upset! So who's the nitwit who did the dirty on 'er?"

"Don't know," said Henley. "She refused to say. Probably doesn't even *know* for sure! She ran away from home a few months ago, almost as fed up with us as we were with her, and since then we've had no idea where she's living, what she's been up to, and frankly, who she might be dinkin' around with. I mean, whoever really knows about stuff like that?"

"Ain't *that* the truth!" said Stan.

"All we know for sure right now is that she's got a serious bun in the oven. Ain't no hidin' it anymore, that's for sure."

"Jesus," said Stan, still shocked at the reality of Tuckerman's life away from Scheckel & Newbury. "And here I've thought all along that either you were childless or your kids were long gone—all grown up and out on their own."

"Like I said, I've always tried to keep the family stuff out of the workplace," said Henley. "And again, we're pretty private people. When we learned she was in the family way, we did our best to keep it a secret. I mean, I've got a prominent profile in this community! Can't afford to have my reputation smeared by something like this. I should think you can see how traumatic this has been for us."

Then he leaned across the table and whispered into Middling's ear. "So I think you'll understand why I'm asking you not to say anything about this to anyone at work—or anywhere *else,* for that matter. Can I trust you on this?"

"Of *course* you can," said Stan. "No need to worry. My lips are sealed! Besides, I'd expect the same from you if it was *my* daughter who got herself in trouble."

"You're lucky you don't *have* a daughter," said Henley. "When they reach their teens, they're damned high maintenance!"

"I can only imagine," said Stan. "So what's your daughter's name?"

"Avis," said Henley. "Avis Ellen. Like the rental car. We named her after her maternal grandmother, because the moment we saw her at the hospital, we couldn't get over how much she looked like her grandmother in her baby picture."

"Avis," said Stan. "Nice name!"

"We thought so," said Henley. "But when Avis turned nine, she decided she didn't like it. And when her fourth-grade teacher told her one day that she was fragile as a bird—'the sweetest little birdie in the lollipop tree,' she cooed—the name stuck. So she's been 'Birdie' ever since."

"Birdie?" said Stan. "What a coincidence! Our son said something about a girl down in Ingleside, and I'll be damned if her nickname wasn't Birdie, too. Never did learn her *last* name, though. In fact, we never even met her. When Clay turned eighteen, he decided he shouldn't have to bring a date home for Daddy's approval anymore."

"There's gotta be a whole lot o' Birdies on the planet," said Henley. "After all, it's just a term of affection. Kind o' universal."

"I'll bet Clay never messed around like Avis did! That boy is smart—*way* too smart ever to have gone out and gotten a girl in trouble!"

"You're damn right," said Stan. "God knows, Clay has his weaknesses—they all do at that age—but makin' babies out of wedlock isn't one of 'em. Besides, even if he'd messed around, he'd never have done so without taking the necessary precautions."

"No doubt about that," said Henley. "Your son was born with a halo on top o' that noggin of his."

"Amen!" said Stan. "When Clay got his driver's license, I sat him down and talked to him, man to man. I said, 'Son, don't ever climb into your hoopty with a hot 'n' ready chick unless you've got a raincoat in your wallet!' And you know what, Henley? He *listened* to me! It was amazing. The message sunk in, and it stayed there, too. It's *still* there. He even thanked me for warning him! Now, it's that kind of guidance that turns a no-good party animal into a fully grown man. Thanks to you, I can tell the world my son's a valued employee. And when they hear where he works, they'll damn well know I'm not shittin' 'em!"

They finished their meal at Sam Wo's with a heightened feeling of father-to-father, employee-to-employee camaraderie. Henley drove home pleased with Stan's obvious empathy, convinced that he could count on him to keep the lid on his daughter's 'condition.' Stan drove home convinced that, in spite of his son's post-adolescent flaws, he was a whole lot more mature and socially responsible than Henley's daughter would ever be. To him, it meant that he was without question the superior father of the two.

Let Tuckerman think he's the Hot Shot around here, thought Stan to himself. *Let him go ahead and take credit for Clay's exceptional performance in the workplace. But it's me—not Tuckerman—who brought a fresh young mind to S&N. And Tuck's just got to understand by now that without an employee like Stanton Middling, there would never have been a Clay. My son's success will soon be his father's triumph!*

Chapter Ten

Nearly two years after Stan and Henley dined at Sam Wo's, the decade was coming to a close. As the Vietnam war raged on, Clayborne Middling was feeling triumphant. He'd finally begun to make something of himself, and because of it, his confidence was climbing higher—and faster—than the temps in an Arizona heatwave. Meanwhile, his father, forced by circumstances beyond his control to live in the far-reaching shadow of a more successful son, continued to struggle with his self-esteem.

Pundits had their hands full with more pressing issues. While taking the pulse of a struggling nation, a growing number of them could see that rank-and-file Americans, understandably exhausted from the political mania and social upheaval of the 1960s, had finally begun to tune out, turn over, and drift off into a kind a calculated stupor, hopeful that when they woke up the next morning they'd find themselves in a more peaceful, more egalitarian decade than the one they'd just endured.

But is that what actually happened? Not really.

It would be foolish for anyone to deny the reality of the cultural upheaval in a decade that became known, understandably, as the Hippie Era. The Flower Child, Make Love Not War mystique hung tough right up to the end of the '60s and beyond. Never shy about its stubborn convictions and counterculture demeanor, the decade went out with a bang, not a whimper, with the Woodstock Festival destined to become the very touchstone of a country in serious turmoil, trying its damnedest to mend its wounds and reset its philosophical compass.

But Clay Middling—who, like his father, was a self-absorbed creature, indifferent to the larger issues—missed the party. He'd moved in with his parents as promised, and he'd needed only a month to realize that coming home again was the best decision he could have made. Instead of being angry with his father for being so harshly critical of him, he found to his surprise that he was feeling closer to him than he had in a very long time. And as his mother watched the two of them rekindling their relationship and actually going places together again—basketball games, movies, or even just a Saturday morning breakfast out— she let go of her disenchantment with her son, warmed up to him again, and began to feel that, in the best sense of the word, the Middlings were once again a *family*.

On this particular evening, Stan, a creature of clockwork consistency, got home right on time. But Clay, who'd recently been promoted and was now putting in long hours, was working even later than usual. It would be a while before they expected to see him.

Meanwhile, Stan and Brooke were enjoying a supper of pan-fried salmon and rice pilaf over the latest episode of *Hogan's Heroes*.

"Klink is such a knucklehead!" said Stan, then scooped up another heaping spoonful of pilaf, spilling half of it down the front of his tie before it had a chance to reach his mouth.

"I know, I know," said Brooke. "He does some pretty stupid things. But he means well. And when he stops strutting around like a drugged-up rooster, he strikes me as kind o' cute!"

"Cute?" said Stan. "If Klink is cute, then Jerry Lee Lewis plays the cello!"

"Don't be silly! Klink's only occasionally, *marginally* cute; Lewis, on the other hand, is downright *sexy* the moment he sets foot onstage."

"Don't you mean on the keyboard?" said Stan. "Playin' footsies with the ivories is his favorite stunt! But I have t' tell you, I don't see anything funny about it. In fact, I think it's kind o' stupid."

"What's wrong, honey? Is my poor little Stanton feeling jealous again?"

"Jealous, my ass!" he said. "Jerry Lee Lewis is a clown—a piano-bangin' madman! If I was his agent, I swear I'd sit him down and tell him I've had it with his ridiculous onstage antics. I might even go so far as to—"

In the middle of Stan's preadolescent tirade, the doorbell rang. Brooke, annoyed with the interruption, hopped up from the couch, turned down the TV, stepped over to the front door, and opened it.

Standing there on the stoop was a young, remarkably attractive woman with long, slim legs and a warm, genuine smile.

"I hope I have the right address!" she said. "I'm Avis—Avis Guertner. A friend of mine, Dorian Breitmeyer, told me your son might still be living here. I've something I need to tell him, so I decided to come by and see if . . ."

"Oh!" said Brooke. "*We* know Dorian! He's a longtime friend of Clay. And yes, Clay's back with us now, for a while anyway. But he's working later than usual tonight. Should be home in half an hour or so. You're welcome to wait in my husband's den, only because Clay will no doubt need a little time to unwind and change into his lounge-arounds."

"That's so nice of you!" said Avis. "But I've had a long day at work, and now I've got to get home and make supper. There's never enough time in a day, is there."

"Never," said Brooke, "never! But are you sure you need to leave so soon? We'd hate to have you miss a chance to talk with our son."

Brooke heard a familiar snoring sound coming from across the room, then glanced back at her husband and saw that he'd fallen asleep. *He must be dead tired,* she thought. *Or maybe he's just being his usual rude, inconsiderate self.*

Then she turned back to Avis. "Sorry," she said. "Stan's over there sawin' logs. By the way, before you leave, how did you come to know Clay?"

"We met four years ago at my friend Tommy's annual Fourth of July bash. I've been going to that party for three years now. It's a really big deal where we live! Anyway, Dori came over to me right after I got there and said, 'Y' know what? I should introduce you to my pal Clay. I think you'll really like him!' He did just that, and he was right. Turned out your son's a really nice guy! We spent a couple hours together, and I could tell right away that he was really intelligent. Thoughtful, too—one of only a small handful of true gentlemen, anywhere you go!"

"Glad to know you feel that way," said Brooke, smiling from ear to ear. "It's what every mother wants to hear. I know Clay can really turn on the charm when the spirit moves him! But I must confess I'm a little surprised that the two of you didn't make yourselves a team. I wouldn't want you to think I'm bragging, but Clay's a lot like a strip of flypaper—the *good* kind, not the bad kind. Girls have been sticking to him in swarms ever since junior high school."

Avis couldn't help revisiting her moment of rapture with Clay up in that second-story bedroom, where they'd made fireworks more than worthy of the Fourth. She turned red as a beet.

"I can easily see why girls are drawn to him," Avis said, feeling increasingly uncomfortable with the way the conversation was going. "No matter how you slice it, Clay is just plain *likable*. Everyone says so! I remember we disagreed about a few things, mostly politics. He was fond of LBJ for some reason, but I detested the man. I mean, what kind of president holds a dog up by his ears? And did anyone really deserve to see that scar on Johnson's fat belly—on nationwide television?"

"It *was* kind o' unsightly," said Brooke. "The belly, I mean. And I didn't appreciate how he treated that poor dog, either!" The two of them laughed convivially for a few seconds, then began wondering, silently, what else there really was to talk about.

"So," Avis said, "as you can see, Clay and I went our separate ways before I ever had a chance to meet the two of you. I'm sure you know how it is!"

"Do I *ever*," said Brooke. Then she turned back and shouted across the room at her husband, a tone of playful ridicule in her voice. "We've all been through it. Haven't we, dear!"

Her loud, jeering pronouncement jarred Stan out of a sound sleep. He had no idea what the two of them had been talking about, but to keep the peace, he cheerfully pretended to agree with her. "Sure," he said. "*Sure* we have!" Then he rolled over, buried his face in the couch again, and did his best to fall back asleep.

"Anyway," said Avis, "like I said, I had something I wanted to talk about with Clay, and I hoped I might be able to catch him here at your place. Guess I'll be on my way now. Have to pick up my four-year-old from childcare."

"Ah!" said Brooke. "Boy or girl?"

"Girl! Her name is Cecelia. She's a real doll, too! But right now she's kind o' hard to handle. It's like her terrible twos never really ended!"

"Oh, yeah," said Brooke. "Believe me, Clay used to be a handful, too! Anyway, so you have just the one?"

"Two, actually," said Avis. "I also have a boy, Brent. He's eleven."

"How nice; one of each. Does your son like having a little sister?"

"Well, he lives with his father," said Avis. "Of course, I wish that wasn't the case, but we can't have everything just the way we want it, can we."

"Amen to that!" said Brooke, sending another dart in the direction of her husband. Avis saw the look of contempt on her face, then immediately decided it was best for her to move along.

"So sorry I've gabbed on and on like this," she said, "but I really do need to go now. In fact, they'll *kill* me if I don't get there by closing. And traffic this time of day is horrible! Also, the teachers don't like having to stay past closing when a parent fails to show up on time."

Then Avis reached into her purse, pulled out a hand-written note, and handed it to Brooke.

"Here's my phone number, Mrs. Middling. Street address, too. Can you please tell your son to call me or drop by when he has a moment?"

"Will do!" said Brooke. "Drive safely, now. And I know you'll make a swell supper for that little girl o' yours."

Once Avis was on her way, Brooke closed the door, then came back and settled into the overstuffed chair across from the couch.

"What a charming young lady!" she cooed. "And *tall*, too. I swear she must be at least a head taller than Clay! Anyway, tall or not, I hope he has the good fortune to meet someone that nice when he's in the market for a mate!"

"Now that's just weird," said Stan. "I don't see why you should get all whipped up about some know-nothing giraffe who spent a couple of hours with Clay two centuries ago, then suddenly shows up right when I'm about to—"

"About to what?" snarled Brooke. "I mean, what's happened to the thoughtful, well-mannered Stanton Middling

I married? Where's *he* gone to? Good thing I was home when Avis dropped by! You'd have been the world's worst imaginable host if you'd been here alone."

"*Enough*, already!" said Stan. "Now how 'bout bein' a *good* wife for a change and getting us something to drink?" He reached up and patted her affectionately on the rear end, and Brooke, touched by his sudden moment of amour, went straight to the kitchen, pulled a couple of Grain Belt Lagers from the fridge, and brought them back to the living room.

"Good timing," he said. "*I Dream of Jeannie* is on."

"Why am I not surprised?" said Brooke, rolling her eyes. "So what's *this* one about?"

"Jeannie accidentally got herself locked inside a safe bound for the moon," said Stan. "Guess we're supposed to believe it's about some NASA experiment having to do with weightlessness. What a crock! I mean, that girl gets into the dumbest situations, doesn't she? Course, now, it looks like poor Hubby's gotta figure out how to get her out o' that safe before they put it in the rocket."

"This is such a ridiculous show!" said Brooke. "Can't we find something else to watch?"

"But I love *I Dream of Jeannie*!" said Stan. "It's always funny. And well-written, too! Sometimes, it can even be stimulating. You know, intellectually."

"Oh, yeah," said Brooke, "intellectually stimulating." She pointed down at her husband's lap, shaking her head in disapproval. "And I know just what's getting stimulated!" Then she jumped up from the couch and turned the TV off.

"I'm not stupid, Stan. I know why you love this show, and it's got nothing to do with the stories! You don't really love *I Dream of Jeannie*; you love dreaming of Jeannie's *boobs*! So how 'bout doing without that mile-deep décolletage of hers just this one time?"

Stan, feeling vanquished, smiled meekly at his wife, left the TV off, then put a straw up his nose and unleashed a noisy, porcine snort.

"You infant!" shouted Brooke. Privately, she couldn't help thinking that what he'd just done was actually rather funny, but she did her best to avoid giggling. "That's the kind of stuff junior high boys do with ice cream sodas to impress the girls. Be a *grown-up*, for God's sake."

Then, while Stan was sheepishly pulling the straw out of his nose, the phone rang. Brooke got up reluctantly from the couch, crossed the room, and picked up the receiver.

"Is Stan home?" bellowed a loud, raspy voice. "My Man of the Hour?"

Brooke held the phone at arm's length to save her hearing. *Oh my God, now what,* she thought. Then she brought the receiver back to her ear and said, "May I ask who's calling?"

"*Me,* of course!" said the voice. "Henley Tuckerman!" He realized he was shouting unnecessarily, then paused, took a deep breath, and started over. "Sorry to bark into the phone like that, Mrs. Middling. I figured you'd have no trouble recognizing my voice by now. I mean, God knows how many times I've had to dial up your husband after hours! Anyway, if he's *there*, get him *here*. I've got some news for him. *Big* news!"

"Really!" she said. "What *kind* of big news?" She prayed he was calling about the raise Stan and she had been yearning for, or, at the very least, about a bonus. *Just in time for Easter,* she smiled, *and spring cleaning. How sweet that would be!*

"Just big news," said Henley, "nothing you'll need to get riled up about." Then he brought his voice down to a whisper. "But if you don't mind, I'd rather have him get it straight from the horse's mouth. No doubt he'll tell you as soon as I've spilled the beans to him. Promise!"

Stan yanked the phone out of Brooke's hand and made contact, then waved her out of the room so he could have some privacy.

"So what's happenin', chief?" Stan was nervous now, wondering what the big fuss was all about, but he did his best, in spite of it, to sound upbeat. "I thought I'd finally cleared up the confusion I created in the Anselm contract this morning," he chuckled. "What'd I do *this* time—leave the dot off another i?"

"Nah," said Henley. "You've got nothin' to worry about, my man. You're doin' fine! The truth is I was just calling to congratulate you."

Stan paused, then stared down at the receiver. "Why the hell would you need to congratulate *me*?" said Stan. "I can't think of anything I've done lately that deserves congratulations."

"Better let me explain," said Henley. "Remember when I took you to Sam Wo's and told you I ran into my daughter and she looked like the friggin' Hindenburg in a hatching jacket? She wouldn't tell me who did the dirty for the longest time, but then, one day, she finally did. His name is Clay. *Clay Middling!* So, congratulations, Stan. I'll be damned if you're not a *grandpa!*"

Flabbergasted, Stan went white as chalk and collapsed into the nearest chair. He sat staring up at the ceiling, a look of anguish on his face, then unleashed a rant.

"Honestly, Tuckerman, if this is some kind o' gag—another one of your elaborate, drawn-out practical jokes—you're wasting your breath. 'Cause I'm not buyin' it! I don't *believe* it!" He banged his fist down on the table so hard that Henley could hear the dishes rattle. "Holy motherfuckin' Christ!" he raged. "What am I supposed to *do* about this?"

"The only thing you *can* do," said Henley. "Give 'em some time! Anyway, here's how it happened: Birdie met

Clay at a keg party a few years ago. Right away they got oiled up with some beer—some cheap stuff, probably—and in less than an hour they were up in the guest bedroom in Dori's house, squeakin' the bedsprings. Just a couple o' horny little hop toads, that's what they were. And now look what they've got for their trouble—a Ball 'n' Chain Baby! A girl! Can't return *that* kind o' merchandise, now, *can* they!"

"I *still* can't believe it," wailed Stan.

"Get *real*, Stan!" he said. "You're gonna *have* t' believe it, now, ain'tcha!"

"Guess so," said Stan.

"I tried my damnedest to hide the truth about the whole revoltin' development—wanted to save my ass in the eyes of the public and the Higher Ups at Scheckel & Newbury—but I can't pretend any longer, can I. The truth is out, and, as Jerry Lee liked to say, it'll soon be all over town."

"Holy Christ!" said Stan. "It means we're no longer just workmates—we're stinkin' *in-laws*!"

"By God, you're *right*!" said Henley. "I can already see it coming: an absolute shitstorm of family get-togethers! Gifts for Every Occasion; there goes my vacation money! And we'll be getting those annoying last-minute phone calls at home, too. You know, 'Any chance you could watch the kiddies for us this weekend?'"

Jesus! Stan grumbled to himself. *That boy's gonna get a piece o' my mind when he gets home. A really big piece!*

"To tell you the truth," said Henley, "I don't really think it's gonna be as bad as it seemed on first notice. The kids will find a way to make it work, and so will we. But one thing's certain: we're not gonna tolerate having two kids in the tribe with no rings on their fingers and an illegitimate baby. They're gonna have to get *married*."

"Clay Middling *married*?" said Stan. "He's not ready to

get married! I'll be waking up one morning with a fuckin' *lady cake* before that happens!"

"I suppose anything's possible," laughed Henley. "But I doubt that would go over all that well with the Mrs. Well, it's about time I got off the phone, isn't it. Doreen wants me to take out the trash. I can feel her tuggin' on my nose ring right now. And believe me, that's one woman who never takes no for an answer."

"Know just what you mean," said Stan. "Adam never should o' handed Eve that apple. It's been hell on earth for the male of the species ever since."

"Forbidden fruit," laughed Henley. "Oh, yeah! Like Seeger keeps singin', 'When Will We Ever Learn?'"

Stan was all set to hang up the phone when he realized he hadn't even asked Henley the most important question.

"By the way, boss, what's the girl's name? I figure I should know at least that much about her if I'm gonna be playin' Grampy."

"*Cecelia*," said Henley. "Birdie told me she named her after her great-great-grandmother Cecelia Koroneva, an accomplished ballerina long before she and her family emigrated from Russia to the States. Performed all over the world, in fact, including the Mariinsky in St. Petersburg! My daughter says CeCe—that's short for Cecelia—is already showing signs of the same stubborn determination her great-great-grandmother was famous for—and at the ripe old age of twenty-four months. Can you imagine? I'd better wish you good luck, Stan. You're gonna *need* it. Sounds like CeCe's gonna be an independent little brat, just like her Mama was!"

Stan had already moved on from the Grampy talk, so he was hardly listening as Henley Tuckerman rattled on about Cecelia and the fateful bite of the apple—the one in Dori's guest bedroom—that led to Cecelia's untimely arrival in their lives.

His next, more immediate challenge—his son, Clay—would be home soon, and Stan wondered what, if anything, he could do to rein in his wayward, irresponsible son.

Clay arrived home right on cue, rang the doorbell, then glided into the living room like a runway model in a fashion house.

"Whatcha doin', Pops?" he said, then hung his sport coat in the foyer, strode across the room, and flopped down on the couch.

"Not much," said Stan. "Too tired to do anything. And you?"

"Just got home. And if *your* day was half as good as *mine*, then you had a damn good day!"

"Do I *look* like I had a good day?" said Stan. "I came home two hours ago, exhausted as hell. So do me a favor, would ya? No more talk about your 'damn good day.'"

"Sorry, Dad. It's just that Henley keeps saying he's really happy with my work. He told me just this morning that there might be another raise in my future—a *substantial* raise!"

Stan wanted badly to come clean and light into Clay for planting a bun in Birdie's oven, but he decided to wait for a time when his anger could be unleashed full-throttle. It wouldn't be good to mix up the issues.

"A raise, huh?" he said, smiling half-heartedly. "Good for you." Then he turned quietly away from his son and talked with his back to him. "Listen, there's something I need you to hear—a practical matter—and it's best not to put it off. Now that you're doing so well at work, I think it's about time we raise your rent."

"Raise my *rent*?" Clay closed his eyes, then took a deep breath and propelled a noisy, disillusioned column of air down toward the carpet.

"Yes!" said Stan. "Raise your rent! My income has pretty much flattened out at this point, and let's face it: a ten-spot doesn't buy nearly as much as it used to. I haven't heard those magic words—*raise* or *cost of living adjustment*—come out of Tuckerman's mouth for nearly five years. And every time I bring up the word *money*, he turns silent as a dinner plate. He can be such a goddam skinflint!"

"Jesus!" said Clay. "Just when I'm starting to make something of myself, when I've finally begun getting ahead in the world—something you've been badgering me to do for years now—now you wanna reach into my wallet while I'm not looking and feather your nest with my hard-earned cash?"

"Not true!" shouted Stan. "I hardly think it's fair of you to accuse a caring, hard-working father of mooching off his own flesh and blood."

"Well, what would you *call* it, then," said Clay, "a Christmas present? A reverse cash advance? I've been telling you for *weeks* now that as soon as my income reaches a manageable level, I'll start looking for an apartment—maybe even a starter home! Can't you see? I'm trying my damnedest to . . ."

Their conversation came to a halt when Clay's mother came shuffling downstairs in her bathrobe, her hair in curlers, her face chalky white from a thick layer of night cream.

"Here we go again," she said, her face locked in a playful, Alice-in-Wonderland grin. "Another family catfight, I see! If you boys aren't careful, I swear you're gonna claw each other's eyes out one o' these days."

"*Girls* have catfights," said Stan. "Men have *confrontations!* I'd advise you to stay out o' the ring, honey. This angelic son of yours may soon be down for the count."

Brooke cut loose with a shrill cackle, then waved her hand dismissively at the two of them. "You can settle your differences with him later, Stan!" she said. "I should think your son would rather hear about the 'special guest' who came by to see him only an hour ago. Don't you?"

Clay stared at her, his brow furrowed. "Are you kidding? Who on earth would want to come here, of all places, to see me? Not one person I know and care about has come to visit me since I moved back."

"Lemme give you a hint or two," said Brooke with an affectionate chuckle. "She was tall and thin, with long legs—I mean *really* long legs. And she was really quite lovely. Kind o' *sexy*, too! And by the way, she described you more than once as a 'really nice guy.'"

Clay went red in the face, then felt a chill of recognition travel up his spine. "I can't imagine who you're talking about," he said, suddenly pressed into lying shamelessly about an encounter that he could never in the world have forgotten. "*Me?* A really nice guy? Sounds like something straight out of a Brady Bunch episode—one o' those dippy things teenyboppers like to say."

"Trust me, honey," said Brooke, "she was no teenybopper! Quite poised and mature, really. Anyway, are you sure you don't remember? She made a fuss about a certain day—July Fourth, four years ago—a day she's obviously never quite forgotten. Said she was at Tommy Dolliver's annual America's Birthday bash that day, and Dori introduced you to her."

Clay could feel his heart pounding away like a hard mallet on a cheap drum. He desperately hoped his mother couldn't tell just by looking at him how much of her—and which *parts* of her—he'd been so passionately drawn to that day.

"Hmmm . . ." he said. "I do remember Dori introducing me to some long-ago high school classmate of his. She was nice enough, I suppose, but kind o' dorky if you ask me—that, and *way* too tall for me. I can't even remember her name."

Stan, who was just around the corner, couldn't help

chiming in. "What's how *tall* she is got to do with it? It's how *hot* she is that matters."

"Your father's right for once," said Brooke. "I'm nearly as tall is your father is, and it sure as hell didn't stop *him*! I should think you're proof enough of that. Anyway, her name is Avis—Avis Guertner. But she said her friends usually call her Birdie." Then she tossed Clay a supercilious, *film noir* look—an expression halfway between sugary smile and cynical frown.

Well, there you are, he thought to himself. *I figured she'd long ago moved on to another conquest—another freakin' one-night stand. And now, wouldn't you know it, she's back again, sniffin' me out for some reason. I wish Dori had never introduced me to her! Sure, she was a damn good lay. But she was also more trouble than she was worth—way more! Maybe it's time for me to admit, long-legged beauty or not, that Avis Guertner was just way too much for me to handle, then move on to greener pastures.*

"And you say she was dorky?" said Brooke. "Jesus, Clay! I suppose I should automatically take you at your word. I *am* your mother, after all. But you know what? I'm having trouble believing any of what you've been saying about her! Listen: the girl who came here today may not have been picture perfect, but she was *anything* but 'dorky,' as some lucky boy obviously found out. She has a four-year-old girl. And an eleven-year-old boy! Dorky? Unattractive? Not an ideal baby maker? I don't think so!"

A four-year-old girl? Holy shit, groaned Clay, his mind racing. *That's how long it's been since I shot my wad on Birdie! I hope I didn't forget to wear that friggin' raincoat! Say it isn't true! And an eleven-year-old boy? How old is this woman, anyway? And where the fuck did that eleven-year-old come from?* He inwardly scratched his head, easily as shocked about Birdie's son as he was dismayed to learn that *he*—Clayborne Middling—may very well have fathered a child four years prior. *It was supposed to be just a one-time thing,* he mused, *a harmless little afternoon diddle.*

He thought and thought, then thought again, revisiting that magical moment of flesh-into-flesh connection. But the more times he ran the tape, the more certain he was that just before he plunged his Big Fella into her Lady Cave, he'd slipped on the French Tickler he'd stolen from the bottom drawer of his father's nightstand. *If I'd forgotten to wrap the sausage,* he mumbled, *I'd have been able to feel the difference, and so would she! Or maybe the bucket simply had a hole in it, straight from the factory. I've heard about stuff like that happening, but if it ever happened to me, I'd sue the bastards who made it!*

"Dorky, schmorky!" he snapped to his mother, back now to reality and once again more or less in charge of his wavering self-confidence. "Baby, schmaby! I don't wanna talk about Birdie Guertner. I mean, why *should* I? If she ever stops by here again, do me a favor and tell her I have a steady now, and I'm nuts about her." Then Clay stormed across the room and bounded up the stairs, badly in need of some time away from his mother's constant dark-side evaluations. *Women!* he grumbled. *Who needs 'em? I can take care o' myself!*

As soon as he was safely inside his bedroom, he locked the door behind him, stripped down to his underwear, grabbed a well-worn, dog-eared issue of *Playboy* from a stack of magazines hidden in his closet, and, like a wrestler heading for the ring, dashed over and scrambled up onto his bed. Once he'd turned off the light and was stretched out on his back, he began slowly flipping through the pages, ignoring the articles and lingering instead over the long march of coy, provocative photos.

When he finally got to the centerfold—this time a pleasingly plump, thoroughly airbrushed cheerleader named Angelique, teasing a tiny, green-and-orange pompom over her densely carpeted, chocolate-colored snatch—his penis was hard as rebar. Then, long past ready to drop his load, he reached down into his skivvies, grabbed hold of his throbbing Johnny, and began vigorously pumping. He needed only a few seconds to jerk himself off, and when he was finished, greatly relieved and feeling more and more certain that he'd done the right thing that day—that he couldn't possibly be the man who'd fathered Birdie's little Love Bundle—he closed his eyes for what he was certain would be a deep, blissful sleep, his bedsheet stained with the wet, sticky consequences of his solitary amour.

I'll clean it up tomorrow, he laughed. *Wouldn't want the Old Lady to find it. Then again, if she did find it, she'd probably think it was just the tapioca we had for dessert last night.*

But he soon discovered that the sleep he'd been yearning so fervently for was anything but deep. He was soon tossing and turning like an infant with a bad case of colic. Then he bolted upright in his bed, his eagerness to escape from his worries sabotaged by yet another maddening episode of self-doubt and confusion. One minute he was a young, proud Daddy, beaming with delight at the prospect of caring tenderly for his beautiful infant daughter; the next minute he was a good-for-nothing Loser, trapped in arrested adolescence and swinging wildly back and forth like an out-of-control pendulum—a frightened little boy in a grown man's body.

Maybe I did get her pregnant, he mused. Then he ridiculed himself for his raw, hare-brained stupidity. *Or maybe that guy named Guertner came back for some more fine pussy after being away from Birdie for so long, then failed to put his cock in a sock before taking the plunge! I mean, wouldn't that make* him *Cecelia's father? Why would it have to be* me?

Oh well, he laughed, *if it* was *me who stuffed her without protection, then Birdie's little squirt could easily have been my doing.* He closed his eyes, then locked his hands behind his head and smiled warmly up into the all-enveloping darkness of his bedroom. *And would that really be such a bad outcome? Cecelia, huh? Nice name! Wonder if I'll ever see my little girl! Wonder if she looks like me! And if she does, then what other proof of paternity would a man need?*

As for the eleven-year-old boy, Clay didn't even want to *think* about how *he* came into the world. Yes, he realized it could have been Guertner's doing. Of course! Or maybe it was some lowlife who took Birdie out one night for soft drinks and polite conversation, then pinned her down like a butterfly in the back seat of his Chevy and had his way with her. Maybe *that's* the creep who did the dirty on her!

But he knew that whoever was responsible for filling Birdie's tank with baby fuel four years ago didn't have to be him. After all, there were other available explanations—other possible perpetrators! More than likely, she'd been intimate with others long before he hooked up with her at Dori's place. It was time for him to face that possibility, however unpleasant it might be for him, however severely it might bruise his frail ego.

The only good news, he laughed ruefully, *is that her Boy Child is* her *problem, not mine! And as for Cecelia, if it turns out she really* is *mine, then I'll have to find a way to deal with her. But how? And why me, God, why me?*

He was feeling desperate now, more than eager to find a way—*any* way—out of the jam he'd gotten himself into. *And all,* he groaned, *for one brief but exhilarating afternoon poke at that Fourth of July party. This whole mess would never have come about if Birdie had just gone ahead and gotten an abortion! It would have been a good, clean break from an impossible situation. Our only problem then would have been keeping it a secret. But no! She had to take off her thinking cap, consult with her heart, and do the 'right' thing!*

The word around high school, said Dori one time, had been that Birdie was one of that increasingly endangered species, a Good Catholic. So naturally, he said, when she found out she was pregnant, she must have begun listening to the Pope whenever he stood on that balcony at the Vatican and chanted that, in effect, abortion is *murder,* and under no circumstances—not even *rape*—could it ever be justified. That must have been when Little Miss Virtue put her hanger back in the closet, bought herself a bassinet and a shitload of diapers, and knitted a drawerful of baby clothes. Full steam ahead, she must have told herself.

Women! Clay grumbled. *They can be so damned impractical!*

Determined to stop obsessing over the uninvited arrival of a baby in his life, he grew quiet, hoping to drift off into something close to sleep again. Then he remembered, fondly, what Ned Beckerman, the head counselor at Camp Sequoia, always warned him and his cabin mates about on orientation day: "Now don't you go gettin' any ideas about sowin' your wild oats while you're here at the Camp," he'd say. "Redwoods—that's the girl's camp just down the road from us—is strictly off limits. So as far as you're concerned, Camp Sequoia needs to be *Alcatraz!*"

Of course, the boys always listened politely to Ned, nodding their heads in agreement, then did whatever they wanted to do when he wasn't looking. They didn't really like his style as a counselor, anyway—they considered him a creep and a loner—so, in private, they took great pleasure in calling him "Sasquatch." After lights-out, they'd pull the blankets up over their heads and then, giggling like a bunch of schoolgirls, they'd make fun of his scrawny legs, his bad breath, and the strange, Quasimodo way he always lumbered around the grounds late at night with his flashlight beaming, checking the cabins out, one by one, for any rule infractions.

Sometimes they'd slip out the back door of their cabin long after Sasquatch had turned in for the night, then sneak over to Redwoods and peek into their cabin windows, hoping to catch one of the campers in her bra and panties.

Those were the days, Clay thought to himself. *And while Ned doesn't know it—I heard he's out of the camping business now—I'm not done sowin' those oats, not by a long shot!*

He came back down to earth again, then tried hard to imagine the way another solution might play itself out: the meeting at the adoption agency; the signing of release papers; Cecelia's introduction to her new parents; the final, painful, poignant goodbye. Then he realized that the scenario he envisioned was more make-believe than manageable.

Staring up at the ceiling, a rueful half-smile on his face, he whispered into the darkness of the room he'd called home for the better part of his checkered, up-and-down childhood. *Besides,* he thought, *I do love that name. Cecelia: it seems like the perfect name for a little girl—my little girl—to have!*

Chapter Eleven

Early in 1971, Clay arrived at S&N one morning and found a brand new state-of-the-art office chair at his desk—no doubt another "I love what you do for us" gift from Henley. Then, just as he was settling into the chair, the phone rang.

"A call for you, Mr. Middling," said Imogene, the receptionist, employing her usual deferential, sweet-as-cotton-candy manner. Clay loved hearing himself addressed as "Mr. Middling," especially the way Imogene did it. This could never have happened at the Flea Market, he laughed.

"Shall I put her through, then?" said Imogene.

"If she's a friend, sure!" said Clay. "If she's a bill collector, tell her nobody named Middling works here."

"Whatever you say, Mr. Middling," she said, this time with a hint of sarcasm in her voice. "But *everybody's* a friend of Mr. Real Estate—right? Anyway, whoever wants to talk with you sounds really friendly. Not an angry client or the typical bill collector, so the coast is clear! You may proceed."

Clay rolled his eyes, then held the phone to his ear and waited. *There are times when I'd like to take that woman over my knee and teach her a thing or two about respect,* he thought to himself. But he knew it was a ridiculous sentiment, because Imogene was at least twenty years older than him, and more matronly than mischievous.

"Clay?" said the voice.

He knew instantly, from the high-pitched, nasal tone, who the voice belonged to. And because he wasn't at all pleased to be hearing from Birdie again, he clammed up, dug in, and refused to respond.

"*Yoo hoo!*" she said. "Can you *hear* me? What are we—disconnected?"

Clay checked to make sure Imogene wasn't listening in, and to his relief he could hear nothing but the sound of his own agitated breathing. *No third-party intrusions,* he grinned.

"Never thought I'd hear from *you* again," he said. "And of all the times and places you might have chosen to call, while I'm at *work!* Then again, why are you calling me at *all?* I figured you'd written me off and moved on with your life—found somebody more to your liking."

"I gave you my number after we . . . you know . . . after we went upstairs at Dori's house and . . ."

"No need to bring *that* up again," he said.

"What? So now you want to pretend it never happened? Tell you what, lover boy: I'm not gonna pretend. I mean, it *happened,* didn't it? And then I left my number at your house, but you never bothered to call me!"

"You're right," he said, "I never called. I had my reasons! But I'm not gonna drag you through the list right now. In fact, it's time we put a stop to this little chit-chat, because I've a ton of paperwork to do."

"And you're asking me why I called? Now that's laughable! I mean, why *wouldn't* I call? *Think,* dimwit!"

She took a deep breath, did her best to calm herself down, then continued. "I know, I know. I suppose it's a bit late—four years late, to be precise—but I thought it was about time I offered my congratulations."

"Congratulations? For what?"

"You have a *daughter,* that's what! And her name is Cecelia! Oh, and then there's the little matter of *child support.* I honestly thought I'd be able to take care of her all by my lonesome, but guess what! Those bills just keep comin' in! And without some help from Daddy-kins, the Good Ship Mommy-kins is gonna sink!"

"Oh, shit!" said Clay. "Here it comes: the Money Grab!"

"You're surprised? You're shocked that I finally realized Cecelia is not just my problem—that she's *your* problem, too? Listen: if you're looking for a way to slither out o' *this* jam, save your breath, tightwad! You'll be hearing from my lawyer in a week or two. And if you don't come across with some serious cash by the first of the month, we'll be garnisheeing your wages!"

"All right!" he shouted. "I've heard you loud and clear!"

He finally realized that there was no way out. He was trapped. If he didn't agree to contribute to Cecelia's upkeep, he'd be labeled a lousy excuse for a father and the courts would hound him relentlessly. And after an exhilarating four years of climbing the occupational ladder, his reputation in the Bay Area real estate community would go up in flames and his job at S&N would be in jeopardy.

"Look," he said, "I'm not an ogre! I can see why you need help with your daughter, but—"

"You mean *our* daughter," said Birdie. "*Our* daughter!"

"I suppose you could say that," he said.

"Ain't no 'supposing' about it! So let me see, Mr. Middling," she sneered. "My guess is that you've never taken a dance class in your life. Am I right?"

"Well, that's at least *one* thing you've gotten right," he smirked.

"Because if you *had* taken dance lessons, you'd know it takes two to tango!"

Clay, who'd finally reached the limit of his tolerance for her righteous tongue-lashing, went silent, refusing once again to respond.

Birdie sighed into the phone, then drummed her fingers on the arm of the chair she was sitting in.

"Well," she said, "have you nothing more to say about this?"

"Nothing more," he said softly. "Nothing at all." He hung up the phone, then sat staring out through the imposing trio of Palladian windows that looked out on the manicured lawn of Scheckel & Newbury.

Our daughter! he thought to himself. Then he glanced down at the small mountain of paperwork staring up at him and wondered what life—that all-powerful, unforgiving Taskmaster of Us All—had in store for him.

* * *

He slept surprisingly well that night, given his long day at work and the harsh, unnerving exchange he'd had with Birdie. The next day was routine—no surprises, no complications, no unpleasant phone calls from his less than perfect past. He'd worked through the stack of papers in record time, then left them on Henley's desk. Later, as soon as Tuckerman had double-checked them for accuracy, he marched into Clay's office and praised him for the all-around excellence of his work.

"You've done a damn good job!" said Henley. "If you keep goin' in the direction you're goin'—I mean, *Up, Up, and Away*—we're gonna have to add your name to our company logo. Scheckel, Newbury & *Middling*. How's *that* sound?"

"Music to my ears," said Clay, blushing cherry red. "But I'm afraid my Old Man would never approve. Unless, of course, there was a Stanton before the Middling."

"No doubt about that," said Henley. "Your father has a right to his dreams, just like any other man upstairs in the trenches, bustin' his hump to earn an honest dollar. But what Stan and all the other S&N stiffs around here have to understand is that there's no room for sentimentality in this operation. Not on *my* watch!

"Of course, your father does a decent job here," he continued. "Always has, always will. But decent is not enough in a competitive world. Only the Best of the Best could ever hope see their name added to the S&N logo. And though I'll soon be retired from the real estate racket—finished here at Scheckel & Newbury after nearly forty years of service—I want you to know, between you and me, that in my remaining time here I'll be doing everything in my power to make sure your last name *will* eventually be added to the S&N logo. It'll be a proud moment for me. And believe it or not, even poor Stanton Middling will finally come around and see what his son has meant to all of us."

Then Henley got up from his desk, took his wallet out of his pants, pulled out a bill, and handed it to Clay.

"Been meaning to give this to you," he said, "but I've got a hell of a lot on my mind right now. And when it gets like this, the wheels don't always turn the way they're supposed to. Now why don't you finish filing the Lewinsky report, then wrap it up at 3:00 p.m. and take the rest of the day off? You've been pushing yourself really hard lately; it's about time you got out o' the Rat Race for a few hours. We'll do fine without you, and you'll come back tomorrow fresh as a springtime flower!"

Whoa, thought Clay. *Fifty bucks!* Unable to find the words to express his appreciation, he took the bill and stuffed it into his shirt pocket. He was blushing all over again, squirming his way through Henley's rapturous anointment of him as S&N's Man to Watch.

Too much praise, especially the gushy kind, had always made Clay Middling uncomfortable. He'd spent years doubting himself, thanks to parents who found more pleasure in finding fault with him than they did in praising him for his accomplishments. Because of that, he'd learned not to trust anyone without careful observation and meticulous analysis.

Can I really be as good as Henley keeps saying I am? he wondered. *Is there an ulterior motive in his never-ending flattery? Either I'm the Second Coming—the John D. Rockefeller of the real estate world—or Henley Tuckerman's an ass-kissing sycophant, an old man near retirement with nothing to do but hand out kudos like chocolate bunnies at the Easter parade. What reason does he have to praise me so lavishly at every turn?*

Henley wrapped up their conversation, and Clay was relieved to get back to his own office—a place where he could reflect on his good fortune, get started on his next project, and plan for what promised to be a glorious future as a member in good standing of an elite trio of real estate gurus: *Scheckel, Newbury & Middling.*

He finished the Lewinsky report by 3:00 p.m. as promised, then stepped out into to the hallway, locked the door behind him, and headed out to his car, grateful for the chance to slip away from work on such a beautiful early-spring day. He found himself whistling as if he were Johnny Appleseed on the way to a planting. *Things could be worse,* he laughed. *I could be unemployed. I could be homeless. I could be terminally ill like my cousin Jimmy, who turned twenty-three a few months ago but learned only a week later that he has less than a year to live. That poor son of a bitch!*

"Nobody loves a whiner!" Clay shouted to no one in particular while driving through his neighborhood beneath a cloudless, sparklingly blue sky. High above the horizon, a flock of songbirds darted and swooped over a long line of rooftops, searching merrily for the perfect place to build their nests. *Mrs. Niederman used to call us whiners back in kindergarten,* he laughed, *and if any of us were dumb enough to fight back, she'd say, "Zip your lip, then get a grip!"*

The gift of free time—a chance to escape for a few hours from the rigors of life as a working stiff—ought to have given anyone an interlude of pure, unalloyed pleasure. But for some reason, Clay had always had trouble with downtime. To keep focused, he needed a game plan of some sort. *Or maybe just a hot little skirt to chase around and obsess over,* he laughed. *Swell, Tuckerman. Thanks for the gift. But I don't have a woman. My dance card is empty! So what am I gonna do 'til tomorrow?*

To kill some time—anything to avoid going home and dealing with the noxious, ever-present cloud of familial tension—he decided to cruise around Belvedere-Tiburon, one of the area's more exclusive enclaves, and do some work-free, parent-free fantasizing.

The homes in Belvedere—some of them breathtaking cliff-hangers overlooking San Francisco Bay—were sprawling, pretentious, and outrageously expensive. Some were so spectacular they were on the National Register of Historic Places. Clay couldn't help imagining what it would be like to live in one of them. *Yacht clubs! Five-star restaurants! Views of the Golden Gate! Maybe—if, with Tuckerman's help, I continue to climb the corporate ladder at Scheckel & Newbury—one o' those seaside castles could soon be mine!*

He finished his fantasy ride through the Land of the Elites, then drove back to a more humble reality—*his* reality—and fought his way through dense, early evening traffic, his radio tuned to Station KSAN and turned up full blast. He finally reached home around 6:00 p.m., feeling more chipper than he'd felt in weeks thanks to his boss and the sneak preview of what he hoped really would become his future. *Tuckerman may be an old fart on the skids,* Clay chuckled, *but he really does have a good side. I just got myself six hours off and a nice, fresh hunk o' change. And by God, there's gonna be a lot more o' that stuff comin' down the pipe. Eat your heart out, Pops!*

Not ready to go inside, he pulled up and parked in front of the house, left the radio and his sunglasses on, then leaned back in the driver's seat, stretched his legs, and finished listening to "We Gotta Get Out of This Place," the one song by the Animals he liked more than any other. *My sentiments exactly,* he smiled while steadily tapping his class ring on the rim of the steering wheel. *I've had enough "Mommy & Daddy" for a while!*

He was remarkably relaxed under the circumstances, and yet his entire body was moving in precise rhythm with the beat, as if he were in bed, dancing solo. He soon found himself imagining what it would be like to have a girl on top of him there in his Mustang, bucking like a bronco, losing herself in the bone-hard ecstasy of the moment. The image was so intense—so shockingly, pleasurably real—that he came full throttle in his chinos, leaving a three-inch wide wet spot dead center of his crotch.

Then, seconds later, a door slammed loud enough to jar him out of his fantasy. He snapped upright, looked out across the lawn, and to his horror saw a large pile of stuff—stuff he instantly recognized as the contents of his bedroom—taking shape at the base of the front porch. Too stunned to know what he should do next, he sat still and watched in astonishment as item after item—his high school track letter, his favorite quilt, armload after armload of shirts and pants, sweaters and coats still on their hangers—and even his framed *Playboy* centerfold of Patti Reynolds—came flying out the door.

He knew his father was the one doing the trashing, because each time another armload of stuff was thrust out the door, he could see the porch light playing off his father's prized Rolex Oyster Perpetual—the wristwatch he'd been given after twenty years of "distinguished service" at Scheckel & Newbury.

Distinguished, my ass, thought Clay. *Daddy was nothin' but an incompetent bum-sucker the moment he strode into S&N and hung his London Fog on a hook. Thinks he's Ricky Blaine in* Casablanca *when he wears that getup! My God,* he chuckled, *Tuckerman must have been completely off his rocker when he put Stanton Middling on the payroll!*

Still boiling over with righteous indignation, Clay shut off the radio, threw his car into reverse, and peeled noisily out from the curb. Then, engulfed in a dark cloud of noxious exhaust fumes, he put his pedal to the metal and headed north.

He came back less than two hours later with a four-by-eight cargo trailer from the UHaul in San Rafael attached to his car's trailer hitch. Though the trailer was modest in size compared to the others, the clerk at UHaul still thought it was too big and heavy for what Clay was driving—a Plymouth Valiant his father had bought for him when he turned sixteen. But Clay, who was easily as stubborn and foolhardy as his Old Man, brushed the clerk off, paid the required fee, and waited while the trailer was attached. Then he drove off toward home, laughing uproariously at the loud clanging sound the trailer made whenever he hit a manhole cover.

It was dusk now, and the porch light at his parents' place was off—a sure sign that they were close to turning in for the night. *Good,* he smiled. *I'll just load up the trailer and get the hell out o' here before the two of us get into another nasty blow-up! He must have been really ticked off at me to do something that radical. But at this point I really don't give a shit what he thinks of me. All I care about is cutting the umbilical with the two of them. Beyond that, and beyond Birdie and Cecelia, I really don't know what the hell I do care about—where I'm going, what I want to accomplish, what evils are lurking round the corner in this fucked-up life of mine!*

He grabbed his emergency lamp from the passenger seat, made his way to the front of the house, positioned the lamp in the crotch of a nearby mulberry tree, then trained it on the stack of his belongings and began loading them into the trailer. When he finally reached the last item—the single-drawer bedside cabinet where he kept his favorite issues of *Playboy* and *Penthouse*—he found an envelope with his name on it attached to the top with a strip of duct tape. The handwriting was clearly his father's. *The bastard always manages to have the last word in arguments,* he sneered. *I should have known!*

Clay tore open the envelope and pulled out two elegant, neatly folded sheets of stationery, each with the words *Scheckel & Newbury* engraved at the top. Inside the letter were a half dozen crisp hundred-dollar bills.

Jesus, he thought, *Dad can be a real tightwad when it comes to the practical stuff—things like clothing and rent— and yet he always thinks he can buy my love by showering me with gifts.* Clay remembered the most costly ones he'd received over the years: the Valiant; the weekend in the Bahamas (when he finally passed his calculus class after three tries); and the brick-red Domino Californian guitar with the body shaped like a pentagon—a real collector's item. After showing off the guitar to his friends, Clay had put it back in its case and never played it again. *Boy, did that ever piss off my papa,* he laughed.

Then he unfolded the letter and read it to himself.

To My Son Clay:

I called Henley last night. Talked with him about Cecelia. It took a while, but we finally put two and two together and realized that you're the father, and Tuckerman's daughter, Avis, is the mother.

Listen: I may be angry that you've gone out and knocked up a girl—that when the chips were down, you didn't have the sense to keep your pecker in your pants like you should have. I thought you had better judgment than that, but I was obviously wrong!

And yet I like to think I'm a good and decent man, and so is Henley. So we want you to know that in spite of your careless mistake and its unfortunate consequences, we're going to love our granddaughter!

We know there's no way you and Birdie can turn the clock back and make the right decision. We're sad about the outcome and yet resigned to it.

But there is one thing you can do, and it will be the right thing to do. You must get married—as soon as possible—and preserve your good standing, not just in the community, but in the marketplace. You're going to need to be gainfully employed, and not just once in a while, the way it used to be, but for good!

Henley assured me he'll keep you at S&N—at this point he can't imagine doing without you—but only if you tie the knot with his daughter and avoid the scandal of having a manager at Scheckel & Newbury whose daughter slept with a born loser.

So! Until you're legally married, don't even bother to show up at work. Henley says he won't let you in the door again unless you have a marriage certificate in your hand, signed and notarized. Until then, you need to find yourself an apartment, rent yourself a tux, and use the enclosed cash to buy Birdie the best damn wedding dress on the market.

Understand? Hope so. And by the way, your Mother hopes so, too!

Love,
Your Father

PS: Sorry, but something had to be done, and that something ended up being the mess you found on the lawn!

I'll bet Mom does, laughed Clay. In The World According to Brooke, everything had to be done by the rules—the ones in that suffocating guide to all things proper, all things conventional. He crammed the letter into his coat pocket, then backed his car, with the UHaul attached to it, out of the driveway. *It works for her and Dad,* he laughed, *but not for me, by God!*

He made it back to Bridgeway, tuned the radio to Station KYA, and out roared Tina Turner's "Shake a Tail Feather," filling up every nook and cranny of his Valiant. *Ain't nobody comes close to Big Daddy Donahue when it comes to sniffing out a sure hit,* he laughed. *He's got an instinct for killer music.* Then Clay headed straight to the Hotel Sausalito with Turner's primitive, driving rhythms fueling the ride.

"Six hundred Benjamins for one goddam wedding dress?" he shouted at the windshield, shaking his head in disgust. "Fuck that! She can get one for next to nothin' at Second Time Around, and her Old Man can pick up the tab!" *Besides,* he chuckled, *I've got a better idea about what to do with Daddy's little windfall.*

When Clay pulled up to the main entrance of the Hotel

Sausalito with his UHaul in tow, the valet on duty dashed out from the lobby and came running up to him, his eyes rolling, his palms outstretched in a gesture of supreme exasperation.

"What are you, deaf, dumb, and blind?" he shouted, then pointed derisively at the UHaul. "You can't park that thing here! You'd be smack in the way of our guests!"

Clay rolled down his window, thrust his head out, then stared menacingly at the man, who couldn't have been more than eighteen or nineteen.

"*Excuse me*," he sniggered. "I *am* a guest. One of *your* guests, in fact! Or I *will* be, as soon you park this crate so I can go inside and register!" Then, to make sure the valet knew he wasn't kidding, he pulled the six hundreds out of his jacket, waved them in his face, then yanked a twenty out of his shirt pocket and handed it to him. "Unless, of course, this dump doesn't need the cash—and you don't want a tip."

As soon as the man realized he'd misread the situation, he apologized profusely. "Sorry!" he simpered. "I should have asked you if you were a guest instead of assuming you weren't. Guess that UHaul sent me a mixed message. But I know, I know: it's still no excuse."

He smiled, then handed Clay a laminated "We're So Sorry!" card. "This is our way of apologizing to our guests for having behaved in a less-than-professional way. You'll want to present this card to the bartender each time you order a drink. For the duration of your stay with us, all of your drinks will be on the house—as long as you stay reasonably sober."

Clay put the card in his shirt pocket, shook the valet's hand, then got out of his car and handed him the keys. "Please take good care of my baby," he said. "It's my pride and joy!"

He slept like a king in his castle that night, his heart warmed by the realization that he would finally be free of his father's never-ending judgments. And the prospect of spending three luxurious nights at the Hotel Sausalito, treating himself like royalty and handing out extravagant tips, made him feel powerful—a young Manager-on-the-Move with a fine career ahead of him.

He spent the next two days hunkered down at the Sausalito, oversleeping, watching X-rated movies from the comfort of his bed, consuming five-star meals prepared by award-winning chefs, and downing as many free drinks as he could handle from the No Name Bar.

Early Tuesday morning, he crawled out of bed, had one last breakfast in the spectacular downstairs dining room, paid his bill, then hopped on the expressway, still disturbingly unsure of his next move.

Would marrying the boss's daughter really solve all my problems? he asked himself while working his way through the morning rush.

I know it'd be the right thing to do; common sense tells me that! But what if I don't really love Birdie? What if I'd be marrying her only to please my father and hang onto my job at S&N? And what if having Henley Tuckerman as my father-in-law would cause friction in the workplace? Clay knew he could easily avoid his Old Man; his office was on the third floor. But Tuckerman's office was two doors away from Clay's; the two of them interacted on a daily basis.

It was all too much for Clay to handle on his own, so he decided to drive straight to Birdie's place, with the UHaul still in tow, and have a frank talk with her. He figured it was early enough that he'd have no trouble catching her at home.

When he pulled up to the address he'd scribbled down on a three-by-five card, the house didn't surprise him. It was one of dozens of post-war cookie-cutter bungalows with manicured lawns and identical front doors with half-moon windows. But the car in the driveway did. Clay knew his cars from years of thumbing through his father's issues of *Motor Trend*. It was a lime green '67 Lamborghini Miura P400.

Holy shit! he muttered to himself. *Where'd a blue-collar girl like Birdie Tuckerman get the cash for an Italian super-car? Either she's found herself a Sugar Daddy or she's shackin' up with a rich boy.*

He rang the bell a half dozen times before Birdie finally came downstairs and cracked open the door, just enough to allow her to peer over the security chain and see who'd come by so early in the morning. When she realized it was Clay, she smiled happily to herself, then flung the door open and stood there gaping at him, her brow furrowed, her eyes half-closed but shining with optimism. She was still in her nightgown, her hair like the snakes of Medusa, her powder-blue slippers worn and faded from years of shuffling around the house. When Clay saw two firm, plump nipples pushing outward from within the pale green satin of her gown, he felt a swelling in his Fruit of the Looms and was more than happy to let it blossom.

"And what can I do for you, Mr. Middling?" she yawned, hoping he'd make a move on her but playing innocent. "Kind o' early for a social call, isn't it?"

"More businesslike than social," said Clay. But he knew from past experience just what she was up to. "I've got some questions, and they need answering."

"Come *in*, then," she said. "No need to be bashful! But I hope you'll forgive me, because the place is a real dump right now. After all, I didn't expect to be entertaining my favorite one-night stand at this ungodly hour."

He hung his jacket on a coatrack in the foyer, then walked over to the couch and sat down. "So what's with the Lambo?" he asked.

"It was a gift from my father," Birdie said. "He just moved up to something newer, so he didn't want it any more. I actually just sold it. Guy's picking it up tomorrow."

Birdie headed straight to the same couch, all set to drop the pretense and snuggle up to Clay. But, to her surprise, he played traffic cop and held up his hand, stopping her cold.

"No you don't!" he snapped. "It may have worked for you at Tommy's party, but it won't work now. Believe it or not, I've grown older and wiser since then. I've got a good job and a reputation to preserve, and it's gonna *stay* that way!"

"All right," she said, "have it your way! It's just that I couldn't help thinking you might still have a tender place for me in your heart."

"Only in my pants," said Clay. "And as you can see, it's never really gone away."

"I did notice that," she chuckled. "And it's clear we're not talkin' 'roll o' quarters' down there!"

"More like silver dollars," he said. "But I didn't come here for nookie, so let's get serious. Do you really need to keep Cecelia? I mean, couldn't you farm her out to a foster family and get your life—your *freedom*—back again? I'm having trouble believing you're actually enjoying takin' care of a baby again. Doesn't seem to me that would be your thing at this point. I mean, wasn't once enough?"

"The only thing you remember about me," she said, "is that I have very long legs, and I knew just how to wrap 'em around that tight little ass of yours. But the rest of me is a whole different world, and you don't know *squat* about *that* world, do you. All *you* did was plant the seed; since then it's been my job to tend the garden. Surprise, surprise! Typical male, typical father!"

"Oh, *that's* cute!" said Clay. "But you don't know much about *me*, either. You know the length of my crank, all right, but not one damn thing about the *rest* of me! I can't help thinking that if you were to—"

A door suddenly slammed shut upstairs, and down came Cecelia, still in her pink bell-bottom pajamas, dragging her favorite teddy bear behind her. Each time she took a downward step, the teddy's head made a loud thumping sound on the staircase.

"You shouldn't do that, honey," said Birdie. "You'll give poor Smokey a concussion!"

Clay's anger dissolved at the sight of his daughter. He felt an immense, hard-to-explain pride in the knowledge that the beautiful little girl standing in front of him was here on earth in part because of him.

"What's a concuzzin?" asked CeCe. Then she turned to Clay and stared intensely at him, her lips pursed, her eyes bursting with a combination of understandable mistrust and childlike curiosity. "Who *are* you? I've never seen *you* before!"

"Questions, questions," said Birdie. "Do you ever stop asking questions? I'll talk to you later. Promise! It's just that right now's not a good time for Q&A."

"What's Cuenay mean?" asked CeCe.

"Shush!" said Birdie. "Where's your manners? Can't you see I've got a guest right now?"

"Jesus!" said Clay, who, to his surprise, harbored a powerful urge to defend his little girl. "She can't help it! She's just being curious! So what the hell's wrong with *that*? I mean, isn't that what little kids are *supposed* to be? I should think you'd want to cut her a little slack! And by the way, I cannot believe this cute little shrimp of yours is only four years old! How can that possibly be? She talks like a freakin' ten-year-old—at *least*!"

"Believe me," said Birdie, "it astounds me, too—every damn day! But I have to say, I'm glad you noticed that about her. I heard just the other day that some dude named MacArthur out in Chicago is getting ready to launch a grant of some kind—a 'genius grant,' they're calling it—any month now. And y' know what? I think CeCe may just end up *getting* one someday! Wouldn't that be sweet?"

"Sweeter than the finest cabernet," Clay said, making what he imagined to be an authentic Wine Country flourish with his right hand. Then he pursed his lips in the French way, and, with a look of genuine envy on his face, said, "Man, I can't help wondering what somebody would do with a windfall like that. Maybe *I* can earn one o' those McCarthys—or whatever they call it—someday."

"You and *me*," she said, shrugging her shoulders. "I mean, who the hell wouldn't want a pot o' gold like that to show up on her front porch?" Then she changed the topic of conversation back to her visitor.

"I'm curious," she continued. "Where have these sudden Daddy feelings of yours have been hiding? I've never seen that side of you before."

"You saw plenty of me at Tommy's shindig that day, didn't you. Just not *that* side."

Then he simmered down and turned reflective.

"Look," he said, jamming a finger into his chest as if he were an elevator button. "There's all sorts of layers on this onion. You've just not been around me long enough to see me peel 'em off. Besides: what reason would you have had to see me since that day? And come to think of it, what reason would I have had to come back to *you*? You never got in touch with *me* again, either. Remember?"

Birdie went silent. She stood up and stepped away from him, then whipped around and pointed at Cecelia. "*There's* your reason," she said. "*Your little girl!* That would have been a damn good reason, don'tcha think? Or maybe you didn't know she's yours!"

"I never thought a little afternoon of 'spin the bottle' would end up like this!" he said. "I swear it's the one and only time I've ever failed to use protection before takin' a dive with a dame."

"A pretty *dumb* dive, if y' ask me," she said. "But done is done, isn't it. The chicken's been hatched. We had our fun, and now it's over. The only question left, as I see it, is what are you gonna *do* about it?"

"I don't *know* what I'm gonna do about it!" he snapped. "Gimme a few days to work through my feelings. I'm a wreck right now, and people never make good decisions when they're in the shape I'm in."

He leapt up off the couch, yanked his jacket off the coatrack, and yanked the front door open. "You'll hear from me again," he shouted over his shoulder, "but don't pin me down about when. Maybe I'm just not ready to do what you probably *want* me to do. You know—the 'right thing.' After all, I really don't know for sure what the right thing is, and as I see it, neither do *you*!" With that, he charged out of the house, slamming the door behind him.

As he prepared to drive off, he could see Birdie standing in the doorway with Cecelia next to her, clinging tightly to her leg. She was clearly upset about something, but he couldn't tell what. Then, without really thinking, he poked his left hand through the car window and waved a small, plaintive goodbye to her. She waved back, then broke away and ran straight toward the car with her arms outstretched, dropping her teddy bear behind her as she ran.

"Daddy! Daddy!" she wailed. "Where are you going? You just *got* here!"

Daddy? he thought to himself. *She called me Daddy!* Startled to learn what she thought of him after only one brief encounter, he put the car in gear and roared away, not ready to engage with her again. He had no idea where he was going, but it didn't seem to matter. And the truth was that at that painful moment, *nothing* really mattered. Nothing, that is, except Cecelia.

Birdie calmed her daughter down, then did her best to explain to her why a handsome young man named Clay had suddenly showed up, uninvited, at their door. Cecelia listened patiently to her mother, pouting and whimpering along the way, but in the end she nodded her head in grudging agreement, then snuggled up to her mother.

'He's a nice man," said Birdie, "a *good* man! I could tell he really liked you. I'm betting he's gonna come back *again*, too—sometime *soon*. So why don't we just go ahead now and get you ready for bed, honey. Brush 'em, brush 'em, brush 'em," she chanted as they marched down the hall together. "I want to see that smile of yours again!"

Once upstairs, CeCe turned off the light, bounced up onto her bed, then waited eagerly for her mother to come and tuck her in. She was feeling better now, so instead of sniffling when Birdie hugged and kissed her, she issued a sweet, childlike sigh of contentment, then smiled up into the warm darkness of her bedroom.

"I love you, Mommy," she said. "But if I had a *daddy*, I'd love you even more! Maybe I'd even love *him*."

"That's very sweet," said Birdie. "And I love you too!" Then she pulled the covers up to her daughter's chin, planted one more kiss on her forehead, and shuffled off to her own bed in the room right next door to CeCe's.

* * *

Birdie got into her bed and turned out the light, but she couldn't sleep. Part of her was surprisingly happy to see Clay again, and not just because it so obviously rekindled her sexual attraction to him. The moment he bumped up so salaciously against her rear end at Tommy's Fourth of July party—and especially the moment she whipped around and saw for the first time the suave, devilish smile on his face—she found him to be easily as hunky and viscerally electric as Ryan O'Neal, or even Christopher Reeve.

But it wasn't only because he was so undeniably attractive, both in the way he was built and in the way he carried himself. She was also glad to see him because, from the very beginning, she simply *liked* him. He was funny—awkward in that disarmingly male way, and unusually polite for a man his age, barely beyond adolescence. That he was nearly a head shorter than her—and a few years younger—might have bothered her the way it seems to bother most women. But to her surprise, his raw, steamy masculinity made the difference in their height and age completely irrelevant. He'd undoubtedly turned her on that day, more than she'd ever been turned on before. And from that moment on, nothing else seemed to matter. She hoped he'd eventually do the responsible thing and agree to marry her. Then Cecelia would finally have the Daddy she always wanted.

Chapter Twelve

For very different reasons, of course, Cecelia didn't fall asleep easily that night, either. Her restlessness came from visions of Clay as a father.

What would it be like, she wondered, *to have a daddy around the house? Would he be like my friend Katie's father? I hate going over to her house when he's home. He's always so grouchy—growls like a dog and throws things around when he's mad! I sure wouldn't want that kind of daddy!*

I'd want a daddy who'd play games with me! Who'd do things with me on rainy days. Who'd take me to places I've never been to, like zoos or circuses!

Suddenly she remembered how much she loved playing outside after dark. Her mother didn't mind her doing that once in a while—especially in the summer—as long as she always stayed close by, on the front lawn, where Birdie could easily keep an eye on her.

Imagine how much fun it would be to have a daddy who'd go outside with me at night! We'd play hide-and-seek, or maybe Wiffle Ball! We'd get the glow-in-the-dark kind. Wouldn't that be fun! And just think: we might even dance together!

Through her bedroom window she could see a plump, iridescent October moon, glowing like a precious amulet from within a dense blanket of twinkling, multicolored stars. A gentle, late-night breeze rustled the leaves of a nearby sycamore, whose long, tentacled branches then came alive and lyrically raked themselves, like a Jamaican *guiro,* against the clapboards of their home.

Transfixed by the music of the trees and the light of the moon, Cecelia tumbled out of bed, slipped into her bunny slippers, then padded gently down the stairs and into the night, as careful as she could possibly be not to wake her mother.

No one but Cecelia knew she loved to dance. That's because she only danced when she was alone. She didn't want anyone to laugh at her, so, as she saw it, keeping her love of dancing a secret meant that no one ever would.

Her passion for dancing had begun right after she learned to her delight that her great-great-grandmother, Cecelia Koroneva, had been a world-famous Russian ballerina. Ever since then, she wanted desperately to become a ballerina herself. So whenever she was alone, she'd work on the moves she'd seen in *The Nutcracker Suite*, either on television or in the movies. She even had a library book next to her bed showing step-by-step how to perform all the basic ballet moves. She knew she should return the book—it was now several weeks overdue—but she just couldn't bring herself to take it back.

Until now, she'd never really thought of dancing outdoors at night, and she couldn't help wondering why it had taken her so long to imagine doing such a thing.

I'm gonna do it right now, she smiled, *and no one—not even my mother—can stop me!* Deep down inside, she knew that this was her moment—hers only—and she felt certain no one would be around to laugh at her.

It was much colder outside than she'd expected. "The frost will soon be on the pumpkin," Birdie was fond of saying; "it's time you wore a coat!" But CeCe had quite forgotten her mother's well-meant admonishment. She thought of going back up to her bedroom to get at least a sweater, then decided against it. *I'll be moving around a lot anyway,* she thought, *and then I'll wish I hadn't gotten it. And besides,* she giggled, *my nightgown, with all the lace and ruffles on it, will make me look just like the Sugar Plum Fairy!*

She decided to pretend she was at the Mariinsky in St. Petersburg, ready at any moment to glide elegantly out from the wings and onto the stage as Princess Aurora in Tchaikovsky's *Sleeping Beauty. I'll be the star,* she laughed. *In the play it's supposed to be my sixteenth birthday; there'll be thunderous applause!*

She began with an arabesque, but with one leg stretched out awkwardly behind her and a bunny slipper dangling from her foot, she felt more like a flamingo than a world-renowned ballet dancer. *I look so silly,* she thought to herself. *Better do something easier for now.*

She took a deep, swimmer-like breath, then spun wildly out across the lawn. But the grass was soaking wet with dew, and in the middle of her spinning she slipped and crashed to the ground, her bunny slipper catapulting high above her into the air.

Rome wasn't built in a day! she giggled, then got up off the ground, laughing, and shook the dew off her hands. She'd heard the saying on an episode of *Sesame Street*—the one in which Big Bird was trying his best to learn how to dance.

One last try, she laughed. *I'm not a quitter; I'll do a pirouette!*

She knew the pirouette has three parts, but while she could do the preparation and placement pretty well for a beginner, when it came to the third part— the rotation—she knew she still had a lot of work to do.

She worked her way through the first and second positions, then crossed her mental fingers and gave the rotation everything she had. And to her great surprise, she did it, more or less right, the very first time.

Exhilarated, she chased down her missing slipper. Then, shivering but ever so proud of herself, she dashed across the lawn to the front door, tiptoed up to her bedroom, threw off her slippers, and dove happily into her bed, too excited to worry about her dew-soaked nightgown.

"I can't wait to show Daddy my pirouette someday!" she whispered. "He'll be so proud of me! I'll even teach *him* how to do it!" As she settled into her pillow, beaming with pride, she was certain that someday, with a lot of practice, she'd be even more famous than her very own great-great-grandmother, dancer Cecelia Koroneva.

* * *

Clay drove aimlessly around for the better part of an hour, dealing with the ramifications of being an actual father. *Me? Really?* Then he decided to stop in at the No Name and have a few beers. *Might calm me down,* he thought. *Nothing else has, so it's worth a try.*

Only two other people were in the bar when he arrived: a lonely, withered old man with crooked, tobacco-stained teeth nursing a Watney's Red Barrel, and, three stools away from him, a young woman dressed to kill and stacked to the heavens, carrying a bright orange Gucci bag and taking deep, lung-punishing drags on what appeared at first glance to be a pretzel stick but was actually a cigarillo. Between the two of them, they'd turned the No Name into a smoke-engulfed, liquor-saturated speakeasy.

There'll be no problem with the woman, thought Clay. *She's too wrapped up in her own me-me-me universe to even notice me.* But the man, clearly anything but bashful, moved right in on him, determined to strike up a conversation.

"Been comin' to the No Name for years," he said. "Decades, actually! But I ain't never seen *you* here. What's your story, young fella?"

"No story," said Clay. "Nothing worth bothering *you* with, anyway."

"Aww, c'mon!" said the man, who by now was drenched to the gills and spinning crazily back and forth on his stool. "You can tell me anything! You've jus' *got* to have *somethin'* to get off your chest. You look like you just lost your best friend in a train wreck!"

Clay got up and moved two stools down from the man, then quaffed down his first beer and ordered another. And then another and another, until he himself was good and smashed.

Nearly half an hour passed before the old man decided to try again. "Well?" he said. "Five straight beers shoulda been enough to open you up. I've been countin'! You ready to talk now? Let the Bad Times flow, my friend!"

Clay thought about it for a moment, then decided there couldn't really be any harm in sharing a few of his woes with the old geezer. *Might even help me clear my sinuses,* he thought. *And besides, I'm never gonna see the guy again.*

"OK, OK," he said. "I'll talk! So what's my problem, you ask? Well, you know—just the usual shit a guy my age likes to wade around in. The truth, and nothin' but the truth, is that I boned a girl at a party four years ago—forgot to wear my raincoat—and found out only a few days ago that I'd knocked her up. And now, wouldn't y' know, I've got a four-year-old daughter to deal with. I mean, holy shit! I must have been out o' my mind that day!"

"More like out o' *Daddy Guards*!" laughed the geezer.

"And let's face it," said Clay, "I'm really not father material." Privately, he wondered if the old man even knew what it meant to 'bone' a girl, but he figured 'had sexual intercourse with' was just a little too formal for bar talk.

"Bad move, Ex-lax!" said the old man, then shifted from crude to philosophical and leaned in close toward Clay, his brows lowered, his eyes squinting like a Japanese Zen Master.

"So you went schlongin' with your dongin', huh? Fine! Been there, done that, and on more than one occasion. Trust me! But a guy's always got to remember to wear his rubbers when it's raining. Didn't your Mommy teach you that? Or better yet, your Daddy?"

"Oh, they *tried*," said Clay. "God knows, they tried! Guess the sermon didn't really sink in, though. But the *jizz* did, and now I'm paying the price for not listening to 'em."

"No need to fret," said the man. "Redemption's only a phone call away!"

"How's that?" said Clay. "I mean, what are you trying to tell me?"

"I'm trying to . . . to . . . no, *forget* that. I'm *telling* you! I'm tellin' you it's time to get off your tricycle and turn yourself into a man! Take a look at your calendar, my boy. Look in your closet. What clothes do you see there? You're no longer a toddler, no longer an adolescent. You're a *grown man*. And that means marriage needs to be right there at the top of your 'gotta do' list."

As Clay listened patiently to the man's lecture, the color began to drain from his face. *Jesus,* he mumbled to himself, *this guy's really been around! He could see right away that I've gotten my tit in a wringer, and he knows it's not gonna be easy to pull it out.*

"So get a *move* on, man!" he continued. "It's time to face the inevitable. The ring on her finger, the ring in your nose. Far worse things than that happen every day!" Then he adopted the best warm, avuncular smile he could come up with, given his condition, and flashed it to Clay. "You've gotta *listen* to me," he said. "Your daughter needs you! Her *mother* needs you! Are you listenin'? Are you *hearin'* me?"

The man reached into his vest pocket, pulled out several quarters, and slid them noisily down the counter, like pucks in a game of shuffleboard. "Now get yourself to the nearest phone booth and feed this chump change into the slot. Sayin' 'yes' to fatherhood's gonna *change your life*, son—and all for the better. I was an absolute shipwreck before I finally faced reality and got myself hitched. So mark my words: if bein' a Daddy could change *my* life, it can change *yours*, too!"

Clay scooped up the coins and crammed them into his pants pocket, then stood up and turned to the man. "Thanks, Pops," he smiled. "You've sure given me something to think about. Now if you'll excuse me, I've got to go and . . ."

"And do the right thing!" said the man. "That's what you've got to go and do. And remember, they're countin' on you!"

Clay watched the Preacher Man slither down from his stool and stumble out into the night, then laid his aching head down on the counter and tried his damnedest to blot out a growing, nightmarish vision of himself as Clayborne Middling, husband, father, and Pillar of the Community in Sausalito. "I'd rather end up in Eliot's fucking *Wasteland!*" he mumbled, then grabbed his last beer and took it down in one swift, noisy guzzle before leaving.

He found the phone he needed in a laundromat, two streets over from the No Name. He fed three quarters into the coin slot, then waited anxiously for Birdie to answer.

"Whoozzis?" said a boisterous, high-pitched voice. Clay knew it was Cecelia, so he played along.

"It's your mama's friend," he said. "You know—the man who came to your house a couple hours ago. So whoozz *you?*"

CeCe caught on right away. "*I* know who you are," she giggled. "You're that man who made my Mommy mad, then left without saying goodbye. Mommy said that was *rude* of you, leaving like that!"

"I'll do better next time," he chuckled. "But for now, do me a favor and tell your Mommy to pack up her clothes and stuff. I'll be over in less than an hour. Tell her we're goin' away, and I won't take 'no' for an answer!"

"Who's goin' away, and where?"

"*We're* goin' away," said Clay. "The *three* of us. You've gotta be patient! You'll find out where we're going as soon as we get there. Like your mother said, too many questions! Now hurry up, honey, and tell Birdie everything I just told you. Understand?"

"Of *course* I understand," she said, genuinely puzzled. "Why wouldn't I understand?"

"Got it," said Clay, shaking his head in continuing amazement at his daughter's precociousness. "You understand! Well, your mother *told* me you were a smart little kid, and now I know she wasn't shittin' me."

"Mommy told me never to use that word," said Cecelia. "So why should *you* get to use it? That's not fair!"

"You're right," said Clay. "Not fair!" He could see he was in for a serious challenge being a father to this girl. *Hope I can pull it off,* he laughed.

Cecelia giggled again, then turned serious. "So what am I supposed to call you," she said. "What's your name?"

"It's Clayborne—Clayborne Middling. But everyone calls me Clay, and you can, too."

"I don't really like that name," she said. "I'll just call you Daddy, cuz Mommy says I *need* one. A *daddy*, I mean!"

"That'll be fine with me," he chuckled, his heart swelling with pride. "'Specially since I *am* your daddy!"

"All right," she said. "Goodbye, Daddy! I've gotta go tell

Mommy what you said about goin' away." Then she hung up the phone, and Clay drove straight to the nearest gas station, beaming into the rearview mirror as if he'd just been told he'd won the lottery.

He checked the oil and filled his tank, then headed back to Birdie's place, marveling at the fact that the most important decision in his life—doing the right thing for the sake of Birdie, Cecelia, and himself—had just come about as the result of a chance encounter with a sponge-drunk geezer in a smoke-filled bar. *We never know when lightning will strike,* he laughed, *or where. I suppose I should thank Old Yellow-Teeth for putting the heat on me—for helping me step up to the plate—but how? Cold, hard cash? Season tickets to the 49ers? In his condition, I don't think he'd be able to make it into the stadium! Maybe, when we finally get hitched, I could invite him to our wedding.*

* * *

As he pulled up in front of Birdie's place and peered across the lawn into her picture window, he could see her and Cecelia darting from one room to another, then racing back to the living room with various essentials—pots and pans, blouses and pants, tableware and kitchen utensils—all to be stuffed into suitcases and a freight train's worth of cardboard boxes they'd lined up on the living room floor. They were shrieking with laughter and throwing things up into the air, just for the fun of it—a madcap, female Abbot & Costello movie short, with the two of them as the stars.

The front door was ajar—a welcoming gesture from Birdie, he hoped—so Clay stepped inside and cheerfully offered to help with the packing. He knew there was really no need for him to explain himself—Cecelia had clearly gotten his message across to Birdie—so as they went about their business, the only sounds in the room were joyful chatter and the helter-skelter clanging of items, one against the other, as they stuffed them carelessly into the boxes.

When everything had been packed and the boxes were sealed with tape, Clay strode across the room to Birdie and, without warning, threw his arms around her. Then he reached up and kissed her tenderly on the lips. He could tell she was in no hurry to put a stop to it, so he kept on kissing—more and more passionately with each additional kiss—while CeCe stood off to the side, pointing and giggling.

"Kissie kissie!" she bubbled. "Mommy's got a boyfriend, and now they're *doin'* stuff together! Kissie kissie kissie!" She made smacking sounds with her own lips, then dashed over to the two of them and wrapped her arms around their calves. "Clayborne's got a girlfriend and CeCe's got a Daddy! It's Christmas!"

"Uh-oh!" said Birdie, then reached down and tugged on her daughter's ponytail. "You've forgotten your teddy! I don't think Smokey'd be all that happy about being left behind. Now *quick*! Run upstairs and find him while we start loading stuff into the UHaul. It's getting dark outside, so we've got to hurry!"

When Clay could see that CeCe had reached the top of the stairs and disappeared down the hallway, he didn't waste any time. He reached up and locked his hands around Birdie's rear end, then pinned her to the nearest wall and caressed her butt cheeks rhythmically, like a baker kneading dough. Birdie returned the favor by plunging a hand into his slacks and stroking him until he was rock-hard and hungry for connection. Then, just as he was all set to drop his load, CeCe came roaring down the stairs with her teddy in hand, and the fun was over as fast as it had begun.

Birdie yanked her hand out of Clay's pants, then spun around, dashed over to the staircase, and caught CeCe as she frog-leapt off the steps into her mother's arms.

"I'll put Smokey in the car," CeCe squealed. "He'll just have to wait until we're all packed up and ready, won't he!"

"Yes, honey," Birdie said. "Now go ahead and get in the car—Clay's car—with your teddy. Back seat only! We'll be out in a minute, and we'll load things up ourselves. As for you and Smokey, don't forget to click your seatbelts. Safety first!"

Once Clay and Birdie were alone again, she turned to him, smiling, and said, "As for you, Mr. Middling, there's no need to worry. She clearly didn't see what was goin' on. And besides," she winked, "we'll get the job done later this evening, won't we. I mean, there's just got to be a night deposit box around here somewhere!"

"Oh, yeah," said Clay, then pointed down at her erogenous zone and, grinning like a seventh-grader, said, "and I'm lookin' at it."

Chapter Thirteen

An hour later, the three of them had finally loaded up the UHaul and put Sausalito behind them. They were winging their way toward the Rockies now, Destination Unknown, with Clay behind the wheel and Birdie as the navigator. CeCe was lying face up on the back seat, reading *Green Eggs and Ham* to her teddy, her knees pointing skyward like miniature twin peaks.

"I'm so glad you've come back," whispered Birdie. "I was sick and tired of being stuck in that crummy apartment—a single mother, short of cash and raising a little brat who soaks up all my time and energy."

"Don't talk so loud!" he whispered. "You don't want to hurt her feelings."

"So where are we going? If we pool our money, we'd be able to go a long, long way from here! But alas," he sighed, "I blew the better part of my cash reserve at the Hotel Sausalito last week. Wanted to live the High Life for a change thanks to Dad, who left me some serious chicken feed when he booted me out. I was so ticked off, I decided to spend some of it on something frivolous—like the Sausalito!"

"Now that really was dumb of you," laughed Birdie. "But you didn't say you blew it all, so how much of it's left over?

"'Bout 350, I guess."

"Well, *hey*!" she said. "Not too shabby!" Then she took a deep breath and turned to Clay with a gleam of renewed hope and high adventure in her eyes.

"Listen, Clay, I'd better come clean with you. I've got around $1,300 from the money my grandmother bequeathed to me in her will a couple years ago. I was saving it for something really special, and I think I've just found that something." Then she reached over and teasingly caressed the side of his face. "So! If we were to put my 1,300 and your 350 together—and the money I got for the Lamborghini—and if we don't blow it on endless cigarettes and fancy hotels, we could actually afford to go a long way away, just like you keep saying you want to do!"

"I like where you're goin' with this!" said Clay. "Tell you what: I'm gonna keep driving eastward—come what may—and while I'm doin' that, you can grab the atlas—it's right there, under your seat—and give me some ideas about where we might go."

"Under my seat? It *can't* be! If there was something down there, I'd *feel* it."

"Under your *seat*," he laughed, "not your ass!"

"Very funny," she chirped, then reached down and pulled the atlas up onto her lap. "Anyway, have you just gone crazy? Do you actually think the two of us are gonna drive somewhere right now—tonight—then buy a house and live there? Just like that?"

"Sure!" laughed Clay. "Crazy like a fox!" Then he stopped laughing, lowered his voice, and, out of pure necessity, turned businesslike.

"Look," he said, "we'll stay in cheap motels along the way, and when we finally get there, three or four days from now, we'll find a 'rent with an option to buy.' Then I'll find a job with a livable wage—plastic will get us through until then—and then, bingo! We'll be sittin' pretty! Now get busy and find me three possible towns, and we'll just go ahead and choose the one that sounds like the best one of the three. It'll be just the two of us!"

"The two of us?" shouted CeCe from behind her book. "You keep sayin' 'the two of us,' but there's *three* of us here. Sounds like a *song*," she giggled. 'One, two, three, what about me! The three of us *together*—can't you see?'"

Birdie smiled back at her through the rear view mirror. "You're right, honey, you're right. Sorry! I should've said 'the three of us'—me, your daddy, and our little Cecelia."

"Wait a minute," said Cecelia. "We forgot Smokey! So make it *four*. And by the way," she pouted, "I'm not *that* little! I'm getting taller 'n' taller! Haven't you noticed?"

"Enough o' that sassy stuff," said Birdie. "We know how tall you are!" Then she closed her eyes and began flipping through the atlas at random, state by state. A few pages later, she stopped flipping, jammed her index finger down, and opened her eyes.

"Well?" said Clay. "Cough it up. Don't make me wait!"

"Georgia!" she said. "Homeland, Georgia. It's just a few miles east of that famous swamp. I can't pronounce it."

"I know the one you're talking about," said Clay. "It's Okefenokee—Okefenokee Swamp. We drove by there on the way to Florida when I was a little kid, and we *hated* the place. Way too hot and sticky. So *no*! Absolutely not! You can Oke-*forget* it!"

Birdie shrugged her shoulders, rustled through several more pages, then banged her finger down again, held it there with her eyes closed, and slowly started counting down. "Seven, six, five, four . . ."

"Cut the countin'!" he shouted. "No more games. Just tell me where the fuck you landed."

"The F word, honey?" said Birdie. "Was that really necessary?"

"I know what *that* stands for!" giggled CeCe.

"Just tell me where the F-word we're *goin'!*" shouted Clay.

"Coldwater, Missouri," shouted Birdie. "Touchy, touchy!"

"Never heard of it," he said.

"Doesn't mean it's a *bad* place. I mean, who knows? It might be a real paradise!"

"Or maybe another friggin' swamp," he said. "With a name like Coldwater, Missouri, it seems likely it'll be a dead-end destination. So I say screw it! Now try again. And if I don't like that one, I'll just pull over and choose one myself."

"Jesus!" she said. "It's not like I have ESP, you know!" She glared at him, then pushed through a half dozen more pages and slapped her hand down so hard that CeCe, who'd begun to fall asleep, sat up and let out a yelp. "Don't do that, Mommy. I'm trying to sleep!"

Birdie ignored her daughter's whining, then lifted her finger up with a flourish and looked eagerly down to see where it had landed.

"*North Dakota,*" she shrieked. "Rugby, North Dakota!"

Clay sped up, roared past a slow-moving livestock trailer loaded with mooing cattle, then banged his forehead on the steering wheel. "You know what?" he said. "I'm *tired* o' this. I mean, who the fuck would want to live in a place called Rugby, North Dakota?"

"Not *you*, from the sound of things," she said.

"But you know what?" he said. "I'm tired o' *driving*, too. I'm tired of wondering where we're gonna land. So let's just *go* there. North Dakota, I mean. Life's a crapshoot, right? You rolled the dice, and up came the Dakotas. So Rugby, North Dakota, here we come!"

Birdie laughed, then made a fist and thrust it up toward the ceiling. "How fuckin' cool!" she said. Then she leaned over to Clay and kissed him on the cheek.

"Bye-bye, Sausalito, hello, Rugby!" she shouted, then curled up against the passenger door, closed her eyes, and listened happily as Clay revved the engine, shifted into fourth, and shot down the highway, indifferent to the posted speed limit. A feeling of heavenly serenity had swept down and enveloped them, and with it came genuine hope for the future.

* * *

As they drove farther and farther away from the Bay Area, Clay could feel the gradual warming of the days—*his* days now, not his parents' days—in his bones. Like a plant curling up through the soil into springtime, his lingering worry about the wisdom of this cross-country caper had finally turned to a growing conviction that his fortunes were about to improve, not just drip by drip but rapidly and dramatically.

Now, he marveled, there would be no more judgmental parents around the corner, looking for more and more things not to like about how he dressed, what he did with his free time, what he read, who his friends were, and who he may have slept with. No longer would he be just two floors away from his father at Scheckel & Newbury. And while it was true that Henley Tuckerman had always been good to him, he finally realized that neither Henley nor the world of real estate held any real charm—any lasting path to fulfillment—for him. That chapter in his life was a closed book now, and for the first time in his life he'd be putting California behind him, embarking on a brand new adventure on unfamiliar soil. And with it he'd have a daughter, a fiancé, and a future he could be proud of—a future of his very own making.

Altogether, they needed four days to get to the North Dakota border, staying first in Winnemucca, Nevada, then Cheyenne, Wyoming, then Billings, Montana. Mile by mile, town by town, there was less and less sunlight and more and more chill in the air. They'd really never taken a moment to consider how dramatically different from San Francisco the weather in Rugby was bound to be. By the time they reached the western border of Montana, it wasn't just cold, it was snowing. They realized, then, that they clearly weren't dressed for the bracing, bitterly cold North Dakota winters ahead of them.

On the fourth day they stopped for a late afternoon meal at a diner on the outskirts of Minot, then reached downtown Rugby around 8:30 p.m.

"We're here!" said Clay, then pulled up to the curb near a convenience store and turned off the engine. Snow was falling heavily now, and while Birdie shook her head in disbelief, Cecelia, who'd never seen more than a flake or two of snow in California, squealed with delight.

"Rugby, North Dakota," said Birdie, "the Paris of the Upper Midwest!"

"But *wait!*" said Clay. "Maybe I made a wrong turn, and we're actually in Alaska! I mean, would you *look* at that snow!"

The temperature continued to drop, so much so that the Valiant's heating system could no longer keep up with it. The three of them could see clouds of chalk-white water vapor pouring out of their mouths, one puff at a time, like smoke belching from a chimney.

Birdie yawned, stretched her long legs out as far as she could in what was, for her, a miserably inadequate space, then rolled down the window and, with her teeth noisily chattering, peered down Main Street through an increasingly dense wall of snow. All she could see were two dim, flickering streetlights and the two rows of timeworn, weather-beaten commercial buildings that lined the street. A few of them looked occupied—Birdie figured they would surely come to life in the morning—but most of them were vacant, abandoned by once-thriving businesses that had run out of hope for the future.

Other than the snap and crackle of the Valiant's cooling, overworked engine, the town of Rugby was eerily silent. As they sat in the freezing interior of their car, discouraged and disillusioned, a scrawny, underfed cat darted across the street and into an alleyway. Birdie couldn't help thinking they'd just been swept up into a chilling episode of the *Twilight Zone*. There was no other human in sight, and the three of them were now trapped and shivering in a living, breathing, blue-collar Currier & Ives print.

"Oh, my God," she wailed, "there's nothing *here*!"

"I thought sure we'd find a ghost town back in Coldwater," said Clay, "but it turns out there's one right here in Rugby!"

"We'll have to sleep on the friggin' *sidewalk*," said Birdie, loud enough to wake up Cecelia, who'd most likely been dreaming about what their new home in North Dakota would look like.

Then CeCe peered out the rear window and let out an ear-splitting shriek. "This isn't a town," she wailed, "it's a *dump*! I wanna go back to Sausalito—right now!"

"Pipe down, honey," said Birdie. "And I hate to tell you, but that's not gonna happen. That world is gone forever. But you mustn't worry! Rugby just has to be a whole lot more than one lone street and a bunch of abandoned buildings. It'll have a school! A playground! You'll have friends!"

"I don't *want* friends," she said, "and I don't need a playground. I want Sausalito!" Then she pulled a blanket over her head, burrowed down into it, sniffling, and did her best to fall back to sleep.

"*Forget* Sausalito!" shouted Clay. "And you can forget Rugby, too. We're goin' back to Minot! It's got to be more civilized than this sorry excuse for a town." Then he carved out a noisy, asymmetrical donut in the center of Main Street, turned back toward Minot, and smashed his foot down on the accelerator. "I saw a Motel 6 just off Route 2, not far from Granville," he said. "We'll be back in Minot in a little less than an hour. And tomorrow after breakfast—God knows where *that* will be—we'll find us a rental. So long, Rugby, hello, Minot!"

Chapter Fourteen

Birdie and Clay needed only a week or two after their arrival in Minot to find a home—a rambling, turn-of-the-century farmhouse on three acres of well-maintained property with plenty of shade trees and a large, fenced-in area where Cecelia could safely play, far away from traffic. While the home was lovely in a nostalgic way, its exterior needed some attention—a fresh paint job, a new storm door, some caulking around the windows. Some of the shingles were missing from the roof—victims of the bitter cold and fierce winds of North Dakota winters—and needed replacing. But in spite of all that, it was in remarkably good condition.

The home was a mile away from downtown, and yet close enough to the business district to make shopping for goods and services easy. The interior woodwork was beautiful. The three bedrooms, two bathrooms, and well-designed closets were surprisingly spacious. And most importantly, the asking price, to their surprise and relief, was only one-tenth the cost of a home of similar quality back in Sausalito.

To make the modest down payment, they had borrowed $6,000 from Merchants Bank in Rugby. During negotiations, the two of them lied and said they were still gainfully employed but had decided, while on vacation, to shop cross-country for a new life away from the West Coast.

"The moment we drove into downtown Rugby," said Birdie, "we absolutely *fell in love* with everything about the place!" Clay could feel her kicking at his foot under the table as she said it, and he struggled not to break out laughing at her audacity. Both the bank and the buyers were eager to sign, so the deal was settled in record time.

The very next day, to make Cecelia happy, they had decided to name their new home *Little Saucy*. "We'll put familiar things all around the house," Birdie told Cecelia. "You know—*pictures* and stuff: the little things that made you happy in your home there. You'll think you're still right there in Sausalito!"

"They should call this place *Frost*-a-lito," said CeCe. "I'm never gonna be warm again living here!"

Birdie paid a local artist to paint the words 'Little Saucy' above the front door, each letter woven with delicate flowering vines. When she'd finished the lettering, she added two tiny songbirds to the sign, one to the left, the other to the right of the words. "It looks so quaint. So sweet!" she said. "I love it! And so will the neighbors!"

"They'd *better* love it," said Clay, who had little interest in either gardening or, with the exception of the nudes in *Penthouse* and *Playboy*, art of any kind. "We just paid that girl a serious bundle o' cash for her work—half a week's salary!"

As soon as they'd signed the papers for Little Saucy, Clay bought a copy of the *Minot Daily News*, and in a stroke of divine good fortune found work immediately as a manager-in-training for Jupiter Discount on Main Street, just half a mile from their home. He knew that after months of praiseworthy performance at Scheckel & Newbury, a job of any kind at a discount store was sure to be a painful come-down. But he also knew it would beef up his resume and keep him on track for more suitable employment. Things, he felt certain, would soon get better.

Birdie, who didn't relish the idea of being a stay-at-home mom, found a baby sitter for CeCe—a diminutive, kindhearted onetime kindergarten teacher named Claudette—then picked up a part-time job waiting tables at the Shirley

Room, a popular cafeteria in the basement of the Minot Savings & Loan Building.

For the next several weeks, she and Clay worked long, hard hours, banking a good portion of their income to cover housing, food, and other basic expenses. Then, as soon as they felt financially secure, they found a justice of the peace in nearby Devil's Lake and made plans for a Saturday, April 19 wedding ceremony in the back yard of their home in Minot.

They were all set to be married as scheduled until they learned, only a few days before the wedding, that the Souris River was rising at an alarming rate. It meant that the flood-prone city of Minot would soon be at the mercy of yet another record-setting, water-fed calamity.

The Souris was expected to crest on the very day of the wedding, so they shelved their great disappointment and rescheduled for April 26. One week later, as they stood together in a quiet, water-logged outdoor ceremony— dressed incongruously in wedding clothes and galoshes— they would soon become Mr. and Mrs. Clayborne Middling. Cecelia was pressed into service as the flower girl, and Wade Hinckley, the local trash collector who came by the Middlings' place every Thursday on his trash route, cheerfully agreed to serve as the witness. To their delight, he even wore a suit and tie. On the lapel of his coat was his prized Elk's Lodge pin, and next to that a corsage from Fresh from the Garden Flowers, given to him by Birdie in return for his involvement in the ceremony.

The sky was still overcast as Birdie and Clay read nervously through the vows they'd written for themselves only an hour before the ceremony—a few poignant words of love, devotion, and sacred promise. Then, just as Clay took the ring from the palm of Hinckley's hand and slipped it onto Birdie's waiting finger, a warm, well-aimed beam of sunlight broke through the clouds and illuminated the two of them. Smiling, the justice of the peace pronounced them Man and Wife, then gestured to Clay to kiss the bride.

It surprised no one that Cecelia turned a rich, flowery pink at the sight of her mother's mouth on the mouth of her new Daddy. The first time she saw them kissing, back in Sausalito, she thought it was weird. But this time she knew that what they were doing was not only a *good* thing, it was the *right* thing. *Makes it official now,* she giggled. *We're a family!*

Moments later, the two of them were walking hand in hand to Clay's waiting Valiant, their daughter skipping happily behind them. Clay held open the car door for Birdie, and she slid inside, still holding up the train of her wedding gown to keep it out of the mud. Then he turned back to Cecelia, swept her up into his arms, eased her into the back seat, and handed her Smokey, the beloved teddy she'd dragged thumping down the staircase the day she saw her father for the very first time. She smiled broadly, then hugged Smokey over and over again.

As Clay started the car, Birdie kissed him gently on the cheek, then ran her fingers playfully through his hair, turning it into a tangled shock of barn straw.

"Look at you *now*!" she giggled, then tipped the rear view mirror toward his face so he could see himself. "Here we are—the very first day of our marriage—and you're already a freakin' mess!" She laid her head on her husband's shoulder, then blew an appreciative kiss to Wade Hinckley as he stood nearby on the lawn, waving goodbye to the three of them. Then the Valiant, with all of the Middlings in it, including Smokey, sped off toward a brand new existence—two happily married, cross-country nomads in a rundown farmhouse 1,600 miles from Stan and Brooke and the traffic-choked, image-conscious town of Sausalito.

Chapter Fifteen

On the day five years ago when he so abruptly packed up and left the Bay Area, Clay Middling hadn't bothered to call and say goodbye to his parents before loading Birdie and Cecelia into his car. Nor had he bothered to call Henley Tuckerman and thank him, as he knew he ought to have done, for his unceasing support and encouragement at S&N. And he had given not a single thought to the fact that he'd managed to avoid serving in Vietnam, thanks to a dubious asthma diagnosis courtesy of the family doctor.

Instead, he'd left the Bay Area angry and disillusioned—clearly for selfish reasons—and never looked back. He'd put the Golden State behind him forever and begun forging what would become a surprisingly satisfying existence in the unlikely state of North Dakota.

In the beginning Birdie and Clay had made sure Cecelia's bedroom was nearly a carbon copy of the one back in Sausalito. But, as life in North Dakota lumbered on, the room grew along with their daughter. Cecelia was now nine years old, and her room was suitable for a nine-year-old living anywhere except, perhaps, the Bay Area.

The summer of '75 in Minot had been long, hot, and intolerably humid—one of the most punishing summers in memory, according to the locals. But now that autumn had arrived, temperatures were plummeting. And after only a handful of years living in the Upper Plains, Clay and Birdie knew from experience that the worst was yet to come.

The novelty of the harsh North Dakota winters didn't especially please the two of them. They'd been sun worshipers from their earliest years, simply by virtue of where they were born. But Cecelia—a young and spirited California transplant for whom the onset of cold weather was still a novelty—could hardly contain her excitement. She was once again dreaming of blizzards, snow angels, and reindeer—especially the one with the red, glowing nose. And she couldn't help thinking her parents were silly, if not downright half-witted, to allow themselves to be intimidated by a little snow and ice—or, for that matter, sandbags and flooding, the two other inescapable realities of life in the Dakotas.

But weather aside, both Clay and Birdie were worried. They couldn't help feeling that their daughter was more than likely going to have trouble fitting in with her classmates. They figured it wouldn't be only because she was growing increasingly sassy and opinionated. More than likely, it would be because she'd begun to dress in unconventional ways. She was fast becoming a Rebel in a part of the country where Religion was King and any act of rebellion—a failure to live by conventional rules, in or out of school—was considered no less than an unpardonable sin.

At the age of nine, she was already at least a head taller than her classmates, including the boys, and taller even than some of the teachers at Cloverton. Birdie may have been proud of her stature—after all, she herself was a head taller than her own husband—but Clay, who'd never really grown comfortable with the difference in their heights, privately harbored feelings of resentment about his daughter's growing size. *She's gonna be taller 'n' me before long,* he realized. *How do y' suppose that's gonna make me feel? And what about her classmates? Compared to them, she's an absolute giraffe!*

But the truth was that, while proud of her stature and her intellectual prowess, Cecelia had begun not to care in the least how she looked in public. Whenever she thought she could get away with it, she'd go to school wearing threadbare jeans with tasteless words scrawled on the rear pockets with a felt pen. She'd roll up her pants like a country bumpkin, indifferent to the fact that the turned-up cuffs weren't even close to being the same width. And, once she was at school, she'd slip into the girls' bathroom and either tease her hair up into a knot the size of a grapefruit or plaster it down onto her skull using the Brylcreem she found in her father's medicine cabinet. To the more conservative teachers at Cloverton, she looked more like a *boy* than the girl they expected her to look like.

At home, her parents were increasingly bothered that no matter where she was—bedroom, bathroom, front porch, dinner table—she was constantly reading. They were sick and tired of seeing her face buried in the pages of yet another pretentious, 300-page book filled with what they considered intellectual gobbledygook.

They complained to each other in private.

"The other kids," Clay railed, "especially the boys, are gonna think she's a snooty little Know-It-All!"

Birdie whined, "The way things are goin', she's *never* gonna get a date when she gets to high school. What self-respecting boy wants to be seen with a girl who cares more about her brains than her body?"

On top of all that, they worried that Mr. Thornwood, Cecelia's fourth-grade teacher, seemed to be cut from the very same cloth—that he seemed to think he was more important than everyone else in town. The first time they saw him, they noticed that, unlike the rest of the male teachers at Cloverton, he nearly always dressed "fancy."

"Probably thinks he's smarter than the Super," they laughed. "Thinks he's gonna take over the school and run it *his* way, and to hell with the Administration!"

But Cecelia didn't think Mr. Thornwood was showy and self-important. On the contrary, she adored the man. Like other children her age, she was hungry for learning. And because she could tell Thornwood loved teaching, she loved *him*, unconditionally. It was something that Clay and Birdie, who'd had little respect for teachers and learning while in school themselves, would never really understand.

Fortunately for Cecelia, Alec Thornwood was a stellar example of that almost mythical creature—an educator who, in spite of being overworked, unappreciated, and criminally under-compensated, was sharp as a tack and more actively engaged than a baker's dozen of his stressed-out, burned-out colleagues. His uncanny ability to understand precisely what a given student needed most, then deliver the goods on time and in glorious excess, couldn't have come at a better time for Cecelia.

When Thornwood realized how intellectually curious Cecelia was, he quietly decided, perhaps against his better judgment, to pay special attention to her needs. He knew she had an enormous appetite for reading—that she thought the books her classmates were reading were silly and juvenile—so he began to call her up to his desk every Friday, show her a half dozen books from his personal library, then invite her to take one home and read it over the weekend. He'd never allowed himself to condescend to his students, so when he learned to his astonishment that Cecelia was reading at a higher level than most high school seniors, he chose only titles that would be certain to challenge her.

The first time around, he brought *To Kill a Mockingbird, Moby Dick, Huckleberry Finn, Oliver Twist, Anne of Green Gables,* and *Frankenstein: or, the Modern Prometheus.* Then he laid them out on the work table nearest the window and asked her to choose one.

He figured she would most likely choose either *Moby Dick* or *Anne of Green Gables*. For one thing, he knew she loved reading books about sea creatures. Moreover, as far as he could tell, there wasn't a girl anywhere in America who hadn't read or at least *planned* to read *Anne of Green Gables*.

So he was more than a little surprised when she dismissively pushed all the others aside, then snatched up Mary Shelley's *Frankenstein* and held it lovingly to her chest, embracing it as if it were a kitten she'd just been given for her birthday.

"I absolutely *adore* scary stories!" she squealed. "But Mommy and Daddy refuse to let me read books they're certain would give me nightmares." Then a storm cloud formed itself over her head, registering her obvious disapproval. "They can be so stupid!" she snapped. "And so . . . so controlling! How can people that old be so silly—so amazingly ill-informed?"

Thornwood tried not to let her see the look of incredulity on his face. He went silent for a moment, then suddenly turned toward her, smiling, and said, "Ever heard of Bruno Bettelheim?"

"I *have*," she said. "Really! But only once, when I came downstairs one day and heard my parents talking about him. They were saying they'd seen him on television—a documentary—and couldn't believe their ears when he actually said stories like 'Hansel and Gretel' and 'Rumpelstiltskin' are *good* for children. 'Children *need* to be scared,' he said. 'Imagining scary things helps them prepare for adulthood.'"

Right away, CeCe had bought into that philosophy. "So I plan to read as many scary books as I can get my hands on," she said, "because I want to be ready for adulthood when it gets here. But when I told Mommy and Daddy I wanted only scary books for Christmas, they kind o' went *nuts*."

She recalled, bitterly, what they had told her that day. "Absolutely *not!*" they'd shouted in unison. "We're not gonna waste our money on sick books like that! We'll give you books for Christmas if we must, but only books that *we've* chosen—books appropriate for your age—books we've approved of in advance!"

Thornwood was crushed to think that a girl as intelligent as Cecelia was being raised by people as culturally ignorant as her parents so obviously were. He listened intently to her, marveling at her sophisticated vocabulary, long, complex sentences, and fine-tuned sense of humor. The more he listened, the more impressed he was with her extraordinarily precocious intelligence. He vowed then and there that as long as he was her teacher, he would do everything in his power to nurture her intellect.

"Tell you what!" he said. "I'll let you take *Frankenstein* home with you, just this one time, as an experiment—the *book*, not the monster," he grinned. "But only on condition that you'll read it only up in your bedroom, after your parents have turned in for the night." Then he winked conspiratorially at her. "I mean, when it comes to perfectly respectable books, what they don't know can't hurt them, can it!"

Cecelia thanked Mr. Thornwood for loaning her the book, then skipped happily out of his classroom and into the long line of children waiting to board their buses for home. Later that evening, after finishing her homework, she brushed her teeth, slipped into her nightgown, and crawled into bed. When she was certain her parents had fallen asleep—she could hear both of them snoring loudly from down the hallway—she very quietly retrieved the book from her closet, where she had hidden it safely inside a pillowcase. Then the climbed back into bed, made a tent out of her quilt with the help of her head and knees, pointed her flashlight toward Shelley's masterpiece, and began reading.

Only a few pages into the story, she realized that some of the words the author used were words she'd never seen. So she tiptoed downstairs, found the dictionary her mother kept on a shelf in the dining room, carried it upstairs, and put it on her nightstand, where she could easily get to it. She figured her mother hardly ever used it anyway; it was coated with dust and showed no signs of ever having been opened.

In the beginning, she didn't find Shelley's book all that exciting. But when she got to page eleven—a paragraph in which Victor Frankenstein attempts to explain his insatiable appetite for learning and his determination to learn only what mattered to him—she was swept away by the eerie similarity of Victor's personality compared to her own:

"My temper was sometimes violent," said Victor, "and my passions vehement; but by some law in my temperature they were turned not towards childish pursuits but to an eager desire to learn, and not to learn all things indiscriminately."

I wonder, she thought to herself, *if when Victor was my age he hated fourth-grade textbooks as much as I do. I mean, they're so simply written, they end up sounding more like 'goo-goo, gah-gah' than actual conversation! I'll bet Mr. Thornwood wishes he didn't have to use them in the classroom. When I asked him about it, he said he really doesn't have any choice in the matter. And by the way, I can't imagine Mary Shelley liking them, either.*

Cecelia loved the way Shelley wrote. So precisely! So musically! Every sentence like a song! So she jumped back in and continued reading, eager to see other ways in which Victor must have thought like she thought.

"Neither the structure of languages, nor the code of

governments, nor the politics of various states possessed attractions for me," he said.

How strange that is, Cecelia thought. *Shelley has Victor talking like a wooden soldier sometimes. 'Possessed attractions for me'? Why didn't she just say 'appealed to me'? Oh, well, I guess even famous authors don't always know just how something should be written.*

But, as exciting as what she'd read so far was for her, it was the very next passage that made her heart leap with joy:

"It was the secrets of heaven and earth that I desired to learn," said Victor. "And whether it was the outward substance of things or the inner spirit of nature and the mysterious soul of man that occupied me, still my inquiries were directed to the metaphysical, or in its highest sense, the physical secrets of the world."

"Wow!" yelped Cecelia, so loudly she worried her mom and dad might have heard her. *What a thinker he must have been! Shelley, too! And I think just like they do!* She pulled her bedsheet up to her chin, then turned contentedly toward the wall, proud of herself and yet more than a little embarrassed for being able to read and understand a book that even her mother and father once said was way too hard for them to read when they were in high school.

Just think! she giggled. *I only had to look up the words 'vehement' and 'metaphysical.' Not bad! They're the kind of million-dollar words Daddy likes to use whenever he's trying to impress people. He must write 'em on his shirt cuffs,* she chuckled. *Probably doesn't even know what they mean. They just sound important to him, make him feel like a Big Shot!*

But she had no doubt that Shelley knew exactly what every word she wrote meant. *The secrets of heaven and earth,* she laughed. *The inner spirit of nature! That's just the kind o' stuff I want to learn about!* Cecelia couldn't help thinking that if her classmates had tried to read *Frankenstein,* they wouldn't have had a clue about what Victor was saying.

She yawned, put the book down, then reached down with her feet and found Smokey at the far end of her bed, hiding beneath her quilt. *I may be as smart as Victor,* she smiled, *but I'm still just a little kid. And I still need my teddy. I'll aways need my teddy!*

She hugged Smokey close to her and tried to fall asleep, convinced that, unlike her mother and father, Mr. Thornwood always listened to her—and actually *under-stood* her.

He must really trust me, too, she thought. *Otherwise, why would he lend me books from his personal library? I mean, who else would ever do that? And I'd never find them at home, because Mommy and Daddy are too cheap to buy them. Besides, they don't read books anyway! Mr. Thornwood must be the best teacher in the whole wide world. And he's not just my teacher, he's my very own per-sonal librarian!*

The first thing Monday morning, Cecelia stepped off the bus, marched into the fourth grade wing at Cloverton, then ran down the hall and burst into the teachers' room. She'd finished *Frankenstein* late Sunday evening—every single page—and couldn't wait to tell her teacher what she thought of it.

"Whoa!" said Thornwood, simultaneously frowning and smiling at Cecelia, the girl who'd very quickly become his all-time favorite student. "You know you're not supposed to come into the teachers' room!"

The other teachers, annoyed that a student—especially Cecelia Middling—would dare to violate their privacy reg-istered their obvious disapproval with a flurry of sharp, condescending grimaces.

"But I loved *Frankenstein!*" she gushed, ignoring them. "I like the way Shelley writes, and the way Victor thinks! I just had to come in and tell you!"

"Alec!" snapped Corrine Federer, whose class was right next to Thornwood's. She disapproved of his laid-back appearance and unconventional methods in the classroom. "You didn't lend that girl *Frankenstein,* did you? Please tell me you didn't!"

Thornwood glared harshly at her, then brushed her aside with one dismissive sweep of his hand and turned to Cecelia with a warm smile on his face.

"I'm glad you liked that book so much," he said. "And, like I said on Friday, there'll be more where that one came from."

"Are you *sure* you're gonna lend me more of your books?" said Cecelia. I'd be so disappointed if—"

"Well, of *course* I'm sure," he said, cutting her off. "Of course! Didn't I just *say* I would? Now *scoot!* And don't forget: you can't barge into the teachers' room any time you feel like it. Next time you do that, you'll have to stay in for recess!"

Thoroughly chastised, Cecelia spun around and went straight down the hall to room 314, red-faced and pouting as she walked. I guess I shouldn't have done that, she mumbled to herself, then stepped inside, hung her jacket on the back of her chair, and settled in for the day. *But I was so excited. I felt sure he'd like it, since it was over a book—not some dippy thing like a sitcom or a boy. That's all the other girls seem to care about—Dennis the Menace and boys, boys, boys!*

As soon as Cecelia left the teachers' room, Nora Leavitt, by far the most prudish teacher in the school, had leaned toward Federer and whispered righteously into her ear. "What's he gonna lend her next, for heaven's sake—*Lady Chatterley's Lover?* I mean, really!"

Thornwood, who could hear what they were saying, got up from the table, then looked down at them, shaking his head in disgust.

"Nora!" he said. "You think no one is listening when you get into your gossiping ways, don't you. But you know what? You're dead wrong about that. In case you've forgotten, it was just last week, right here in this room, that I overheard you telling Corrine how much you liked *Peyton Place Revisited.* Then you told her you have a boxful of paperbacks a whole lot naughtier than that—books you said you loved reading when you and Corrine were in your teens—up high in your bedroom closet, where your parents couldn't find them! Am I not right about that?"

Nora was *Scarlet Letter* red by now, squirming like a worm on the end of a fishhook. But Corrine, who couldn't help being amused, did her best to hide the 'Gotcha!' grin spreading triumphantly across her face.

"How many times have you reread *Odd Woman Out?*" he continued. "I should think *that* one must be worn to a *pulp* by now! Sorry 'bout the pun," he said. "But fear not, ladies: there's no naughty, girl-on-girl stuff in *Frankenstein!*" Then he grabbed his grade book off the table and strode out of the room, pleased with himself for having flushed Nora's niggling hypocrisy out into the open for everyone to hear.

Five minutes later, Thornwood was back in his classroom, a more welcoming environment filled with the laughter of happy, well-adjusted children, warm of heart and eager to learn. He plopped his grade book down on the desk, then clapped his hands three times to settle them down.

"All right, kids," he said, "it's Show-and-Tell time! You were told to read at least the first chapter of a book of your choice over the weekend—a book you never thought you'd want to read—then step up in front of the class this morning and tell us first why you chose the book and then how you felt about it. After five minutes, you'll be dismissed with one ring of my bell. Got it?"

An odd mixture of enthusiastic yelps, noisy 'got-it's and uneasy chatter rippled across the classroom.

"So who wants to go first?" he said. "And this time it needs to be a *boy*. After all, we don't want to be guilty of discrimination, do we!"

Every one of the boys waved his hand wildly in the air, hoping to be the Chosen One. And since Timmy Lancaster was the most animated one of the lot—always the one most hungry for attention—Thornwood chose him.

"Your turn, Timmy," he said. "So tell us what book you chose. We're eager to hear from you!"

Timmy pulled a dog-eared, badly worn paperback from the back pocket of his jeans, then held it up in front of him so everyone could see the cover. On it was a man crouched down inside a storefront of some sort, pointing a loaded pistol toward a woman just outside the window. The woman wore a bright red jacket sweater, a low-cut strapless gown, and a look of abject terror.

"We don't have a library at home," said Timmy. "I don't have a library card, either; Mom says they're too expensive. So I snooped around the house while Mom and Dad were outside doing yard work and found this book under their bed. It's called *Too French and Too Deadly.* Funny name, huh? I don't really know what they mean by "Too French," but I'll bet it isn't good!"

Thornwood smelled trouble, and its name was Timmy Lancaster. He wondered if he shouldn't just pull the rug out from under his well-intended project and go back to the timid, clean-and-proper fourth-grade textbook he was required to use in the first place. But, at this particular moment, he just hoped the children couldn't see how red his face had grown as Timmy continued speaking.

"Anyway," said the boy, "there was stuff going on inside the book I've never even heard of—stuff my parents probably think I'm way too young to know about!"

Thornwood shuddered, then steeled himself and waited for what was coming next. He feared the worst.

"You aren't gonna believe this," said Timmy, "but in Chapter Three, some scary guy named "Two-Ton Tony Dee" tries to force a woman named Julia Boni into the back seat of his Chrysler! She tries to get him off her, but . . ."

"All right, Timmy!" said Thornwood. "I think that'll be quite enough for now. Glad you're reading. But the next time, for heaven's sake, *check in with me* before you choose your next book!"

Whew, thought Thornwood, shaking his head as Timmy walked back to his desk, proud of what he'd brought to the Show-and-Tell. *I don't even want to think about what happened in the back seat o' that Chrysler. Think I'll just leave that to Timmy.*

"So who's next?" he said. "And this time it will be a *girl.*"

Cecelia jumped out of her chair and dashed up to the front of the class, waving her borrowed copy of Shelley's *Frankenstein* triumphantly over her head.

Here it comes, thought Thornwood. *Another curve ball, right down the middle. Guess my granddaddy was right: "A loose tongue always leads to a tight spot."* Then he leaned down and whispered nervously into Cecelia's ear. "You *cannot* tell the class I lent you that book!" he said. "If you do, we'll both be in big trouble! Now go ahead and do your review. But remember: Mum's the Word!"

Clearly exasperated, Cecelia scowled her disapproval, then pulled herself together and began speaking.

"Like I was gonna say, some people think the creature Frankenstein created was this big, scary monster with scars all over his body, bolts sticking out of his head, and a really mean expression on his face," she said. "But they've got it all wrong. He was actually *kind-hearted*—unless, of course, he was provoked by some rude human saying bad things about him. He even loved animals! He would never have harmed them, not in a million years!"

The more excited she got, the faster she talked—the words tumbling out of her mouth like coins from a slot machine. She paused for a moment to catch her breath, then got back to work.

"The only real monster in Shelley's book," she said, "was Victor Frankenstein, the man who created the alleged 'monster' out of body parts from dead people—from corpses!"

The few children in the class who already knew what a corpse is groaned in unison, right on cue. The rest either sat fiddling with their pencils or stared blankly at Cecelia, wondering what on earth she was talking about.

"I know it's kind o' gruesome," she said, "but you'd have to have read the whole story to understand how nice the 'monster' was in the beginning, and why Doctor Frankenstein created him in the first place." Then her eyes grew large and her brow arched downward. And even more gruesome was what happened later in the story, when . . ."

Enough is enough, Thornwood thought to himself. He knew that the more she said about the more sinister details in the book, the more likely it was that her classmates would rush home and tell their parents. So he banged down hard on his desk bell, then stood up and motioned to Cecelia to return to her chair.

"Time's up!" he smiled, doing his best to sound upbeat and supportive. "I could tell right away that you've read the entire book, and that you really enjoyed it. But—"

"But I'm not *done*!" she wailed. "I haven't told 'em . . ." She looked down at her notes to see where she'd left off, then continued. "I haven't told 'em what happened later on, when the monster sneaks into Elizabeth's room on her wedding night and—"

Suddenly, a series of sharp, angry raps on the door brought an abrupt halt to Cecelia's review. Then, to everyone's shock, Clay Middling, who'd been listening quietly from the hall, charged into the classroom with a look of uncontrollable rage contorting his face.

"You're *not* gonna make my daughter read trash like *Frankenstein* in your class, Mr. Burnwood!" he roared. "And just in case you've forgotten, I'm the parent. You're just the teacher! So you see, *I'm* the one who'll decide what's proper reading for my children—not you!"

Humiliated, Cecelia shuffled back to her desk, laid her head down, and turned away, her eyes full of tears, her cheeks burning red. *He must have snuck into my room right after I dozed off,* she thought. *I thought sure I'd hidden the book under my pillow!*

Thornwood could feel his heart beating wildly inside his sport coat, but he wasn't about to make a fool of himself in front of his students. So instead he took a deep breath, quieted them down with a finger to the lips, then calmly confronted Cecelia's father.

"I don't mean to be rude, sir, but it's *Thornwood*, not Burnwood."

"Thornwood, Burnwood, *Dead*wood," he snarled. "Frankly, I really don't give a damn *what* your name is!"

Then, while Thornwood would have much preferred to walk casually over to Middling and slam his face down on the nearest table—a *film noir* moment he'd often dreamt of pulling off—he went the professional route and pinned a warm, patently dishonest smile onto his face.

"Perhaps we should step out into the hallway, Mr. Middling," he said. "I feel certain it would be best for us to discuss this issue in privacy—don't you think?"

"Don't I think?" said Middling. "I do *indeed* think, and I happen to do it very well. It's *you* who obviously doesn't!"

Clay then leaned down at Cecelia's desk and whispered to her to get her books together and put her jacket on.

"So tell you what, Mr. Something-wood: what I'm thinking right now is that I'll see you in the principal's office tomorrow morning, eight o'clock sharp. No excuses! Don't worry; I'm sure they'll find a sub. And for God's sake, I hope the one they find has more brains than *you* do!"

Then he yanked Cecelia up out of her chair and stormed out of the classroom, dragging her behind him as if she were a stuffed teddy bear, not his daughter. On the way out, he slammed the door so hard it shook the glass in the transom.

* * *

"I'm so sorry this happened," said Thornwood quietly to the class after they were gone, "but I'm especially sorry that it happened here in school, right in front of you. I'm sorry that you—a captive audience—were forced to witness this encounter!"

Privately, he couldn't help wondering if it was really possible for a nine-year-old—hardly more than a fresh young flower, only just beginning to blossom—to have become so thoroughly disillusioned. In the case of Cecelia, the answer couldn't have been anything but yes. By now it was clear to him that her disillusionment must surely have taken form long before the moment her father burst into her classroom and made such an ass of himself in front of his daughter. Anyone who'd been there and was still looking for evidence would only have needed to watch the tears as they traveled, slowly and inexorably, down her defeated, debilitated face.

He thought about Cecelia—how humiliated she must have felt—then decided it was time to offer some badly needed advice to his students, not just for their sake but for Cecelia's. So he hopped up onto his desk, loosened his tie, and began what he hoped would be a brief but timely sermon—a message to his students about the importance of being kind, compassionate, and supportive to a classmate in need.

"Listen," he said. "We all love Cecelia! We all know how intelligent she is—how driven she is to excel. And we also know how much she goes out of her way to support and encourage her classmates!"

Many of the students, who'd been helped by CeCe countless times when they were in a pinch, nodded their agreement.

"All of this is wonderful stuff, of course, but when she comes back here next Wednesday, it will not be an easy return for her. Do you understand that? So I'm asking you to find within yourselves the best gifts you have to offer, then share them with her, gently and unpretentiously. She would not want you to feel sorry for her! She doesn't need to be preached to about why this incident happened and what she might have had to do with it. All she needs is your love and understanding! Can you do that? For me? For yourselves? But especially for a loyal, caring classmate?"

There was a long period of silence following his address, punctuated only by the shifting of chairs and the clearing of throats. Then, suddenly, a thunderous round of applause filled the classroom, and Thornwood knew at that moment that his students loved Cecelia, and—dare he think it?—*him.* The spontaneous, heartfelt display of affection reminded him of why he'd decided, so many years ago, to become a teacher, not a lawyer or a CEO.

"Thank you for your response to my little homily," he said, half tearful, half chuckling. "It means a lot to me. And remember: *you're* gonna mean a lot to *her* when she comes back on Wednesday! Now get along home, and don't forget to crack those books tonight. Your midterm is looming like a North Dakota 'Nado, so you'll have to be ready. *Class dismissed!*"

* * *

Alone now, Thornwood devoted another hour or so of his teacherly existence to after-school tasks, then stuffed his grade book into his attaché case, slipped into his jacket, flipped off the lights, and headed out to the parking lot. It would soon be dark, and, as was his habit before going home, he settled into the driver's seat, dozed off, and lapsed into an imaginary, sound-asleep sermon, delivered entirely from within the privacy of his Volkswagen.

But this time, instead of being Alex Thornwood, a small-town school teacher of humble origins, he was the celebrated Father Mapple, thunderously orating from high up in the elaborately configured pulpit of the Whaleman's Chapel—a quaint, turn-of-the-century seaside church in the village of New Bedford, Massachusetts. And with each passing minute, the weather outside was growing more and more ominous.

In the closely packed pews was a crew of raw, thoroughly inexperienced seafaring recruits about to sail across the Atlantic in search of Captain Ahab's nautical archenemy, *Moby Dick*. And as Mapple saw it, it was his sacred duty to prepare them for the soulful but incomparably treacherous profession of whaling.

They were hardly men of means. Some were honest citizens in need of a livable income and a sense of pride in a job well done. Others were newly arrived from criminal activity and eager to avoid prosecution for crimes ranging from trifling to heinous. Most of them came from low educational and social circumstances. Not all were Caucasian. It was a melting pot of people from every imaginable underpaid, disrespected walk of life.

Not surprisingly, every last congregant in the church that evening was a male of the species. If a woman happened to be aboard a whaler, it was only because she was married to either the captain or someone else of high standing in the ship's hierarchy. Any other woman unfortunate enough to have been mixed in with such a motley crew of thugs and ne'er-do-wells would have been in mortal danger the moment she set foot on the ship.

As the weather in Alec Thornwood's dream grew more and more threatening, Father Mapple ranted and raved to his congregation for what seemed like an Eternity, condemning indolence and dishonesty, and demanding loyalty under threat of either summary dismissal or death by drowning. For any incident of outright mutiny, he roared, death alone would not be sufficient punishment unless preceded by a series of unspeakable tortures.

To the enormous relief of the recruits, Mapple finally finished his evangelizing. Then, as he and the congregants were reaching for their hymnals, he looked across the congregation and noticed a young girl—a sudden visitor—standing exhausted at the rear of the chapel, dressed as if she'd just stepped off an oceangoing schooner. Her jacket was smeared with whale fat, and her arms were cradling what appeared to be a stack of weather-beaten, waterlogged books—more than like likely her reading material from a just-completed expedition across the Atlantic.

"Give the girl a hymnal!" shouted Mapple to the men nearest her. "Whatever the reason she has entered this, the House of Our Lord and Savior, she cannot be deprived of the opportunity to sing His praise with us!"

One recruit handed her a hymnal, and then the singing began—more a cacophony of indecipherable sounds than singing as one would commonly call it—and in spite of the flood of tears cascading down the girl's face, she joined in.

The congregants, who'd never seen their Sudden Guest before and had no idea either where she may have come from or why she was crying, were so moved by her arrival and the magnificence of her voice that they sang with even more conviction than usual, raising their own voices to the heavens as if they'd just witnessed a miracle.

As the thrown-together choir finished the last rousing verse of "Abide with Me," Thornwood abruptly woke up, set up straight in his car, and shook his head in amazement.

What a sermon! he laughed. *Maybe I should have become an evangelist, not a teacher! And the remarkable thing is that I can remember it as if it were a movie!*

But who on earth was that girl in the back of the chapel? he wondered. *And why should she suddenly show up in a chapel filled with a gnarl of grizzled, sea-hardened sailors?* Then he remembered the weeping, angelic expression on her face—and the waterlogged stack of books she was carrying—and realized to his astonishment that it was Cecelia he'd been dreaming about, coming back from a lifetime of trials and tribulations that one as young as she was should never have had to endure.

He started his car, adjusted the rear view mirror, and drove off into the night, wondering—and indeed fearing— what was in store for the finest student he'd ever had in all his years of teaching.

* * *

As Clay and Cecelia walked away from the confrontation with Thornwood, Clay was still letting off steam. "Don't you ever bring home another filthy book like that, young lady!" he growled. "Whatever made them hire a jerk like that? Your Mr. Burnwood would make a better *dog catcher* than a classroom teacher! Now get yourself into the back seat. There'll be no TV tonight! And you'll be going straight to bed after supper. Understand?"

"It's *Thornwood,* Daddy, not Burnwood," she said, trying her best to be polite when she was really far beyond furious.

Somebody has to be mature right now, she thought to herself, *and it clearly isn't gonna be my father.*

"And he didn't mean any harm, either! He just wants me to read good books by famous authors—not those silly 'Dick and Jane' books the other kids read. I guess it's all they can handle! And really, Daddy, *Frankenstein* isn't a 'filthy' book! There's not one filthy word *in* it—just lots of really hard words and a whole lot of scary things—stuff I really enjoy reading! Remember what Bruno Bettelheim said? He said being scared is good for kids! Gets 'em ready for the real world! I heard you telling Mommy about that just last week."

"Maybe you're right," he mumbled, eager to get home, have some supper, and relax. "But only about *this morning,* not Bettelheim." Listening to his daughter talk about pretty much anything, these days, had become a lot like listening to Alistair Cook introduce his evening guest on *Omnibus.*

"This morning?" she said. "What *about* this morning?"

"About the way I behaved!" he snapped. "Maybe I shouldn't have said what I did—at least not the way I said it. Maybe I was a little too hard on Mr. Burnwood. But you know what? You can do me a big favor and just *shut up* about that quack

Bettelheim! I'm not in the mood to hear about his silly ideas. And by the way, no more big-word fancy talk, either! OK? I've had enough of that shit for one day!"

When he looked into his rear view mirror and saw her curled up like a caterpillar, sniffling and trembling, waves of fatherly guilt began to wash over him.

"But honestly, honey, I swear that school of yours is tryin' to *poison* you with their highfalutin ideas!"

Poor Mom and Dad, thought Cecelia, who by now was at a loss for words to challenge the things her father was saying. *They should have read more books when they were my age. Or any books, come to think of it. I should think something would have been better than nothing!*

Alec Thornwood, in spite of all the trauma he and Cecelia and her classmates had just suffered through, was not about to give up on Cecelia. He vowed then and there to find a way, no matter how difficult it might prove to be, to continue to nurture Cecelia's astonishing intellect—her hopes, her dreams, her every aspiration. It would be a rare opportunity for him, and for any teacher, really, to have a lasting influence on a young, inquisitive, adventurous mind.

The very next Friday, after his confrontation with Clay Middling—and with the full support of the school's administration, which had always encouraged innovative projects—Thornwood moved Cecelia from Tier Three of his classroom roster to Tier Seven, the academic level reserved exclusively for gifted students.

The meeting with Clay and Natalie Furbish, the Principal, went much better than Thornwood had expected it to go. Furbish did herself proud by defending Alec Thornwood for his sound judgment and all-around professionalism—but especially for his well-thought-out position in the matter of what a student should or shouldn't be allowed to read at school, and why.

Clearly, Middling himself must have taken the time and initiative to cool himself down after his ugly encounter with Thornwood, because he was surprisingly civil toward both Furbish and Thornwood while expressing his opinion about Thornwood's choice of reading materials for Cecelia. That fact alone made Thornwood feel better. He knew that if he were hard on her father while in the principal's office, it would get back to CeCe and cause her even more pain and conflict at home. As for Clay, maybe it was just contrition, combined with shame, that made him finally rein in his fury.

Middling may have acted conciliatory during the meeting with Thornwood and Furbish, but at home one day after school, he was right back to singing a very different tune.

"So what'd you do today, Little Miss Smarty Pants?" Clay was always confrontational when something or someone reminded him of his insufficiencies.

"Plenty," said Cecelia, *"plenty!* Today we learned about the worst of the countless ways men, women, and children were mistreated—dehumanized, really—after they'd been rounded up and taken to the concentration camps in— can you believe it?—*cattle cars*. I can hardly bring myself to *think* about it!"

"So why *do* you think about it?" said Clay. "Why do you want to mess up that mind of yours worrying about stuff like that? We're not even sure all that camp stuff— you know, the ovens, the lampshades—ever actually *happened!* Where's the *proof?* I mean, how the hell does Thornwood think he can get away with peddling that kind o' leftist rubbish in the public schools? It's *my* tax dollars they're using to spread harebrained ideas like this in the classrooms of America!"

Enduring yet another painful confirmation of her father's hard-core, recalcitrant bigotry made Cecelia sick to her stomach. So instead of battling with him over his ill-informed grasp of history, she went straight upstairs to her room, slammed the door behind her, and left him standing there, wondering all over again why his daughter never seemed to approve of anything he said.

Meanwhile, Alec Thornwood clung tenaciously to his principles. Cecelia would now be working with students who, while not nearly as precocious as her, were much better prepared to deal with the intimidating reality of her intellectual prowess. And they quickly learned that while their new classmate might be annoyingly opinionated and excessively talkative, she was also unusually generous for a child her age—more than willing to help them with any problems they couldn't solve or facts they couldn't recall. It was almost as if they had another teacher in the classroom. Since the students liked her as a classmate, it meant that instead of being threatened by her intelligence, they stood in awe of it and found themselves praising her lavishly for her accomplishments as a student. If she'd been playing softball instead of reading books, she'd have earned the Most Valuable Player award without even trying.

In Tier Seven, Cecelia thrived as she'd never thrived before, spilling over with happiness to finally be in an environment in which learning was actively encouraged and open-minded inquiry was considered a supreme virtue.

Still, Thornwood was painfully aware of conditions in Cecelia's home. Neither of her parents had high expectations for themselves. They'd apparently never been high achievers in school, so it was next to impossible for them to understand or even acknowledge their daughter's burning desire to feed her intellect and enrich herself in every way she could.

To make sure she was being challenged intellectually at every turn, Thornwood set aside an hour a day, five days a week, for her to be excused from Tier Seven for an entire hour of independent reading. Mrs. Furbish agreed to allow her to use a small, well-appointed room adjacent to her office for her reading sessions—a room ordinarily reserved exclusively for either meetings with parents or off-the-record school board meetings. Then he had Harvey Cornelius, the school's head janitor, install a free-standing bookshelf for her with a sign above it, created by the school's art teacher, that said *Cecelia Middling's Tree of Knowledge.*

Each Monday morning, Thornwood would arrive at work with another half dozen of the most challenging books from his personal library in the trunk of his Volkswagen. Then he'd bring them inside, line them up on the shelf, and instruct Cecelia to choose the one book that excited her the most. In return for the privilege of having a room all to herself, she would be required to write a brief report about the book, then leave it on his desk no later than two weeks from then. Thornwood couldn't help wondering if she'd really be able to finish the report in just two weeks, but he soon discovered that not only was she a skilled, attentive reader for a nine-year-old, she was also an exceptionally strong, eloquent, and fast-moving writer. To his delight, she nearly always got her report in a few days ahead of Thornwood's deadline, and it was always impeccably well written and astonishingly insightful.

From the moment Thornwood began lending his books to Cecelia and allowing her the luxury of reading alone each day from the Tree of Knowledge, her ability to read and fully comprehend complex material, whether fiction or non-fiction, science or history, literature or the arts, skyrocketed.

Not long after the incident with Cecelia's father, which had been telegraphed throughout the building by word of mouth, there was talk in the teachers' room about the possibility of allowing her to sit in on high school classes or even audit courses at the local community college. Only a handful of the most progressive teachers thought it was a good idea; the rest thought she was getting pretty damned uppity for a fourth-grader.

"We're spoiling her!" said Trudy Ballentine, the school's guidance counselor. "We've got kids in this school who deserve special treatment a whole lot more than she does. Our Little Miss Middling has a *way* too high opinion of herself!"

"I mean, just who does she think she *is*?" asked Valerie Swingle, the school nurse.

"Well," said Flora Heinrich, one of the school's more frequent substitutes, "I don't know who she *thinks* she is, but I happen to know, from personal experience, who she *actually* is!"

"And who, may I ask, might that be?" asked Valerie Swingle. She looked around the room, clearly fishing for a smart remark—another pithy, poisonous dart of condemnation. But when there was no response, she went back to work on her tuna fish sandwich and waited for an answer.

Finally Heinrich—always eager to earn points with the regulars for another of her legendary, well-timed barbs—came to Swingle's rescue.

"She's a little *snot* if you ask me! A spoiled-rotten, silver-spooned brat from . . . what was that town? I forget."

"From Sausalito," said Trudy. "You know, one o' those West Coast tourist meccas from the Gold Rush State. I mean, lah-de-fucking-dah!" she sneered. "Who really cares?"

"Trudy!" whispered Valerie. "Keep your voice down! The children can hear everything when they walk past here."

Then Heinrich picked up where she'd left off. "Anyway, as I was saying, the other day a teacher's aide told me she watched in amazement as Cecelia marched right up to the chalk board and corrected the spelling of a word

Alec Thornton had just written on the chalkboard. Can you believe it? I mean, the *insolence* of it!"

"That's disgusting!" sneered Heinrich. "Believe me, if I'd been there and seen her do a thing like that, I'd have slapped that girl silly! Back o' the hand—it's the only thing that works with some kids!"

"The *hell* you would have!" said Valerie. "Don't you know there are laws against corporal punishment here in North Dakota? I'm tellin' you, Flo, you'd never have gotten way with it. It's just not . . ."

Then they heard the familiar sound of spiked heels against linoleum and knew it was Mrs. Furbish, on her way to yet another parent/teacher conference with a stack of manila folders in one hand and a cup of coffee in the other.

"Oh, *shit,*" said Trudy. "Guess who's comin' to dinner!"

"Breakfast," said Flora. "It's 7:30 in the morning, for Christ's sake!"

"You'd better hope she didn't bring her axe to work this morning," said Valerie. "If she heard what you were saying, she might wanna do a Raskolnikov on you!"

Furbish set the folders and coffee down on a detention desk in the hallway, then stepped inside wearing a fierce, disapproving glare. She walked over to Trudy, and stared intimidatingly down at her.

"I'd know that magpie voice of yours from five miles away, Trudy!" she said. "And sometimes I'm glad to hear it, but not this morning! The words I just heard you uttering here in my school should give no one pleasure. They're offensive! They do not belong at Cloverton! Nor do they have a place anywhere in the town of Minot, the state of North Dakota, or for that matter, all of education. Cease and desist, or you'll be looking for work in a school far away from here—if you can find one that wants to put up with that kind of thinking. And if I ever hear that you actually laid a hand on one of my students—including Cecelia—you'll never set foot in this school again!"

Once Furbish had gone on her way, the mood in the teachers' lounge turned sullen.

"Well, now!" crowed Trudy. "Nothin' like a trim-down from the Assassin to get us all into teaching mode!"

"She'd bump off her own mother if she thought it would keep her in power," said Flora. "That's all she really cares about—showin' 'em who's boss!"

"I'm beginning to think it's *Cecelia* who's actually the boss around here," said Ballentine. "How'd we ever get to the point where a brainy little misfit like Cecelia Middling gets royal treatment?"

"If y' ask me," said Valerie, "it's about time we *dethrone* that little bitch."

"And while we're at it," said Trudy, "we should find a way to take down *Thornwood*, too. We've got way too many Goody Two-Shoes in this school. Time to get down to business. Time to weed the garden!"

From that day on, they did their best to change the chemistry at Cloverton—to tilt things their way, philosophically. But no matter what efforts they made over the next several months to rid their garden of what they considered an invasive species—teachers and students with high ambition and sophisticated, big-city thinking—they failed miserably.

In the process, they managed to make everyone around them miserable, firing a calculated, never-ending barrage of toxic innuendoes and public condemnations that clearly gave them intense pleasure—a pleasure which, sadly, they made no effort to conceal.

Trudy Ballentine went before the school board and demanded that the district look into allegations that Alec

Thornton was forcing his students to read "inappropriate literature" replete with violence and vulgarity, meant only for adults without high moral standards. For some reason, they considered Mary Shelley's *Frankenstein* "filth" and demanded that it be banned from every library in North Dakota.

Flora Heinrich rounded up several sympathetic neighbors and persuaded them to come with her to the monthly PTA meeting, where together they accused Thornwood and several other teachers of favoring Cecelia Middling while turning their backs on students who, in their opinion, deserved special care infinitely more than Cecelia did.

Valerie Swingle went straight to Janson Kefauver, the superintendent of schools, and claimed that Cecelia was reading "dirty books" from Alec Thornwood's personal library, then whispering the more titillating passages to children at recess.

Soon, the entire town was aware of the growing scandal at Cloverton. Cecelia's parents were no longer included in neighborhood gatherings; Birdie was shunned when she went on her weekly shopping trip to Red Owl; Clay was abruptly cut out of Friday night poker at the local Elks Lodge, with the entirely fabricated excuse that because of "seniority issues," there would no longer be room for him at the table. And, without explanation, Cecelia was no longer being invited to her classmates' birthday parties—even the ones for those she considered her closest friends.

Conditions were bad enough for Cecelia at school, but at home they were much, much worse.

Disciplining her—even for the smallest, most common-sense infractions—was a formidable challenge. Not only was her intellect a constant reminder to her parents of their own intellectual weaknesses, she was also a hidebound maverick and a born Rebel, simply not built to take 'no' for an answer without fighting back, sometimes ferociously. She often felt as if she'd been trapped in some diabolical, inescapable role reversal—a ridiculous state of affairs in which she was expected to bring her parents into adulthood long before she herself would have a fighting chance to mature.

For Clay and Birdie, who weren't even close to being ready for the task of parenting, raising a girl like Cecelia was an assignment fraught with exasperation, stress, and open conflict.

When Clay would order her on occasion to clean up the chaos she'd created in her bedroom—to change her dirty bedsheets, pick up the food scraps she'd tossed on the floor, or vacuum the carpet—she'd fight back, using the strongest weapon in her arsenal—her formidable, insurmountable logic. "If no one but me ever comes in here," she would shout, "then why on earth should I worry about trivial things like cookie crumbs and banana peels? If I'm the only one who ever sleeps in my bed, then what do I care if it smells funny and has hair curlers and candy wrappers in it? I mean, if this is really *my* room, then why should I have to make it look like *you* want it to look? You're not making sense, Daddy!"

When Birdie would take Cecelia aside and try to explain to her how 'real' girls should dress and groom themselves—how attracting boys requires learning to 'walk and sit like a lady'—Cecelia would stomp her foot, double her fists, then glare violently at her mother. "That's ridiculous!" she'd shout. "I'm *book*-crazy, not *boy*-crazy! Any boy I'm ever be attracted to will have to love books as much as I love books! And if he can't do that, then I'll have no use for him!"

And when Clay would tell her she was grounded for a week because she'd watched television longer than she was allowed to on a school night, she'd flash her most innocent smile, then say, "You're right, Daddy. I'm sorry. I won't do it again!" Then, as soon as she knew her parents were upstairs, fast asleep, she'd tiptoe down to the family room with Smokey and a pillow, turn on the television, and watch whatever she felt like—but with the sound so low it was barely audible. *It's way more fun when I secretly do stuff they don't approve of,* she'd whisper to herself. *And besides, Daddy can be such a doofus. Can't he, Smokey!*

Chapter Sixteen

In spite of Cecelia's bodily insecurities, by her sophomore year—it was 1983, and she was sixteen now—the hormones had really begun to kick in. She began to wonder in earnest just what society's endless preoccupation with sex—with "doin' it"—in books, magazines, films, and especially the girls' locker room at Cloverton—was all about. Indeed, she'd begun to have strong, undeniable sexual urges herself, and on her own initiative had gone out of her way to read, in great detail, about how babies are made. And yet the more she learned about human sexuality, the more sordid it had all begun to seem to her.

Still, she was too smart and too intellectually curious not to be a realist about the changes in her body. *I mean hey,* she laughed, *everyone eventually wants to know what 'sexual intercourse' is like.* To fuck or *not* to fuck: it was the Question of the Hour at Cloverton. *Shakespeare was young once. He must have wondered, too. So maybe it's about time I find out,* she giggled.

Tired of being known around school as a Late Comer—a term she'd coined while in study hall one day, secretly devouring D.H. Lawrence's *Sons and Lovers*—she decided to do some serious "field research" on the subject, then put it to the test.

But what, she wondered, *would I do if, God forbid, I were to end up pregnant—an unwilling incubator for the white, gummy product of some pimply, adolescent creep—and at the worst possible time in my life?*

She wasn't really all that worried. After all, she was no dummy. She'd learned long ago what the word "protection" means, and because of it, she vowed to always be more than adequately well-prepared for any South-of-the-Border contingencies.

The next morning she headed down to the nearest drug-store, armed with a note she'd forged to appear as if it had been written and signed by her father, and bought a box of Lucky Dip condoms, each one sealed in a bright red package with playful, banana-yellow lettering. "*Banana yellow*," she laughed. "How appropriate!"

The clerk, a young, stylishly dressed *femme fatale* with a twinkle of sexual awareness in her eye, was clearly skeptical about the authenticity of the note. But she was also old enough—and experienced enough—to know, without a doubt, just what was going on. She smiled, rung up the sale with a flourish, and sent Cecelia off with a near-audacious wink of womanly complicity.

There will be no 'preggo,' Cecelia told herself, *simply because I'll be sure to head off any aggressive spermatozoids at the pass, long before they have a chance to get there.*

But who would be her partner in crime? Right away she thought of Arnold Legume—the boy next to her in Human Anatomy, who was always playing with himself, arranging the contents of his "package" when he ought to have been listening to Mrs. Langlois. She wondered what it would be like to watch a boy's strange, dangling noodle grow hard as a screwdriver, then burrow into her most secretive Lady Bits.

The truth was that Cecelia felt genuinely sorry for Legume, a struggling, patchwork adolescent with low self-esteem, no one to lean on, and little if anything to make him libidinously desirable. *I understand loneliness,* Cecelia mused. *I've grown up with loneliness!*

The more she thought about climbing into the sack with Arnold Legume, the more it struck her that by doing so, she'd be killing two birds with one pair of stones: a one-on-one anatomy lesson for her, and a moment of what she felt certain would be intense pleasure for him.

Sounds like a good deal to me, she laughed. *A fair trade-off. And who knows? Our little Arnold may know just what to do with that little wee-wee of his! All I'll need to do is wake it up, make it bigger, and make it do the Boogaloo for me!*

She knew that Legume, the neighborhood loner, could nearly always be found on weekends slumped lugubriously over a table at Conklin's Foam Bucket, a nostalgic, fifties-style soda fountain not far from her home. She knew he had no siblings and few if any friends. She also knew, from the never-ending gossip around school, that his parents—who, for some inexplicable reason, were a whole lot more well-adjusted than he was—were more than glad to have him out of the house as often as possible, especially on weekends, when they could indulge in the bedroom amusements their son had never had the pleasure of experiencing. The truth is that they couldn't have cared less about what, if anything, their son's sex life might be like.

Cecelia picked up a copy of the *Pierce County Tribune,* jotted down the Saturday hours at Conklin's, then showed up there at 7:00 p.m., an hour before closing. She told her parents she was going to an open house for her and her fellow honor students. She knew she didn't need to worry that they might find out there actually *wasn't* an open house. She also knew, all too well, that they would never have bothered to show up anyway.

Sure enough, Arnold was there as predicted, curled up like a potato bug in a booth at the far end of the café. There were no other diners, so she knew it was likely the two of them would be alone until closing, where no one else would hear them talking.

"Mind if I join you?" said Cecelia.

"Me?" said Arnold, looking first baffled, then genuinely shocked. "You want to sit down with *me*?"

"I don't blame you for being surprised," she said. "I'm just kind o' pissed off at my parents right now and needed to get as far away as possible from them. Thank God for Conklin's! Anyway, it would be helpful to talk about it with someone."

"Listen," he said, "I've been pissed at *my* parents since I was ten years old! Maybe we can sit here for a while and compare notes. I'd benefit from opening up to someone about my *own* anger and disillusionment. No one has ever given me the opportunity!"

"Sure!" said Cecelia. "When do you have to be home? I've got a lot on my mind, so it's gonna take a while."

"No particular time," he grinned. "Bonnie and Clyde—that's what I call Mom and Dad in my journal—are at another Drink-a-Thon over in Granville. Guess it's their idea of High Culture. Anyway, they could stay there forever far as I'm concerned! But of course they won't do that. They'll stay and party their asses off there, then come home totally blasted. They usually get back by 3:00 or 4:00 a.m. Doesn't matter, though; I'll likely be sound asleep when they stumble in through the side door. Then again, I always know they've arrived when I hear 'em puking in the driveway. Happens every time."

She was blushing inwardly now, surprised at how alert and articulate he was, then ashamed of herself for having failed to take him seriously in the past. Her classmates' opinion of him was obviously ill-conceived, and she ought not to have fallen for it. He'd been severely ostracized at school, and their treatment of him, by both students and teachers, was unfair, uncalled for, and patently cruel.

But she was also ashamed of what she was about do with—and to—an innocent, well-meaning young man who clearly deserved better treatment than he'd been subjected to while a student at Cloverton. *This will be a growing experience for me,* she thought to herself. *And who knows? Maybe I'll even like the sex!*

"Tell you what," she said. "This place will be closing soon, right smack in the middle of our talk. And since your Mom and Dad are out on the town, why don't we do our talking at *your* place? Think they'd mind? And is there a nice, comfortable couch in the living room?"

"Oh, yeah," he said, "a really *nice* couch!" He wondered why on earth she'd ever care about another person's couch, because he only cared about his own.

"I've always loved vintage European furniture," he said. "How 'bout you? We've got several pieces of it scattered around the house—even a Rennie Mackintosh—and believe me, anything with his name attached to it is worth a bundle! I know because we subscribe to *Architectural Digest*. I read it all the time!"

Poor Arnold, she laughed. *I swear the boy just missed my cue by at least a mile or two. My God! Can anyone in this day and age really be so sexually untutored? Of course, I realize I don't have a whole lot o' cred in the sex department, either. But I'm still gonna do what I can to give my little stud muffin a memorable experience. It's the least I can do under the circumstances. After all, I've got a reputation to uphold, at least in my mind. I wouldn't want anyone to think I don't know the ropes!*

As they walked down Kensington toward his place—a mustard-colored split-level ranch with pampered lawns and a faux Georgian entrance flanked by a pair of out-of-kilter, bargain-basement lions—she imagined Arnold and her writhing merrily around on that couch, undies down, asses pumping.

But holy shit, she squealed. *All he can think about is a friggin' piece of period furniture! Oh, well: I'll just ignore the zits and concentrate on that six-shooter of his.*

It took less than ten minutes for them to reach Arnold's place. Once they were politely positioned on the couch, she engaged in the socially required small talk—a minute or two of bland, linguistic foreplay—then dropped all pretense, sidled boldly up to him, and blew, gently but persistently, into his waxy, shell-shaped ear. *Eww!* she grimaced. *And it has a foul odor, too!*

But this time she could see that he clearly hadn't missed the cue. She looked down and watched with womanly amusement as what only moments ago had been little more than a flaccid, eminently forgettable rope of flesh alchemized into a battle-ready Soldier of Fortune—and a Damn Big One, too, she noticed. To be ready for action, she grabbed one of the Luckys and cupped it in her right hand where he couldn't see it.

Seconds later, her bra was on the floor and Legume's hands and mouth—greedy, enraptured Partners in Crime—were aggressively seeking. He went first for the nipples—*don't they all,* she laughed—deftly licking and nibbling them into firm, twin shrines to the nobility of straightforward, unbridled sexual pleasure.

He jerked her panties down to her knees, then yanked his throbbing penis out of his Jockeys and stood there like some sort of city-dwelling scarecrow, wondering just what it was she expected him to do next. *My God,* she thought to herself. *The guy's absolutely clueless!*

She unwrapped the condom and handed it to him, figuring he'd at least know what to do with *that*, but she soon realized to her amusement that he didn't.

"Hold still," she giggled. "You ain't goin' anywhere without your raincoat on!" She quickly wrestled the thing onto him—*Damn: I should think they'd come in bigger sizes than this!*—then guided him into her and let him have at it. *Wahoo*, she yelped, *we're off to the races!*

In and out of her he went then, with lightning speed but not one iota of sexual finesse, delivering the goods into his synthetic love glove in what surely must have been record time. She was ever so thankful, knowing they'd landed *there* instead of in *her*.

It was just as they warned me, she mused afterwards while he was down the hall, disposing of the condom. *Boy gets jazzed, girl gets nothin.' Nothin' but a whole lot o' friction and precious little reward. I'd have had a better experience with a hand job,* she laughed. She pulled herself together while he was gone, hoping to make a quick, clean escape from the mess she'd gotten herself into. She really wasn't angry with him, though. After all, it was she who'd sought him out, not the other way around.

He came back a minute later and joined her on the couch, still in a condition of wonderment that he, Arnold "The Loser" Legume, had actually done the dirty with the most esteemed, most intelligent girl in the school.

"Ready to talk?" he asked, too embarrassed to mention what had just happened. "You know, about *parents* and stuff like that! Things have been even crummier than usual at home lately—so bad I'm about ready to bail out. How 'bout *you*?"

Cecelia, who to her shame had never really intended to talk with him about anything, came up with a lame excuse for leaving.

"Sorry 'bout the *conversa-tus interrup-tus*," she purred, "but wouldn't you know, I forgot I have an appointment with the dentist in less than an hour! Got to have a bridge redone."

"A bridge?" said Arnold. "A *bridge*? At 9:30 in the evening? What kind of dentist keeps hours like that?

"Dentistry is not a cookie-cutter profession," she said. When you're a freelancer, the hours you keep are *your* business."

"But what about *us*? I mean, when are we gonna get together again?"

"Don't really know," said Cecelia. "Maybe next month. Maybe next year. Maybe never."

"But I don't understand!" he said.

"You don't *need* to understand," she replied. "That's *my* job! Right now, I just need to get my face back in shape."

"You mean you didn't like what we . . ."

"Fair to middling," she laughed half-sarcastically, reasonably certain he hadn't picked up on the double entendre. "Fair to middling. Sure! But it was quite enough for now, thank you. *More* than enough, in fact."

"What the fuck?" he shouted. "You've led me on! I don't think that was very . . ."

"Class in session!" she snarled. "So you still haven't learned? An N and an O together spell *no*. So guess what, Arnie: it looks like wettin' that Willy of yours again will just have to wait. But don't despair; there's always Amsterdam—right?"

Arnold finally realized he'd been had—that he'd been shamelessly taken advantage of. He felt humiliated, and as he watched her imperiously gather up her belongings and disappear out the front door, he stood there like a store mannequin stripped bare, wondering what on earth he'd done—or not done—to make her lose interest. "I . . . I actually thought I did a pretty good job!" he stuttered.

Cecelia went home that night doubly ashamed of herself for having treated Legume so roughly after trapping him into a sexual moment he'd never asked for and never expected. But she also felt certain he'd never talk about their sexual encounter with friends, simply because he'd have been too ashamed to acknowledge that it was only his first time and he hardly knew what he was doing. *Besides,* she laughed, *who would he tell? He doesn't have any friends anyway!"*

What she'd just heard herself saying about Legume left a bad taste in her mouth. *What's happening to me?* she wondered as she climbed into bed. *Was I just sowing my wild oats, carte blanche, like boys have been doing since Cave Man times? Or am I actually a whole lot less emotionally intelligent and socially responsible than Thornwood always said I am?*

The truth was that she didn't feel very good about herself *in general* because of her treatment of Arnold. *Would it not be fair to call what I just did a kind of 'soft rape'? Or am I merely guilty of ringing his bell a little too aggressively? I should have known that, like other adolescent boys, he has a sensitive trigger, and yet I went ahead and pulled it for him!*

Others might have asked God to forgive them for such a transgression, but there was one little problem for Cecelia: she was not really a Believer. In the matter of religiosity, she was more on the side of Hitchens and Russell than Swaggart and Graham. And that meant she'd have to find a more secular way to forgive herself for her loathsome conduct.

The thought that she might actually have the worst of Clay and Birdie Middling deep inside her, shaping her morals and ethics, made Cecelia feel sick to her stomach.

With each passing day, they seemed less and less like a mother and father to her and more and more like an unfortunate complication in an otherwise happy existence. *Did I ask for them to be my parents? Did they really want me in the beginning? Is there any evidence that they need me now?*

She turned to the wall and pulled the quilt up over her head, as if by doing so she could somehow put the evening's disturbing events behind her. It would be, she hoped, as if they'd never actually happened.

Chapter Seventeen

Over the next two years, through blistering hot summers, bitterly cold winters, and the ever-present curse of the springtime floods for which Minot had become so infamous, Cecelia Middling continued to outshine virtually every other student at Cloverton. There had been only one glaring exception: a cold, dark November in grade nine when she'd earned a C– from Mrs. Charbonneau, the French teacher, for "failing to master her declensions" and a D+ in Citizenship for being "generally disruptive and disrespectful in the classroom." Prior to this, she had never earned less than an A in any of her classes.

Despite her well-deserved reputation as a difficult student, the accolades for her scholarly achievements continued to pile up, fast and furious, from both within and well beyond the school system.

She received the Model Student Award for three consecutive years—an unprecedented accomplishment at Cloverton—and the Most Likely to Succeed Award in grades 7 through 11. An article about her academic prowess appeared in the *Devil's Lake World* in 1983, extolling the virtues of her work ethic and applauding her for her "breathtaking accomplishments as a student."

"Surely Miss Middling should have no trouble finding a good fit for herself in one of this country's most prestigious universities," wrote the Opinion Page editor. "Harvard, Yale, UCLA, and dozens of other top-ranked colleges will be at her beck and call! And the good news is that she won't even have to try, because they'll soon be clamoring for her to enroll. All of us here in Greater Minot urge our

Favorite Girl to shoot for the moon, and we have nothing but the highest hopes for her as she prepares to enter the work world."

Then, after all her remarkable courage in the face of constant criticism, shunning, and open ridicule, what everyone in Minot knew was bound to happen finally came to pass. Cecelia Middling was named the valedictorian of her senior class. At the award ceremony, late on the evening of June 19, 1985, she was offered more scholarships from prestigious colleges than all of the other seniors put together.

As Cecelia's awards were announced—more than a dozen of them altogether—only a small handful of people in the gymnasium bothered to applaud her. The rest of them registered their disapproval by either going completely silent or continuing to chatter amongst themselves about things having nothing at all to do with the most accomplished student ever to graduate from Cloverton.

Cecelia, deeply hurt by the audience's palpable indifference to her achievements, fought back tears, then looked anxiously around for her parents, hoping against hope that they, of all the people in attendance, might understand how it felt for her to have been openly, callously shunned by an auditorium full of people interested only in themselves and their own petty, provincial lives.

As she wound her way through the crowd after the ceremony, her spirits were lifted by the certainly that she would soon be greeted with a pair of broad, beaming smiles. *Sure,* she thought, *we have our problems. Big problems! But I've no doubt that deep down inside, my parents love me. And tonight, at least, they must be really proud of me!*

But when she finally caught sight of them and ran toward them with open arms, she saw not smiles of pride but frowns of disapproval on their faces. She dropped her arms to her sides in defeat. She could tell right away that they were more annoyed than excited about the tidal wave of honors and scholarships she'd just been awarded.

"Sorry it took so long!" she said, feeling more and more as if she'd somehow let them down. "I know it's hot in here, and those bleachers are no fun to sit on—especially for two and a half hours! Everyone here hates them."

"Honestly," said Birdie, "I thought the whole thing was never gonna end! And speaking of 'ends,' I'm gonna have to soak my *rear* end in a tub o' hot water when I get home."

Clay, trying his best to look and feel upbeat, gave his daughter a polite hug followed by a perfunctory kiss on the cheek. "Good girl!" he said quietly, sounding more resigned than enthusiastic. "I guess you've been studying harder than we thought, huh!"

"Sure have!" said Cecelia. "I mean, really! Who in her right mind would want to come out of school dumber than when she went in? *I* sure wouldn't! And besides, Mr. Thornwood says I'm one of the smartest students he's ever had. I know he would have been so disappointed in me if I'd been a slacker. That's why I worked myself to the bone. I wanted more than anything else in the world to please him!"

"But not to please *us*?" said Birdie with a flash of child-like petulance. "C'mon, CeCe! You don't want to give Thornwood too much credit, do you? I mean, he's just your *teacher*. We're your mom and dad!"

"He's not 'just' a teacher!" snapped Cecelia, no longer able to conceal her disgust for her mother. "None of the teachers at Cloverton are 'just' teachers. They've been the most import-ant people in my life, and I'm gonna miss them terribly!"

"All *right*, already!" hissed her mother. "You can stop making a scene here right now, young lady! And just think," she said, turning to her husband—"on this, her Special Day!"

"You really shouldn't have said that," said Clay.

"Maybe I shouldn't have," she responded. "Maybe I should say I wish I hadn't missed *Three's Company*. But wouldn't you know—that damned ceremony just kept droning on and on. I nearly fell asleep!"

"Sorry I spoiled *your* Special Day," sneered Cecelia. "Now can we please just go home? I'm in the middle of *Schindler's Ark*, and I'm dying to get back into it!"

"It's *Noah's Ark*, not *Schindler's Ark*," said Clay as the three of them headed out to the parking lot with Cecelia in the lead. "Even *I* know *that* story! He led the animals two by two—right?"

"No, it's *Schindler's Ark!*" shouted Cecelia over her shoulder. "The book by Thomas Keneally. It's all about the *Holocaust*. You've heard of that, haven't you? And for your information, the movie's *Schindler's List!*"

"*Thank you, Miss Know-It-All,*" said Clay.

But Cecelia was too far ahead of them now to hear all of what her father was saying.

Clay turned to his wife and slipped his arm into hers, and as they walked side by side to the car, he carried on with his smug little diatribe.

"And I also don't know why the hell a girl like Cecelia— or maybe I should say *any* girl—wants to read morbid stuff like that. The Holocaust? I mean, what good is knowing all about the Holocaust ever gonna *do* for her? Before long, she's gonna have to go out and find herself a *job*. Until then, she needs to be reading something *useful*, for Christ's sake—not that goddam bleeding-heart pablum they'll no doubt be feeding her in college!"

On their way home, the only audible sounds in the car were Tanya Tucker crooning "Delta Dawn" over the radio and Cecelia Middling, Recent Graduate, quietly mourning the loss of her once sky-high and indestructible optimism.

Dawn? What dawn? she whimpered to herself as the

sun worked its way down to the horizon. *The only thing I can see right now is darkness.*

She curled herself up into a corner of the back seat, closed her eyes, and did her best to escape from the ugly realities of being trapped in a ramshackle farmhouse on the outskirts of Minot—the Folsom Prison of the Dakotas—living under the same roof with parents who had less and less in common with her and made no effort at all to understand her. *If only there were a train to a Better Place!* she lamented. *I'd buy myself a one-way ticket, put my hopes and dreams and books in a suitcase, and be gone forever from this sorry excuse for a town!*

When they got home, Cecelia tumbled out of the car, slammed the door behind her, entered the house through the side door off the laundry room, then dashed upstairs. *Forget supper,* she grumbled, *I'm not gonna give them the satisfaction of pretending everything's just fine in the Middling family, because it most certainly isn't!*

As she stared down from the window overlooking the front yard, she could see the two of them standing motionless in the driveway, two crumbling tombstones in a long-neglected graveyard. Clay was staring forlornly down at the black-and-beige penny loafers he'd not worn since Scheckel & Newbury's annual award banquet nearly a decade earlier. Birdie had just pulled a handkerchief out of her purse, and Cecelia could see her wiping away a small river of crocodile tears as they streaked down her cheeks, leaving a trail of mascara in their wake.

"What a waste of time!" said Clay. "She didn't even thank us for coming!"

"And to think I made such a wonderful meal for the three of us, just for this occasion!" said Birdie.

"Thoughtless as usual," said Clay. "I'm afraid that girl was just *born* thoughtless!"

"And I'll bet you a million that while we're sitting down there in the kitchen, eating our baked salmon and chocolate cake alone, she'll be upstairs in bed, pouting like a spoiled little rich kid!"

"Nothin' new 'bout that," said Clay. "But hey! Let her sit up there and pout! There's no need for us to allow the Teacher's Pet to spoil our supper."

"You're right, honey," said Birdie. "To hell with her and her Major League tantrums! She can find herself one o' those fat, brainy books of hers and read herself silly, all by her lonesome!"

"Probably deep into *Crime and Punishment* right now," laughed Clay, "or maybe *Journal of the Plague Year.* Nothin' like a good, light-hearted beach read to send you into the Land of Nod, huh?"

"Hmmm," said Birdie. "Lemme sleep on that and get back to you." Then she leaned over, smiling, and pecked her husband on the cheek. Moments later they were in the house, and in less than an hour they were stuffed full of salmon, all jammied up, and in for the night.

Upstairs, Cecelia tucked herself into bed as fast as possible, greatly relieved to have gotten as far away as she could from her parents.

How, she wondered, had she managed to become the product of two smug, proudly ignorant people with an abundance of bigotry in their blood? She was starting to understand just how twisted and ill-informed their take on the world really was.

Parents? she thought to herself. *Not really! More like two mentally fucked-up strangers named Birdie and Clay, pretending to be someone's mom and dad. They're nothin' but phonies! Imposters!*

Dead tired and emotionally exhausted, she drifted toward a deep, mind-numbing sleep. She wondered if the way she felt at that moment was the way she'd feel when she was actually on her deathbed years from now. *What, me worry? I can think of worse ways than this to call it quits.*

Chapter Eighteen

Now, instead of being upstairs in a decaying farmhouse on the outskirts of Minot, North Dakota, she found herself standing, bleary-eyed and yawning, on the edge of a country road not far from the Atlantic, in a place she'd never been to before.

The landscape, a dry, flat, inhospitable topography with patches of low-hanging, water-starved vegetation, seemed almost extraterrestrial. And yet the bright early morning sunlight, the dazzlingly blue skies, the fast-moving clouds—and everywhere around her the pungent, ocean-born aromas of seaweed and saltwater—made a living, breathing sonnet of the place.

Ahead of her in the mist she could just make out a tar-stained telephone pole with a series of weather-beaten signs posted on it, each one mounted haphazardly above the other. The sign at the top had the words "Scudders Lane" scrawled on it. *Horrid!* she thought. *Couldn't they see it needs an apostrophe? What kind of planet have I just landed on, anyway?*

The next sign down read "Welcome to Barnstable, Massachusetts!" in colorful letters. *Well, it's at least a good beginning,* she laughed. *But where's the barn? And the stable?*

The sign at the bottom read "Hinckley/Scoggins Pond" with an arrow pointing right.

She did what the sign said, and before long she saw a large white clapboard home ahead, set well back from the road and surrounded by a grove of tall, stately trees with leaves only recently brought to life by a steadily warming springtime sun. The lawn, if one could call it that, was badly in need of water, and both the roof and the siding of the home showed evidence of having been subjected to decades of harsh Cape Cod winters.

Such a magnificent old farmhouse, she thought. *I wonder who's lucky enough to call a place like this home.* She wanted badly to know, but she knew it would be terribly rude of her—a complete stranger from some faraway place—to walk up and ask if she could come in uninvited.

She stood there for the better part of a minute, trying to decide which angel to listen to: the maddeningly cautious one, or the insatiably curious one.

She could see from a considerable distance that on either side of the steps leading to the front entrance were complementary stands of fragrant, fresh-bloomed lilac bushes. Drawn in by their intoxicating scent, she made her way up the path and inhaled deeply. Then, without really considering the audacity of her move, she rang the doorbell, not once but several times.

Eventually she heard heavy footsteps coming toward her from inside. Then, finally, a man with a gravelly, high-pitched voice shouted, "I'm *coming,* dammit! Didn't I just say I'm coming?"

Sounds like an old geezer, laughed Cecelia. *And what a grouch—just like my father!*

When the man flung open the door, Cecelia's jaw dropped.

"You've got to be kidding me!" she shrieked. *"Kurt Vonnegut?"*

"The Real Thing," he laughed. "The One and Only!"

She rubbed her eyes in disbelief. "I've read nearly all of your books—finished *Deadeye Dick* just last week. Was absolutely nuts about *Cat's Cradle*—read it *twice.* But I never dreamt I would ever see you in person. I must be hallucinating!"

"Not really, honey. Promise! No phonies allowed in Barnstable."

"Well, I'm not a phony, Mr. Vonnegut. At least I don't *think* I am."

"I sensed that right away," he said. "And by the way, you can do me a favor and can the 'Mr.' stuff. Just call me Kurt; I'm not big on formalities. Around here, I'm just the guy with the Volvo dealership and a few books on the market, and I prefer to keep it that way."

"All right, Mr. Vonnegut," she laughed. "I'll call you Kurt, but it won't be easy. I hope you'll be patient with me."

"Well, of *course* I'll be patient!" he chuckled, then flashed his trademark impish smile. "Most of the time, anyway. Now, I don't know what brings you to these parts, young lady, but would you like to come in? I mean, for this time of year, it's already unusually hot out! Even better, I just pulled a fresh batch of homemade Indian pudding out of the oven, and with a scoop of Breyer's on it, you'll think you've gone straight to Ice Cream Heaven."

She stepped inside, then followed him into the living room and, at his invitation sat down on the couch opposite him. She was quietly astonished at how quickly she felt entirely comfortable in the presence of an author as famous as Vonnegut.

"Now *that* kind of heaven I could live with," she laughed. "It's the other kind—the *biblical* kind—I have trouble believing in."

"Oooh—so young to be such a hardcore skeptic!" he cooed. "Then again, for a person your age, I consider that an accomplishment! You may be Younger than Springtime, but I get the distinct impression that you've already read a lot and seen a lot. Intellectually, it seems to me you're way ahead o' the game."

"I wish my *parents* could see that," she said. "But they

either can't see it at all or they know it's there and refuse to acknowledge it. I'm constantly reading—been reading since I was three years old—and yet I can't remember the last time I ever saw them look inside a book. Maybe their *checkbook*. I suppose I should give 'em credit for that."

"They never read books?" Vonnegut shook his head. "People like that can put a writer like me out o' business!"

"I could keep *you* in business without even *trying!*" she laughed. "I'm a one-woman reading machine. And as for you, I swear I'd be happy to read your *grocery list* if I knew for sure you were the one who wrote it!"

"Nice that you read so much," he smiled. "But do you write just as often? That's my greatest concern."

"You *bet* I do," she responded.

"Good! So you're a writer! But where can I see your writing? Are you published?"

She shrugged her shoulders, then looked sheepishly down at the floor. "Not yet," she sighed, "but I'm sure I will be someday! Mr. Thornwood—he was my high school English teacher—says it's inevitable. He says I'm that good with words."

"I *like* your Mr. Thornwood," said Vonnegut. "I've no doubt he knows what he's talking about, too. But I'm also sure he'd be the first one to agree with me that in all endeavors, the proof is in the pudding—or, in this case, the writing. Confucius say, 'Don't tell me, show me,' and I've been told he was a pretty smart fella. A little too rotund for my tastes, but he must have had a whole lot of active brain matter 'tween those ears of his."

"*Confucius* said that? I thought it was *Chekhov!*"

"Of *course* it was Chekhov! A writer needs a sense of humor, too, don't you think?

"Sorry," said Cecelia. "Guess I missed that one. Usually nothing gets by me."

"I can tell!" said Vonnegut. "By the way, in case you haven't noticed, writing's a tough business. So, like all the other wannabe writers who ever lived, the time for you to put up or shut up has come. For the aspiring writer, at least, it's never later. It's always *now*."

Cecelia smiled, then jumped up from the couch, shook off her backpack, reached into it, and pulled out a manila envelope with a sheaf of stationery inside.

"Well, I do happen to have one small sample I'd be willing to share with you," she said. "I always carry what I'm working on with me, just in case I suddenly want to make on-the-spot improvements. It's the beginning of a short story I've been working on about what it was like the night we arrived in Rugby, North Dakota."

"Ah, Rugby," said Vonnegut. "Drove through there one summer on the way from Ogden to Chicago. Lecture circuit. All I really remember about North Dakota is some nice scenery. But no mountains. None at all! Flatter 'n a pitch-poor singer! At least they've got their *flatness* to crow about. That and those flakey *krumkakes*. Anyway, where were you coming from when you landed in Rugby?"

"Sausalito," she said. "Sausalito, California! I loved it out there—most of it, anyway. We were right near the ocean! There were all sorts of ethnic restaurants, too. And, best of all, bookstores by the dozens!"

"Really!" he chuckled. "I had no idea people in California can actually *read*."

"They sure can! You haven't heard of Stanford? And UCLA? California has an ocean, too. Just like you!"

"It must have been quite a culture shock, coming from a town like Sausalito to a dusty little afterthought like Rugby. And I've heard it's colder 'n a witch's tit in the Dakotas come November!"

Cecelia was used to that kind of locker room talk from

her high school days, but from a literary legend like Kurt Vonnegut? The fact that he had no trouble being so openly, in-your-face colorful—and to a complete stranger, young enough to be his granddaughter—made her love the man even more.

"But enough o' this Chevrolet-in-the-USA stuff," he said. "Never did like Doris Day. So let's have a look at that writing sample!"

As she handed him the envelope, an unsettling combination of swelling pride and abject fear turned her face a deep scarlet. *Kurt Vonnegut critiquing my writing!* she tittered. *If I was religious—which I decidedly am not—I'd be down on my knees right now, thanking God for this opportunity.* Then she remembered her earliest muse, Mr. Thornwood. *Wouldn't he be proud—and, if I know him as well as I think I do, probably pants-peeing envious, too!*

Vonnegut decided to leave his guest alone on the couch and go where he knew he could really concentrate: his study.

"Help yourself to the books," he shouted as he left. "There's lots o' good writing up there. In fact, some of it's even mine!" Then, once he was alone, he sat down at his desk, lit up a Pall Mall, and began reading.

Malinda and her sister, Margie, arrived in downtown Rugby late on Christmas Eve, smack in the middle of a raging, Hazel Miner blizzard. Malinda, always wanting to be completely in control of things, was driving; Marge cheerfully but grudgingly agreed to be the navigator. They'd come home to visit friends—a half dozen one-time high school classmates they hadn't seen in years.

Vonnegut had no idea what a Hazel Miner blizzard was but figured he'd soon find out.

They hadn't been back to Rugby in nearly a decade, so it was hard for them to believe that the town they drove into that night—rundown, dreary, badly in need of repair—was the lively, meticulously groomed village they'd grown up in. The difference between the then and the now rekindled fond memories of the little Christmas-themed snow globe Granny Winston displayed in the drawing room of her farmhouse over the holidays. Granny was gone now—taken from them too soon by a fierce, relentless cancer—but there would always be a place for her in their hearts.

Whenever either Margie or Malinda picked up the snow globe, shook it, and watched the snow settle gently to the bottom, they couldn't help wondering what it would be like to actually live in a village as beautiful as the one inside that globe. Rugby could never hope to compete with this little paradise, they'd think to themselves.

They couldn't understand why Mom and Dad chose to live in Rugby. And the fact was that Granny couldn't understand, either.

"This part of the country—especially up near the Canadian border—is flat as a pool table," she'd say. "It's either hot 'n' sweaty or cold 'n' icy, and nothing in between. And if that ain't enough to make you hate it, they get enough flooding up here every year to make an ocean out of a mud puddle. Noah's Ark would've been right at home in North Dakota, at least in mud season. And whoever makes them thousands o' sandbags every year must be filthy rich by now!"

Vonnegut stopped reading for a moment, then peered absentmindedly out the window above his desk, wondering how it was that a feisty, intellectually alert girl named

Cecelia Middling—an unlikely transplant from the West Coast—should suddenly show up on his doorstep unannounced, sharp as a tack and fiercely independent.

That girl has some serious writing chops, he mused—*and yet she's so young and fragile and wet behind the ears. But not in her writing! She's got the natural rhythm of conversation down pat. My sense is that she can paint either a pretty picture or an ugly reality, whichever one she needs at the moment, and do it damn near flawlessly! To do that so effortlessly, so early in her development as a writer, takes genuine talent.*

He lit another cigarette—he was a three-pack-a-day smoker—then continued reading.

The sidewalks in Rugby were deserted now. Any footprints that might have been there half an hour ago were buried under an ever-deepening blanket of snow. But Malinda, who hated winter, wasn't really surprised. "Nobody in his right mind would be out in weather *this* severe," she said. "A person could disappear into a drift and freeze to death!"

"You don't remember Clifford Thompson?" asked Margie. "They say he used to walk in all *kinds* of weather—conditions no one else would've been dumb enough to walk in."

"How could I *not* remember?" said Malinda. "The article I found on microfiche at the library—it was from the *Bowbells Tribune*—said he was more than eight feet tall! He couldn't step out of his house without being pointed at, laughed at, and even photographed without so much as a 'Do you mind?' Some kids even threw stones at him, just to watch his long legs flop around as he galloped away. Unbelievable!"

This doesn't even sound like fiction, thought Vonnegut. *It sounds like real people from the Real World—people I might have overheard at the bus station or ballpark in any American town. Sweet! Most authors take years to learn to write like this. Some never get there. The Land of Fiction is littered with failed writers and broken dreams. But my, oh my—Cecelia's train is already at the station! It's just sitting there on the tracks now, waiting for another North Woods Grace Metalious to get on board, head down to the Big Apple, and become an Overnight Sensation!*

He glanced up at the clock over his desk and realized it was getting late. He needed to finish reading and leave time for his own writing, so he got back down to business with Cecelia's manuscript.

"At least Thompson's parents were smart enough to get the hell out of Rugby," said Margie. "They packed up and moved east—as far away from the Dakotas and the gawkers as they could possibly get."

"Ha-ha!" laughed Malinda. "He was known as the Paul Bunyan of Wisconsin."

"The Big Cheese!" said Marge.

The two of them broke out in raucous laughter at the thought of Thompson trudging down Main Street during a blizzard, hunched over against the wind, his beard caked with ice, completely oblivious to his surroundings.

"His body might be in Rugby," said Marge, "but his mind was somewhere else—someplace far, far away from the Dakotas."

"Maybe on a cattle ranch in Abilene," said Malinda, "or a mountaintop in Tibet. Worse things have been known to happen."

"Hope they had a McDonald's there," said Marge. "He'd have been a little quicker on his feet with some fast food in his belly."

"Oh, *stop* it!" shrieked Malinda. "I can't take any more o' this silly talk. I swear, if you say one more thing as silly as that, I'm gonna . . ."

Vonnegut put the manuscript back in its envelope, then stretched his arms high up over his head, yawning.

Enough of this for now, he chuckled. *I don't need any more proof of her abilities as a writer! Ain't no doubt about it: with some savvy marketing, and a whole lot of personal discipline, Cecelia Middling's gonna ripen like a Florida orange in a heatwave. And when her debut novel is released—likely a year or two from now—readers are gonna stampede into America's bookstores. And I'm gonna do my part to make sure it happens!*

Then he stood up, strode back into the living room, and handed her the manuscript.

"Finished!" he said, a warm, appreciative smile widening across his long, Twain-like face. "Good stuff. *Damn* good stuff!"

Too stunned to find the right words, Cecelia sat there, silent as a statue, smiling warmly at him. *Yes, damn good stuff,* she thought to herself. *The feelings I'm having, I mean. Way better than good, actually.*

"You have the *Gift*, honey!" said Vonnegut. Then he bent down and firmly but politely hugged her. His gesture soon opened the floodgates, and tears of pure, uninhibited joy tumbled down her face.

"I *do*?" she replied. "The *Gift*?"

"You most certainly do," he said. "Now I want you to sit down and have some lunch with me, then go straight home and get to work on this story and then a *novel*. I've already got a publisher in mind—a longtime friend of mine who lives down in New York City—who'll take to your writing like a kitten takes to milk! I've known her for years, so trust me: she knows a bestseller only five pages into a submittal. She's the Angel who got me started as a fiction writer."

Oh, my God! whispered Cecelia to herself, too embarrassed to actually look Vonnegut in the eye. *A writer of Vonnegut's quality—a writer whose work I fell in love with on first reading—wants to help me, Cecelia Middling—a bucktoothed nobody from Rugby, North Dakota—get published!*

"Do me a favor, Mr. Vonnegut—sorry, can't help it—and *pinch* me. I just *have* to be dreaming!"

"Pinch the cheek of a soon-to-be-celebrated author?" laughed Vonnegut. "That would be inexcusable! Then again, if that's what Ms. Middling really wants, who am I to refuse her?"

Just as the renowned Kurt Vonnegut reached out to affectionately tweak the cheek of young Cecelia Middling, Best-Selling Author-to-Be, a series of violent pounding sounds broke through the calm, sweet poignancy of their exchange. Cecelia sat up abruptly in her bed and listened with alarm as the pounding on her bedroom door continued unabated.

Holy shit! she thought. *I must have been dreaming! Me and Kurt Fucking Vonnegut—the Literary Titan—together! And now my Old Man's come and spoiled it. He's ticked off for some reason. Nothin' new about that!*

Soon the poundings were punctuated with an angry staccato of obscenities—epithets hurled violently into the darkness by her father.

"Unlock the goddamn *door*," he shouted, sounding more than a little tipsy. "We've told you a thousand times not to lock your bedroom door at night. I mean, what if you needed help for some reason? How would we get in? Anyway, you've obviously been talking in your sleep—making so much noise, your mother and I can't sleep! And by the way, what was all that crap about *Mr. Vonnegut*? You mentioned his name at least half a dozen times. Sounded like you were having an Audience with the freakin' *Pope*! But really, what the fuck do you know about Kurt Vonnegut? Not much, by God, but *I* do. I know *plenty*! The man's a shitty writer—and a raging Socialist to boot!"

Stunned by the ferocity of her father's ill-informed rant, Cecelia fought back.

"You *bastard*!" she shrieked. "Have you been drinking again? When you talk like this—when you remind me how astonishingly ignorant you are—I'm ashamed to call you my father! By the way, in case you haven't noticed, I'm no longer a child. So you can just knock off the bullshit about locking my door."

Clay, who had indeed had a few too many nightcaps, went silent for what seemed to her like a good ten minutes. Then, ashamed of himself, he decided to settle down, play the compassionate father, and address her civilly.

"I'm sorry, honey," he slurred, "but . . ."

"Don't you *dare* call me 'honey,'" she snarled. "I'm not your honey. Never was and never will be! Don't be surprised if you wake up tomorrow morning and find an empty bedroom where your daughter used to sleep. I think I've finally had enough of the two of you!"

He stood there in his pajamas, motionless and still as a stone, wondering what, if anything, he should do next.

"Look, I know you're furious with me," he said, "but the last thing I'd want you to do is leave home! What can I do to make things better for you here? Tell me!"

"What can you *do*?" she said. "Anything you want to, as long as it doesn't include *me. That's* what you can do!"

He thought long and hard, checking off a mental laundry list of possible things he could do to appease her and keep the family together. *I'd never survive at work,* he thought to himself, *if they found out that my daughter—my beautiful, one-and-only child—had packed up and run away from home!* Then he suddenly remembered what he'd intended to tell her on the way to the awards ceremony. *I'll give it a try,* he mused. *It might just work.*

"Listen," he said. "Your mother and I had planned to tell you this on the way to the ceremony, but I . . ."

"I don't wanna *talk* about the ceremony!" she roared. "It was supposed to be a celebration—a way of honoring smart kids who actually give a damn about learning and *act* like they do. But you wouldn't know anything about that, would you! I mean you and Mom. For me, the 'night out' you're talking about wasn't a ceremony—it was a goddam *nightmare.* So please! No more 'ceremony' ever!"

"I wasn't gonna talk about that," he said. "It's done and gone! I just wish we hadn't gotten into that awful argument this evening. I should have known better. When I was a kid and Mrs. Langhorne caught us fighting on the playground during recess, she'd always say, 'It's a perfectly nice day, boys! Why spoil it with a spat?'"

"Guess you weren't listening, huh? Poor Mrs. Langhorne! And by the way, what happened just now between the two of us wasn't a 'spat'—it was a *showdown.* The 'High Noon' kind! You always try to make a molehill out of a mountain! Anyway, get to the point, would you? What were you going to tell me?"

"What I was going to tell you . . ." He paused, then turned red in the face and continued. "What I was going to tell you is that Brent Guertner, the half-brother you've never met, is going to come and live with us. We're finally gonna be a complete family again!"

"Oh, my fucking Christ!" she roared. "Why do you want Brent Guertner to live with us? Why would *I* want him to live with us? You can't even handle having *one* offspring under your roof, let alone *two*. So *tell* me, Dear Daddy. I can't wait to hear your answer!"

The idea of having to deal with yet another difficult personality at home was more than she could bear. *Three cats in a gunnysack is bad enough,* she thought. *Why tempt fate with a foursome?*

"We thought you might really enjoy having a brother!" said Clay. "Someone close at hand who you could share your hopes and dreams with! Besides, your mother loves Brent every bit as much as she loves you! He's her child, for heaven's sake!"

"As much as she loves *me*? Can't be very much then, can it!"

She wanted to leap out of bed, charge out of the house, and never come back again, but she realized that no matter how angry and disillusioned she was about things at home—especially her parents' failure to understand anything about her—leaving home might not be the smartest thing to do at the moment.

What am I thinking? she said to herself. *I have no job! No one I can think of to share my feelings with! To me, this place is more like a prison than a home. And yet I have no choice but to stay here for now.*

"I know your mother can be difficult at times," said Clay. "And don't forget: I have to put up with her little eruptions too, y' know. Welcome to long-term marriage! But it's different with you. When she gets rough with you on occasion, there's always a reason—a *good* reason. Please try to remember that when she's layin' into you about something! She has only your best interests in mind. Incidentally, it seems to me you know next to nothing about Brent Guertner. So instead of convicting the poor guy before you've even selected a jury, why not give him a chance to prove himself?"

She took a deep breath, fought back her tears, and then, feeling defeated, turned to her father.

"All right. Look: I'll stay for a while. But only until October, or maybe November, long enough to decide whether I can continue to stand living with the two of you—and on top of that, a total stranger—a guy barely out of his adolescence, lightyears away from maturity! I've had it up to *here* with guys like that! It was the only kind we had at school. So for the last ten minutes, I've been asking myself: does my half-brother read books? Does he have a job? Does he love learning as much as I do? Or is he just another 'dumb jock' type—a clueless sex fiend who sits around drooling over the photos in the latest *Penthouse* and has no high ambition other than gettin' into another pair o' panties? I'll give him one month to prove he's got something other than boobs and pussies between those jug handles of his!"

"I wish you wouldn't talk like that around me," said Clay. "We never used that kind o' language when we were your age."

"What would you rather I'd have said, 'mammary glands' and 'birth canals'? I'll bet you didn't use clinical words like that when *you* were in high school. Now if you don't mind, Daddy," she sneered, "I'd like to get some sleep. I'm gonna need all the energy I can muster for when Mr. Dumb Jock shows up."

* * *

Brent Guertner arrived early on September 12, 1985, sprawled out like a well-dressed garden snake in the back seat of a bright red VW Bug with a sign on top saying "Small Wonder Taxi—the Only Way to Travel!"

"All right, so he's *here!*" Cecelia said. "Wonderful! But why'd he take a *taxi*? Doesn't he have a car?"

"Yes, he has a car!" said her mother, clearly perturbed. "It's just that he got into a little trouble a few weeks ago—a minor DWI incident—and won't have his license back until late April."

"Well, shit!" said CeCe. "Just like I figured it was gonna be. No car, no job! He'll be on the dole before he even gets his bed made. By the way, I've never heard of a 'minor' DWI incident. Have you?"

"Don't worry about it!" said Birdie. "Your brother really has learned his lesson; he'll be back on the road by Easter. Promise!"

Birdie looked out through the living room window and saw her son walking up the driveway, dressed to kill and carrying a duffle bag, a hockey stick, and a portable television.

"He's coming in right now!" she said. "Now I want *you* to do the welcoming. It'll make him feel like a part of the family right away. And mind you, I expect you to be on your best behavior. So don't you dare mention that business about the DWI! Understand?"

"Yes, Mother, I understand. *Everyone* understands you; it's a *requirement!* Tell you what: I'll just start the conversation by asking him all about his AWOL father. Bet *that'll* get things off to a good start!"

"Like hell you will!" said Birdie. "Like *hell* you will! Listen, he's about to ring the doorbell, so get over there—be a good sister—and be ready to greet him!"

As soon as Brent was inside, he dropped his things down on the carpet, smiled inauthentically at the sister he was seeing for the very first time, then strode over to

Birdie, hugged her warmly, and dutifully planted a glad-to-be-here kiss on her forehead. He had to bend over to reach her, because he was a good six foot four—well over a head taller than his mother. And with a brand new pair of bright turquoise Saucony Jazz Originals knotted together by the laces and draped around his neck, he looked for all the world like the classic Mall Rat, just home from a successful jaunt to the local shoe store.

Nothing but the best for my boy Brennie, Birdie thought, glowing with pride at the way her son looked now that he was all grown up. *We always wanted nothing but the best,* she laughed, *even when makin' babies.*

Brent settled in right away, working from a hidebound presumption that he was doing the Middlings a favor by agreeing to stay with them in the first place. In less than a week it became obvious to everyone around him—except, of course, his mother—that he didn't understand the concept of teamwork and wouldn't have honored it even if he did. Birdie's hen-on-an-egg approach to motherhood meant that, in her mind, Brent Guertner could do no wrong. So instead of offering over the next few days to pitch in and help with chores, he concentrated on making adjustments to every room in the house, entirely to accommodate his own selfish needs.

The biggest battle was destined to be fought in the bathroom, and from the very first week of Brent's arrival, it raged.

Thanks to him, CeCe now had to share the towel rack across from the bathtub with her half-brother. "That crummy little towel was taking up too much space anyway," he told her. "And by the way, what'd you expect me to do with my towel—hang it off the ceiling light? It's twice as big as yours. Why? Because I'm twice as big as *you*! It's about time for you to use that little brain bucket of yours, sister!"

Thanks to him, the space where she'd always kept her toiletries was reduced overnight by more than half. And when she complained about it, her mother found an empty shoe box in the hallway closet, brought it straight to her daughter, and shoved it into her arms. "There," she sneered, "your very own medicine cabinet! Just for you, Darling Daughter!"

And thanks to Brent, the toilet seat—the one they had no choice but to share—the one he never bothered to lift up before his morning pee—was nearly always sprinkled with his very own piss: a pungent, foul-smelling liquid excrescence more the color of hard cider than genuine urine. And, not surprisingly, it always seemed to be CeCe who had either to clean up the mess he'd made or squat down on it unintentionally, doubling the humiliation.

As for Clay, he wanted to lay into Birdie's son right away and tell him to get his act together. But to keep the peace in the family—and especially to avoid conflict with his wife, which was always, inevitably, ugly—he held his feelings close to his vest. The way he saw it, they'd already had enough marital conflict to last a lifetime. So why in the world would he want to pour kerosene on a marriage that was already about to change from a bed of smoldering embers to a fierce cauldron of flames?

It was when CeCe learned one day, quite by accident, that her parents had set up a special bank account to pay for Brent's college education—something they'd shrugged off as a waste of money whenever she asked for help with her own schooling—that her growing resentment reached its zenith.

She finally realized that with Brent Guertner in the house, being excessively babied and lavishly praised, she would never have the satisfaction of being treated as an equal and respected for her accomplishments.

So, without saying a word to them about her accelerating discontent, and without being rude or combative in any way with Brent, she quietly, slowly, and deliberately planned her getaway. *They won't even notice I'm gone,* she laughed. *It'll make my exodus from this madhouse that much more satisfying!*

For the next two weeks, she waited until well after midnight, when everyone else had turned in for the night, to begin packing. When she could tell from their snoring that they were sound asleep, she worked down a list of things she would need to survive on her own, checking them off one by one.

First on the list was toiletries. She would be leaving home with a little less than $130 in her purse, money she found in her mother's sorry excuse for a bank—the long-forgotten cookie jar on the top shelf of the pantry. She needed to take as much of it as she dared for genuine emergencies, with a little left over, she hoped, for what she affectionately called her "feminine dainties."

To save the purloined money for more urgent matters, she helped herself to the basics—deodorant, shampoo, hand soap, toothpaste, washcloths, and, just to tweak her half-brother's nose in absentia, a beach towel from his duffel bag with the words "Come & Get Me, Sweetie; I'm a Hunka-Hunka Burnin' Love!" printed on it. *No modesty in that boy,* she snorted.

She knew he wouldn't miss any of those items until at least a month after her departure, simply because he was shamelessly filching the very same items from Clay and Birdie's bathroom cabinet and storing them under his bed. Sponging off their supply of necessities allowed him to keep all the pocket money he needed for things like beer, cigarettes, snacks, and French Ticklers—the typical post-adolescent Boy Toy that makes the male of the species feel all grown up when he's anything but.

While rifling through Brent's bag, she came across a large, multipurpose pocket knife—the kind hunters and campers use to solve problems they encounter while in the woods. *Now that's a real beauty!* she smiled, then slipped it into the side pocket of her jeans. *He'll never miss it; he's too busy sniffin' out the ladies.*

To augment her dwindling supply of maxipads, she helped herself to the stash hidden behind her mother's quilt rack. She wouldn't touch the cosmetics; she considered them to be a frivolous, self-absorbed waste of money. The dollars she saved by avoiding them allowed her to spend more on books, pens and pencils, bus fare, an occasional movie, basic over-the-counter medical supplies, and—when really needed—a new bra or an assortment of playfully themed, brightly colored panties.

She already had a dildo—a shocking pink Hitachi Magic Wand she'd bought on the sly after school one day, using what was left of her grandmother's Christmas gift money. "Works like a cinch in a sexual pinch," her friend Ashley loved saying, and because CeCe had faith in All Things Ashley, she didn't bother to compare brands before buying.

Back home in her bedroom that evening, she'd removed the wand from its package, stroked its beautifully designed contours, and decided to name it Buzzy after a memorable figure from her past—Buzz McSworley, the blue-eyed, wavy-haired beefcake who had sat next to her in trigonometry. McSworley had little interest in anything academic—especially higher math—so instead of paying attention to the teacher as he ought to have been doing, he stared unapologetically at Cecelia's chest area, hoping he might one day give his life meaning by catching a long-desired glimpse of the proud, protruding nipples beneath her sweater.

But that was high school, and, happily, that phase of her life was over. Cecelia Middling was now a young woman of great energy and idealism, eager to learn and increasingly wise in the ways of womanhood. And on top of all that, she was fed up with her home life, hungry for freedom, and more than ready for whatever adventures might come her way. *Why,* she would ask herself over and over again—especially late at night, when she was alone—*do my parents never say that they love me? That I'm beautiful? That I'm intelligent and they're proud of me because of it?*

With CeCe's escape only hours away now, she realized she was more and more focused not on the past or present, but on the future. And yet she figured there were still things worth doing, right there in the Here & Now. So as soon as she'd finished packing, she climbed into her pajamas, scrambled into bed, revved up her Buzzy, and, to celebrate her imminent evacuation, took a long, gratifying ride on her do-it-yourself Tilt-a-Whirl.

Works like a charm, she panted when it was over. Then, once she was back down on solid ground, she lulled herself into a blissful sleep by reading from her deluxe, richly annotated edition of Shelley's *Frankenstein*—the novel Mr. Thornwood had so thoughtfully given her on the day of her graduation from Cloverton.

She slept better that night than she'd slept in months. *I'll soon have a future worth living,* she smiled. And she was comforted by the reality that she wasn't alone in her elation, because Smokey, her beloved Teddy, was right there beside her, smiling every bit as contentedly as she was. She would be leaving her half-brother behind less than a month after he arrived, and, looking back, she would wonder how she'd ever managed to endure him that long.

Chapter Nineteen

On Thursday, October 7—a day she knew she would never forget—Cecelia got herself quickly dressed, wriggled into a faded blue-jean jacket she'd discovered the night before in the hallway closet—probably her mother's, but she really didn't give a damn *whose* it was—then grabbed the travel bag and her teddy and slipped quietly out the back door of the house into a chill but optimistic autumn morning, her eyes moist with tears.

Go figure! she wondered. *Why should I want to cry at a moment like this? I'm escaping!* But she knew with certainty that the droplets, small and surprisingly unaggressive, were tears not of sadness but of joy—watery expressions of pride in having finally found the courage to leave, flavored with welcome relief from what had become an untenable situation within the Middlings' onetime ever-so-sweet, *Leave It to Beaver* household, now gone terminally sour.

She knew there was a municipal park with a zoo in it somewhere well beyond the outskirts of Minot—called Roosevelt Park, if she had it right—so she immediately struck out toward the edge of the city, determined to find it. Only a few days ago, a postman had assured her that just beyond the far side of the park she'd find a dense stand of tall, stately trees with leaves the size of elephant ears. "They're absolute whoppers," he'd shouted from his mail truck; "you'd have to be blind not to see 'em!"

"Great," she laughed. "They'll make a really good cover!" She figured that if she were to get there sometime after dark, she'd have no problem; she'd be able to find either an out-of-the-way park bench or a hard-to-detect clearing, then sleep there for the night with the trees as refuge.

After a long, arduous walk, she arrived at the park and found a well-marked path to the zoo. Walking quietly, she tried not to make any noises that might cause someone—a policeman, or perhaps a night watchman—to wonder what she was doing in the park, all alone, so long after closing hours. As she passed by a dimly lit enclosure, she heard the familiar twittering of penguins, a sound somewhere between a scrawk and a gurgle. She'd always loved penguins: the peculiar, high-pitched way they converse amongst themselves, the Chaplinesque quality of their walking. But tonight, at least, she wished for her sake that they'd give their overworked beaks a rest and remain silent for a change.

Eventually she arrived at what must have been the southern perimeter of the park, then came to an abrupt halt, stared all around her, and shook her head in dismay.

A stand of tall, stately trees? "Bullshit!" she cried. "I've been hoodwinked!" Instead of the trees with elephant ears she'd been promised, she saw only a broad, gray ribbon of asphalt choked with traffic, and high above it a sign saying Burdick Expressway East.

She stared as a long, steady stream of vehicles—mostly eighteen-wheelers, but with a few tiny sedans sprinkled amongst them here and there—moved steadily along, the exhausted drivers eager to make their cross-country deliveries and call it a day.

Welcome to Middle America, she grumbled. *There's no pedestrian overpass!* Then she heard the ear-splitting shriek of air brakes mingled with an unholy chorus of honking horns and squealing tires. She watched in exasperation as the traffic came to an abrupt, grinding halt.

"Well, *shit!*" she groaned. "I'll be here until sundown or

worse, waiting to get across!" Then it dawned on her that the delay was more a blessing than an inconvenience.

"What the hell's wrong with me?" she mumbled, half in amusement and half in an all-too-familiar ritual of self-denigration. But she also knew it was time to dispense with the self-pity. After all, she was on her own now, and while brooding would get her nowhere, some action—a plan and the courage to implement it—*would*. "I'll hitchhike!" she yelped. It'll get me out o' this mess fast. What was I gonna do, anyway—call a taxi? I'd blow at least half o' my travel money with that!"

With a plan in place, her old optimism returned full force. *There just has to be a restaurant somewhere east of here,* she thought. *I'm famished.*

She scampered down the incline to get closer to the traffic, then ran her eyes along the sides of a half dozen stalled semis and zeroed in on the one with the words *Beanz Meanz Heinz!* along the entire length of its side panels. She shouted at the driver, but because his windows were up and the honking horns were so loud, he obviously wasn't able to hear her. He couldn't see her, either, because the cab's windows were coated with a nearly impenetrable layer of grime accumulated while traveling hundreds of miles across the prairie in all sorts of weather.

To make contact with the driver, she doubled her fist and pounded as hard as she could on the passenger door. Finally, she managed to catch his attention, and down came the passenger side window.

"What the fuck do y' think you're *doin'*, little girl?" roared the driver over the growl of the truck's idling engine, an unwarranted sneer of masculine superiority chiseled into his granite-hard expression.

Never one for timidity, she hurled his insolence right back at him. "Asking for a ride! *That's* what the fuck I'm doin'! And for your information, I'm not a little girl!"

The driver, a freight train of a man with bulging biceps, a long, bedraggled ponytail, and a wiry blanket of hair on his chest and forearms, saw the fire in her eyes, shed his aggravation, and burst out laughing.

"All right, whatever! I like your style! So come on up and climb in!" He extended a generously tattooed arm down to her and offered his assistance. "But be careful," he laughed, "it's a long way down to Planet Earth from up here. And don't worry, honey. I'm harmless. Really!"

She shouldered her backpack, dismissed the offer of assistance, then grabbed the side bar, lumbered up into the cab, and plopped herself down on the passenger seat. She was relieved to see his smile but annoyed that he'd had the temerity to describe her—a woman who'd obviously put her childhood behind her by now—as a 'little girl.'

The air in the cab was an olfactory horror show—a repulsive amalgamation of diesel fumes, body odor, and the rank aroma of what appeared to be a trio of half-eaten, long-forgotten Happy Meals gone green with mold. Because there was never enough food in one Happy Meal to satisfy his hunger, he always bought three of them whenever he got off the expressway. After all, they were cheap, and he liked the little toys that came with them. After every completed long-haul, he'd bring the gifts home and present them proudly to his grandchildren.

With just one snap of his gnarled, grease-stained fingers, he'd transformed himself from a cantankerous old geezer into a kind-hearted, avuncular Santa clone.

"So where you goin', young lady?" he boomed. When the line of traffic began to move again, he wheeled smoothly out along with it.

"East," she said, still a little winded from what it took to climb up into the rig. "As far east as you can take me."

"All *right,* then," he said. "East it shall be! I mean, I don't really have a lot o' choice in the matter, now do I. Gotta work my way down to Pittsburgh 'fore the end of the week. By the way, in case you haven't figured it out, I'm a fiercely devoted Archie Bunker fan. That's why I called you 'little girl' before. It's funny! Honestly, there was no other reason!"

"Oh, I noticed the Archie resemblance, all right," said Cecelia. "Only had to look and listen! But more like Oscar Madison, I should think."

"We do make a rather Odd Couple, don't we!" he smiled.

"Couple, my ass!" she snapped. "I've known you for less than ten minutes. Hasn't happened, ain't *gonna* happen!" Then, remembering how easy it had always been for her to lose her temper when affronted, she cooled herself down and looked slowly around her.

"But really," she continued. "Just *look* at this!" She pointed down at the dense thicket of blackening banana peels, gnawed-on apples, and gummed-over, rancid-smelling cigar butts, then shook her head in dismay. "Your cab is filthy! A pigsty on wheels! I mean, just take a whiff; it smells like a pool hall! Hope your home's in better condition than this."

He slowed down along with the trucks ahead of him, then glanced over at Cecelia for a moment, a mildly derisive smile on his face.

"OK, so you're a Neatnik," he chuckled. "Fine! How sweet! But that kind o' thing isn't for me. Fact is, I'm happy as a pig in shit here in my rig. *Better* be, too, 'cause that's where I've been spending my life for the last quarter century." He looked over at her again briefly, then up at the rear-view mirror. "If you wanna know the truth," he blushed, "I see my dashboard ten times more than I see my Old Lady. Not supposed to be that way, I know. But when you think about it, it's probably a good deal all around."

"Oh, c'mon," she laughed. "She can't be all that happy about it, can she? I mean, about hardly ever seeing her husband!"

"Oh, you'd be surprised," he grinned. "She probably jumps up and down like a goddam *cheerleader* right after I close the front door and head out for another assignment. I know *I* do. I mean, I do a freakin' *Fred Astaire* as soon as she stops wavin' her fat little hands out the window at me and goes back to those stinkin' soap operas. What a phony baloney hypocrite that woman can be!"

Cecelia tried to imagine the man sitting next to her in his truck suddenly back at home in the kitchen, a frilly pink apron tied round his bulbous, hirsute belly, doing the dishes or making lamb chops for supper. But she just couldn't make it work. She knew he'd never change his ways, so as the jam eased up and they were on their way again, she dropped the subject and let him jabber on.

"By the way," she said, "you haven't even told me your name."

"By God, you're *right*!" he shouted, banging the butt of his left hand on the steering wheel. Time to fess up. It's Fenton! Fenton Clevenger, to be thorough. Some people call me Fent, and that's fine with me. You can, too. The truth is that the Clevengers were a very big deal around these parts a century ago, but you might say we've kind o' gone to seed; nothing much came of us, unless you want to think of a long-haul trucker as Royalty."

"King of the Road!" said Cecelia. "I should think that's Royalty!"

Clevenger smiled broadly, then glanced over at her, his eyes rolling. "And *your* name? I mean, a pretty young thing like you can't possibly be an Isabel, or, God help us, an Adeline! Say it isn't so!"

"No thanks to those," she laughed. "It's Cecelia! Cecelia

Middling. I'm fine with the first name, but not with the last one. The truth is I'm trying hard—*really* hard—to cut myself loose from that one."

"Skeletons, huh?" said Clevenger. "No need to go there again. Better to stay right here in the present, right? Nothin' to worry about here—at least not right this moment." He shrugged his shoulders, then returned to his more nonchalant demeanor.

A half mile down the road, he turned on the radio, and Chuck Berry's "Back in the USA" came roaring out of the KLH speakers he'd mounted at the left and right of the cab. CeCe loved Chuck Berry, but the volume was excruciating. Even worse, the current craze for songs with hyper-patriotic themes never failed to get on her nerves.

"Looking hard for a drive-in, searching for a corner café," sang the man who'd made "My Ding-a-Ling" a number one hit. "And a jukebox jumping with records like in the USA."

And then came the inevitable clarion call for flag-waving, heart-pounding patriotism: "Well, I'm so glad I'm livin' in the USA! Yes, I'm so glad I'm livin' in the USA! Anything you want, we got right here in the USA!"

"Jesus!" she shouted over the hard-driving rhythms of the song. "How 'bout turning that radio down? I mean, I'm still gonna need my ears when I finally get out o' this road coffin!"

"Road coffin?" said Clevenger, frowning. "*Road coffin*?"

"It's just wordplay," she laughed. "Just trying to be funny. So what's the harm in that?"

"No harm, I suppose. Unless, of course, you happen to be an undertaker—or maybe a brand new cadaver, fresh out o' the refrigerator. Anyway, would you mind telling me why a fragile young thing like yourself, a regular Flower in the Meadow from *my* perspective, is traveling like this—all alone, for God's sake!—on the highways of America? It can be pretty damn dangerous, you know. A lot o' really bad dudes out here, guys on the prowl with nothin' to do but make your life miserable! I know, because I've tangled with a few of 'em myself. You might say they're truly an obnoxious exception to the Rules of the Road as I've experienced them."

"I hope you weren't the *reason* for those entanglements," she bantered. "Men can be so stupid! I mean, why make trouble where there *isn't* any? Why do they do that?"

Genuinely insulted by her youthful insolence, Clevenger hit the air brake, swerved off the highway, and came to a noisy, inelegant stop.

"So you think I'm stupid?" he shouted. "You think I'm uneducated?" He reached over, grabbed a beat-up, coffee-stained paperback off the dashboard, and waved it aggressively in her face. "Here!" he roared. "Have a look at *this*!"

Cecelia yanked the book out of his hand, turned it over, and mouthed the title quietly to herself. *Tropic of Cancer. Holy shit!*

Cecelia had read *Tropic of Cancer* cover to cover, late at night by flashlight, when she was thirteen. She was smart enough to know that if her father had found out she'd been reading a book as sexually explicit as *Tropic of Cancer*—a book, she found out later on, that Mr. Thornwood had read and thoroughly enjoyed—he'd have had an absolute fit. *Guess I owe those dudes Big Time,* she laughed. *Thornwood for admitting to me that he'd read the book and enjoyed it, and Miller for writing it in the first place. Thanks to them, I know a whole lot more about sex than I might otherwise have known.* The book had also taught her the importance of never allowing herself to feel ashamed of anything having to do with sexuality.

She put the book back on the dashboard, then stared straight ahead of her, at a loss for words.

"Why so silent?" he said. "Are you surprised to learn that a hairy, ham-fisted guy like me—a man who drives a semi for a living—also happens to read some really heavy-duty books in his spare time? Does the truth about me offend you in some way? Have I shattered your image of what a working stiff is supposed to look like, do, and be?"

"None of the above," she whispered. "I guess I was just a bit surprised that you'd be reading a book like *Tropic of Cancer.*"

"I don't know why!" he said. "I mean, it's just another book, right? And a damn *good* one, too. It's about a whole lot more than kinky sex and wild abandon. But of course you wouldn't know that, would you. You really should read that book sometime. It's a real humdinger! Then, by God, you'd know."

Cecelia winced at his snide remarks but decided not to stir the conversational pot by telling him she'd already read it—and a whole lot earlier in her life than he had. Besides, she was exhausted now. She figured that without all the mental badminton, she might actually have a chance to fall asleep, then wake up tomorrow morning refreshed.

But Clevenger wasn't done. "I've also read Kafka's *Metamorphosis,*" he said, ready to provide her with a long-winded, self-congratulatory litany of the beloved Classics he'd devoured over the years. Proof positive, he presumed, of his undeniable literacy.

"Shelley's *Frankenstein!* Russell's *Why I Am Not a Christian!* I even wrestled with *Principia Mathematica* for a while back in high school. You know, the one he wrote with that flaky number-cruncher Alfred North Whitehead. Finished it in just three days, too! But guess what? Old Man Quackenbush, my calc teacher, gave up on it only three pages in. Said it was way too hard for him. When my classmates and I found out about that, he became the laughingstock of the entire school. I wanna tell you, we really had that old geezer's number!"

He leaned back, caught his breath, then waited patiently for her to be gobsmacked at his literary prowess.

"So!" he said. "Wanna hear more? Or maybe it's better you don't. Maybe your heart couldn't take it!"

"*No mas*, Mr. Thuringer," she said quietly, testing the sophistication of his taste in humor.

"I like black forest a lot more," he quipped. "But just in case you don't remember, it's *Clevenger*, not Thuringer. Anyway, what's your next move? What's the Man Upstairs got in mind for you?"

"To be honest," she said, "I don't give a shit what the 'Man Upstairs' has in mind for me. I'm a hard-core skeptic, not a True Believer. Right now, all I believe in is a decent meal and a safe place to stay until I decide what's best for me next."

"You mean like a motel, or maybe a youth hostel? Somethin' cheap, minus the bedbugs?"

"No! Like a place outdoors, under the stars—a place that won't cost me one red penny. I love the outdoors! Even sleep outside on occasion, just because it feels so good. Nothing fancy, of course; just enough tick-free space to accommodate my worn-out carcass. I even like to *dance* outdoors on occasion, usually late at night. That's the best time of all."

"I'd sure as hell love to see *that*," he said. "It's not every day—I should say, *night*—when you can see a comely lass like yourself prancing about in the woods. But alas—no camps or parks in the immediate vicinity. By the way, why at night? What's so special 'bout that?"

"The *moon*," she said, "that's what's so special. It's cool and delicious, that moon. And the Man up there? *He* is, too! I can easily lose myself in the moment, dancing by moonlight. And to tell you the truth, it's almost as if Mr.

Moon is down here on the forest floor with me, and we're dancing together, cheek-to-cheek. It's so divine!"

"Oh, you're just *chock full* of surprises," said Clevenger. "I'm lucky. Old Man Trucker just got to hear the *poetic* side of you!"

"I hope you're not making fun of me," she said. "Trust me! I was dead serious about that moonlight thing. The Man in the Moon is one smart dude. He may be all alone up there, but not really! He has innumerable friends with him up in the heavens, but they keep their distance. They know their place in the Scheme of Things. And they're so damn magnificent, every last one of 'em! So mysterious! And so refreshingly inscrutable, too! There aren't any Know-It-Alls in the Firmament; they're all down here on earth, makin' life miserable for people like me."

Captivated, Clevenger listened intently to Cecelia's inspired ramblings. He was deeply moved by her sensibilities—swept away, briefly, into a world without long lines of road-hogging semis, impossible deadlines, and truckers' hemorrhoids.

Why aren't there more Cecelia Middlings in the world, he lamented. *Why is there not a Cecelia in* my *life?* Then he remembered he was much older now, and, at his age, sweet perfection—everything in its place and the fondest dreams come true, exquisite and eternal—would never quite be available to him again.

Wondering why Clevenger had suddenly become so silent, Cecelia reached over and tapped him gently on the shoulder.

"Where have you gone, Mr. Trucker?" she asked him. "What mysterious detour have you taken from the Highway to Heaven?"

"Oh, just a little side trip," he said, doing his best to conceal his real emotions. Yes, the well-intended tap had done what she wanted—brought him back to some semblance of reality there in the sometimes stifling confines of his cab. But he wasn't altogether happy about it. And, because he was no longer in the mood to look for answers to the Big Questions, his mind began to drift.

The great authors—the thinkers and doers of the world—had given him intense pleasure and lots and lots of intellectual rewards. Russell, Dostoevsky, Sontag. But had they really offered him answers to questions about affairs of the heart? Or had his countless hours on the road, lugging crates of goodies to obscure destinations, kept those answers out of reach? *Maybe I'm spending too much time worrying about me,* he pondered, *and too little time considering the wants and needs of others.*

He sat there in the driver's seat, fidgeting with his gear stick while keeping his eye on the traffic. Then he remembered, suddenly, that Cecelia had asked him a question but he'd failed to answer it.

"CeCe!" he said, much too loudly. "You said you want a safe place to stay outdoors, and I've just come up with an answer: The Experimental Forest! It's only a few miles east of here, just off Burdick East in Denbigh. I could get you there in less than an hour."

"I don't need a friggin' experimental forest," she snarled. "I need the real thing!" She could hear how silly her little rant must have sounded to him, so she did the smart thing and simmered down. "Anyway, if you think that place fits the bill, then take me there, Mr. de Soto."

"Oooh! A *history* buff, too!" he laughed. "Is there anything this girl doesn't know?" He kept his eyes on the road, then smiled to himself, jammed his rig into high gear, and sped happily down the highway.

Most of the nomads I pick up while on the road are duller 'n a sink full o' dishwater, he chuckled. *Real 'no-future' losers. But this little chickie—now here's a girl with actual blood in her veins! She's obviously smart as hell, and though she may not realize it yet, oh, so friggin' pulchritudinous!* He blushed a deep salmon pink, then pulled himself together. "Please, God," he whispered into the rear view mirror, suddenly flung back into his recklessly libidinous adolescent years. "Make me young and irresistible again!"

When they finally reached the western perimeter of the Experimental Forest, a heavy rain was falling—the kind of violent, soaked-to-the-skin downpour that can suddenly turn to ice and make even the most stouthearted drivers head for the nearest underpass. Clevenger knew that hailstones in North Dakota can turn a brand new car into a junker in less than a New York minute, so he was thankful that the weather was still warm.

"Well, we're almost here," he said, doing his damnedest to smile in spite of the sudden realization that he really didn't want her to leave.

"Guess it's the end of the trail—the end for *you*, anyway. As for me, I've got nearly 1,300 miles to go before I can get out o' this sardine can and flop down on a bed—preferably my own bed, not one in some cheap motel in Shitty City."

"You know, I'm truly sorry to hear that," she said. "But hey: it's *your* reality, not mine. I just need a little sleep. As long as I finally get it—and as long as it isn't in this gas guzzler—I'll be happy. Of course, I can't afford to be all that picky 'bout where it's gonna *be*. Truth is I *hate* it around here. The place is so ridiculously flat! The lack of anything taller than a bus token actually depresses me!"

"That bad?" he frowned. "Y' know, everywhere on the planet you can find things to be disappointed in. But it's never the whole story. Never! When you open your heart and mind, the bad things are soon dwarfed by all the good things, right there for the taking. It's not as if they suddenly appeared out of nowhere like a flying saucer. They've always been there, just for Yours Truly. I mean, *think* about it!"

"Well, I suppose Minot wasn't really all that bad," she said, surprised and even a little touched by the realization that, deep down inside, Clevenger—a burly, snarling beast of a man—was a world of tenderness that she'd obviously failed to see at first. It occurred to her that she should give the man a chance to reveal himself on *his* terms and *his* schedule, not hers.

"I've learned to *like* some things about this region," she confessed. "The eerie, never-ending silence of life in Minot compared to the cacophony of life in the Big City; the astonishing lack of anything approaching 'traffic'; the outrageously friendly people—even complete strangers— around every damn corner. But in my home? With my alleged 'parents'? Thanks to them, Minot had become a living hell for me!"

Clevenger wondered if he'd been too harsh and too hasty when he sized her up so negatively only moments after she'd climbed into his rig. Looking back on that moment, he knew she hadn't deserved the way he'd treated her at first.

"Listen, honey," he said, "I know I'm full o' bluster a lot o' the time. Some would even call it bullshit! But really, it's just my way of coping with so much time on the road, my ass numb from all the sitting that goes with the job. It's pretty much a solitary lifestyle, and it can get damned lonely out here! Only rarely do I ever come across the kind of good-na- tured back-and-forth you've brought into this cab."

Cecelia glanced over at him, then watched with quiet fascination as one large, pearl-shaped tear began forming in his eye, preparing for descent. He knew she'd seen it, and because of that, he quickly brushed it away with the back of his hand.

It was obvious that he wanted her to think it had never really happened, so she looked away and said nothing. For the next two or three minutes, the only sounds in the cab were the back-and-forth of their steady breathing, an occasional yawn, and, from the outside, the relentless thump-thump-thump of the truck's tires as they rolled over the cracks between road slabs.

It was Clevenger who first broke the silence.

"Tell you what, Ms. . . . Ms. . . . ."

"Ms. Middling," she replied. "Cecelia Middling. By the way, it's nice to know you're up to date on the salutations. I never did like being referred to as Miss. I mean, Miss what? Far as I'm concerned, they can save that stuff for the beauty contests."

"Oh, yeah," he said, "sorry! I've never been good at remembering names. Anyway, as I was about to tell you, instead of tryin' to sleep outside, in a cold, dank forest, no doubt crawlin' with gnats and mosquitoes—and probably black flies big as horses—how 'bout sleeping right here in my bunk?" Then he jerked his righthand thumb over his shoulder, kept his eyes on the road, and waited, smiling to himself, for her to say something— anything, really.

But instead of responding, she went silent, turned her back to him, and huddled up against the passenger door, as far away from him as possible. He wondered what he'd done to make her turn against him, and then suddenly he understood.

"Oh, *Jesus*!" he shouted. "I didn't mean with *me*! I meant you'd sleep in my *bunk—alone—*right there behind you. See? And *me*, I'd just keep on drivin' while you get some rest! Check it out: It's got curtains all around, and the walls in there are padded, so you'd hear a lot less road noise. There's even a nice little Port-o-Potty back there, right behind the bunk. Lots o' privacy for M' Lady, right? I mean, a guy couldn't hear the Upper Falls from in there!"

"I'm no dummy, Mr. Clevenger," she growled. "Been around the track enough times to know where the finish line is." *He'd understand me better,* she thought, *if he knew what I did on Arnold Legume's couch that night.* "At this point in my life, I must confess that, other than Kurt Vonnegut, the only male of the species I've come to trust and respect—unconditionally—is my onetime high school teacher, Alec Thornwood. He was a real gem! Treated me like an Intelligent Being—fed my hunger for learning in the most imaginative ways! And now, to my great disappointment, he's no longer in my life."

She slumped down in her seat, feeling deflated, then laid her head back and stared listlessly at the ceiling.

"I guess you can tell by now that, thanks to a long series of star-crossed encounters with the male animal, I've learned to be very choosy—ever so cautious—about who I spend time with."

Then she turned toward Clevenger and, with genuine, heartfelt emotion, addressed him. "Listen, you seem nice enough! I'd have to be a real dimwit not to see that! But y' know what? I'm not taking any chances, even with a sensitive, well-read granddaddy like yourself. So how bout doin' me a favor? Pull this rust bucket over—right now— and let me get the hell out o' here!"

He could tell she meant business, so he did as he was told, hit the brakes, and pulled off to the side of the road. The moment the rig came to a halt, she grabbed her backpack off the floor and, before he could stop her, shoved open the passenger door and scampered down to the ground. The rain had tapered off, so she figured she wouldn't have trouble walking anywhere.

"Thanks for the ride," she said, looking wistfully up at

him. "I really do mean it! But, in case you haven't noticed, I'm a Modern Girl, not a Delicate Flower. I'm quite capable of taking care of myself."

"Swell!" he shouted over the roar of the idling engine. "So you're sensitive. And you're delicate. Good for you! And just a little bit too full of yourself, I might add—good at playing the victim. But how *practical* do you allow yourself to be when practicality is precisely what's needed?"

He continued: "Listen, you might be surprised to know that people can be simultaneously intelligent and practical! They can walk and chew intellectual gum at the same time, just like the High Rollers—the Intelligentsia! But really, Ms. Middling, you need to ask yourself just how competent a judge of character you really are! It takes *seasoning*. I mean, can't you see? I would never have taken advantage of the situation! I would never have harmed you. I'm a *trucker*, not a rapist! People have this idea that long-haulers are all the same—that we're either night prowlers or hatchet murderers or both. But it's not true. Promise! And by the way, what were you gonna do, hitch a ride on a cement truck? Grab some roadkill for supper? Shit in a ditch? You could do a whole lot worse than this!"

He gave his anger a chance to subside, then continued. "Now get your tail feathers back up here and let Mr. Heinz do the long-haulin'! You can help yourself to some snacks—deli sandwiches, boiled eggs, trail mix, sodas—right there in the cooler above your head. Then you can wriggle up into that bunk and get some shut-eye. Third Avenue North is only twenty-some miles from here. Once we get there I'll hang a right, and we'll have you down to that Forest in Denbigh 'fore the frogs are done croakin'!"

Goddammit, she thought to herself, *he's right! Without him and his state-of-the-art semi, where the fuck would I eat? Or take a dump, for that matter? I mean, Ol' John Brown's been knockin' on my door for the last half hour. And there's just got to be toilet paper in this rig, 'cause I sure as hell don't have any. Even worse, do I really want to be thumbin' it again? I'd have to be out of my mind to want to do that.*

She looked up at him, shrugged her shoulders, then climbed back up into the cab.

Clevenger took care not to appear to be gloating, but he knew that having persuaded her to trust him in spite of her skepticism was a personal victory, and he couldn't help being proud of himself.

Cecelia, more hungry than embarrassed now, had her hand in the cooler before he'd even managed to pull back out onto the highway. She gnawed feverishly on a stone-cold meatball sub, took a swig of Dr. Pepper, and gnawed again. When she was done, she unleashed one long, thunderous belch of satisfaction, wiped her mouth clean, and turned to him.

"And don't you dare gloat, Mr. Clevenger. I despise people who gloat!" Then she made her way back to the Port-o-Potty, did her business, and climbed up into the bunk. In less than ten minutes she'd fallen sound asleep, greatly relieved to have allayed herself of her worst apprehensions.

Jesus, chuckled Clevenger to himself. *Smart as a whip, cute as a pin-up, and a champion belcher to boot! Wish I was always this lucky on the road. Work's been fun again! But it won't be once this little Smart Girl jumps ship.*

He'd hoped to make good time—more for her sake than his—but this time around, fate had another plan for him. Eastbound traffic slowed to an intermittent crawl, and the taillights ahead stretched on farther than Heinz could see. The cause was yet another gruesome vehicular catastrophe—this one when a Datsun 240Z, traveling in excess of 90 miles an hour, blew a tire and smashed into a bridge abutment. The Datsun then caught fire, consuming not only the car and its driver but the driver of the car it had torn into on the way to the abutment. Clevenger, who'd suffered more than his share of costly delays over the years, took this one in stride. *Probably another wreck. Ain't no way around it,* he chuckled, *so no use gettin' my pants in a bunch.*

Fortunately for Cecelia, the sirens and ambulances were too far away to disturb her, so she slept straight through the delay.

To cope with the inevitable downtime, Clevenger tuned in to Froggy 99.9—his favorite Country Music station—and waited it out with the able assistance of Waylon Jennings, Loretta Lynn, and a long string of lesser luminaries. Nearly two hours later, the truck passed the bottleneck. Clevenger took the exit for the Experimental Forest, then stopped the truck on the shoulder near the park entrance. "Time to get up, wild thing," he laughed, reaching up and banging his fist on the bunker. "We've reached the Promised Land!"

Groggy and disoriented, Cecelia crawled down and into the passenger seat. "Damn," she laughed, "I hope that's not the way you wake up your *wife* in the morning!"

"Need to use the ladies' room?" he asked, pretending he hadn't heard what she just said. "Gonna be pretty damned uncomfortable, doin' your business out there on the grass. Bound to be lots o' little ass-nibblers down there, lookin' for a snack."

"Guess my *ass* would be *grass*, then, huh?" she laughed. "But really, *fuck* the little ass-nibblers! What me and my nethers do, and where we do it, is a private matter, don't y' think?" She loved his playful honesty and derived great pleasure from dishing it back out to him, in equal proportion, at every opportunity.

Clevenger had hoped for one last warm moment with her. He couldn't help adoring not just her cheeky sense of humor but pretty much everything about her—but his wish was not to be granted. This time, when she grabbed her knapsack and climbed out of his truck, he knew she'd not be getting in again.

She looked up at him, a faint, wistful smile of appreciation on her face, then flashed him the Peace Sign, spun around, and headed toward the entrance to the Experimental Forest. Seconds later, she winced as a large bundle of twenties, held together with a pair of rubber bands, sailed over her left shoulder, barely missing the back of her head.

Clevenger watched affectionately as she picked up the bundle, stuffed it into her coat pocket, and continued walking without even a nod of acknowledgment. *She's grateful,* he chuckled, *even if she's too proud to say it.*

As soon as Cecelia was far enough away so he couldn't see her, she undid the bundle, flattened out the bills, and put them in a zippered money bag she'd remembered to put in her backpack the day she left home. *I just knew that thing would come in handy someday,* she smiled.

Clevenger released the hand brake, then rumbled back out onto Burdick East and, eventually, 79 South toward Pittsburg. As he jerked the truck up into high gear, his copy of Miller's *Tropic of Cancer* slid off the dashboard and crashed down into the wheel well, landing, pages open, on top of a bowl of ripening, malodorous potato salad. The smell of the mayonnaise, mixed with the cab's low-hanging cloud of cigar fumes and his own unwashed feet, made his eyes water. *Not to worry,* he smiled, waving the stench away with his hand. *Plenty o' good readin' where that one came from, right back there in my travel chest. And besides, I've read Tropic three times; don't need to read it again.*

Cecelia needed less than half an hour to find a place where she could set up camp without easily being discovered. The spot she chose—a modest declivity of land tucked behind a sharply protruding slab of granite—would be just enough space for her to stretch out in, hidden by the boughs of a dense gathering of junipers.

As she walked quietly around, exploring the area, she could see the stars twinkling high above her from within a stand of bur oaks. From a distance, she could hear the sweet, melancholy hoo-hoo-hooing of what must surely have been a saw-whet owl.

Great-Great-Granny Koroneva would have just loved it out here, Cecelia mused. The mere thought of her famous relative sweeping grandly across the stage at the Mariinsky in St. Petersburg—her silvery tutu shimmering in the imaginary moonlight—brought tears to Cecelia's eyes. *Grammy's mom and dad must have loved seeing their daughter performing so superbly. I'll bet they were constantly praising and encouraging her, too. And it must have made her feel like a million dollars. So why didn't my parents do the very same thing? It hurts just to think about what it would have been like to have that much encouragement!*

Why, oh why did I have to be born when I was born? I so wish I could have seen my very own great-great-granny dancing there! And after every performance, I would have watched her, right along with her parents, as an adoring audience tossed dozens of bright red roses onto the stage to express their appreciation for her artistry!

She looked lovingly up toward the heavens, just as she'd done back in Sausalito years ago, then inhaled the intoxicating perfume of North Dakota forestland and began dancing. But this time, instead of bunny slippers and a nightgown, she was wearing a pair of hiking boots, blue jeans with the cuffs rolled up, a sweatshirt, and the jacket she'd snatched from her mother's closet the morning she left home. *An outfit like this wouldn't have cut it at the Mariinsky,* she thought, *but I'm not at the Mariinsky, now, am I!*

She also knew that without a pair of pointe shoes, she would never become a ballet dancer. But, true to her temperament, the lack of proper equipment didn't stop her from trying. *A pirouette in shitkickers?* she laughed. *Well, why not! I'm like a kid in the drive-thru at Burger King: I'll have it my way!*

When a stiff breeze came up, rustling the leaves and pushing the clouds along, she moved to an imaginary downstage center and did her best to execute a series of strenuous, flat-footed arabesques. She stood still long enough to catch her breath, then listened with pleasure as a small ensemble of crickets fiddled away in the darkness.

Next, she glided from stage left to stage right, performing a danceable necklace of pirouettes along the way. As she spun around and performed the same maneuver back toward stage left, she imagined she could hear the lush, evocative tapestry of a full orchestra as it carried her triumphantly along.

Done at last with her valiant attempt to earn the flowers and praise of a grateful audience, she fell exultantly backward onto the grass, exhausted but filled to overflowing with happiness.

And yet, to her wonder, the music continued.

What's this? she whispered, then rose up onto her elbows and looked quietly around her.

A short distance away, the invigorating sounds of a single violin wove themselves into the farthest reaches of the clearing. Enchanted, Cecelia waited patiently to learn where they were coming from.

When the playing was done, two mysterious figures—a man and a woman—stepped out of the mist, hand in hand, and approached her, wide-eyed and smiling. They were dressed in clothing so unconventional—so inexplicably exotic—that it was as if the two of them had either just stepped off the stage from a Victorian melodrama or emerged from a still-warm, long-traveling time capsule.

The man's hat, a rakish stovepipe affair, was positioned precariously atop an unsightly cascade of long, stringy hair more worthy of a sheepdog than a vagabond. His complexion, uniformly smooth and walnut in color, was complemented by a coarse, parchment-colored shirt with lapels broad as the wings of a pelican. Completing the ensemble was a faded, Lincolnesque jacket embroidered top to bottom with vintage folk art designs.

No less provocative was the appearance of the woman standing proudly next to him. Her long, velvety hair was crowned with an elaborate headdress of multicolored ceramic beadwork punctuated by a crescent of beautiful, expertly crocheted flowers. Her dress, wide-pleated and dusty rose in color, was enhanced by a Swiss-style apron with deep side pockets and, at the bottom, a broad expanse of elegant turn-of-the-century lace. Her dark, satin-smooth forearms protruded from a blouse whose exquisitely sewn sleeves were delicately flowered and billowy as a summertime cloud.

The woman spoke first. "Such a beautiful dance!" she said.

"Absolutely magical!" said the man.

"And such fine musicianship!" said Cecelia. "I've always loved Monti's music—especially 'Czardas'—and I must say you've done it great justice with your playing."

"You *know* that melody?" said the man. "You must be a musician."

"No," said Cecelia, "not a musician, but a music lover. Found the record in a thrift shop, dust-caked and scratchy, and fell in love with it. I've played it dozens of times since then, and yet I've never failed to think the melody is absolutely rapturous. I swear, every time I hear it, I swoon. It's unavoidable!" Then she came back down to earth and turned her attention back to the two of them.

"By the way," she said, "I don't recall having invited anyone to my 'recital'—if one could reasonably call it that." Her right to privacy had just been violated, and she wasn't especially happy about the intrusion.

"We meant no harm!" said the woman. "We often walk in the Experimental Forest at night, but usually we're the only people here. And as far as we know, we're the only ones around here who'd ever want to *do* such a thing!"

"She's right," said the man. "We never expected to see anyone here. But when we saw you dancing in the moonlight, we were entranced. And since I had my violin right here—we're buskers, you know, so I always have it with me—I couldn't resist responding to your performance, and in the best way I know how."

"But it wasn't really a performance! said CeCe. "Not a *public* one, anyway."

"Call it what you will," said the woman, "but to us it was pure poetry! You see, anything done spontaneously, straight from the heart, is nothing short of miraculous. Guess it's the gypsy in us."

Cecelia smiled to herself. She liked what she was hearing. "First things first," she said. "Who *are* you?"

"Well, I'm Renowin," said the man, then gestured toward his mate. "And this is my partner, Mahala. We're the Chilcotts, and we're in it for the long haul!"

"Yes," said Mahala, smiling tenderly up at him. "The long haul! But not just Until Death Do We Part. We're in it for All Eternity! And *your* name?"

"Cecelia! But you can call me CeCe for short. That pretty much sums up who I am right now, for better or worse."

"No *last* name?" asked Renowin.

"Oh, there *is* one," said Cecelia, "but it's not worth mentioning here. For personal reasons, I've never really liked my last name. You know, *intrafamilial conflict*—the kind of term the shrinks love to toss around. I'll soon be getting rid of it."

"As you wish," the two of them said in unison, touched by her spontaneous moment of candor. While they thought it more than a little peculiar, they nodded their heads in approval anyway.

Then it was Renowin's turn. "Look, we don't know why you're out here camping in the woods, but we do know it's unusually cold this evening! So if you'd like, we can offer you a warmer, more comfortable place for the night. How 'bout coming home with us? I think you'd like it there! It's not far away—just a little beyond the perimeter of the Forest—and it's, well . . . colorful!"

"Yes, *colorful*," laughed Mahala. "Kind of like a dozen heavenly rainbows, all in a row."

Cecelia looked over at the area she'd chosen to sleep in, then back toward the Chilcotts. "I dunno," she said. "I've always loved sleeping—and dancing—by moonlight. But you're right. It is pretty damn chilly out here. And you *are* awfully nice. So what the hell! There'll be other moonlit nights, I suppose. So the answer is *yes*. I'll be happy to come with you."

They walked to the nearby Visitor Parking Lot, then piled into the Chilcotts' car—a battle-weary, pea-green 1949 Chevrolet Loadmaster with more dents and rust spots than paint. But it ran well enough, in spite of its less than awe-inspiring appearance—that and the chunk-chunk-chunk of its wheezing, sputtering engine.

Cecelia decided not to ask her new friends why they were driving a tow truck instead of a sedan. Given that she'd known them for only a short time, it struck her as a rude question. Besides, she figured the derrick protruding from the rear might come in handy in a road emergency. She thought Renowin must be a very resourceful fellow, because he was probably the one who had added a small section of what appeared to be a former church pew to the space beneath the derrick, facing out from the back and positioned in such a way that as many as three passengers at a time could enjoy the receding vista as they traveled.

Cecelia figured that being transported by two colorful strangers in a post–World War II tow truck would surely end up being the most memorable moment in what had already proven to be an unforgettable evening. But then, as they neared the end of a long, winding driveway, CeCe got her first glimpse of the Chilcotts' home.

The first thing she noticed was that it looked remarkably like a long-abandoned turn-of-the-century trolley car. On closer inspection, she realized it was actually *two* of them, imaginatively reconfigured and then welded together to make a two-story home. *They must surely have done the work themselves,* she marveled. *How skillful! How wonderfully creative!* She couldn't help envying the Chilcotts for their raw, untethered ingenuity.

Graced with a quartet of elaborately painted cast-iron wheels, the entire structure was perched on a bed of gravel inside a handcrafted rectangular frame. Embedded in the gravel were two railroad tracks which, other than in the fertile imaginations of the Chilcotts, led absolutely nowhere.

The outsides of the paired-together cars were coated with chipped and faded paint in a series of poorly matched colors—the result of what must have been a long history of hasty, ill-considered re-paintings. Once the three of them were inside, Cecelia saw to her delight that the interior was as much a marvel of human ingenuity as the structure itself: cleverly designed, artfully cluttered, and crammed to capacity with a stunning array of eccentric, playfully arranged items.

She fell instantly in love with everything about the Chilcotts and their idiosyncratic lifestyle. The Chilcotts had struck a chord of compatibility in her that she had never heard before; she could feel it resonating right down to the tips of her toes. *The Chilcotts are dyed-in-the-wool, free-wheeling wanderers,* she smiled, *and so, apparently, am I!*

And yet, in spite of its obvious appeal, the place also rekindled within her a host of negative feelings about the relative blandness of her home in Minot and, most importantly, her parents' utter lack of anything approaching style or imaginative, fresh-from-the-oven thinking.

Cecelia thought about her parents—something she had mostly avoided doing since leaving their home. Clay and Birdie Middling wandered the planet with no real purpose in mind other than the accumulation of All Things Material and the money to purchase them. To her, those two people she'd called Mom and Dad weren't really human. They were merely cardboard cutouts—a pair of aging, ersatz *Homo sapiens*, pretending to be socially engaged when they were actually little more than card-carrying members of the Walking Dead.

Mahala thought it odd that, while Cecelia obviously appreciated their home, she'd yet to say even one little word about the place. So she decided to go fishing, politely, for a reaction.

"Excuse me," she said, "but after so much conversation, you've suddenly gone silent. Is everything OK? I mean, are you all right?"

"Of *course* I'm all right!" said Cecelia, embarrassed to have disappeared so completely into her very own, very private universe. "My apologies, to be sure! It's just that

I was so completely mesmerized by everything around me—everything you've accomplished—that I forgot, for a moment, where I actually am and who brought me here!"

"No harm done," said Mahala. "You aren't the first to have that kind of reaction to our home, and I've no doubt you won't be the last."

"You must be tired," said Renowin. "Why don't you come with us now and we'll show you where you'll be sleeping. Something tells me you're not going to be disappointed!"

As the three of them approached the far end of the car, Cecelia could see a magnificent, intricately embroidered curtain, apparently put there to allow whoever might be behind it some privacy. Mahala reached up and drew the curtain to one side, and Cecelia immediately felt as if she'd just been invited into the pages of an epic romance about life in the Land of the Arabians. Her bed for the evening—a tightly woven, multicolored tapestry atop a mattress made from multiple layers of Bactrian camel wool—was at the center of a miniature Bedouin yurt, so evocative and so mysterious that it brought tears to her eyes.

"This is *so, so* beautiful!" she gasped. "Ever since my arrival you've been astonishingly kind and welcoming! Honestly, what have I done to deserve such obvious solicitude?"

"It's the way of the Gypsies," said Renowin, bowing slightly toward her. "I beg of you not to believe the many negative things you're heard about us. We're not mere mindless wanderers—one-note tinkerers of kitchen utensils. Quite the contrary! We—the Gypsies, I mean—are the Poets of the Desert, and even more than our hard-won freedom, we value kindness toward all whose lives we've had the good fortune to pass through!"

That was a sweet bucket o' slush, thought Cecelia. It was all a little too saccharine for her tastes. *And since when do gypsies build permanent homes?* And yet she supposed there really was something inherently poetic about those sentiments—something Don Quixote and his crowd would certainly have understood. She decided to put the lid on her trademark cynicism for once, plead no contest, and quietly tolerate the romantic notions of her hosts.

Next to the bed was a small table lamp and a hammered brass bell. Mahala pointed to it, then turned to Cecelia. "The bell is for you to use, without apology, whenever you need something," she said. "A glass of water, a good book. We've an extensive library just beyond the kitchen. Or perhaps you'd just like a moment or two of companionship! You're our honored guests this evening, so please don't hesitate to either call us or pull down a book and lose yourself in it!"

Smiling, the Chilcotts nodded good evening to Cecelia, then pulled the curtain shut and walked silently back to their end of the car, hands once again locked together. Cecelia, who in one brief hour had endured enough *kumbayah* to last a year or two, was grateful to be alone again. *I wonder if anyone has ever drowned in a pool of smarm,* she thought. *It wouldn't surprise me.*

She draped her jacket on a chair, followed by her jeans and sweatshirt. Then she deposited a few personal items on the table—a scattering of coins, a bottle of aspirin. She pulled a book out of her bag, then set the bag down next to the bed. She wasn't worried about her valuables. *Ozzie and Harriet would be a greater threat than those two,* she laughed.

Happily self-tucked into bed now, she admired the book—Kahlil Gibran's *The Prophet*—running her fingers lovingly across its ruby-red velveteen cover. She opened it to page seventeen:

In the sweetness of friendship, let there be laughter,
  and sharing of pleasures.
For in the dew of little things, does the heart find its
  morning and is refreshed.

"Well, why the hell not?" she whispered into the soft, soothing darkness of the yurt. "The more goo, the merrier!"

She'd read Gibran's book many times, so one achingly beautiful aphorism was quite enough for now. She reached over and pulled the chain on the table lamp, then closed her eyes and fell into a deep, soul-mending sleep.

* * *

She woke up the next morning feeling remarkably refreshed, given what she'd been through in recent days, but with a slight headache and decidedly mixed feelings about her encounter with the Chilcotts.

They're beautiful people, she mused, *but they're a couple in love, while I'm just a lonely wanderer—a woman with no permanent address, no real family, no plans for the future. Who could possibly love someone like that? What does a drifter like me have to offer someone as nice as Renowin? Lucky Mahala! And on top of all that, messy hair or not, he's so damned handsome! I shouldn't be surprised that he took no more than one polite, perfunctory glance at me on first meeting. He must consider me a rather queer-looking duck compared to Mahala. And let's face it: who wouldn't? Oh, well.*

She slipped into her grungy jeans, then found a clean blouse in her bag and put it on. As she began buttoning the blouse, she suddenly had the distinct feeling that someone nearby was watching her. It was the very same feeling she'd had while dancing the night before at the

Experimental Forest. She paused, then turned back and saw Mahala and Renowin peering at her through a gap at the end of the curtain, heads stacked one above the other like two little clowns in a puppet show.

Cecelia just waved to them, trying not to feel as if her right to privacy had once again been violated.

"Sleep well?" asked Mahala.

"Sure did! And I have to say it was that bed—and the two of you—who made it possible! But really, it's time now for me to hit the road. I don't mean to be rude, but I've got a whole lot o' challenges ahead of me. Can't afford to dawdle!"

"Fair enough," said Mahala, "but I do hope you have time enough for breakfast before you leave! Renowin cooks a mean omelet—big and delicious! You wouldn't have to eat again at least until sometime tomorrow, if *then*."

"Well, I suppose I have time," she said. "I'd love to have breakfast with you! But first I've got to comb the rats out of my hair and make myself presentable. Where can I find a mirror?"

"The upstairs bathroom," said Renowin. "It's right above where we are right now. Tell you what: you go ahead and clean up, and in the meantime I'll go downstairs and get the dining room set up for breakfast. Hah-hah: some dining room! It's actually just a cute little table at the far end of the fruit cellar 'neath the lower trolley. Works for us, and it's nice and cool down there in the summer. See you in ten or twenty minutes!"

Cecelia grabbed a novel from the Chilcotts' bookshelf and made her way to the bathroom. After using the toilet, washing up, and combing her hair, she sat down on a stool at the foot of the ancient claw-foot bathtub to read until breakfast was served.

Meanwhile, the Chilcotts wasted no time. While Renowin was down in the kitchen, frying bacon and whistling

"Czardas," Mahala stayed upstairs. As soon as she was certain the coast was clear, she searched around the room Cecelia had slept in, found the backpack, stood it up on the bed, and rapidly, systematically rifled through its contents.

"The usual shit," she mumbled. "Deodorant, a bar of soap, a hand towel, a spare tampon. *Eww,*" she whispered, "and a pair of lavender lace panties with stains in the crotch. How tacky!"

Just below Cecelia's hardbound edition of Shelley's *Frankenstein* ("Well, *la de dah,*" Mahala laughed, "no dime novels for *this* girl!"), she saw something slender and metallic protruding from the tangle of travel essentials.

"Wahoo!" she yelped. "A Hitachi! A real beauty, too; Renowin probably wouldn't approve, but I wish it was mine!" She wanted to turn the dildo on and listen to its soft, titillating purr, but she realized it wasn't a good idea under the circumstances. So she put it back where she'd found it, then kept digging. Moments later she came across a small navy blue bag—a money bag with the words *Sausalito Savings* on it. She eagerly unzipped it and found just what she'd been looking for: an inch-thick stack of twenty-dollar bills stained with engine grease and what appeared, oddly, to be hardened smears of catsup.

Holy shit, she whispered. *A serious head o' cabbage! Wait'll Renowin sees this!*

Mahala heard a pair of clicks as the bathroom door opened and closed, then the delicate shuffling of footsteps in the hallway. She crammed the money bag back into the backpack so it didn't appear to have been tampered with, left the backpack on the bed, then scampered out of the room and down the stairs only seconds before Cecelia returned to the bedroom.

I should put that bed back in shape, thought Cecelia. *No one likes a messy house guest!* She pulled the spread back into place and plumped the pillow, then looked around the room to make sure everything else was in order.

That's odd, she thought. *I could have sworn I put my backpack on the floor last night.* She shrugged her shoulders, then flipped off the bedroom light and headed downstairs to the fruit cellar.

The breakfast was delicious—letter-perfect in every way—and Mahala and Renowin were as warm and entertaining as a pair of vaudeville comics. They thanked Cecelia for staying with them, then wished her well on her journey.

"So what's next, Time Traveler?" said Mahala.

"*Only The Thumb Knows,*" laughed Cecelia. "I never thought it would happen, but it turns out hitchhiking suits me just fine. If my *next* ride is as rewarding as the *last* one, I'll never again park my ass in a plane, train, or—pardon me—trolley."

"Hah-hah!" said Renowin. "Very funny! No offense taken! Those feet of yours are made for walking, and they've got minds of their own. So go where they take you, Ms. Middling, and may you arrive at the destination of your dreams!"

"By all means," said Mahala, "I second that emotion! But let us give you a ride back to Burdick East. No need to overdo it with the footsies."

A few minutes later, Renowin pulled up to the southern perimeter of Burdick East, dropped the engine into neutral, then waited patiently with Mahala as CeCe gathered up her belongings and scrambled out of the truck.

"Once again," she smiled, "thank you for your hospitality! If I ever pass this way again—when and why, I really can't predict—I'll be sure to look you up."

She stood there and blew the two of them a kiss, then watched tearfully as they drove off toward their home. The last thing she saw was the back of Mahala's head, cradled lovingly in the crook of Renowin's neck.

For All Eternity, thought Cecelia. *What a long time that would be!* Deep within her, the mere idea of such heartfelt commitment between two people provoked another disarming episode of melancholy. *With my luck,* she frowned, *I'll be lucky if I make it to the end of the decade!* A moment later she was back on the road, putting her thumb to work again.

Chapter Twenty

She needed only ten minutes to snag another ride—this time from a genuine Ma Kettle lookalike who was decked out, paradoxically, in freshly pressed bib overalls and a pair of squeaky clean Betty Boop sneakers. She was well into her eighties and immaculately groomed, and while her car—a fire-engine red '57 Chevrolet Nomad—was crammed full of hay bales and miscellaneous farm implements, it managed, in spite of its cargo, to come across as if it had just rolled off the assembly line. Fortunately, there was just enough room up front for Cecelia.

"So where y' goin', cupcake?" asked the driver. Her twittery, high-pitched voice was a perfect match for her; she looked less than five feet tall and fragile as a hummingbird. Anyone farther away than Cecelia would have thought that behind the steering wheel of the car was a tiny child dressed as an adult and pretending to be a farmer on the way to market.

Cecelia wanted to burst out laughing at both the woman's cotton-candy voice and her odd appearance. But she decided that not only it would it be improper to treat a woman of her age with such disrespect, it would accomplish nothing.

"Oh, just east," she answered. "Beyond that, I don't really have a plan—not at the moment, anyway."

"*Well*, now!" said the woman. "If y' ask me, not havin' a plan don't sound like a plan worth havin'!"

"But I didn't *ask* you, now, did I?" said Cecelia, unable to contain her irritation.

"Didn't mean no harm," said the woman, then reached over and patted Cecelia affectionately on the knee. "Tell y' what, honey. I'm goin' only as far as Michigan this mornin'. Gotta deliver a shitload o' bales to some old coot with a barnyard full o' horses." She waved her hand back toward the rear of the car. "You can't *smell* 'em?"

"Oh, I can smell 'em, all right," said Cecelia. "No doubt about that! But Michigan? That's a hell of a long way to drive just to deliver a carload of hay bales, isn't it?"

"Not *Michigan*," laughed Gertie. "Not the *state*, I mean. Michigan *City*: that's where I'm goin'. The way I see it, the Mitten might's well be on Planet Jupiter! There's nothin' to do there, nothin' but them silly Great Lakes to gawk at. Whoop de doo! I mean, what's so damn great about the Great Lakes? Compared to the Atlantic, they're nothin' but a string o' rain puddles! So why would I ever want to go there? Anyway, sorry 'bout the odor. Hay can smell pretty awful after it's been sittin' out in a cloudburst. But business is business, ain't it? Gotta do whatcha gotta do! I know, I know! Wish I could get you farther 'n that, but I have to go straight back to my place afterward and do some serious sleeping. It ain't easy, gettin' up every morning at 3:00 a.m. to take care of a barn full o' hungry bovines—know what I mean?"

"Well, *sure*. I really do understand, Miss . . ."

"Miss *nothin'*," said the woman. "Gertie's the name. Gertie Glidden."

"Nice alliteration," said Cecelia.

"If you say so," said Gertie, who had no idea what the word meant. "My first name's actually short for Gertrude. I always hated that name, so I figured, why keep it? That's when I went ahead and took the 'rude' off the 'Gert'! My Old Man was really pissed, but Mama—bless her heart—went right up to him with her chin stickin' out like a battering ram and said, 'Listen, darlin', It's *her* body, so she can call it whatever the hell she *wants* to. And so the name stuck, and by God, I'm keepin' it!"

"Lucky you!" said Cecelia. She hoped Gertie hadn't seen her rolling her eyes in something fast approaching disgust. She was already exhausted from listening to the woman's meaningless chatter, and it was a relief to know the ride would be ending at Michigan City.

"And believe me, sweetie," Gertie continued, "you'll be glad you got to see that town. Not everyone does, y' know. I mean, the place is *famous*! In 1945, right after the War was over, a Great Northern passenger train ran right up the rear end of another train just outside o' town. Three hundred 'n' nine injured, thirty-four of 'em deader 'n a toilet full o' turds. Most o' the victims were young, grass-green squaddies returning home from the front right after doin' their Patriotic Duty against them horrible Nazis. Stinks, don't it?"

"All right, Gertie," Cecelia said. "Thanks for the history lesson. Sorry it happened! Now, about that name change: I understand! And if it'll make you feel better, I wouldn't have wanted to get stuck with a name like Gertrude, either! Anyway, Michigan City will be just fine with me. All I'm looking for tonight is a place to eat and a nice, clean bed. Can't afford anything fancy."

Gertie's eyes lit up like the headlights on her Nomad. Then she glanced over at Cecelia, smiling broadly. "My God, child, I know *just* the place for you, for the food *and* the bed! It's Strickland's Chow-Down & Sleep-Inn! Friendly folks! Good food! Private bathrooms with flush toilets! Can y' imagine! And they finally got rid o' them pesky cockroaches—just last month! Anyway, cockroaches or not, the place is just outside of Lakota, so I'll have you there quicker 'n a cow with the shits can make a pancake!"

"Lakota? Never heard of it!" said Cecelia, sighing more audibly than she should have. "But that's all right, Gertie. It's all I need to know. Promise! Now if you don't mind, I'd like to do some serious sleeping myself!"

"Be my guest!" said Gertie. "But before you drift off, I just wanted you to know I think it's kind o' stupid to call a town with less than three hundred people a city. Don't y' think? I can't imagine what the Founders were thinking when they . . ."

Gertie needn't have continued, because Cecelia was soon fast asleep and wouldn't have heard a knock if it had been smack on her forehead.

When she finally woke up, the first sound she heard was Gertie's less-than-mellifluous voice as she croaked her way through the lyrics of "Summer Nights," the song that helped make John Travolta and Olivia Newton John famous.

"'Tell me more'?" said CeCe. "Whaddaya mean, 'Tell me more'?"

"Hah-hah!" laughed Gertie. "Perfect timing! Truth is, I was about to tell you we've just reached Strickland's. Time to Chow Down and Sleep Inn, girl!"

Cecelia sat up, yawned and stretched, then reached over to Gertie and embraced her warmly.

"Now where the hell did *that* come from?" said Gertie, blushing. "Last time I got a hug like that, it was from my Aunt Cordelia down in Glenfield—on my eightieth birthday!"

"I really don't *know* where it came from," said Cecelia. "Maybe it's 'cause I hardly ever got a hug back in Sausalito—which means I never gave anyone a hug myself, either. No problem there, because nobody ever *deserved* one."

"Sorry 'bout that," said Gertie. "But let me tell you: if you'd grown up in *my* house, you'd have had bruises all over your body from all the hugs you'd gotten. The Gliddens were Major League huggers!" Then she looked at the dashboard clock and came back to reality. "Listen, honey, I really do have to get along now. That geezer wants his hay, and he ain't known around here for his patience!"

Cecelia hopped out of Gertie's Nomad, glad to be rid of the pungent odor of sopping wet hay, then waved goodbye as Gertie drove off. Cecelia crossed Main Street and headed toward a sign that read *Welcome to Stricklands: The est Place in the World to Chow Down & Sleep Inn!* In place of the missing letter were the remnants of a once-inhabited bird's nest, now torn apart and sagging down toward the top of the window just beneath it.

Well, shit, she thought to herself. *Who could've blamed that little birdie for flyin' the coop? This place is an absolute dump! What was Gertie thinking, anyway?*

But what Gertie had been thinking was no longer relevant, because Cecelia was exhausted—so much so that had Strickland's been half burnt to the ground, it wouldn't have stopped her from trying. So in she went, and in her wallet, to her delight, was more than enough cash to cover the cost of a one-night stay.

She checked in at the front desk, got her key, and found her room. It was shabby, with torn curtains and stained carpet in a God-forsaken hodgepodge of mismatched colors. She sniffed the air and detected the faintest hint of urine. She left her backpack and other items in her room, then made her way to what passed, barely, for a restaurant.

There were plenty of booths to choose from. One would have reasonably expected a crowd at breakfast-time—the essential meal for travelers—but other than Cecelia and two weary, droopy-eyed waitresses, the place was empty. She could see why, too. The red and white checkered floor tiles were chipped, the red and white checkered table-cloths were stained, and the red upholstery on the seats and stools was torn and faded. Whatever allure the 1950s diner décor once held had been lost long ago. *Bet the wait-resses are wearin' red and white checkered panties, too,* laughed Cecelia. *I won't even ask about* their *condition!*

Cecelia picked a booth and opened the menu. It wasn't exactly cosmopolitan, but for anyone who enjoyed 'eating local' and loved mealtime adventuring, it was a culinary dream come true.

For her entree, she chose fleischkuekle, a Russian–German meat-filled pastry close to the hearts and bellies of North Dakotans. As a side dish, she added kase knephla (locally known, affectionately, as cheese buttons). Then, to top off her repast, she chose the ultimate North Dakota comfort food, kuchen. The pastry could feature a wide variety of fruits, but she went with apricot, one of her childhood favorites.

For a place with just one hungry customer, the meal was a long time coming. But once it arrived and she'd sampled the items, she knew it had been well worth the wait. The kase knephla, a deep-fried dough filled with a sharp-cheese combination she couldn't quite identify, was delicious—the perfect appetizer for a cheese-aholic like Cecelia. The fleischkuekle was cooked to perfection, leaving an aftertaste so strong and so satisfying that it could have been a second helping. *This place may be a dump,* Cecelia thought, *but the cuisine is five-star. Go figure!*

She took her sweet time with the meal, savoring what would come to have been a rare interlude of well-deserved peace and tranquility.

It wasn't until she was polishing off one last, irresistible mouthful of apricot kuchen that another customer—a bearded, bespectacled young man perhaps in his late twenties—arrived with an impressive stack of books under one arm, sat down without hesitation in the booth directly across the aisle from her, and began poring over the menu.

Must be a regular, she thought. *And not just any regular. Not only did he know exactly where he wanted to sit, he just happens also to be devastatingly handsome!*

She found herself blushing, with a smile of approval and a stirring in her loins that no other man had ever been able to engender.

Oh, my God, she laughed inwardly, *I can't let shit like this—a Leaping Libido—cloud my judgment! And besides, why would a babe cake like him have any interest in a drab wallflower like me?* Knowing better than to stop and stare at him, she swept her bill up off the table, then stepped over to the cash register to pay up.

"Good meal?" said the waitress.

"Oh, yeah!" said Cecelia. "Every last bite!"

"Good! That'll be $13.87. Sorry 'bout the tax! Them Baby Kissers up in Bismarck don't give a damn about the Little People."

"That's fine. I mean, food like that's worth every damn penny, Baby Kissers or not! Take cash?"

"Sure!" said the waitress. "In fact, we're short of fives and tens right now, so that would be helpful."

Cecelia opened her wallet and pulled out the bills left in it. As she counted through them, she realized to her horror that there wasn't quite enough money to pay for her meal.

"Oh, *shit!*" she said, then blushed a deep red over her choice of words. "Excuse the naughty vocabulary, but I don't have enough to pay! But not to worry; I've got plenty of money up in my room. Be right back!"

She turned and headed to the exit, too annoyed with herself to notice that the man with the stack of books on his table was unapologetically staring at her—*ogling* her, really—up, down, and all around, assessing both the quality of her figure and what he must have considered the provocatively feminine swagger in her way of walking. *Ahh,* he recited to himself, *the liquefaction of her clothes . . . that brave vibration each way free.*

Back in her room, Cecelia rifled through her backpack, eager to get her hands on the bundle of twenties Clevenger had so compassionately tossed to her, then go back to the restaurant and pay her bill. But her earlier horror was multiplied tenfold when she realized the bundle was missing. "God-fuckin' dammit!" she screeched. "It's *gone!*"

Now in full panic mode, she considered the possibilities. *Let's see: Maybe I stashed the money somewhere else.* But she had no other bag, and the bundle was too big for a pocket. *Maybe the housekeeper went deep-diving into my backpack and came up with the Big Fish that should have been my catch, not hers.* But the bed was still unmade; there was no sign of a housekeeping visit.

I mean, what else? she moaned. *What other explanation can there be?*

Then another possibility struck her like a bolt of lightning straight up from the Bowels of Hell. *Mahala! She must have snuck into the bedroom yesterday and stolen that bundle while Renowin was down in the kitchen and I was right down the hall, usin' the can. That two-faced, counterfeit bitch!*

Holy Mother of God, she snarled. *I'll deal with that later! But right now I've got to go back downstairs and tell that waitress I'm flat broke and can't possibly pay for all of the foods and beverages I've just consumed in good faith.*

When she arrived at the cash register, the waitress was still standing there, this time with a half-smirk on her face, tapping her long, dirty fingernails on the counter.

"Don't do freebies at this joint," she said. "Gotta cough it up, honey!"

"But I don't have anything to cough up! Just found out I've been ripped off, Big Time!"

"What a *shame,*" said the waitress. "Tsk tsk. But shame don't pay the bills, do it! Excuses don't pay the bills, either!"

"C'mon now!" said Cecelia. "I paid for my room up front yesterday—every last penny of it. Please! Have a heart! I'm heading east now, and as soon as I get home I'll send you the balance—and more—because of the inconvenience I've caused you. *Please!*"

The waitress eyed her with suspicion. "And where might that home of yours *be*? I mean, which side o' the Atlantic? You don't exactly sound like you come from around here."

None o' your business, smart-ass, thought Cecelia. *And I don't like people snooping around, digging into my past.* To get away as soon as possible, she decided to make something up on the spot.

"West Mifflin," she said, "a little town southeast of Pittsburgh. Fun place to grow up in! Had an amusement park called Kennywood." Cecelia knew about West Mifflin only because her Aunt Minerva, who grew up in Pittsburgh, loved to talk about how much fun she'd had there as a child.

"Listen," said the waitress, "I'm sorry, honey. I really am! But the Boss Man said he'll fire me right on the spot if I go easy on the hard-ups. And believe me, we get a whole lot o' hard-ups here—people with one more pitiful sob story about some horrible thing they claim happened to 'em just a day or two ago! What a coincidence, huh?"

Then the waitress suddenly stopped frowning and pointed at the man with the stack of books on his table.

"Maybe that young man over *there* can bail you out," she said.

The man with the books got quietly up from his table, ran his fingers through his hair to make himself more presentable, then strode up to the two of them, smiling just short of unctuously. He was tall, slim, and well-built, a pleasurable mixture of letterman athlete and esteemed intellectual.

"I promise you I wasn't eavesdropping," he laughed, looking straight down at Cecelia with twinkling eyes. "But

I couldn't help hearing, just now, that through no fault of your own you've managed, somehow, to come up short of enough cash to settle your account with this woman. Of course I don't know either of your names, but . . ."

Blushing, Cecelia remained silent. But the waitress, who'd never had a problem with shyness and was always eager to make a good impression—especially with a virile young man like this one—dove right in.

"Miss Bentley," she giggled, unaccustomed to dealing with men as handsome and mannerly as this man was. Because of it, she was blushing even more deeply than Cecelia. "But you can call me Sally, 'cause that's my name!"

"And yours?" said the man, ignoring the waitress and turning instead toward Cecelia.

"Oh, just another run-of-the-mill, unavailable Vaginoid," she chuckled. Privately, she wondered what on God's earth had just compelled her to say such a thing. "Name's not really worth mentioning."

"As you wish, Ms. Vaginoid," he smiled, his brow arched. "As you wish. I shall make no more inquiries!" Then he turned back to the waitress.

"All right, Ms. Bentley," he said, toying with her obvious naïveté. "From this moment on, 'Sally' it shall be, whenever I happen to be in town. But until then, here's twenty dollars to cover this woman's bill, including a generous tip. I mean, if we aren't here to help our fellow humans, then what can we possibly be here *for*?"

"A *twenty*?" yelped the waitress. "But she only owes us . . ."

"Doesn't matter," he said. Then he handed her the twenty, turned back to Cecelia, and gestured toward his table. "Tell you what," he purred, "why don't you come and sit with *me*? I seldom have an opportunity to play the

Chivalrous Shark, so I should think it would be more than foolish of me to miss this one!"

Sally, annoyed at having been brushed off so summarily by her *Don Juan* diner, left her post in a huff and headed back to the kitchen.

But for Cecelia, it was different. Given the intensity of the stirrings south of her waistline, she knew right away that her feelings for this man, though entirely spontaneous, were real. Even worse, she realized that she couldn't possibly say no a man who'd just opened his billfold and come to her rescue.

She followed him to his booth, wondering what in the world the two of them—complete strangers by any definition—could possibly have to say to each other that would be worth saying. But how she felt about this and that and other things didn't really matter. *As Cole Porter was fond of saying,* she laughed, *when you're down and out, Anything Goes.*

Once they'd settled in, the Man Without a Name carefully perused the menu. Then he looked up at Cecelia, and, with the same earnest expression that had charmed the hell out of her only a moment ago, spoke directly to her.

"Dessert?" he chimed. "What's a cup of fresh-brewed coffee without a slice of pecan pie and a scoop of Bridgeman's to enliven it?"

It'd been a very long time since Cecelia had been treated so warmly and respectfully by a man, so she wasn't about to turn him down.

"I'll *take* it!" she replied. "Haven't had a decent piece of pie since I was a tiny thing. By the way, Bridgeman's Chocolate Delight was the Pride of Minot; I'd have eaten an entire gallon o' the stuff at one sitting if only my parents had allowed it. But it never happened, because they were too damn stingy—not just about ice cream, but about *everything*—to spring for it."

"I'm sorry to hear that," said the man. "Parents can be problematic, can't they."

She nodded in agreement. At that moment, moved all over again by his charm, his remarkable eloquence, and his razor-sharp wit, Cecelia knew she wouldn't care if the ice cream came warm in a plastic bag. To her alarm, she realized she was hooked and there would be no turning back.

He waved to the nearest waitress—this one a short, chunky woman named Queenie with an excess of lipstick and a mile-high head of hair—and seconds later she arrived at their table. But instead of addressing the young man, she spoke to CeCe.

"Is your name Cecelia?"

"Uh . . . yes. Why?"

"Someone just called here with a message for you. Sounded kind o' anxious, too! Said he needed to talk to you and that it was urgent. You can go ahead and use the phone, honey. It's just down the hallway from here."

The waitress handed Cecelia a slip of paper with a telephone number on it.

"Be right back," said Cecelia to the young man, her brow furrowed with concern. Then she made her way to the telephone and dialed the number.

"Cecelia?" said a vaguely familiar voice, and yet more gravelly now than she remembered.

Oh, my God, she panicked. *Buzz? That pimply little pervert who sat across from me in trigonometry and was always trying to sneak a peek at my noogies? Sounds like him. Please don't let it be him!*

"Yup," she answered. "So who's this?"

"You don't recognize my *voice*?" he replied, sounding simultaneously disappointed and distressed. "*Jesus*, girl, it's your *father!*"

Shocked, Cecelia paused, too confused and alarmed to say anything.

"Well?" he said. "How 'bout at least a warm *hello*—or maybe just a few words of recognition! You know, with at least a hint of *emotion* in 'em somewhere."

"How the hell did you find out where I am?" she snapped. "If I'd wanted you to know that, I would have told you long before this, don't you think?"

"Believe it or not," he said, "a onetime co-worker of mine saw you walking down the road outside of Lakota. He's a traveling salesman now. I've been calling every hotel and restaurant in town."

"You know what, Daddy? I don't give a flyin' *fuck* what your friend does for a living. And I don't give a flyin' fuck about *you*, either! Have I made myself clear?"

She could tell he was crying now. "Please, honey!" he sobbed. "Don't do this to me! I need to know you still . . ."

"I still *what*?" she shouted. Then she remembered where she was and cupped her hand over the receiver. "Still *love* you? Don't kid yourself! Did you love me when my mother whined about missing her favorite TV show to come to my award ceremony? Did you love me when you marched into my classroom at Cloverton and humiliated me in front of my classmates by attacking my favorite teacher?" Then, doing her best to speak softly, she hissed, "Get real, Mr. What's-Your-Name. You're no longer my Daddy! And your wife—what was *her* name? Susan? Camille? I forget!—is no longer my *mother*. Understand? We're finished! End of story! So why don't you just scurry on home and call your plumber, or maybe your tax preparer. Maybe one o' *them* would enjoy your company. Or maybe a suicide hotline— something you could actually *use*!"

"I won't be calling any of those," he whimpered. "The plumbing's just fine here! I do my own taxes! And I won't be calling any suicide hotline, either. But you know what? Your mother called one! More than once, in fact. She was even more upset than I was when she discovered you'd run away from home."

The news that her mother had actually considered suicide—more than once—shook Cecelia to the core. And yet so great was her anger with both of them that she slammed the receiver down—hard enough, she hoped, to give him a permanent earache—then leaned against the wall, sobbing quietly to herself.

So many questions about myself, she grimaced. *So many questions!*

But the answers weren't coming easily. She'd begun to wonder, for instance, why in recent weeks she'd taken to swearing like a drunken sailor—a shit here and a fuck there, far more often than in the past—and in response to the most ridiculously minor moments of disagreement.

She liked to think it was only because she'd grown up in a family—and in an Era—where people didn't read much and swearing was more and more socially acceptable, a convenient placebo for the lack of a more sophisticated vocabulary. *I swear,* she laughed, *if I'd been a Catholic, I'd have been more than happy to tell the priest on duty to go fuck himself if he didn't like what I'd just told him in that little booth.*

But more disturbingly, she'd begun to see a strong connection between the frequency of her epithets and the intensity of her anger about everything from minor social offenses to deep, fundamental differences in the values and conduct of people closest to her. And not just to them, but with people she'd never seen before and would never see again.

The way she saw it, not only was there no God in her value system to offend—no Bible-based list of linguistic no-no's—there was also no reason, if swearing made her feel better, to put an end to it—no reason at all.

Five minutes later, she was still trembling, still boiling over with rage. *Jesus Christ,* she mumbled. *Suicide? Guess I can't really blame her, though. Living with that man all these years must have been slow-dripping torture.*

But why her? It should have been me! Not her, not my father, not that bitch down at the Post Office in Minot—the one everyone hated because she was so fundamentally rude and ignorant. It should have been me.

Back she went into the restaurant, her eyes red and swollen from her encounter with her father. She composed herself and sat down. Then, to escape the trauma of that phone call, she reengaged with the man across the table from her. *I hope my face isn't still red as a lobster,* she worried. *It usually is after I've had a good cry.*

"What's with all the *books,* professor?" she teased, looking for a path—any path—to meaningful conversation. Or at least conversation that might keep her from thinking about her suicidal mother.

"Are you all right?" he said. "You look a little flushed in the face." *Worse than that,* he thought to himself. But he didn't want to upset her, so he didn't push his luck.

"I'm fine," she said. "Really! Just an unpleasant encounter with an even more unpleasant man from my past. Anyway, about those books!"

"Yeah, the books," he laughed. "Everyone wonders! But I'm not a professor—just a raging bibliophile, hungry for knowledge and incapable of kicking the habit. By the way, my name's Christian Danvers. So now you know me, up close and a little bit personal. There can be no holding back now. We're both in for the ride, aren't we! Time to balance the scales of social justice. So your name is Cecelia. Cecelia what, please?"

Christ! she thought to herself. *'In it for the ride'? What'd he mean by that? And did he just wink at me when he said it? I mean, holy shit! From toe in the water to complete Baptismal Immersion, all in one fast-moving morning. Hope I'll remember how to swim.*

"You can call me CeCe," she said. "Everyone else does. But we can skip the last name. OK? Really, it's irrelevant when you think about it."

"CeCe!" he said. "I *like* that! Anyway, you asked about the books. You can see the titles yourself right there in front of you, so you won't have to listen to me going on and on, telling you where this Inquiring Mind of mine often takes me. It's all right there on the spines."

Wondering what *his* spine might look like, she rifled through the stack and saw books there that made her heart sing with approval: Dostoevsky's *Crime and Punishment,* Orwell's *1984,* Russell's *Why I Am Not a Christian.* And finally, to her amusement, Miller's *Tropic of Cancer.*

"Very impressive!" she said. "So you've read Bertie's *Why I Am Not a Christian*? Me, too! But I must confess, I'm more than a little worried about your first name."

"Ha-ha!" he laughed. "That my mother's ever-present gallows humor for you. She and the Old Man are actually hard-core, card-carrying atheists. They must have laughed long and hard on the day I was born: 'Let's give the little bugger a name that'll scare the crap out of our church-hating acquaintances,' they must have said."

"My God," roared CeCe, "an atheist named Christian! Kind o' like a Bible Thumper named Beelzebub!"

As they were laughing Queenie arrived with two plates of fresh-baked pecan pie, each one accompanied by a generous scoop of Caramelicious. Then, between spoons full of ice cream and the playful crunch of glazed pecans, they smiled warmly, laughed energetically, and traded overtly flirtatious glances—a steady barrage of visual love notes, tinged with undeniable lust.

"Listen," said Christian, suddenly more animated than usual. "Speaking of laudable, eminently readable books, I've got one *upstairs* that's a real gem. Wanna see it?"

"I don't know," said Cecelia, feeling a sudden surge of common-sense apprehension. "Upstairs? *Really*? I mean, just who am I actually dining with here—Christian Danvers or Anthony Perkins?"

"No Anthony here," he replied. "Just me: Christian! Or you can call me Chris if 'Christian' sounds a little too pious for you."

"Neither one," she said. "I think I'll just stick with 'Book Boy'; it's no doubt the way I'll remember you. Anyway, I really don't have enough time to do justice to the book you mentioned. I've got to be on my way. You know, Miles to Go Before . . ."

"Before you sleep," said Christian. "Frost had a way with words, didn't he? But back now to the moment: where's your sense of adventure? Seeing this book will be like finding the most exotic imaginable gift under your Christmas tree come December; the thrill is always in the discovery!"

By now it had dawned on Cecelia that the time for her introduction to genuine, truly desirable sexual activity—for that very human craving that her biology textbook euphemistically referred to as "copulation"—may very well have arrived. *How bone-chillingly clinical is that word,* she thought to herself, even while marveling at the double entendre she'd just hatched. *I can do better! And I can certainly do better than Arnold Legume.*

To her, what they did back in Minot that night wasn't really sex in the romantic sense of the word. Far from it, in fact. *More like a poorly played game of couch tennis,* she laughed. *But in that particular match, the balls—his balls—never quite made it over the net.*

The truth is that long before the onset of puberty, Cecelia

had harbored an intense reluctance to—and perhaps even an active revulsion for—the idea of 'sexual intercourse' as described in pulp novels and *Understanding Your Body* manuals. In the locker room afer PE class at Cloverton, a small handful of girls—a well-known, unsavory tribe of troublemakers—were inordinately fond of quizzing her, crudely and aggressively, about her sex life, desperate to know if she'd 'done it' with anyone yet.

Two of them could be especially cruel and insensitive while interrogating her. "So: has CeCe put a Weenie in her Pee Pee yet?" cooed Diana, who by the tenth grade had been up close and personal with enough male members to stage an after-game hot dog roast for the Cloverton Dakotas.

Her close friend Angela, known throughout the school as 'Available Angie,' was even more blunt about what she and her girlfriends considered an essential rite of passage—the only way, they believed, that a girl could prove she had what it takes to be a worthwhile prom date. "What?" Angie would shriek. "You mean you still haven't Done the Dirty yet with Mickey the Dick? Everyone else has! What are you *waiting* for, girl?"

Their nonstop preadolescent impertinence truly disgusted Cecelia, but her strong constitution and sky-high ideals—acquired, she figured, from years of insult and abuse in the capable hands and questionable intellects of her own culturally ignorant family—would simply not allow her to lower herself to their level of social misconduct. *Not only are those bitches super dimwitted,* she'd told herself, *they're flamingly jealous of me! They know how intellectually superior I am compared to them. All they have to do is read the honor roll every six weeks. The one flat-out, undeniable truth—their jealousy—is eating them alive!*

And on top of all that, Cecelia had already endured enough negative comments about sex and the male anatomy over the years to imbue her with an irrational but intractable fear of 'doing it' with anybody. Undoubtedly, the memory of her half-brother's Neanderthal behavior—that and her father's notorious foot-in-mouth social ineptitude—contributed significantly to her revulsion. *What self-respecting woman,* she shuddered, *could be sexually attracted to that?*

In the privacy of their bedrooms during pajama parties, Diana, Angela, and other like-minded Cloverton girls were known to speak with hair-raising honesty about what they considered the aesthetic virtues and practical attributes of the male genitalia, calling them "indescribably beautiful" or "ugly as sin but astonishingly good, on a good day, at what they were built to do."

But others, shortly after their first sexual experience, could hardly wait to tell someone—someone dumb enough to listen, that is—that "Eddy's 'hard-on' was softer than a glazed stick from Dunkin," or "They told me Snake Rawlston was gonna send me straight up to heaven, but I gotta tell you, I didn't feel *one* damn thing that night. I'm not convinced he ever got it in there in the *first* place. He just *thinks* he did. Poor delusional, under-equipped Rawlston!"

But that was then and this is now, Cecelia mused. *And let's face it: I'm not getting any younger. Time to stir the batter and bake a cake!*

Of course she had absolutely no desire to be pregnant, only to learn—once and for all—what it must be like to have a *true* man's estimable phallus pay her a welcome visit Way Down Under. She took a certain pride, however unfounded, in having a sixth sense about the motives of the male animal—motives nearly always sexual in nature—and as far as she could tell, what Danvers had in mind while upstairs with her, admiring that book, was anything but Christian.

Christian swept the bill up off the table and went up front to pay, and Cecelia gathered her things and followed him to the register.

"Thanks for bailing me out," she said. "And for dessert, too."

"My pleasure," replied Christian. "And besides, having some time with you over coffee was worth a whole lot more than the cost of lunch and a piece of pie and a scoop of ice cream."

"*Pecan* pie," said Cecelia, licking her lips.

"And Caramelicious," said Christian. "We mustn't forget *that!*"

As Cecelia opened the door to leave, Christian positioned himself strategically behind her—perhaps a bit closer than a true gentleman ought to have been—and gently but intentionally brushed himself up against her buttocks. *Oh, the possibilities,* he chuckled. *I be a Bad Boy!* Then he pulled back, laid a hand gently on her shoulder, and followed her outside.

Did he just do what I think he did, she wondered, *or did I only imagine it? Maybe I knew exactly what he was doing, and kind o' liked it! It's probably time for me to stop being so damned prudish. Who knows—maybe I can learn to like a man who knows just what he wants to do, then takes me somewhere, without my permission, and does it. Maybe my time to stop saying no has finally come.*

The book Christian had been so eager to show her—a beautiful, richly annotated facsimile edition of Martin Luther's *95 Theses*—really was everything he had insisted it would be, and more. *But is it not ironic,* she reflected, *that a book so obviously admired by a man named Christian should have as its author one of the most fabled, most influential Christians of all time? This may very well be a subliminal message to me: You Go, Girl!*

While Cecelia perused the book, spellbound by its breathtaking elegance, Christian slipped an envelope with a quartet of fifty-dollar bills out of his vest and laid it down on a nearby dresser. *I'll present it to her right after I'm finished with her,* he chuckled. *It's the least I can do to thank her for allowing me to 'know' her before she goes on her way.* He knew, somehow, that sitting there together over coffee, chatting and grinning like two high school sweethearts, just wasn't going to be enough for him. *I'll need more than that to feel sufficiently compensated for my generosity,* he laughed.

They stood side-by-side over the book then, running their fingers over its stained-glass illuminations and inhaling the leathery scent of its artfully designed, hand-tooled cover. She could feel the warmth and solidity of his body against her arm now, and she wondered if he'd intentionally moved even closer to her. *The only man I've ever come across,* she mused, *whose physical presence, intellectual passions, and ways of speaking compare favorably with those of Mr. Thornton. Oh, my God! Maybe I had a crush on my English teacher, too! Anyway, if there really is a God, may He forgive me for having the hots for a living, breathing replica of the best damn teacher I ever had!*

To her delight, Cecelia realized she was quickly growing impatient for some action. When, she wondered, would the lightning she was yearning for finally strike? To learn whether she'd only imagined his attraction to her, she pressed subtly back against him from shoulder to thigh, then waited for his reaction.

It came without either hesitation or any suggestion that it might not be fully authentic, and the temperature between the two of them immediately and precipitously climbed.

Directly behind them was a queen size bed, and on the wall opposite was a reproduction of Edouard Manet's beloved masterpiece *Olympia,* poorly framed. *Very cool, and yet very hot,* laughed Cecelia, who, thanks to the art-loving Mr. Thornwood, knew the painting very well. On the nightstand next to the bed was an alarm clock that would mark the precise moment of their imminent encounter. *Legume was just an underperforming warmup,* Cecelia thought, her heart pounding in anticipation.

Danvers stepped over to the window and quietly pulled down the shade, creating the illusion that it was dusk, not early morning. Then he spun himself around, swept her up into his arms *film noir* style, tossed her playfully onto the bed—face down—and scrambled up on top of her. She recalled, later on, that she'd experienced two unforgettable sensations at that moment: the rock-hard tubularity of his penis and the swift, nimble movement of his hand as he unzipped his pants to give it swift passage.

She needn't have worried that she might not be ready to receive him; the urgent liquidity of her Lady Bits was all the evidence the two of them would need.

In he went then, deep enough to make her squeal with a half-erotic mixture of intense pain and indescribable pleasure. Seconds later, he was wildly plunging into and out of her, as if he were the one essential piston at the very heart of one of Leonardo's more diabolical war machines.

It was over far too quickly, given the undeniable pleasure it gave her, and yet not soon enough, thanks to the obvious pain it caused her—a series of sharp, dagger-like jabs which on first entry were every bit as emotional as they were physical. *I suppose I could have handled more of those intrusions,* she whimpered, half crying and half laughing at the absurdity of her first real introduction to full-throttle copulation. *But the loss of my dignity? What about that? I feel more like a wild animal than an aspiring author right now! What would Vonnegut have had to say about this?*

Danvers was sprawled out on his back now, panting like a tiger but smiling as if he were some proud, triumphant warrior just back from the battlefield.

"So! Did you like it?" he asked her.

"Well, a *little*," she replied. "Sure! A *little*. But the pain? I didn't expect the pain!" She went silent for a moment, then added, "Well, a *lot*, actually. The pleasure, I mean! But you know what? I don't really want to talk about that right now."

"You *don't*?" He was a little baffled by her reluctance. *Women*, he thought, *they're so damned inscrutable—and so temperamental!*

"I mean, I'd rather just *think* about it," she said. "You know, like a poetry lover who's just finished reading the finest poem she's ever come across, then wants only to remain stretched out on her divan, relishing the experience! That's all I think a decent person should *want* to do after an event as emotional is this one was, for me at least!"

"Only if one happens to *be* a decent person," he laughed. Then he flashed her a sly, quizzical smile. "By the way, you admit you liked it, but what, precisely, did you actually *like*? I need to know!"

"What we just *did*, for Christ's sake," she replied. "Don't be a doofus!"

This time he laughed outright at her response. Though he couldn't quite see her expression in the dim room, he could tell just from the impish tone of her voice that she meant what she'd just said, and for all the right reasons.

"So you *did* like it, then!" he continued.

"Jesus! Didn't I just *tell* you, not once but twice, that I liked it?"

"Well, yes, you *did*, by God!" he chuckled. "You did indeed say that very thing!"

"And that was the *last* time I'll ever say it!" she said, increasingly irritated by now. "To *you*, anyway!"

He winced at the implications of her smart remark, then continued, unconcerned. "Well, then! Since you *liked* it so much, what say we do it again? You know, 'Double your pleasure, double your fun!' Remember that ad?"

"Oh, I remember it, all right," she said. "Another dumb jingle from the marketing 'experts.' But just so you'll know it, one intrusion was quite enough for me. So do me a favor, big boy, and keep that serpent in your pants, right where it belongs. I do believe I've had my fill for the day."

He figured she was just joking around now. After knowing her for only a few hours, he already loved the naughty, suggestive tone of her repartees. He knew that he would never have enough of her. So he sprang up from his sitting position and scrambled playfully back up onto her. This time she was lying face up, so he knew to his delight that he'd now have an opportunity to watch her expression as he buried himself in her bush again. *How I do love those patches,* he laughed. *You never really know for sure what you're gonna find down there. Such fun!*

But this time, her response was different. As he re-entered her, there was no discernible pleasure, only acute physical pain. And this time, its emotional component was even more severe than before, simply because, while she'd emphatically said no only a few moments ago, she realized he'd chosen to interpret it as meaning yes. This time she wasn't merely hurt—she was also humiliated.

Danvers had clearly failed to get her message, so while he was busy trying to force his half-spent member back into the most intimate part of her anatomy, she fought back.

"*Stop* it," she shouted. "It's not funny, so why are you laughing? You're not pleasing me. You're not amusing me. You're *hurting* me!"

He pulled out of her, then looked straight into her eyes, his penis dangling pitifully downward toward her belly, and sneered at her.

"Don't give me that crap, you little slut! You've given me every reason to think you wanted it! Green light, green light, green light! I knew even before that pie arrived that the dessert you were really looking forward to was *me*!"

Cecelia squirmed out from under him and off the bed. "You pig!" she spat. She lit into him as she angrily yanked her underwear and jeans on. "You led me on! You tried to impress me with your knowledge of literature and your love of books, then lured me up here with the promise of allowing me to cast my eyes on that priceless facsimile of *95 Theses*. And now look at what I've gotten for my trouble—for my rare, idiotic moment of trust in you!"

Before she could put on the rest of her clothes, he jumped off the bed and backhanded her across the face so hard that she fell to the floor. Then he hauled her up and pinned her against the nearest wall, knocking the lamp and the alarm clock off the nightstand in the process. He could see a widening rivulet of blood traveling down from the left corner of her mouth now, and the sight of it only deepened his rage.

"You sick son of a bitch!" she screamed. She tried to get away from him but could not. He had her pinned to the wall with the force of his weight.

He seemed shocked momentarily at the intensity of her anger. Then, still unapologetically buck naked, he grinned sadistically. He moved his face very close to hers, as if he were a deranged ophthalmologist, and studied the terror in her eyes.

Danvers trembled as he grew more and more red in the face. He grabbed her by the throat and tightened his vise-like grip. "So whaddaya have to *say* about yourself?" he howled. "Do I get an apology for your insolence? Are you gonna put out like a Good Girl now? I got you out of a jam this morning by paying your bill! And then, because that wasn't enough for you, you sat there and said nothing while I picked up the tab for your dessert. You'd obviously intended all along to rip me off with your cunning ways. Say it's true, now. *Say* it!"

"I'll be *damned* if I'm gonna say it!" she wailed. "Why are you *doing* this to me? Am I plain awful as a woman, or do you just hate *all* women? Fucking lunatic misogynist!"

"Say it, or pay the price!" he shouted. "*Say* it, goddammit!"

"Fuck you! Fuck all men *like* you," she ranted. Then, redoubling her resolve to survive the ordeal, she dug in deep, unwilling to cave in to his demands. "You seem not to understand my position in this matter, Mr. Danvers," she said, reaching into the pocket of her jeans. "Maybe this will make it clear to you!"

She flipped open the knife she'd taken from her half-brother and, with all the strength she could muster, jammed the entire length of the blade into Danvers' thigh.

He was on the floor now, writhing in pain. *Perfect timing,* she laughed. *Good to see that fucker suffer for a change!*

She was certain it was over now, but then she watched with almost clinical detachment as he pulled the knife out of his wound, struggled up onto his feet, wound up like an MLB reliever, and delivered the full, destructive power of his doubled fist straight into her jaw. She slumped down onto the floor, spitting out two of her front teeth as she fell.

"Bitch!" he shouted down into her bruised and blood-ied face. "I was gonna leave some serious money for you in return for a little roadside pussy—a little 'Traveler's Delight.' But not now, honey—not *now*!"

He kicked her in the ribs for good measure, then turned around and grabbed the envelope with the two hundred dollars in it. "I might be a bit of a werewolf on occasion," he smirked, "but no one's ever gonna accuse me of bein' a *tightwad*! If you'd delivered the goods, you'd have been paid, fair and square!"

He got dressed, stuffed the envelope safely back into his vest, then headed downstairs and left through the rear, ground-level entrance. He remembered the sight of Cecelia's motionless body on the floor as he left the room. *Gotta give that girl some credit,* he laughed. *She's a damn good actor—a real ham! Just hope she doesn't croak. That might just prove to be a problem. Or not. I'll be gone before anyone finds her.*

* * *

When Cecelia regained consciousness, she knew something was wrong. She was no longer sprawled out on Danvers' bed, waiting eagerly for him to seduce her. She was on the floor, naked from the waist up. Whatever happened had clearly been pushed back into her subconscious, because she had no clear memory of it.

When she tried to get to her feet, a shock of pain in her ribs took her breath away. With great effort she got up, went to the window, and peered behind the shade. It was pitch dark out. Her chest was caked with blood. She realized there could be only one answer: she'd been attacked and beaten. Given how sore she was in and around her vagina, she must surely have been raped as well.

She began searching around the room, hoping to see some evidence of who might have done it to her and why. Surely Christian hadn't done this to her; it had to have been another guest—or perhaps someone from outside the motel, she reasoned—a prowler or some other sicko.

Then she saw a shiny object on the floor—a knife of some sort. The blade was covered with dried blood. She picked it up, then realized it was *her* knife—the one she'd taken from Brent.

I was smart enough to use the knife, she thought. *But how in heaven's name could I have been dumb enough to put myself in a position to actually need it?*

Suddenly, the pieces of the puzzle began reassembling themselves. She remembered what she'd used the knife for, and a flood of vivid, deeply disturbing images brought her back to reality.

"Christian!" she shouted. "Christian Danvers!"

Shouting made her mouth hurt. She tried to lick the half-coagulated blood off her lips. And when she felt the tip of her tongue travel through a wide, slippery gap where two of her front teeth ought to have been, she gasped.

She could have gone and looked at herself in the mirror in the bathroom, like most people would have done, but for some reason—perhaps pure animal instinct—she got down on her hands and knees instead and began searching frantically for the missing teeth. Within a minute or two, she managed to find both of them—one hiding under the nightstand, the other trapped, incongruously, inside a bedroom slipper that Danvers must have left behind him when he escaped.

"Goddammit!" she roared. *How can I go anywhere looking like this? And where the fuck am I gonna get enough money to put my face back together? I look like a demented jack-o-lantern without my two front teeth. I could just murder that bastard.*

She slowly finished getting dressed, then left Danvers' hotel room and went back to her own room, grateful no one was in the halls to see her bruised and bloodied. But in the morning, she realized there would be no way around it: front teeth or no front teeth, she would have to go downstairs and check out. She hoped the desk clerk would have some compassion, stick to business, and not ask a bunch of nosy questions.

She sighed, turned off the bedside lamp, and plopped down in the faux leather armchair that every cheap motel room in America seemed to have—a utilitarian anchor in a tempestuous sea—then laid her head back and began to sort through her feelings about what she'd been through.

The sex had felt good the first time around, pain of entry aside. But the second time? No! Anything but! What ought to have been an absolutely thrilling moment for her—a grand introduction to a lifetime of sexual fulfillment—had instead become a violent ordeal, a nightmare without justification. *Why, oh why was once not enough for him?* she thought. *And how did I not see it coming? How could I have been so naïve—so downright stupid?*

At that moment, trapped between red-hot anger and the most absurd, irrational self-denial, the question foremost on her mind was still whether she'd actually *been* the victim of a rape. *Do all rape victims suffer this uncertainty, or am I the only one?*

To calm herself down, she dragged her armchair closer to the window and looked out into the all-consuming darkness. She wanted badly to believe the sky was alive with the sounds of insects; for her it would have been a moment of soaring optimism. But in November in North Dakota? It wasn't going to happen. And yet, with the help of a shimmering, lemon-hued moon, the few clouds she could see were glowing like a springtime horizon in the late-night sky. *At least,* she smiled, *there's the moon!*

Chapter Twenty-one

The moon was as much a fascination for CeCe now as it had been in childhood. To her it was a shining Necco Wafer orb of surpassing beauty and mystery. There had been moments in her young life when, deep down, she truly believed that, like Neil Armstrong, she'd actually *been* there. It was high in the sky, yet it seemed so close to her that there were moments when she was certain she could reach up and touch it whenever she wished. But try as she might, it remained stubbornly, maddeningly unavailable to her.

And yet the moon's formidable distance from Planet Earth—a daunting 239,000 miles of cool, crepuscular, impenetrable darkness—was still not enough to stop her from interacting with it in her own understandably limited way. That way was—and always would be—dancing.

As she sat there in her room at Strickland's, she set aside thoughts of Christian Danvers' violent attack on her that morning. The moon reminded her of that magical moment when, at the tender age of four, not long after meeting her father for the very first time, she became Princess Aurora and danced happily with the moon, entirely in harmony with the heart-melting music of Tchaikovsky. *The dashing Mr. Moon was my partner that night,* she laughed, *my shining, milky-white dance mate. And how beautifully he danced! For one unimaginably exultant moment, we were Together as One.*

She got out of her chair and peered out the window to see if the coast was clear. To her delight she saw only a half dozen cars scattered across the parking lot, all of them a good distance away from the room she was staying in. *Good,* she laughed. *No nosy humans!*

Then she slipped into her robe, tiptoed down the stairs, and stepped out onto a large, frost-bitten swath of lawn just beyond the motel. At one end of the swath was a rectangle, roughly thirty feet square, designated for dog-walking and surrounded by a six-foot high enclosure of hibiscus. *Perfect,* she smiled. *I'll be hidden from any sick-minded voyeurs. It'll be just me and Mr. Moon, and I really don't think he'd mind seeing me down here, doin' my thing. After all, he's used to it!*

After weeks of thumbing herself across the Upper Plains, she felt, more than ever before, free of any social conventions. And because of it she no longer felt obligated to repeat, over and over again, that imaginary moment when Cecelia Koroneva, her great-great-grandmother, would dance to wild applause and a cascade of roses at the Mariinsky in St. Petersburg. *Tonight,* she resolved, *will be my night and no one else's. And I just know she'd understand! I'm feeling more Isadora Duncan than Cecelia Koroneva, and it's a wonderful feeling. Time for me to forge my very own path to fulfillment, just as my great-great-granny did so many years ago.*

When she was reasonably certain that everyone in the motel's rear-facing rooms was sound asleep—she could see that the blinds were down in every window—she decided there was no good reason for her to be discreet. *Haven't I had enough of that nonsense by now? I've been such a prude! But now, thank God—whatever that is—it's goodbye to all that!*

Alone in the early morning chill, she allowed her jacket to slip silently down onto the lawn. Then she took off her shirt and bra, pulled off her jeans, and stepped out of her panties and stood there, entirely unencumbered by clothing, proud to distraction of being the free-spirited, devil-may-care woman she'd become since leaving home. *Nothing,* she whispered—*not the November cold and not lowlife predators like Christian Danvers—can ever rob me of my right to self-expression!*

The temperature had fallen precipitously now, and a brisk, late-autumn wind, traveling rapidly down from Canada, made her body come to life in a way that Danvers and his kind could never have done.

Would you look at that face! she thought to herself while staring reverently up at the Moon's bright orb hung on the vast, star-studded tapestry of darkness. *I do believe I've turned my Man on,* she laughed. *He's not just smiling now, he's leering!* She enjoyed being the object of a man's desire, even from such a vast and inviolable distance—even when it was the yearnings of a man more imagined than real.

But the memories of her great-great-grandmother, so far away in-long-ago St. Petersburg, continued to haunt her. So in spite of her rock-hard determination to think entirely for herself—to cut the suffocating ribbon of dependency—she couldn't help hearing the opening notes of an imaginary overture far off in the distance.

In response, she extended her arms upward toward her Lover, employed her long, elegant legs to execute a series of classic scissors maneuvers, then artfully pinwheeled herself across the lawn.

Once back on the ground, she stood proudly at attention, caught her breath, then looked up and blew the Moon a kiss. She could swear that he returned the favor with a sweet celestial kiss of his own, as only her Man in the Moon could do it.

She was all set to perform another series of maneuvers when a loud, sharp noise—a slam of some sort—pierced the air from high up behind her. Startled, she spun around and saw a man hanging half-out of his second-story motel room, wearing an Army cap and ogling her with the help of what appeared to be a pair of heavy-duty military binoculars. Then she realized he was easily high enough above her to see everything over the top of the enclosure, including her in all her stark-naked glory.

Jesus Christ! she snarled. *They're probably infrared, too. The fucking asshole!*

"I'll fix that bastard," she whispered. "I didn't play softball for nothin'!" She grabbed a sizable rock off the ground, leaned back, and pitched it straight up at his window, knocking the binoculars clean out of his hands and down to the ground. Then she watched with glee as he cracked the top of his skull on the window casing while trying to pull his head back inside.

He finally managed to reach out and close the window, but not before he hurled a noxious spray of Grade A obscenities down at her, words so over-the-top offensive that even *she*—a gifted connoisseur of the art of the epithet—found both deplorable and, on purely moral grounds, inexcusable.

Thornwood and the moon excepted, she grumbled, *another good reason for me to hate the male of the species.*

Then, shivering from head to toe, she slipped back into her clothes and scurried across the lawn and back to her own room. She didn't bother to check out the binoculars. *After all,* she laughed, *I've no plans to be a nighttime stalker.* Instead, she went back to her room, crawled into bed, and slept the night through.

* * *

The next morning she got dressed, gathered up her courage, ran a comb through her hair, and without bothering to look into the mirror reported to the motel's service desk to check out officially. She intended to keep her talking to a minimum and get out as soon as possible, hoping the clerk wouldn't notice the dark, cavernous gap in her smile.

But her strategy failed. The moment she opened her mouth to say good morning, the clerk—a chubby, diminutive brunette with gray-green eyes and a built-in smile, probably in her sixties—stared and then gasped.

"My *God*," she shrieked, "what on earth has *happened* to you?"

"Don't know what you mean," Cecelia mumbled. "I mean, just another typical day in the life of a drifter."

"But your *teeth!* And those *bruises*! You must have gotten into a tangle with *someone!*"

"Listen," said Cecelia, "I can't stand around and talk right now. I need to check out! Have to get back on the road, ASAP."

"But the entire left side of your face is puffed up like the cheeks on a squirrel! Somebody—some *asshole*—must have *done* this to you!"

Oh, *shit*, moaned Cecelia. *I've been turned into a goddam carnival attraction. Thanks again, Mr. Danvers!* She decided to trust her better instincts and, without going into detail, tell the desk clerk what had happened to her.

"An infatuation gone bad," she said, her lips quivering, her eyes moist. "I thought a guy who offered to help me yesterday was a real gem—a man of high character, as decent as he was beautiful. He was so sincere! But then I let my guard down and went upstairs with him, and, as you can see, I paid dearly for my foolishness."

"Do you want me to call the police?" asked the clerk. "I really *should*, you know."

"Do what you have to," she sighed. "But honestly, I can't afford to hang around and get mixed up with the cops right now. I've spent too much time on the road already and don't have a whole lot to show for it. Got to get my thumb back in action and catch a ride west."

"All right, honey!" said the clerk, "I'll call 'em. But I sure do hope you'll get yourself patched up right away. Honestly, your face is an absolute *mess* right now. And for heaven's sake, stop trusting people you hardly know, just because they 'look good' and seem to be 'sincere.' Creeps like that are good at what they do. They're gifted actors! And now you know: it just isn't *worth* it. Anyway, here's your receipt. Sign at the bottom, then give me your room key, and you'll be on your way. I'm so sorry to see what's happened to you!"

Cecelia signed the paper as directed, then felt a tap on her shoulder. She turned around to see where it came from, and there, looking compassionately down at her, stood a tall, frumpily dressed man with dark, slicked-back hair and an expression on his face more suited for a funeral home than a motel. Right away, he reminded her of that repulsive toad in Alfred Hitchcock's "Road Hog" who gets his sweet come-uppance when his thoughtless, self-serving driving results in the death of a boy on the way to the hospital.

"Somethin' *bothering* you?" said Cecelia, who was in no mood for yet another man with an agenda. Lately, in fact, she'd begun to feel as if that described every man in her life.

"Nothing. Not at all!" said the man. Then he pulled a business card from his shirt pocket and handed it to her. "I just wanted you to have this."

"No thanks," she said, making sure there was plenty of sarcasm in her response. "I don't know what you're selling, mister, but I can assure you I don't need any!" She took the card from him, then flicked it down onto the floor without bothering to read it.

"But I can *help* you!" he said. "I've no bad motives! I just like helping people who are clearly in a jam, and from the looks of you, you certainly seem to fit the description. Furthermore, there would be no charge! Do you hear me? No charge!" Then, clearly a bit offended, he turned on his heel and left.

"What a jerk!" said Cecelia.

"Not really," said the clerk. "He's a regular here, and we have no reason not to trust him. In fact, we *like* him. If I were you, I'd pick up that card and see what he was offering to do for you. It may be something you'd be *thankful* for! Yeah, I know he's kind o' unsightly. Not *my* cup o' tea, anyway. Yours either, I imagine! But I didn't see any evidence that he was up to something dishonest. He's just the helping type! We need *more* o' that type around here."

"All right," she snapped, "go ahead and read the damn card!" Then she picked it up and grudgingly handed it to the clerk.

"Daniel J. Mortimer, DMD," she read. "Maxillofacial Orthopedics. Hmmm . . . I always wondered what the man does for a living," she chuckled. Then she continued reading: "My Specialty. Pay What You Can for Selected Cases. Available 24/7. For emergencies, call 211-878-YANK! Well, one thing's certain, the man's got a sense o' humor!"

But Cecelia never heard the last remark, because she'd already claimed the card and headed to the nearest phone booth.

She made the call, dashed out to the highway, stuck out her thumb, and waited to see what unlucky stiff would be giving her a lift this time. "All I really want again is my two front teeth!" she laughed.

The ride she snagged was surprisingly uneventful. The driver, a sullen, taciturn man easily in his nineties, was a dead ringer for the Ancient Mariner she'd learned about in high school. He clearly was not in the mood to talk—a fact that pleased Cecelia, because she wasn't in the mood to talk, either.

"Where to?" he croaked.

"Daniel J. Mortimer," she replied, "a dentist. Here's the address. I've got to get some work done on my teeth."

"Don't need the address," he said. "Know just *who* he is and right *where* he is. Fact is, he's just a couple miles from here."

"Good news," she said, smiling, but not so widely that he might see the condition she was in. But he could hear the rush of air as it whistled through the wind-tunnel opening in her uppers, and because of it he knew she badly needed some tooth work.

"Mortimer worked on my great-granddaughter after she fell down on the sidewalk while roller skating. The man's an absolute *magician*."

"Well, *that's* encouraging!" mumbled Cecelia.

"No need to worry," he said. "You'll be in good hands with Doc Mortimer."

"Good *pliers*, too," she responded.

He pulled up in front of a lovely, tree-lined home with a sign on the lawn shaped like a tooth, proclaiming his name and profession. The posts on either side of the sign were shaped like oversized toothbrushes, one bright red, the other a more subdued aqua. The bristles appeared to have been made from the truncated straws of a whisk broom.

"Better get out, honey," he chirped, almost smiling. "Got an appointment with my cardiologist in less than ten. Now listen: All you've got is a little hole in your face. Temporary! Easy to fill! But me? Well, that's another story. I've got so much plaque in my arteries, they'll need Roto Rooter to get it out of 'em."

"So sorry!" said Cecelia. "Life isn't always fair, is it." Then she hopped out of the car, walked briskly up to the entrance, and rang the doorbell. *Cross my heart and hope to die,* she laughed to herself, *I'll get my shit together again; just gimme a week or two!*

Mortimer greeted her warmly, then welcomed her inside. He talked a mile a minute, but with a gentle, ministerial tone that managed, somehow, to put her at ease not just about the appointment but about the recent downward spiral of her very existence.

Once she was in the dentist's chair, he took the two teeth from her and stored them in a clear plastic capsule with her name on it. Then he went right to work, inspecting the gap where the teeth had been. And since she was now a captive audience, he went ahead and gave the surviving teeth a good cleaning.

"So how much is *that* gonna cost?" she mumbled. "The cleaning, I mean."

"Don't worry about it!" he laughed. "I just happened to notice your teeth could use some TLC. Glad to oblige. It was the Christian thing to do!"

"Not much into that sort o' thing," she replied, wishing he'd not spoken that word. It brought back a torrent of emotions about the ever so un-Christian Christian who'd betrayed, attacked, and disfigured her only a few hours ago. "The *Christianity*, I mean. I suppose I'm just another run-of-the-mill heathen," she laughed, "but hey: I have only the best of intentions—no plans to harm others. Except, perhaps, the man who did this to me."

"I'm sorry it happened," said Mortimer. "Really! But I know you don't really mean what you said just now. You're too nice for that!"

If only the Good Doctor knew how much I'd love to slam that bastard's fingers in a desk drawer, she thought, *or maybe just lop off that little Jimmy Dean of his and run it through a meat grinder.* But out of respect for Mortimer—his remarkable generosity, his all-around Christ-inspired kindness—she kept her real feelings about Danvers to herself.

Not only did Mortimer promise to have her two teeth back in place in a matter of days, he listened to her with remarkable patience and genuine empathy as she lay there in the dentist's chair, her mouth all agape, and mumbled through the saliva around the suction tube about life in general and her most recent calamity—the nightmarish encounter with Danvers.

When he was finished, he pulled the wads of gauze out of her mouth, handed her a small paper cup full of dental rinse, and instructed her to swish it around, gargle it, then deposit it in the spittoon bowl. Then he put the gauze back in place and instructed her to leave it there for at least an hour.

"Can't afford to be casual about the choppers," he laughed. "They're the gateway to all other health issues!" Then he brought her up into a sitting position and released her from the chair. "Kind of sad, really, seeing how poor the average patient's dental hygiene is. I like to help people stay on top of that issue."

"Amen to that!" said Cecelia, appalled by her own shameful hypocrisy. She hadn't been to a dentist in nearly five years. "So how much do I owe you?"

"You didn't read the card I handed to you down at Strickland's?"

"Actually, the *clerk* read it to me," she said, blushing. "Sorry I was so rude to you this morning. I was an emotional wreck. But no matter what that card said, I want to pay you *something* for your services. You've been a real life saver!"

"I'd be more than happy to have you pay me," he said, "but not until you have your new teeth in place—and not with money. After all, you obviously don't have a whole lot o' the green stuff right now."

"Not with money?" she said. *Please, God,* she frowned, *not another benevolent perv!*

Mortimer, across the room now with his back to her, writing her a prescription for a painkiller, didn't appear to be listening.

"Can you type?" he asked.

"Can I *what*?" she responded. "Did you say 'can I *type*'?"

"Yes, *type!* Tappity-tap-tap! And are you a fast reader, a good speller, and a quick study for obscure medical terminology?"

"All of the above!" she said. "I type like a demon, and I can handle any words you throw at me—even big ones like 'maxillofacial.' But why? I mean, what does all that have to do with me?"

"*Everything!*" he replied. "You see, my medical secretary's in the hospital right now giving birth—her second pair of twins! Can you believe it? And right now there's a ton of paperwork on her desk waiting to be processed. You need money, and I need a secretary—a reliable, competent, hardworking secretary who can help me catch up—right away. I liked you from the very first moment I saw you at Strickland's and heard your story. You have qualities I've always admired in people. So if you're willing—and if you're up to the task—I'll pay you the going rate for two weeks' employment. And the good news is that I also happen to have a mother-in-law apartment—a cozy little habitat personally designed and decorated by the Mrs. But there's no mother-in-law to live in it! You could stay there while pushing papers for my practice. Even share *meals* with us! And as the card said, *No Charge for Selected Cases.* So. Will it be yes or no? I need that office work done by the twentieth. Somebody's got to do it, and it may as well be *you.*"

Cecelia delivered a resounding yes, and for the next two

grueling weeks she went systematically through reams of medical documents, checking spellings, making textual improvements, and verifying the accuracy of all personal information. She even made lasting improvements to his filing system.

The mother-in-law apartment was a Gift from the Gods—a chance for her to right her emotional compass and fine-tune her equilibrium as a survivor. Fortunately, the apartment's floor-to-ceiling bookshelf was overflowing with ambitious titles by world-class writers. *That's one smart dentist,* she laughed. And by the time Cecelia had finished her two-week assignment, she'd read nearly a half dozen of them, including Dostoevsky's *Crime and Punishment* and, on a lighter note, George Sand's *The Mysterious Tale of Gentle Jack and Lord Bumblebee*, each night after work and well into the morning hours.

The morning after her last day as a medical secretary, with her teeth back in place, she tapped on Mortimer's office door to thank him again, profusely, for his astonishing generosity and extraordinary compassion.

"When will I receive my check?" she asked after saying her goodbyes. Her eyes were filled with tears of appreciation as she spoke to him.

"There'll be no check," he smiled, then handed her an inch-thick accordion-style envelope. "There are moments when I think it's not really a sin to keep the Tax Man at bay. You know, maybe just a small white lie, long as it's good for everyone involved." Then he stepped up and gave her a fatherly, well-deserved hug for what she'd done for him.

"Now stash that away in your backpack," he said, "and *this* time, don't lose track of it! You can't afford to endure another theft of either your hard-earned money or your precious dignity. Oh, and don't you go squealing to the IRS about my little gesture. I'd get a big, fat fine—or worse—for pulling a stunt like this."

As Cecelia closed the door of Mortimer's office behind her and followed the snow-carpeted path to Main Street, her heart quickened—the result of a curious combination of unprecedented joy over the way she'd just been treated and a vague but palpable anxiety about what her next move should be.

Odd duck, she thought, *but that man was the father I never really had. I couldn't have been dealt a better hand! Maybe I've been a little too hard on the Bible Thumpers.* The encounter reminded her that she'd been meaning to read *Why I Am Not a Christian* again. But she wouldn't have told a kindly believer like Mortimer one word about it.

Chapter Twenty-two

Cecelia was aware that long-distance walking, especially in chill morning air tempered by a wealth of sunlight, was good for her. It always helped clear her mind. But after more than an hour of plodding along, lugging a heavy backpack, she decided to stop somewhere and rest. Then, just ahead of her, she saw what appeared to be a little mom-and-pop eatery—*Clara's Casual Cookery*, said the sign. She slipped inside and sat down at a table for two just inside the entrance.

Because she finally had some serious cash on hand again—*Thank God*, Mortimer would have said—she decided that, for now at least, she didn't really need to be frugal about feeding herself. She skimmed through the list of breakfast specials, then stepped up to the service counter and ordered the one called *On the Sunny Side: Two Scrambled Eggs, Three Strips of Bacon (or Sausage Links), The Toast of Your Choice, and All the Coffee You Can Drink, Just The Way You Like It.*

While waiting for her meal to come, she dug down into her backpack and pulled out the envelope Dr. Mortimer had handed her. Inside was the two weeks' compensation he'd promised her—no surprise there. But then, to her amazement, she found a smaller, separate envelope in the first one with another $300.00 in cash, all in crisp, mint-condition twenties.

Attached to the bill on top was a large, banana-colored Post-It with a message written in tiny cursive letters. "Dear Ms. Middling, Wish you were my daughter. You're an absolute Gem! A Feisty Young Female and a Credit to the Species!"

"Holy shit!" she gasped, "I do believe I be livin' on Easy Street!" Her heart swelled with deep appreciation for everything Mortimer had done for her.

Being financially flush again, however brief and tenuous it might be, lifted her spirit and fueled a growing sense that she may just have finally turned the corner and regained her footing. *To hell with the past,* she laughed. *I'm goin' Back to the Future now!* Then she laughed inwardly at what she'd just said. *That'd make a swell title for a movie, wouldn't it! Just you wait: somebody's surely gonna do it one o' these days.*

Her breakfast finally came, and after a long, luxurious repast seasoned with hopeful conjectures about her brightening future, she paid up, put Clara's Casual Cookery behind her, stepped outdoors, and began walking due west, bubbling over with optimism.

This time she had her thumb out for less than five minutes before a dark-haired young man behind the wheel of a bright red Ferrari F40 pulled up beside her and rolled down his window.

"Need a ride?" he asked, grinning from ear to ear, his voice dripping with sincerity. She couldn't quite pin down his accent, but one thing she was sure of: it had nothing to do with the good old US of A—nothing at all.

It also struck her that, under the circumstances, it was a truly ridiculous question. *After all, why else would someone be walking down a busy highway, 'neath a crisp, late-autumn sun, staring straight ahead of her with one crooked thumb pointed over her shoulder?*

She noticed right away that running down the side of the car from headlight to rear bumper was a wide glow-in-the-dark stripe with three distinctive colors—green, yellow, and blue—stacked one on top of the other. Cecelia knew, thanks to Brent, her car-crazy half-brother, that R40s came in only one standard color—a bright, fiery red—evidence that the owner had either added the strip himself or paid someone else a hefty fee to do the work for him.

"A ride?" she responded. "Maybe yes, maybe no—but first, what's with the stripe? I know this fancy-pants car of yours didn't come with one. None of those models ever did."

"Look at my *plates*," he teased. "If you know your geography, they'll have the answer you're looking for."

She stepped back to the rear of the car and saw, in bold black letters against a saffron yellow background, the word *CHIHUAHUA*, and beneath that, in smaller letters, the words *Fronterizo Privado Automovil*.

"Frijoles puercos!" she squealed. "The more you eat, the better you feel! Wish I'd had some with my breakfast this morning."

"So let's have beans for every meal!" he laughed. "Now hop in, and I'll get you wherever it is you're going."

He had a wholesome, aw-shucks way about him that made her want to trust him. *But why should I?* she wondered. *Can people really be this foolish—this ridiculously inconsistent?* Apparently, she admitted, the answer was yes.

Once inside, she slumped against the passenger door and peered out the window, looking for nothing in particular.

"So you're from Mexico?" she said, hoping to generate conversation and get her mind off the possibility of any negatives.

"Si, Señorita!" he said. "I am indeed from that country—a quaint little village, right on the border between Ciudad Juárez and El Paso. And no, I'm not dumb enough to go cruising around, picking up helpless little *muchachas* just for sport. I'm just—you know—the archetypical Good Samaritan."

"Oh, *sure*," she said, "I can *tell*." Then she quietly checked her pants pocket to make sure the knife she'd used to ward off Danvers was still right where she'd stashed it, at the ready.

"*Muchacha*?" she continued. "*C'mon*, now! I haven't been a '*muchacha*' since high school! By the way, I also want to assure you I'm *anything* but helpless! And while I like and appreciate a Good Samaritan, you'll be smart to *stay* that way. Truth is, I don't have a lot of tolerance for the bad kind."

"Don't be silly!" he laughed. "I'm less a threat to you than a doubter at a church picnic! So just tell me where you want to go, my friend, and I'll get you there *apresuradamente!*"

Friend? Here we go again, she thought. *I mean, what is it with this 'friend' thing? Everyone suddenly wants you to be his friend!* She decided not to confront him about how absurd it was for him—a man she'd known less than ten minutes—to chum her up with that over-done expression.

"Look, if you could just get me to York, or maybe Rugby, I'd be ever so grateful."

"No *problemo!*" he said. "Me, I'm headed for Helena. A hell of a long way from here, but a beautiful town. Worth the drive! York, I know, is just a stone's throw west of here. What is it they say in America? 'In a jiffy'? That's how fast we're gonna move!"

"Jiffy won't be fast *enough*," she snapped. "Just do what you can, quick as you can." Then she took off her jacket, wadded it up into a pillow, and settled in for a nap. *He's harmless,* she mused. *Maybe a bit of south-o'-the-border, Manly Man machismo—but a girl can't have everything, can she.*

She'd been asleep for a good half hour when the sharp, whiny sound of a spinning tire jerked her up out of her slumber.

"What the *fuck!*" she shouted. "Where *are* we?"

"Oh, just a momentary setback," he said. "Got off the highway to show you a favorite out-of-the-way destination of mine, but forgot it's kind o' swampy-snowy around here—icy, too—and then I got sunk down into the slush. *Damn!* But don't worry. I'll have us out in a . . ."

"*Jiffy?*" she roared. "In a fuckin' *Jiffy?*"

He tried and tried to free his car from the slush by gunning the engine, then grabbed his car phone and started dialing. "I have AAA!" he said. "They're usually quick to respond around here. Betcha we'll have 'em here before the . . ."

"*Cut the bullshit!*" she cried. "I'm not waiting around for some goddam AAA loser to show up!" She grabbed the door handle and tried to jerk it open, but it refused to budge. *Jesus!* she realized, in full-throttle panic now. *He's locked the doors on me!*

"Hey, hey, *hey,*" he cooed, "you need to calm yourself *down,* little lady!" He reached over and grabbed her firmly by the shoulders, then yanked her into his arms, reached up through the back of her sweatshirt, and tried to unhook her bra. His foul breath made her involuntarily retch.

"Let me *go!*" she screamed, then pushed him away with her left hand, made a rock-hard fist with the right one, and landed a powerhouse punch straight into his face.

Dead center! she laughed. Then she sat back and watched with pleasure as he tried but failed to stop the flow of blood from falling onto his shirt. She could see that while his head was pointing east, his nose, crumpled up and bleeding profusely, was pointing decidedly *west.* Seconds later, while simultaneously moaning and choking, he spat out two teeth—the same two she herself had lost only two weeks ago. They bounced off the seat and landed by Cecelia's feet.

"An eye for an eye!" she laughed, "a tooth for a tooth!" Then she swept the two teeth up off the floor, found the release button, jammed her right shoulder against the passenger door, and tumbled out onto the ground.

The man was ranting uncontrollably now—foul south-of-the-border epithets she'd never heard before.

"Perfect!" she crooned. "Exquisite!"

Then she got up off the ground, tossed the two teeth into a nearby puddle, and ground them into the muck with the heel of her boot.

He can buy himself a new pair, she chuckled, *or just learn to do without 'em!*

She began walking, and as she stumbled through the underbrush, she could still hear the wheels of the Ferrari spinning maniacally in the distance as he worked him-self and his prized automobile deeper and deeper into the rut he'd created. She was enormously relieved—even euphoric—to have gotten away from her attacker, but increasingly worried about her judgment. *I never should have gotten into that car,* she thought to herself. *What is it with me about 'trust'? Why am I such an easy dupe for my own self-imposed stupidity?*

Eventually, she saw a sign pointing toward Route 2, her last remaining ticket to freedom, ahead of her in the distance. She made it there in a minute or so, then began walking west again, feeling better about her prospects in spite of the unpleasant weather and her fragile, unpredict-able self.

What should have been a moment of triumph—her cou-rageous, no-nonsense response to a violent assault by a wandering predator—soon descended into what could only be described as a growing, festering Slough of Despond, a sickening feeling that her life in general had taken yet another turn for the worse and she was now in deep, irre-versible trouble. The reality of her consistently poor judg-ment—that, and the sorry circumstances she'd once again gotten herself into—had begun to take precedence over her long-held conviction that she was a strong, intelligent, invulnerable woman.

Why this endless shitstorm of worthless, self-absorbed boy-men in my life? she asked herself. *What is it about so many allegedly 'adult' males that makes them care more about themselves than anyone else they come in contact with?*

She began counting them off. *Clayton Middling—my arrogant, culturally ignorant, know-it-all father; Brent Guertner—my pitiful preadolescent half-brother who thinks he's a hunk while his mother thinks he's a genius; Renowin Chilcott—a self-proclaimed 'poet' with a propensity for the most flagrant dishonesty; and Christian Danvers—a Major League bullshitter with the face of a saint but the heart of a sadist!*

She knew there were still a handful of decent men on the planet, but as far as she was concerned they would always be more aberration than example. *Fenton Clevenger, the trucker who was so kind and compassionate to me in my time of need! Mr. Thornwood, the finest teacher I've ever known—a man who moved heaven and earth to respect my intelligence and nurture my intellect! Daniel J. Mortimer, who gave me back my smile and repaired my damaged hope for Humankind!*

Why so few of that kind of man? What the hell was God—if there really is a God—thinking when he built the male brain?

The truth was that she'd begun to think there might be an easier way to remove herself from proximity to all men like the ones who'd made her life hell since the time she was just a tiny thing.

Wouldn't it be a more efficient, more expeditious solution to all of my problems? If I were entirely out of the picture, wouldn't my absence from the tumult finally put an end not just to my personal misery but the misery of everyone around me—to all of those people who've been so unhappy with me for so long?

I could think of it as an exquisitely flawless, truly egalitarian strategy, she laughed, *the definitive Quick-Fix Solution to all my problems!*

Of course, I wouldn't be dumb enough to get my scarf caught in the axle of a sportscar. Nor would I load the pockets of my trenchcoat with rocks, then take a one-way early-morning stroll into the River Ouse. I mean, come on, now: only a real whacko would do things like that!

Then again, I could always stick my head in an oven. After all, I love cooking! But what if that oven happened to be on at the time? I should think it would make an awful mess of things—my kitchen, my children if I had any, my reputation—and especially my ever-so-photogenic self!

She began to write down her ideas in a little spiral notebook she'd purchased in Rugby a year ago—a list of the things in her life most in need of attention and the many ways, ranging from prudent to reckless to self-destructive, she might address them.

But she clearly wasn't ready yet for the most radical one of all. Even she knew that.

For now, she decided, the only thing she could bring herself to do would be to keep walking until she couldn't walk anymore, then snag another ride and instruct the driver to deliver her to York, the next town west of Leeds. Once there, she could find a cheap room, have a late-night meal and a good night's sleep, then continue her cross-country trek—by now a meaningless, snowbound Pilgrimage to Erehwon—the very next morning.

It was well past noon now, and while the sun was still high in the sky, it had become bitterly cold outside. Still, she figured it was exhaustion, not the falling temperature, that had suddenly made her feel so miserable. She walked and walked, then walked farther, trying without success to regain control of her crumbling self-esteem. Her back was sore, her feet blistered, her sense of a future worth living all but obliterated. She shuddered to think how many more hours of walking—*and for what good reason,* she wondered—were still ahead of her. She'd run out of drinking water more than an hour ago, so her lips were parched, her throat dry as sandpaper.

Other than an odiferous garbage truck and an unsavory trio of cyclists wearing Brodie helmets and leather jackets emblazoned with skulls and swastikas, she hadn't seen another vehicle on the road—another *human,* even—for more than an hour. *I pray those creeps were the only ones who actually live around here,* she fretted.

Then she heard the deafening roar of air brakes, and when she spun around to see where the sound came from, she watched with amazement as an eighteen-wheeler with the message *Beanz Meanz Heinz!* on its side—and Fenton Clevenger behind the wheel—came to a screeching halt.

Chapter Twenty-three

"Cecelia!" he shouted from high up in the cab. "What in God's name are you doin' *here*? I thought you were long gone from this part o' the world!"

"I thought so, too," said Cecelia, coated head-to-toe with road grime and ice crystals and wearing a look of bone-deep exhaustion on her face. "But bad stuff happens, doesn't it! The world makes a wrong turn, and sometimes we have no choice but to turn along with it."

Clevenger, shocked and then disturbed by her condition, laid a blanket down on the passenger seat, swung the passenger door open, and ordered her to come around and get in. And this time there was no hesitation—only a feeling of deep gratitude for his authentic blue-collar humanity.

Once she was inside, she leaned toward the passenger door, made a pillow out of her jacket, and settled in for another badly needed nap. She'd done the same thing the last time she rode with Clevenger, and she found herself wondering if his eighteen-wheeler had become the closest thing to an actual *home* for her.

Clevenger was eager to learn more, but out of respect for her, he decided to keep his mouth shut and give her a chance to rest. So he got back on the road, continued driving west, and left the radio off for a change.

He drove for another twenty minutes or so, determined not to make any sudden sounds that might disturb her, but his resolve didn't last long. The moment he heard her shifting around, trying to find a better position, he spoke up.

"Cecelia," he asked, "I don't want to pry into your personal affairs, but can you at least tell me you're on the right track now in your life—that you're doin' OK?"

"As OK as anyone who's gone through some rough moments can expect to be, I suppose."

"Rough moments? I've been through a few o' those! If you want to open up and share 'em with me, I'm all ears." His fatherly inclinations made him want to reach over and pat her affectionately on the shoulder, but he resisted the urge.

"Not ready to talk about the 'rough moments,'" she said, "so please don't ask. But if you could get me as far as Rugby, I'd sure appreciate it. For now, I'm afraid it's just Over 'n' Out; I've got to get some rest!"

She quickly fell into a deep, restorative sleep, and when, an hour or so later, they reached the outskirts of Rugby, he nudged her awake.

"We're in Rugby now," he said, "but as you know, around here, at least, Rugby's a genuine *metropolis*. Kind o' like Chicago or Beijing! So which part do you wanna land in?"

"Any place where I can find a motel," she said. "Or better yet, a *bunch* of 'em. I can afford to be choosy."

"Anywhere near the Prairie Village Museum!" he said. "Been there twice. It's a real nice area. Lots of history. Friendly people, too! And there's a nice little motel not far from there."

She'd mellowed considerably in her attitude toward Clevenger since the last time she saw him. *Matured, even,* she laughed to herself. No longer was he a threat to her; he'd become a *comfort* instead, and she was more than thankful for his reappearance in her life.

"It was so good of you to come by and help me out again!" she said. "Wish there was a way I could pay you back for your kindness."

"No need to pay a person back for basic human decency. It's always its very own reward. Don't you forget that, Ms. Middling!"

"I assure you I won't!" she smiled.

Then, to Clevenger's surprise—and Cecelia's, too—she leaned over, threw an arm around him, and gave him one of the very few authentic hugs of affection she'd given to a man—*any* man—since the day she said goodbye to Mr. Thornwood after graduation. A moment later, there wasn't a dry eye anywhere in the cab of that eighteen-wheeler— only two quietly happy people with hope in their hearts and a deep, inviolable feeling of gratitude.

Ten minutes later, he dropped her off near the front entrance to Prairie Village. They said their goodbyes—only a few poignant words were necessary this time—and from there she needed to walk only a block or so to reach the motel he'd mentioned, called North Dakota Digs.

The place was in less than ideal condition, with threadbare carpeting, torn curtains, stained blankets that reeked of mothballs, and, in her room at least, a toilet that leaned like the Tower of Pisa and roared like a trapped animal when flushed. *So much for pooping discreetly,* she laughed. *Everyone in town will know I just pinched a loaf!*

And yet, in spite of its obvious flaws, she liked the place. It had a certain devil-may-care, counterculture charm about it, so she decided to hunker down for an entire week. *After all, it's cheap,* she smiled. *And it makes sense for another reason: I've a whole lot of work ahead of me— and a whole lot of thinking to do—before I move on.*

The room had many endearing decorative touches: a pair of eerily silent, eternally metamorphosing lava lamps, one on each side of her sagging twin bed; a turquoise '50s-era corner cabinet crammed full of knickknacks right out of Lucy Ricardo's breakfast nook; and a ceiling fan with a galloping bison on each of its blades.

An entire herd of bison on one little ceiling fan, she laughed. *Who wouldn't be charmed by that?*

She got up early the next morning, ate her complimentary "breakfast"—a cup of bitter, lukewarm coffee and a gummy 'everything' bagel with everything in it but any hint of taste—then went back to her room, sat down at her desk, and composed a statement to a small handful of carefully chosen people from both within and beyond her family.

She'd thought long and hard about how best to send a message to them about their cruelty—their obscenely self-centered inability to acknowledge any redeeming qualities in her. She'd suffered long enough from their indifference; it was time now for her to drive what she was certain would be the final nail into the coffin of their hate-infested attitudes. *I'll lay the groundwork over the phone,* she thought, *with a simple message. There's no time to do it any other way! And it'll be a whole lot more personal, too.*

First she needed to compile a list of phone numbers. Numbers for her parents, for her half-brother, and for the three Cloverton bitches—the guidance counselor, the nurse, and the substitute—would be easy to come by, but not those for the Chilcotts, Christian Danvers, and the man with the Mexico plates on his Ferrari. But Cecelia loved solving the unsolvable, and she quickly found ways to track down the more obscure numbers. It remained for her, then, only to call and leave the message. If anyone was actually home when she called, she'd hang up without saying a word, then call back later when they were either away or asleep.

CHAPTER TWENTY-THREE

Dear ________________,

This is an invitation for you—and others yet to be named—to be my honored guest at *Cecelia by Moonlight,* a very special event I've planned for Friday, December 17, 7:30 p.m., at the Experimental Forest in Denbigh, North Dakota, just off Route 2 and 13 minutes east of Granville.

Your presence here will finally allow me to deliver to you a well deserved *mea culpa* for the many transgressions I've committed over the years. I know I haven't always been the most pleasant person to be with.

She couldn't help laughing, inwardly, at the "conciliatory" tone of her apology. After all, she had no reason at all to apologize to anyone, either at Cloverton or in her family. On the contrary, *they* needed to apologize for their reprehensible behavior toward *her.*

Think of it as a *Winter Solstice* celebration, but with a spiritual component and an unforgettable twist that will be unlike anything you've ever experienced. Promise!

Now, about the setting for this event: Perhaps some of you will recall that I've always been fond of darkness, especially the kind of alluring, romantic darkness one can experience only while alone outdoors, late at night, when the rest of the world is fast asleep. I used to write about it in theme papers during my Gifted & Talented classes.

As a little girl growing up in the West Coast, Bay Area town of Sausalito, I'd sneak out of my bedroom after Midnight, then slip outdoors and dance to the very same moon that illuminated *your* nights.

Different time, same moon! Don't really know why, but for me it never failed to be a magical experience. And I never revealed to my mother what I was doing while she was sound asleep upstairs, just down the hall from me. So special—so deliciously private—were those moments that I wanted to reserve them for *me* and no one else.

That dark-of-the-night pleasure has never left me. I'm still dancing by moonlight whenever I can, but the difference now is that I'm dancing in beautiful, rustic North Dakota instead of the money-mad, tourist-choked, eternally sunny West Coast. The only other difference is that this time around, *you*—and a handful of other guests whose identity will remain secret until the day you arrive—will be with me while I'm dancing!

By now, of course, you must wondering whether you can really afford to travel from so far away to an event this seemingly insignificant in the Grand Scheme of things—and in a part of the country that you and so many other people consider remote, desolate, and undesirable.

But with all due respect, I must say that you would be *dead wrong* to think that way! North Dakota is not the environmental wasteland—the cultural burial ground—we've been led to believe it is. It has a wide array of hidden, unpretentious pleasures—qualities which over time can be every bit as rewarding as they are beguiling. I was also blind to its virtues in the beginning, but I soon saw, to my delight, quite the opposite of what I'd been conditioned to expect.

You needn't worry about the cost of accommodations around here! They're absolutely dirt cheap compared to those on the West Coast. No surprises there! And they'll be even cheaper for you, because

I've negotiated an across-the-board 40% reduction for you at Howling Coyotes, the motel you'll be staying in. (Don't worry: all the rooms there are guaranteed soundproof; you'll never hear 'em talking to each other out there on the prairie.)

Believe me, you won't regret having come here! In fact, my guess is that this adventure will prove to have been one of the wisest, most entertaining investments you've ever made for yourselves. And as a bonus, you'll be able to experience the Christmas Spirit as only the North Dakotans can do it!

One crucial favor, though: I need you to confirm your intent to attend *Cecelia by Moonlight* by mailing a note saying, "C by M YES!" to Cecelia Middling, % North Dakota Digs, PO Box 737, Denbigh, ND, 58788, no later than Friday, December 10 at 5:00 p.m.

Incidentally, getting to the actual forest will be easy. As you come within a mile of the place, watch for a large white sign with forest-green lettering, saying *Welcome to the Denbigh Experimental Forest*! You'll find a visitor parking lot just a short distance from Route 2, and you'll need only to take a brief walk from there to *Cecelia by Moonlight*. Just follow the little green-and-white "C by M" signs I've mounted on trees along the way.

See you on the 17th! And by the way, you would be wise to dress warmly in advance of your arrival in Denbigh. North Dakota nights can be a challenge this time of year; you'll be glad you took the necessary precautions.

Sincerely,
Cecelia Middling
Proud Alumna, Cloverton Regional High School

"Sincerely"? "Proud Alumna"? Now there's a couple o' laughers, she mused.

She needed a little more than an hour to complete the calls—five altogether—employing an entirely manufactured tone of contrition. She was also meticulously careful to sound upbeat and sincere, like a reformed onetime social miscreant.

Then, one by one over the next few days, the responses arrived in the North Dakota Digs mailbox and were slipped under her door by the on-duty desk clerks. And to Cecelia's genuine surprise, not one of the recipients failed to say yes to her invitation.

They were initially beyond puzzled to have heard from her, then offended to have been invited to a bizarre event staged by someone they pretty much universally detested. And yet, in spite of their initial reluctance, they were intrigued enough to realize they were going to show up at *Cecelia by Moonlight* whether they wanted to or not. A very human curiosity was clearly the driving force in their decision to attend, but their interests were more malignant than sincere, and she knew it.

The ten guests each had strong feelings about their invitations.

"What the *fuck*!" said Birdie. "She treats us like shit, then invites us to a freakin' 'dance recital' out in Yahoo Land?"

"She must be feeling pretty damn guilty about the way she treated me when I called and tried to make peace with her," said Clay. "It's the only possible reason!"

"That little *snot*!" said Brent, who was still living at home and mooching off of his parents, unable to cut the cord and, as Cecelia had, actually take charge of himself. "And to think Little Miss Goldilocks robbed me blind before running away, then expected me to forget that it all happened.

What'd I ever do to deserve this kind of treatment? Some sister! If y' ask me, she's a real *bitch!*"

"We'll show up, all right," said Birdie, "but only because we're morbidly curious about whatever the hell it is she's cooked up for us."

The Chilcotts were equally indignant. "That shameless little twat!" said Mahala. "Go figure!"

"Where's the beef?" said Renowin. "Just another little Bay Area rich kid. I mean, did she really need all that money? She had more chump change in her *backpack* than we have in our 401(k)s!"

Trudy and Valerie—and Flora, the substitute—sat in the teacher's lounge at Cloverton, railing about what they considered Cecelia's outrageous impudence.

"Why should we get an invitation from *her?*" sneered Trudy. "She's just playin' games again. She ain't nearly as smart as she thinks she is!"

"Not by a long shot," said Valerie. "And I'll bet she was playin' games with *Thornwood,* too!"

"Oh, yeah," said Flora. "My guess is that he was lending her a lot more than books, if y' know what I mean. Wouldn't surprise me if they end up gettin' *married!*"

"'Specially when Mr. Know-It-All finds out he's gotten his favorite student fat 'n' preggo," said Valerie.

"Another shotgun wedding at Cloverton," laughed Trudy—"the Las Vegas of the Dakotas. So which one o' you will be the maid of honor? 'Cause it sure as hell ain't gonna be me!"

Unlike the others, Christian Danvers was more than pleased to get an invitation. "*Thank you, God!*" he snickered. "I'll *be* there! But when I get done with Little Miss Muffet, she sure as fuck won't be glad I came!"

The Ferrari driver couldn't imagine why on earth he'd been invited, considering what he'd tried to get from CeCe and what she'd turned around and done to him. *Are all the Americans this crazy?* he wondered. *Or maybe she's decided she was wrong and he was right about what happened. I mean, I just wanted to have a little fun,* he snickered. *Maybe, if I show up at her little wingding, I'll have a chance to get even with her for bein' such a party pooper! I didn't get mine, but you can bet she's gonna get hers!*

Until the moment of their arrival in Denbigh, Cecelia decided to spend her remaining days at the Digs, rereading the three novels she'd wisely stuffed into her backpack the night before her escape from life in Minot. Books—her loyal friends and saving grace—had always gotten her through the rough spots, and she felt certain they wouldn't fail her this time, either.

She began with *Their Eyes Were Watching God,* Zora Neale Hurston's tale of bigotry, betrayal, and abuse in an obscure, long-ago Florida village.

Just who am I? she asked herself while working her way carefully through the story, page by page. *And what, I keep thinking, is to become of me? I feel like a modern-day Janie Crawford, who just happens to have been born White instead of Black!*

But abuse is abuse, isn't it? And misogyny is misogyny, no matter what its source and who the perpetrator. You'd think I've had enough of the Logan Killicks and Joe Starks in my life by now! When am I gonna learn to see trouble coming, then do whatever I have to do to avoid it?

After two nights of Hurston—one sure way, she'd learned, to pour salt on the wounds she'd inflicted on herself—she turned to Sylvia Plath's novel, *The Bell Jar. Why do I keep coming back to this book?* she laughed. *I've already waded through it a half dozen times!*

She adored Plath for her superlative, gut-wrenching command of language and emotions, but the dark, fatalistic tenor of her poetry reminded Cecelia altogether too much of the downward spiral her own once self-assured, supremely optimistic life had taken in recent months.

Maybe it's about time for me to give myself a little credit, she laughed. *I mean, at least I haven't been dumb enough to stick my head in an oven like Sylvia Plath did. So far, anyway!*

To do such a thing, she pondered, *Plath must have been at the end of her emotional rope. And by the way, where the hell was Ted Hughes while her personal crisis—her active propensity for depression and self-destruction—was so steadily gaining momentum? Could he not see it coming? Like so many of the men I've known in my short life, he seems to have chosen not to acknowledge it. Maybe he was just too deeply immersed in his own soaring ego and precious poem-building to make time for her. How awful! How tragic!*

Yes, Cecelia loved Hurston and adored Plath. But given how many men had made her life miserable, it was more than a little ironic that, among the three authors she was reading, the one she cared most about was a man.

She'd saved Sherwood Anderson's novel, *Winesburg, Ohio,* for her last night at the Digs. She considered it a monumental achievement—a loosely constructed but elegantly written paean to the kind of quirky, unsettling sensitivity generally thought to be found more in women than in men. Anderson's insights into the human psyche, presented always with uncanny, spot-on accuracy, were profound, and reading his books was like being in the presence of a doctor who could take the pulse of an ailing patient, then miraculously find a cure, then and there, that no one before him had ever been able to find after years of trying.

Who could forget Wing Biddlebaum, the onetime Winesburg schoolteacher whose hands had been in perpetual motion ever since he'd been unfairly accused of sexually abusing one of his students?

Cecelia considered Biddlebaum's predicament—that of a man once admired and respected, now shunned by nearly everyone around him for a crime he never actually committed—to be a remarkably precise metaphor for her own restless, troubled psyche.

Yes, there was something unsettling about those hands. But there was also something unspeakably *beautiful* about them. And yet even those truths couldn't fully tell the story of the man and his hands, because there was also something inherently *tragic* about them. Biddlebaum's hands were actively talking to anyone willing to listen carefully to them and learn their language. But, tragically, few people in the village of Winesburg ever really tried to hear what they were saying.

George Willard could hear the hands. Unlike the men in town who—entirely without evidence—wanted to form a posse and hang Biddlebaum from a tree, Willard had listened carefully to the hands and understood what they were trying so hard to say.

Cecelia needed only two readings of Anderson's story to understand that, like Biddlebaum, she'd been yearning since her earliest years for someone—but especially her parents—to understand her as well as George Willard understood Biddlebaum.

And like Biddlebaum, she seemed now to be running away—as far away as she possibly could—from a steady drumbeat of crimes she knew in her heart she'd never committed.

First there was her father, who never seemed to take her seriously and had the lowest imaginable expectations for her. Next, there was her half-brother, Brent, who, like his mother, thought he was perfect in every way and somehow, without evidence, inherently superior to his sister.

And then there were Christian Danvers, Renowin Chilcott, and that nameless Mexican macho man—three ducks in the same misogynistic pond. She found their hubris—their arrogant presumption of God-given male superiority—to be both obnoxious and inexcusable.

What was it about her that made men in particular want to underestimate her, deny her intellectual gifts, take such advantage of her, even physically harm her? Whatever it was, she was beginning to feel even more like George Willard, who, after bearing witness to so many injustices everywhere around him, decided to leave Winesburg forever.

Cecelia Middling, she mused. *West Coast hatchling, North Dakota transplant, cross-country vagabond. But to where, and for what purpose?* What had happened to her imaginary Winesburg? Where had it gone, and where was she going? Could there ever be another Winesburg for her? And in fact, had she ever really had one?

The grim reality of her circumstances—unanchored, misdirected, flailing—made her feel as if she'd just been flattened by some heavy, indefinable object, hurled for no apparent reason from the fourth floor of a multistory apartment house. To cope with the trauma of her raw, untethered emotions, she went straight back to her hotel room, pulled down the blinds—it was still only 11:00 a.m.—and downed a half dozen sleeping pills. Soon she drifted into a deep, anesthetizing sleep which, had she actually been awake to experience it, would have seemed easily as permanent as death itself.

Chapter Twenty-four

Two days later, on the eve of checking out from North Dakota Digs, she walked downtown, found a convenience store, and purchased the food she figured she'd need when she finally reached the Experimental Forest. From there she went to Hostler's Mom-and-Pop Hardware—All the Tools You'll Ever Use!—and, to be a well-prepared happy camper, bought three balls of twine, a sack of sheetrock screws, a hammer, a hand saw, a hand drill, a Phillips-head screwdriver, two cloth tarps, a pair of short-handled pruning shears, an awl, a length of rope, a spool of wire, a box of strike-easy camping matches, a kerosene lantern, a small jar of kerosene, a pocket lighter, and, to carry everything, a canvas tote bag.

The next morning, she checked out of the Digs, went to the nearest phone booth, and called a taxi. She'd rifled through her backpack the night before and, to her relief, discovered just enough cash for transportation and some last-minute essentials. *Without Doc Mortimer,* she thought to herself, *I may very well have been either living in a homeless shelter by now or dead in a ditch somewhere north of Nowhere. So many ways to die: what will my way be?*

The taxi—a squat, tomato-red Ford Fiesta hatchback with a missing hubcap and, on the driver's side, a swarm of key scratches—showed up promptly at 10:00 a.m. as promised. Its driver, a frumpy, ruggedly bearded man easily three hundred pounds and even more squat than his taxi, was quiet but amiable, and he got CeCe to the Guest Parking Lot of the Forest, without incident or conversation, in a little under half an hour.

"Need help with that tote bag?" he finally croaked as she stepped out of the taxi and gathered up her belongings. To her, he sounded more like a toad than a taxi driver. "That's a whole lot o' weight for someone as tiny as you!"

He could be talking about himself, she laughed. "No need to worry," she responded. "Trust me. I've handled a lot bigger loads than this one."

She'd fully expected him to ask her what was inside the bag and why in the world a defenseless young thing like her would want to be dropped off at the Experimental Forest, of all places. But as a gesture of respect for her and her right to privacy, he only smiled and tipped his hat. She was so touched by his discretion that, against her better judgment, she gave him a ten-dollar tip, then saluted him as he pulled out onto Route 2 and continued west. *A sweet teddy bear of a man,* she mused. *Kind of like my little Smokey, only all grown up. Wish there were more men like that cabbie!*

She slipped her arms under the straps of her backpack, then slung the tote bag full of tools over her left shoulder and strode off into the woods. It was dark now—well after closing time—so she knew she would need to be quiet. She couldn't afford to be found by a forest ranger, or, worse, a local policeman with a low tolerance for rule-breakers.

She'd gone out of her way to memorize the path to the clearing she'd stayed in on her first visit to the Forest, and it had clearly paid off, because she needed only twenty minutes to make it to the clearing and find the protruding slab of granite she'd been looking for.

She dropped her backpack and tote bag into the declivity behind the slab—it had made a perfect outdoor cradle for her on her first visit—then stretched out on her back and, with her backpack as a pillow, looked straight up into the heavens, where dozens of tall, slim pencil-shaped trees came together against a vast blanket of twinkling blue stars.

She always seemed happiest when she was outdoors and alone: no claustrophobic enclosures; no memories of nagging, ungrateful parents; no noisy automobiles; no artificial lights; no thoughtless, self-absorbed males of any kind. She needed only a minute or two to shed herself of all negative stimuli, then disappear into a serene, flawless world of her very own creation.

The moon was climbing high up into the sky now, and while she wanted desperately to get up and dance—to rekindle her longtime love affair with moonlight—her most immediate need was rest. She pulled a small wool blanket from her backpack, wrapped it tightly around her—especially her feet—then fell into a deep, badly needed sleep. The dancing would have to wait; she figured the moon would be back again tomorrow.

* * *

She woke up early the next morning to the sound of chattering songbirds, swaying trees, and gusts of wind. She found a place to do her business—*hope those leaves weren't poison ivy!* she laughed—broke her fast with a boiled egg and a cupful of trail mix, then immediately set about the task of preparing for *Cecelia by Moonlight.*

There was no time to waste. She'd timed her arrival perfectly, allowing herself just one long day to prepare her surroundings and rehearse the routine she'd choreographed entirely in her mind in just three short days. Her guests would begin arriving shortly after dusk, and she had to be ready for them.

If my great-great-grammy could be here tonight, she

mused, *she would be so proud! But would she forgive me for my choice of venues? I hope so! I know I'll never appear on the stage of the Mariinsky, and yet I should think dancing outdoors, in the meadow of my choice, by the light of a Necco Wafer moon, is in its own way every bit as noble as appearing in the great opera houses of Europe.*

She emptied the canvas tote bag onto the ground, arranged the tools she'd purchased into a convenient semicircle, then opened her notebook and compiled a list of chores she would need to complete by late afternoon.

First she would need a ladder. She found a pair of tall, slender saplings, sawed them off at their bases, and cut a dozen sixteen-inch rungs from them. Then she secured the rungs vertically on a large tree—one of a towering quartet of Scots pines roughly forming a square—that she was certain would be tough enough to withstand her weight as she climbed.

Then, from the other sapling, she cut a series of much longer lengths and wove them together, using twine, into a small platform just wide enough and strong enough to support her a good twenty feet off the ground. It would provide her with both a commanding view of her assembled guests and the perfect aerial lectern from which she would deliver the message she wanted so badly for them to hear.

Next, she scrambled twenty feet up the remaining three trees, limb by limb, marking them so that all four trees supporting the platform would be the same distance from the ground. Then she used a primitive pulley system she'd seen in a Scouting manual to haul the platform up into position and mount it securely between the four pines using her hand drill and the screws. When she was done, she ran a length of wire across one side of the platform, then flung the cloth tarps over the wire, side by side, to serve as an ad-hoc North Woods stage curtain.

Once she was safely down on the ground again, she stood in the clearing and stared upward, proud of what she'd done. Then she laughed out loud—easily loud enough to scatter the assemblage of forest creatures who'd been watching her as she worked. To her, the platform looked remarkably like a raft—the kind of raft Huck Finn might have made, only much smaller—traveling up into the higher reaches of a manmade forest in a remote corner of North Dakota prairieland.

It was nearly 4:00 p.m. now. She had just enough time to make three planned runs through her routine before curtain time. She felt good about it, too, because she knew instinctively that her great-great-grandmother Cecelia—a notoriously driven perfectionist—would have expected no less from her. And the simple fact that she'd been blessed with the very same name made it all the more urgent for her to perform flawlessly.

The first run-through would be purely technical. There were no hard-and-fast rules, no inviolable script. She needed only to reassure herself that, under the circumstances, her loosely conceived, free-spirited choreography would work reasonably well. And really, why should she worry? After all, she alone was the choreographer, and she alone would be the performer. It was *her* show, and she knew ahead of time that no one in the audience she'd assembled would know how to critique it anyway. *Perhaps,* she laughed, *they might even learn something. Imagine that!*

Thanks to careful planning and favorable weather, the first run-through went off without a hitch.

The second one, more physically demanding and emotionally charged, lifted her spirits and made her even more determined to turn in an unforgettable performance. For this one she'd worn the beginnings of what would be her final costume: sprigs of fresh-picked winterberry in her hair; a makeshift skirt of brightly colored, strung-together autumn leaves around her middle; and, on the front of each shoe, a small, pungently aromatic branch of Siberian larch. She would become a North Dakota Earth Goddess, a creature fully in harmony with the elements and entirely free of big-city noises, artificial light, and outdated, misguided ideas about what the "ideal" woman should look like and how she should conduct herself.

Winded now from her exertions, she got her lantern—it would provide just enough light for her to move safely around the platform after dark—and climbed up the ladder. She rested on the platform and made adjustments to her costume. From there she would also be able to watch her guests arrive and take measure of their moods, one by one. *Now that's gonna be entertaining,* she laughed.

She wanted especially to deliver a powerful message to her mother and father who, as she saw it and lived it, had been such abysmal failures as parents. After all, it might very well be their last encounter as a family—a likelihood she figured would be just fine, not only for her but for all concerned.

And if this is indeed destined to be their very last impression of me, she sneered, *it must be an authentic one! Mommy and Daddy—yeah, sure—need finally to understand that I'm not the helpless, forever-adolescent female they've painted me to be, but a fully developed woman with a beautiful body—yes, a beautiful body!—and a formidable intelligence—Mr. Thornwood said so—qualities which, out of raw envy and the most shameful imaginable pettiness, they'd never been willing to acknowledge.*

Did they ever tell me how beautiful they thought I am? Did they ever say, "My, oh my—how wonderfully intelligent is our daughter"? I mean, isn't that what loving parents are supposed to feel—how good and decent parents are supposed to behave?

She was all set to come down from the platform and do her final run-through when, to her dismay, she realized she'd lost all sense of time and her guests had already begun to show up. She quickly pulled the two halves of the curtain together, leaving just enough room between them to peer down from the opening without being seen.

First to arrive were Renowin and Mahala, the Chilcotts. They were dressed just as she remembered them the first time she saw them, he with his dusty, absurdly asymmetrical stovepipe hat and pelican lapels, she with her beaded headdress, billowy blouse, and lace-trimmed apron.

She wondered: *Have they come here in hopes of helping themselves—again—to the contents of my backpack while I'm busy dancing? Or perhaps they're hoping to see me fall flat on my face and make a fool of myself in front of everybody. I might even do better than that,* she laughed. *They might get more than their money's worth. Wouldn't they be surprised!*

Gypsies! she twittered. *I had such romantic ideas about the lifestyle of the Romani—but, it turns out, like the rest of us, they're only human. How ridiculously gullible I was!*

Fast on their heels was the trio of cutthroat staffers from Cloverton, their shrill tangle of voices brazenly disrupting the late-night tranquility of the forest. *Oh my God,* she grimaced. *The Witches of Cloverton! They're the last thing the Forest needs! And yet I wanted them here, didn't I. So I guess I've gotten what I deserved.*

And yet, somehow, she really was glad they came, because she'd finally have a chance to show them what she was made of while simultaneously reminding them of their own shameful ineptitude as educators. Trudy Ballentine! Valerie Swingle! And that beastly cunt Flora Heinrich! *Why, oh why,* Cecelia marveled, *did Mrs. Furbish ever allow that woman to trash-talk her way into the teacher's lounge—or for that matter, anywhere else in the building?*

She and the others seemed to derive their greatest pleasure from dropping turds into the conversational punch bowl at Cloverton whenever they could get away with it.

The five were soon joined by a sneering, stumbling Christian Danvers, limping along with the aid of a crutch thanks to the knife Cecelia had so pleasurably inserted into his thigh during his attack. After Christian came the Ferrari driver. She was pleased to see how twisted and swollen his nose still was, and even happier to see that he'd yet to have his missing teeth replaced. In his beady, jet-black eyes she could see a deep, lingering thirst for revenge for what she'd done to him.

She wanted badly to begin dancing—the moon, plump and glowingly luminous, was fully visible now and calling to her—but she wasn't about to move even one little toe until her mother and father and her half-brother, Brent, had arrived. *After all,* she seethed, *they're the greatest reason I put together this event in the first place. I want 'em to suffer at the mere sight of me and whatever follows. Stay tuned!*

A good ten minutes went by as she waited impatiently for the Middlings to arrive. The others were shuffling aimlessly around, avoiding eye contact, and actively wondering who on earth the other guests were and why they'd been invited to the Forest. Tonight, they were more like ants on spilled sugar than the actual people she'd once known all too well, then proudly learned to detest.

Finally she gave up—*I guess my family's not coming, goddammit!*—then pulled the curtains aside and began her descent.

She was less than halfway down the ladder when, to her delight, she caught sight of the three Middlings walking single file into the clearing.

Brent carried himself with his usual arrogant, dismissive swagger. *This is my sister?* he grumbled. *Could we really have come from the same mother?* He still hadn't found room in his heart for even one small speck of affection for her.

Clay, his stepfather, wore the usual look of cynicism and contempt on his face—a look Cecelia swore he must have been born with. *Who does she think she is, anyway,* he smirked. *What kind of game is she playing this evening?*

Birdie, the quietest of the three, appeared to be more depressed than irritated. She walked with her shoulders slumped, her head bowed low to the ground. *My mother has become nothing more than a sorry spectacle,* thought Cecelia. *Why is this happening? It's demeaning, seeing my mother this way!*

By now, all ten guests were loosely assembled in the clearing. When one by one they finally caught sight of Cecelia coming down from the platform, they stared upward, transfixed by the sight of a more mature Cecelia Middling than they'd ever seen—a woman now of the most exquisite beauty, with berries in her hair, leaves around her middle, and a smile of transcendent happiness on her face. And yet her serenity was tempered by a look of fierce determination, a message to all of them that something unique—something very, very special—was about to happen.

Cecelia could tell right away that the Man in the Moon, handsome as always, was unusually well dressed for the occasion. She also sensed that he was even more alive than usual, clearly eager to dance with her again. She looked lovingly up at him and felt honored to have him in attendance. *And he's not just a man,* she smiled, *he's a good man—the only kind worth knowing.* She knew in her heart that he was smiling down at her and *only* her. *He loves me,* she swooned. *He loves me as much as I love him!*

Caressed by the shimmering moonlight, she began dancing, her eyes glistening with tears. She was moving artfully about the forest now, gliding, darting, swirling from one majestic tree to another, her long, dark hair swaying in sweet harmony with a gentle, steadily quickening wind. She thought of her namesake, Cecelia Koroneva, and wept openly at the reality that her great-great-grandmother, the pride and passion of the ballet world, couldn't be physically here with her to share what for Cecelia was a moment of sublime, inimitable triumph.

Exhausted, she leaned against a tree just long enough to catch her breath and take a quick measure of the mood of her guests.

Brent, alone now and clearly indifferent to the spectacle of his stepsister dancing, was sitting on a fallen tree, dragging on a nasty-smelling brown cigarillo. The possibility that it might eventually land on the ground and cause a conflagration appeared to be the farthest thing from his mind.

Flora Heinrich and her colleagues were no different that night than they had been at any given moment while at Cloverton. They laughed and sneered and gossiped amongst themselves, incapable, as usual, of being moved by anything even approaching artistry. Their contempt for Cecelia was so blatant that anyone nearby could have *tasted* it.

The Chilcotts seemed every bit as indifferent to the moment as Christian Danvers, her attacker, so clearly was. The three of them were huddled together now, standing deliberately apart from the others, whispering and clucking what appeared to be their palpable disapproval of her 'conduct.' *What could they possibly have to share with each other,* wondered Cecelia, *other than open ridicule, pride in their history of criminal behavior, and outright hatred for the good things and good people of the world?*

She'd saved her assessment of her parents for last.

Her mother? Well, to Cecelia, Birdie was Birdie and would always be abrasive and judgmental. She was not quite a mother, because to be a true mother—to be consistently, authentically nurturing—would have required too much self-sacrifice. When it came to selflessness, she simply wasn't up to the task.

Not surprisingly, Birdie was staring fondly not at Cecelia but at her son, Brent—the Chosen One—the unfortunate product of a failed marriage. In her eyes, he could do no wrong. He was the only thing in the Experimental Forest that night with the power to capture and hold her attention.

To Cecelia's great surprise, it was only her *father* who managed to telegraph a disturbingly mixed message to her. Was the moistness in his eyes the result of that acrid cloud of smoke hovering over the head of his stepson, or was it the result of his own gnawing, festering guilt—his deeply rooted shame over the way, thanks to his own deeply entrenched insecurities, he'd underestimated her gifts and devalued her accomplishments over the years?

On and on Cecelia went with her performance, by now so entirely in communion with the moon and nighttime that she'd nearly forgotten that because of her and her alone, she was being watched by the very people she most detested in life—people who under normal circumstances would never have been on her guest list. The truth, she knew, is that she wanted them not merely to see her dancing. She wanted them to be *hurt* and *humiliated* by it—by the realization that here in the Experimental Forest, deep in the North Dakota prairieland, was a woman born to be creative, blessed with a rich imagination and a level of intelligence—of intellectual sophistication—that they themselves would never be able to attain.

As far as Cecelia was concerned, they were the most grotesque, most abject failures in every area of their lives, and she wanted desperately for them to realize it, then pay for it emotionally.

It was colder now, with clouds moving quickly westward, having their way with the moonlight she loved and so urgently depended on. And yet, in spite of the chill, she'd become overheated from so much unrelenting exertion. *Too bad I've got an audience,* she grumbled. *If it wasn't for them, I'd strip down and finish au naturel.*

On first arrival, the guests had seemed genuinely interested in—or at least curious about—her performance. But it soon became painfully obvious to Cecelia that they'd come not to see and appreciate her dancing but merely to *laugh* at her—to ridicule her for having had the audacity to stage the event in the first place. She realized that to them she was little more than a one-woman freak show, and then her annoyance soon turned to rage.

Why do I care what they think of my dancing, she lamented, *or anything else about me? Am I really fully in control of my life now, or am I still groveling for the approval of the very people I so deeply resent and disrespect? I'll just keep dancing, and if they don't like it, they can go fuck themselves!*

She was sweating profusely now, her skin simultaneously clammy and tingly, her muscles growing more and more strained by the concerted effort of her dancing. To deal with her growing discomfort, she decided to remove the offending costume, beginning with the leaves around her waist and the combs that were holding her hair so tightly in place. But it clearly wasn't enough. So without really thinking about it, she stopped in her tracks and took *everything* off—blue jeans and sweatshirt, shoes and socks, bra and panties—and left them in one lopsided, inelegant heap on the forest floor.

For the first time in years, she felt fully, exultantly free of every last vestige of her need for approval. If they were offended by her nudity, it was *their* problem, not hers. She loved the cool earthiness of the soil between her toes, the sweep and tumble of her liberated hair, the erotic bounce and sway of her breasts as she resumed her dancing. Any concern that she was being brazenly, unjustly ogled was gone forever now. After all, what did she care? She was once again the North Dakota Earth Goddess she'd imagined herself to be, only far more authentically so than before. From her perspective, the guests began to look even more ridiculously out of touch—more suffocatingly prudish and conventional—than when they first arrived on the scene.

Not surprisingly, some of those in attendance were amused by her nakedness. Others were either shocked at her boldness or just plain disgusted with what they saw as exhibitionism, pure and simple.

Birdie thought her daughter's behavior was pathological. *She's clearly gone out of her mind. That's what you get when you run away from a perfectly good home and two loving parents!*

Clay, obviously more embarrassed than titillated by his daughter's conduct, turned away, refusing even to acknowledge her unclothed presence. As for Brent, he just stood there as usual, shaking his head in disapproval, openly and adolescently jeering at her. *Jailbait!* he sneered. *Does she really think anyone would be interested?*

It would have been enough for the average sensualist just to be outside, gloriously free of clothing, reveling in the elements. But "enough" was never good enough for Cecelia. So, when the wind suddenly picked up and a fierce, heavy rain began pelting her, she was beside herself with joy. She imagined herself to be lying face up in the bed of a voluptuous, rapidly moving river, the water dancing concupiscently down into the very contours and interstices of her libidinous body, caressing her into a state of the most marvelous receptivity.

She watched with amusement as her guests scrambled to find shelter from the rain. *Poor, poor weaklings,* she laughed. *So cowardly, so easily intimidated.*

The sight of that polished, glowing orb never failed to remind her of the opening stanza of one of her favorite Amy Lowell poems, "Crescent Moon."

Horned. Cecelia had always wondered why Lowell chose to weave such a peculiar, idiosyncratic word into an otherwise tender, heartwarming passage. She didn't like the way it scanned, either. And yet, somehow, it really didn't matter. She loved Lowell's poetry, and she knew in her heart that were Lowell here with her tonight, the two of them would be dancing together, paying homage to the incomparable magic of moonlight.

Then Cecelia raised her arms worshipfully up toward the heavens and spoke directly to her distant, unembraceable soulmate.

"Oh, Kindred Spirit," she chanted as coy rivulets of rain made their way down her body, "why must you be so maddeningly distant? So haughty, so aloof? Will you not finally come down and *dance* with me?"

Surely Lowell must have asked the very same question countless times, beginning in her privileged, Boston Brahmin childhood. But tonight, here in distant Denbigh, North Dakota—geographically and culturally lightyears away from the poet's childhood home—it was Cecelia Middling's responsibility to ask it, and hers alone.

It was as if that glistening pale disc, shining eternally down on them from On High, were a lover Cecelia and Lowell had willingly shared across generations, only to have him stolen from them, locked away in the firmament and forever out of reach.

What, precisely, is the connection? she wondered. *Why Lowell, and why me?* She knew Lowell preferred ladies over men, and lately she'd begun to wonder if it might also be true of herself. *I mean, other than Thornwood and Clevenger, what have men done for me lately? Oh, well! If they're lucky, they'll never be able to see me again. And after all, would it really matter?*

Maybe I should wean myself off the masculine set. Lots o' luscious ladies out there! To the living, every opportunity is up for grabs—there for the taking! But for now it's strictly me and Mr. Moon. And to be fair, he has both the physical allure of a man and the sweet sensibilities of a woman. My sweet, androgynous lover! My precious Yin and Yang! He has everything I've been looking for, and for that I love him to distraction!

As she continued dancing, the wind was coming now in savage, unpredictable gusts. Then a spectacular bolt of lighting slashed down through the sky, followed a second later by a deafening clap of thunder so powerful it shook the platform she'd so lovingly built, toppling the lit kerosene lamp and setting the curtains on fire. As the wind picked up, a note she'd written listing the order of her performance was swept down to the ground.

Horrified at the growing fire, Cecelia stopped dancing, raced over to the ladder, and scrambled up onto the platform. Still naked, she tried to extinguish the flames before they spread up into the adjacent trees and set the entire Experimental Forest—the one place where she'd found the most comfort and security—on fire.

Cecelia's guests, who until now had had no real inclination to congregate, came abruptly together and began arguing amongst themselves over what, if anything, they should do to help her.

"She'll put it out," said Clay. "She's no dummy!"

"Don't be too sure," said Brent, who loved countering his stepfather, then watching him squirm. "If she was dumb enough to put this whole ridiculous show together, what makes you think she's gonna be smart enough to put that *fire* out? Anyway, as usual, she's makin' a whole lot o' ruckus over nothin'. I mean, the rain's gonna put it out *for* her!"

"Dumb?" shouted Clay. "I don't *think* so! CeCe's got more brains in the tip of her *pinky* than you've got up there between your ears!" He knew she was making a spectacle of herself, and yet the more he listened to the others taking cheap shots at his daughter—especially his own good-for-nothing step-son—the more he resented them for their cruelty.

"Sorry," said Valerie Swingle, "but I'm with your son on this one. I mean, let's be honest! She's smart, I suppose, but not as smart as Thornwood kept sayin'! And speaking of honesty, what a waste o' time it's been for me—and all of *you*—to show up here! We must have lost our minds!"

"Uh huh," said Trudy Ballentine. "Here we are, out in the middle o' nowhere, watchin' CeCe Bardot parading her privates around in a driving rain. How smart can *that* be? I didn't drive all the way out here to see those god-awful tits of hers flopping around!"

Clay wanted to strangle the woman then and there for what she'd just said about his daughter, and yet there was a part of him that wondered if he could ever forgive CeCe for doing exactly what had offended Ballentine so much. Cecelia's bare breasts were beautiful—he could see that, and so could the others—but they were the last thing about her that he, as her father, had ever wanted to or expected to see. He knew he had many faults, but erotic yearnings for his own flesh and blood weren't one of them.

The Chilcotts stood side by side, hand in hand, unmoved and indifferent to the spectacle. "She *made* this mess, didn't she?" said Renowin. "Right! So as far as I'm concerned, she can clean it up—and without any help from us!"

"I'll second that emotion," shouted Birdie, then turned to the others. "I don't know about all of you," she said, "but I've *had it* with this nonsense! Little Miss Trot-It-Out can take her bare ass and big ego back home. And that's where *I'm* goin', too! Stay if you want to, or follow me back to the parking lot—back to something like sanity!"

Then, like McCloskey's ducklings, they all formed a line, with Clay and Birdie in the lead, and waddled back to the parking lot. They were free now to return to their ostrich-like, Cecelia-free existences—but not until they'd collectively taunted, jeered at, and ridiculed the one person in the Experimental Forest that night with the kind of fundamental decency that makes the world a place worth calling home.

The Middlings left the Forest certain that their daughter would eventually return to a rewarding life with them in Sausalito, ashamed of her conduct and committed to making amends to them in every possible way. *With our help,* thought Brooke, *she'll become the very model of the ideal daughter—and a half-sister Brent can finally be proud of.*

But since long before the performance, Cecelia had clearly had other ideas. She'd vowed never to set foot in her parents' home again. *Not a chance,* she laughed. *They should have been able to see, from how I looked in my performance—and most importantly, how I carried myself—that I was never really the person they imagined me to be and will never become that person.*

Alone now, still high up off the ground, she watched the flames ebb and flow, hoping the fire would finally lose its momentum and lay quietly where it had landed, smoldering. But then the flames came to life again, this time much more aggressively.

She grabbed what was left of a tarp and began beating frantically at the flames. She was making progress, too.

But then she accidentally stepped on one end of the tarp, lost her balance, and crashed backward down onto the platform. And before she was able to right herself, the tarp she'd been flapping caught fire again, sending a ball of flames roaring down the front of her like an out-of-control semi. She flipped over onto her stomach, then rolled furiously around, trying desperately to snuff out the flames that were now licking away at her.

Why did I ever think puttin' a lit lantern on that platform was a good idea? she wailed. *All I wanted was for all of them to see how beautiful I looked and how well I danced. I wanted to make a statement they'd never forget! But now look at me. I've been cheated out of my Moment of Glory! Instead of becoming the lovable, irresistible daughter I wanted to be for them, I'm about to become little more than a strip of overdone bacon!*

If the forest creatures had been listening more carefully, they would have heard Cecelia's animalistic howling and, behind it, the crackle and sizzle of her burning flesh. Then the howling abruptly stopped, and only an eerie silence was left in its wake.

The moon Cecelia cared so deeply for, always unfailingly loyal, continued to look lovingly but helplessly down at her. Then, out of respect for her and her privacy, it lessened its gleaming and slipped behind a cloud.

An owl hooted plaintively in the darkness, answered by the disquieting chirps of a long-tailed weasel likely foraging for earthworms trapped beneath the wintery crust of the forest floor. Other than that, the only remaining sounds were the crackling of embers and the squealing of tires as her guests, fed up and thoroughly disillusioned, left the Forest.

Not long afterwards, a distant pair of clumping feet and two low-pitched, agitated voices broke through the calmness.

"I don't understand," said Clevenger as they approached the clearing. "I could tell right away, the very first time I picked her up along Route 2, that she was a tightly wound young lady—smart as a whip and yet, in some fundamental way, deeply troubled. The second time she thumbed a ride with me—I was on another westward haul—she was in even worse shape emotionally!"

"She was pretty wired at Cloverton, too," said Thornwood. "That and her hyperactive intellect really got under the skin of some of the adults around her. They didn't like being upstaged by someone only a fourth their age—someone they considered a smart-ass, precocious little Know-It-All."

"Doesn't surprise me," said Clevenger. "She didn't allow herself to be intimidated by anything I said while we were on the road. If that girl wasn't valedictorian, I'll be not just shocked, but *pissed*!"

"Well, she *did*," said Thornwood. "She *was* the valedictorian that year! You mean she didn't tell you that? I was so proud of her! But being top of the class didn't stop the smaller minds at school from doing whatever they could do to make her life miserable. And, the way I see it, that was bound to happen, because she was at least five times as intelligent as nearly all of the teachers at Cloverton! Correction: make that *all* of 'em! The truth is that there were days when I couldn't keep up with her intellectually, either. *Nobody* could! And hey: I was known around school as the Brainy One—the bookworm philosopher. Most folks at Cloverton didn't like *me*, either. They deeply resented me for going out of my way to nurture Cecelia—to feed her voracious appetite for knowledge and insight. It was a joy, knowing her. Made me glad to come to work every day!"

"I can only imagine," said Clevenger. "Anyway, I hope we're not too late to catch some of her show!"

"Me, too," said Thornwood. "I'm so glad Doctor what's-his-name—Mortimer, wasn't it?—tipped us off about this. Can't imagine how he knew about it. By the way, I must confess I was a little hurt that she didn't invite me, but I know deep down inside that there must be a reason I wasn't on the list—a *good* one, not a bad one."

As they approached the starting point of *Cecelia by Moonlight,* Clevenger suddenly stopped in his tracks, looked far off in the distance, and sniffed the air. A small cloud of smoke hovered over the area—*maybe a smoldering campfire?*—obscuring the better part of what appeared to be a half-unmoored structure of some sort, suspended a good twenty feet above ground level and swaying precariously in the wind.

"Jesus," he said, turning white with anxiety. "Flesh! Burning human flesh!"

"Out *here?*" said Thornwood. "Don't be ridiculous! I smell something, too, but burning flesh? *C'mon,* now! How could that even be possible?"

"Trust me," Clevenger snarled. "I know the smell of burning flesh! Did two years in 'Nam! The carpet bombing! The napalm! Don't tell me I don't know what I'm smelling! Corpses out there were more common than botflies and frangipani. We had to step over 'em, hour after hour, just to make it back to our posts in one piece."

"*All right,*" said Thornwood. "Burning flesh! If anyone can identify the smell of burning flesh, I guess it would be you. But *human* flesh? My guess is that it's only an animal. Anyway, we'd better find out where that smell's coming from! Incidentally, where are all the *people*? Mortimer said there'd be a crowd."

"You're right," said Clevenger. "No crowd! There's got to be an explanation. Maybe we really did miss the whole thing. *Goddammit!* Maybe they had a cookout afterward, and I'm just smelling the leftovers. If my hunch is right, there should be a roasting pit somewhere around here. Look for some smoldering embers; that'll be all the evidence we need."

The smoke had finally begun to dissipate, and what they'd missed gradually became visible. Thornwood, who was now several feet ahead of Clevenger, was the first to see the crosspieces of wood nailed to the trees. "A ladder!" he shouted. "Fine! But a ladder to *what*? No doubt *Cecelia* was responsible for this. There's nothing she can't do when she sets her mind to it. But now I want to know what on earth she was *up* to. I'm gonna see for myself!" He raced over to the tree and began scrambling rapidly upward.

"Don't be a fool!" said Clevenger. "Those steps don't look all that secure to me. You could fall and break your friggin' leg. Then what would we do?"

Ignoring Clevenger's admonishments, Thornwood kept climbing, and in less than a minute he'd made it to the underside of the platform.

"Well, now we know, at least, where the smell was coming from," he said. "Horrible!" He paused and retched violently from the stench, then climbed up one more rung and lifted his head over the rim.

There in front of him was what was left of Cecelia Middling, though at first glance it would have been hard for anyone, even her closest friends, to be certain. Her limbs were contracted, spider-like, toward her torso, her arms and legs pocked with a gruesome array of blisters. More than half of her face was unrecognizable now, melted down into raw clumps of flesh by the intensity of the flames.

The few parts of her that had been spared the torment—especially the delicate ears and the distinctive teddy bear earrings that she'd always worn on Dress Down Day while at school—told him instantly who he was looking at.

Thornwood could also see that she was completely naked, and must have been so even before the fire consumed her. A feeling of unbearable shame swept over him when he realized he was seeing more than he ought ever to have been allowed to see of one of his most treasured students, lying there helplessly in full view without a stitch of clothing. He was crying uncontrollably now.

"What's happening?" bellowed Clevenger. "What'd ya just find? You gotta *tell* me, man!"

"You don't wanna *know*," whimpered Thornwood. "Do me a favor, would you? Get back to your truck—fast as you can—and call 911 from your car phone. She's still breathing!"

Clevenger did as he was told, and shortly afterward a pair of young EMTs arrived. In less than twenty minutes, they had brought Cecelia down from the platform, and gotten her into the waiting ambulance, where she was put in a sitting position and given oxygen. Then, once she was down on her back and safely secured to the gurney, Thornwood was allowed to lean over her and offer her some words of encouragement.

"Cecelia!" he whispered. "Can you hear me? It's *me*—Mr. Thornwood! I'm so sorry I got here late and missed your performance! I *so* wanted to see you dance!"

He wanted to believe she'd nodded in the affirmative, but because she was reflexively twitching and writhing, he couldn't be certain. She was obviously in enormous pain, and yet her face and lungs had suffered so much fire and smoke damage that she was able to do little more than moan, softly, into the upper regions of the ambulance.

"No time to waste," said the lead EMT. "We need to get her to Trinity, and *fast*! And from there, she'll have to be taken by helicopter to Avera McKennan in Sioux Falls—the nearest burn center."

CHAPTER TWENTY-FOUR

"Holy shit!" bellowed Clevenger. "That's nearly five hundred miles from here!"

"Yup," said the EMT, "welcome to the Northern Plains medical establishment! Now *stand back.* We've got to get out o' this jungle and back on the road to Minot! Incidentally, there's enough room for just one extra passenger in this rig; which one o' you wants the honor of being there for your friend?"

Right away, Clevenger spoke up. "Look, I'm gonna make it easy for you, chief. This"—he gestured toward Thornwood—"is the man she needs to be near the most. I know their story! She adored him as a teacher, and he adores her. So there's no contest. He's your man."

Then Clevenger walked quickly over to Thornwood, hugged him, and thanked him for having taken such good care of Cecelia while she was a student.

"I've got a delivery to make, and so do you," Clevenger smiled. "Just promise me you'll let me know, soon as possible, how that girl's doin'! She didn't like it when I called her 'girl' the first time I met her—roughed me up pretty badly over that one. But hey, that's what she *was* to me—a *girl.* Still is! By the way, I'm not all that religious, but what the hell? I mean, you can bet I'll be prayin' for her as hard as any self-respecting Bible Thumper would do!"

Clevenger stepped away from the ambulance and headed back to the parking lot, and as he walked away, Thornwood could see tears welling up in his eyes. *He'd be the perfect Grampy for her,* he mused, *and with any luck, he'll be able to become just that. I'll make sure of it!* Then Thornwood climbed into the ambulance, took his place next to Cecelia, and settled in for the trip to Minot.

He wanted badly to lean down and hug her, but he knew that for medical reasons he shouldn't. Like Clevenger, he wasn't formally religious, so, as he saw it, praying wasn't an option. Instead, he just sat there staring helplessly down at her, hoping fervently that the news at Trinity would be good and she'd soon be back on the path to success he'd always envisioned for her.

Chapter Twenty-five

As the ambulance shot westward down the highway, sirens blaring, Cecelia's mind was racing in spite of her injuries.

No doubt they'll think it was an accident. But was it really? Yes, the storm tipped the lantern over. And yes, I ended up getting caught in the flames. So was it a freak accident? Maybe it was, maybe it wasn't. Deep down inside, maybe it was what I wanted all along to happen!

We all deserve to be the author of our fates, don't we? And why not? I mean, haven't I been through enough misery at the hands of the very people I ought to have been able to trust? Wasn't that pretty much enough already?

But I didn't really want to die. I wanted only the satisfaction of knowing, ahead of time, that all those disgusting guests of mine would be right there in the Forest, watching me dance by moonlight, every bit as artfully as my great-great-grandmother Koroneva always did. I wanted them to suffer because of what they did to me—what they stole from me! My self-esteem, my flaming idealism, my hunger for knowledge. My pride, against the worst imaginable odds, in a job well done!

So many failed relationships! So many ugly incidents! So much hatred and cruelty, unjustly administered! But worst of all, so much small-mindedness!

A mom and dad? You've gotta be shittin' me! A stray dog would've done better!

A half-brother? Brent Middling is the very definition of an asshole. If the word hadn't existed, they'd have had to invent it to describe him!

The Chilcotts? Born bullshitters! They fed me a good line, then robbed me! They brought nothing but shame to the idea of who the Romani are and what they stand for.

That creep in the Ferrari? Never got that bastard's name, but I sure as hell gave him a permanent reminder of me, now, didn't I! Makes me laugh just to think about the look on his face right after I bashed the two front teeth out o' that smirk of his!

Christian Danvers? Looks aren't the answer! Intelligence isn't the answer! False advertising isn't the answer! That boy didn't want companionship, he wanted some roadside pussy, and he thought his charm and good looks entitled him to it!

I can't bear to think about those Cloverton bitches, either. Educators? Hell no! Cunts, every one of 'em! They should be banned from the public schools of America!

Every last one o' my ten guests appeared to have at least one thing in common: they openly despised me for being so much more intelligent than they were. I have an excess of brain matter—mine a formidable mountain, theirs a piddling assemblage of molehills. I didn't ask to be born so intelligent—so intellectually curious! So why should a person like me be constantly punished for the quality of my mind?

Was it because I'm a daughter instead of a son? A woman instead of a man? Is that why my parents so relentlessly favored Brent while gleefully trashing their daughter?

Alec Thornwood understood and respected me. Fenton Clevenger understood and respected me. Dr. Mortimer understood and respected me! So why was it so easy for them to do so but so impossible for everyone else?

My worth to the world has been subjected to the most unimaginable scrutiny. I've been tried by a jury of people in no way worthy of being called my peers, and a decision has been made. A verdict has been reached. The answer? I lack any measurable value to those around me. I'm expend-able—not worth keeping for anyone, anywhere!

At that moment, Cecelia Middling had no real family, no real friends, and no loving companion. All she had to show for her time on earth were twisted limbs, a torso riddled with third-degree burns, and a face charred beyond recognition. *Who'll ever look at me again,* she wondered, *and actually like what they see? Would the world have not have been better off if I'd just gone ahead and snuffed myself out, like I'd planned to do all along, well before they got me to the Burn Center?*

But she *hadn't* snuffed herself out. The moment the ambulance arrived at Trinity, a trio of top-notch medical professionals hustled a still-alive Cecelia up to the helipad and into the chopper, and moments later she was on her way to Avera McKennan in Sioux Falls and a precarious, tension-filled appointment with Fate.

* * *

Three days later, Clay and Birdie were back in their Minot farmhouse, huddled over a late-morning breakfast. Because they never watched the news, they had no idea where CeCe was now or what she might be doing. And after a less-than-satisfying taste of Denbigh, Minot had never felt as good to the two of them as it did now.

"What a fuckin' waste of time *that* was!" mumbled Clay through another mouthful of corned beef hash. "I don't know why we ever agreed to spend time in that wasteland!"

"And then to stand out there in that ridiculous 'artificial forest,'" said Birdie, "freezing our sorry asses off—and for what? A chance to watch CeCe Middling parade her privates around for all the world to see—including her own *parents.* Can you believe it?"

"You're right," said Clay. "We must have been out of our friggin' minds!"

"If she really *loved* us," snarled Birdie, "she would never have asked us to go all the way out to such an ugly part of this state—and for such a silly reason. Think of all the things we've done for her over the years! And yet she's been so appallingly ungrateful. How did we manage to bring up such a spoiled little wretch, anyway?"

Clay listened more and more uncomfortably to his wife as she bitterly attacked and condemned their one and only daughter. *Good God,* he wondered, *is that how I've always sounded when I was talking about her?*

He also couldn't help wondering if the two of them hadn't been guilty of being more than a little too hard on her over the years, all in the name of "discipline" and "character development." He remembered the time when he charged into her classroom at Cloverton and railed against Mr. Thornwood, the teacher she'd loved to the point of worship. That and the night when, after the award ceremony, the three of them got into a heated confrontation over their having missed their favorite sitcom in order to be there for her. When he looked back for a moment at the dramatic difference between the ways Birdie treated Cecelia and Brent, he felt a sudden wave of the most intolerable shame wash over him.

"Listen, honey," he said to his wife. "I know CeCe was a real pain in the ass on occasion. I know she was pretty damned uppity about her high grades, those high-toned books she bragged about, and the avalanche of awards she got for being what they like to call a 'scholar.' But more than anyone else, I blame *Thornwood* for it! That prissy little egomaniac was always feedin' her fancy books by 'The World's Great Thinkers,' as if what we taught her right here at home wasn't good enough! But y' know what? My guess is that, even when CeCe was givin' us grief, she meant well! Maybe we should have taken a moment to look deep into *ourselves*. Maybe, sometimes, we judged her just a little too . . ."

"A little too *nothin'*!" shouted Birdie. "If anything, we—allow me to correct that: *you*—smooched her little butt way too many times. And look what you got for your trouble! I figured that when Brent came back into the fold, she might actually *learn* something from him. But no! All she 'learned' was where he kept his valuables! He told me all about the stuff she stole from him the night before she ran away from home! And believe you me, when she gets back here in a few days, I'll make damn sure she *pays* him—in full and *worse*—for what she took!"

"You really think she'll be coming back?" he asked.

"Are you *kidding* me? That girl's always known who butters her bread. Besides, she's not smart enough to live on her own indefinitely! Mark my words, Clay: your Daddy's Girl will be back all too soon, suckin' off our bank account, just like in the Good Old Days. And if experience is a teacher, you'll be dumb enough to let it happen!"

Also back in Minot, the Witches of Cloverton were gathered together in the teachers' lounge, digging for dirt—their favorite pastime.

"Can you believe it?" laughed Trudy, then took a deep, lung-punishing drag on her Menthol. "Lucinda Carlyle's fat 'n' pregnant!"

"Don't go jerkin' me around," crowed Valerie. "It ain't possible! Last time I talked with Lucinda, she said the only bone her hubby can get any more is from a dead chicken!"

"Maybe someone *else* planted that seed," Flora cackled. "Word around school is that she's been spendin' a whole lot o' time down at LeMay's Tavern, chummin' up with Turnell Flabin, the bartender. I'm tellin' you, he's a *major* hunk! Have you seen him lately? If any bone could put

Carlyle in the family way, it'd be Flabin's. My God: what a package that man has!"

"Cut it out," said Valerie. "Lucinda is old news. The more *timely* story has got to be *Cecelia Middling*, don't y' think?"

"What *about* Cecelia Middling?" said Flora. "Haven't we had enough of her for now?"

"Connie LaFleur told me she's in the hospital somewhere a long away from here," said Valerie. "She wouldn't tell me why, though. Said she promised not to mention it to *anybody!*"

Like the Middlings, the three Witches never read the newspapers or watched the news, so they were as far out of the loop as it was possible to be.

"Probably all pooped out from that crazy *dancing* she was doin'," said Valerie. "Wouldn't *you* be?"

"Maybe *Thornwood* knows," said Trudy. "We can wring it out o' him soon as he comes back."

"Comes back from what?" said Valerie.

"From his *sabbatical*," said Trudy.

"Sabbatical, my ass!" she snorted. "He and that little Princess of his have probably *eloped.* Probably tied the knot in Vegas, just like we *said* they'd end up doin'!"

"That's ridiculous," said Valerie. "If y' ask me, that little faggot is prob'ly in San Francisco. By the way, I wonder why Cecelia didn't invite him to her big bash."

"Maybe she finally realized what a vapid little twerp he really is," said Flora.

"All right," said Trudy. "I think we've had about all the fun we can with those two. CeCe's in the hospital. Thornwood's on sabbatical. Doesn't get better 'n that!"

Then the room grew quiet.

"*Think* about it," Trudy continued. "We flew out to Minot. We saw God's Little Angel stumbling around in the forest, swingin' from the trees, shakin' her booty and calling it 'dancing.' Then we came to our senses and flew back to Normal Town. So enough is enough, I say! We've gotta find ourselves a fresh bone to gnaw on."

"You're right," said Flora. "A *fresh* one!"

"*I've* got one for you," whispered Valerie. "Ted Benchley, the boys' soccer coach, said he was in the bathroom yesterday after practice, takin' a leak, and right there next to him was Alec Thornwood, the Cloverton Scholar, scratching his little nut sack over and over again. Looked like Chippy the Squirrel, stockin' up for the winter."

"Sounds more like *herpes* to me," said Trudy.

"For heaven's sake," hissed Flora, "how 'bout keepin' it down? You never know when Attila the Hun's gonna show up!"

"*Attila the Hun*? Who the hell is Attila the Hun?" said Valerie.

"The *principal,* numb-numb!" said Trudy. "Time to go back to school, read your history, and learn from it!"

"Yeah, *history,*" said Valerie. "But if y' ask me, history in *this* school is pretty damn sordid! I'm tellin' you, ladies, it's about time we pull ourselves together and find a way to . . ."

Then the bell rang, putting an end to yet another steamy, clandestine early morning kaffeeklatsch. And as with all the klatsches held by Cloverton's Three Witches, this one was best forgotten.

"Well, guess that's enough o' the chatter for now, girls," said Flora. "Time for us to get back to our Chosen Profession and put all those little snotnoses to the grindstone, huh? Hard way to make a buck, but hey: *somebody's* gotta do it. So *Let's Go,* Team!"

* * *

Thanks to favorable weather, the chopper made it to Sioux Falls in record time. The staff at Avera McKennan leapt into action and wheeled Cecelia into the burn center. Alec Thornwood had no choice but to wait in the lobby, scared to death that Cecelia might not survive her ordeal.

CeCe listened as the doctors and nurses huddled over her, taking her stats and mapping out the most urgent protocols, all while engaging in the usual tension-relieving small talk.

"Oh, my God," said a nurse. "She's an absolute train wreck!"

"Pipe down!" whispered the anesthesiologist. "She may still be alert enough to hear you. You should know that by now!"

"But Laney's *right*," said the head nurse. "There are obviously some third-degree burns. And yet all in all, she appears to have been a very lucky girl. Trust me: I've seen a whole lot worse! Anyway, if everything goes her way, she could be out of here in eight to ten weeks."

"Maybe," responded the surgeon. "But y' know what? It's her *face* I'm most worried about. Aggressive facial reconstruction has to be done in stages. We can tack five or six months onto her recovery time if we want her to leave here looking anything like she did before those flames got to her! And then, of course, there's always that fastball down the center: Yer *out*! Here today, gone tomorrow! The human body's jus' chock full o' surprises, ain't it."

Doctors, raged Cecelia, unable to form words thanks to swollen, blistered lips and a severely scalded windpipe. *They think they're so damn smart—so superior! But they're really no different than we are. It's all guesswork, even in hospitals! 'Think she'll survive the burns?' 'Don't know!' 'Will her face be sweet 'n' kissable?' 'Maybe!' 'Will her own loved ones even recognize her?' 'Better Not Tell You Now.' 'Ask Again Later!' It all makes me sick!*

I keep thinking I should've just lain there and let that fire finish me off, she thought to herself. *They'd have been better off without me!*

Shouldn't logic—or maybe just some good old-fashioned common sense—prevail? she wondered. *Wouldn't it be easier now if I just kind o' fade away like the proverbial Old Soldier? Do I really want to go through burn rehab? I can tell from everything they said—most of 'em so friggin' certain I'm too far gone to hear 'em—that even if I do survive, my chances of living a happy, fulfilling life are less than minuscule.*

She tried repeatedly to roll over onto her left side—the side she'd preferred to sleep on from the time she was little more than an infant in her crib—but to no avail. The truth, she realized, was that she no longer had the strength to do so. And yet she was still conscious enough to know that they wouldn't have allowed her to do it anyway.

And so, resigned to what she imagined would be her fate, she closed her eyes, lay still as a tombstone, then watched in wonder as what appeared to be a small universe of bright, crystalline stars and faraway planets spun majestically around beneath the cool, tissue-thin canopy of her eyelids.

It's moonlight, she marveled. *And stars!* And then, as a sweet, caring cloud of the most remarkable serenity embraced her, the pain lessened, and somehow she knew with certainty that she and her beloved Man in the Moon— the only kind of man she'd ever yearned for and the one man who'd stood by her at every turn—would soon be side by side for real, dancing for Eternity.

About the Author

Maine arts multiple Ross Alan Bachelder, author of *Happy Dawg Walks the Sad Man: The Remarkably Varied Adventures of a Confirmed Arts Multiple* and *Revenge: Tales Best Read in the Twilight Hours,* has enjoyed a long, rich life happily immersed in the fine and performing arts.

A writer, musician, theatre professional and multimedia visual artist, he's traveled extensively in the service of all things creative, attending concerts and plays, performing solo recitals, playing in pit orchestras, and touring museums in England, Scotland, New Zealand, Canada, Reykjavík, Paris, and Amsterdam. He's also visited museums in Boston, Philadelphia, Cincinnati, Detroit, Chicago, Indianapolis, New York, and many other cities.

He's currently working on his fourth book, *Blue Collar Essays*—an in-depth study of his Blue Collar roots and their effect on him in childhood, in high school, at Eastern Michigan University, and well beyond.

Like Mark Twain (1835–1910), who arrived on Earth the same year Halley's Comet made an appearance, then died in the year of its celestial encore, he plans to go out with the same inexhaustible flash of creative energy that's propelled him in all of his endeavors for so many years.

Drawing of the author
by New Hampshire artist Tom Glover